Abby Rosmarin

CHICK LIT

(And Other Formulas for Life)

Abby Rosmarin

Printed in the United States of America

ISBN: 978-0-9966313-0-3 (print)
ISBN: 978-0-9966313-1-0 (ebook)

Cover design by Pixel Studios

For Chloe

Abby Rosmarin

[From *The South End Collections Employee Newsletter*]

"Choose Your Own Chick Lit Adventure"

by Katy Sinclaire

Feeling down and out about your writing? Having writer's block? Still hoping you could be the next big hit on the bestseller's list? Create your very own chick lit novel using this simple outline and you'll be on your way in no time (remember, you can always choose more than one option!):

Your main character is:

A) *A melodramatic girl who is impossibly smart, impossibly good-looking, and has some sad secret about her past.*

B) *A melodramatic girl who is impossibly smart, impossibly good-looking, and the other characters have yet to realize it.*

C) *A melodramatic girl who is impossibly smart, impossibly good-looking, and has some type of terminal illness.*

D) *A melodramatic girl who is impossibly good-looking, absolutely pathetic, and everyone around her is strangely attracted to her.*

Her name is:

A) *Exotic and uncommon.*

B) *A name that means "beautiful" or "alluring" in another language.*

C) *Completely made up.*

D) *Fairly common, but spelled in a ridiculously uncommon way (like "Sarah" spelled S-e-h-r-r-a).*

She meets her love interest:

A) *At a coffee shop.*

B) *Through him saving her life.*

C) *In the empty kitchen of a raucous party.*

D) *Through actions on the man's part that would be considered stalking in most states.*

The problem the girl deals with is:
A) *Something from her past that has been haunting her (but can be easily reconciled within 200 pages).*
B) *People who have taken an unnatural interest in her relationship with the man and want to drive them apart.*
C) *Terminal illness.*
D) *A superfluous tragedy of petty proportions.*

By the midway point, the guy and the girl:
A) *Are forced to break up due to outside forces.*
B) *Have a dramatic but mutual break up.*
C) *Have a dramatic and one-sided break up.*
D) *Think about breaking up.*

But by the finale, the girl:
A) *Ends up together with the man — happily ever after.*
B) *Ends up together with the man — before he dies.*
C) *Ends up together with the man — before she dies (of cancer).*
D) *Ends up together with her best male friend who has been secretly in love with her since the beginning (and who turns out to be the one for her after all).*

I highly recommend that my fellow coworkers utilize this before I end up making a killing as the next chick lit author. I personally plan on writing about a girl who falls in love with a guy who saves her life in the kitchen of a coffee shop, where both break up with the other, only to get back together and die.

Chapter 1

A double row of books started to tumble off the shelf and towards Katy.

Katy's head darted up as she heard the books scrape against the metal shelving. She stared at the books – frozen like a deer in headlights – as the first section started to fall down beside her.

Just moments before, Katy had found an entire bottom shelf empty, its books scattered across the floor as if someone had kicked them out from the aisle over. She had knelt down by that emptied bottom row, starting to sort out the books, wondering how in the world the day could get any worse.

Katy braced for impact as the second section landed directly on top of her. She covered her head and gritted her teeth as the books hit. Each book landed with a sharp *thud* as they bonked against her head and her back before sliding and bouncing to the floor.

The fallen books settled and a quiet quickly took over. In the next aisle, Katy could hear the maniacal squeals of a little boy as he jumped off one of the store's stepstools and ran away down the aisle. Katy surveyed the area, her hands limply dropping down to her sides.

"I hate my life," Katy stated, her eyes numbly gazing at the books around her. "I hate my life."

Katy breathed out the sentence a few more times as she leaned forward, pressed her forehead to the floor, and covered the back of her head with her arms.

Ben peered around the corner and looked down at Katy.

"Katy…what are you doing?" he said in a sweet, almost singsong tone.

"Assuming the fetal position until I'm no longer working at this dumbass job," Katy stated, her voice muffled by the floor.

"Can't you come out beforehand?"

"No."

"Not even for cookies?"

Katy raised her head and looked up at Ben.

"You have cookies?"

"Well, no…but I could get some."

"Then get some. And make them double chocolate chip."

Ben paused.

"That bad a day?"

Katy whimpered out an affirmative.

Ben knelt next to Katy as she propped her head up onto her hands.

"Listen, why don't you go outside for a bit," Ben offered. "Get some fresh air. I've got to finish up some new arrivals, but we can deal with this when you get back. All right?"

Katy sat up and nodded. Ben pushed against his knees and stood back up. He surveyed the mess one last time before helping Katy to her feet.

"You're too kind." Katy steadied herself and gathered her hair into a handful behind her shoulders.

"That's only because I think you might've suffered brain damage."

Katy let out a small, tired laugh. She turned and tiptoed through the wreckage of scattered books before walking past the registers and out the door.

Once outside, Katy leaned against the red brick exterior and closed her eyes. Her head was throbbing. No, it was more than throbbing. Her head was positively hammering. It felt like her brain was pressing against her skull in a desperate effort to escape. Was there any aspirin left in the store's first aid kit? Maybe she could make use of her time outside and take a trip to the convenience store for a bottle of aspirin. Maybe even two bottles.

Yeah, definitely two.

She pushed herself away from the wall and started to walk down the street. The sounds of late lunchtime traffic surrounded her. People were walking up and down the redbrick sidewalks, strolling in and out of the nearby stores and restaurants. Someone was playing classical music at full volume from an upstairs apartment. It was a gorgeous spring day, a rarity for Boston in April. It felt wrong to spend such a gorgeous day at the store.

To be honest, these days, it felt wrong to spend *any* day at the store.

All she had wanted to do was open up the bookstore, avoid the registers at all costs, and retreat into the backroom until she could clock out. She had no drive, no energy, and certainly no motivation.

It was definitely the wrong type of day to spend at work.

But – really – what was wrong with just wanting to do her shift and go home? It didn't seem like too big of a wish. Now, after the morning she just had, all she wanted to do was take the rest of the day off.

Long before she was pummeled with books – before she had even placed her bag in her locker – she had found out that an employee had called out sick. At a tiny store where every employee counts, an employee had called out sick.

And it was a shipment day – a day when they need all hands on deck and then some – at a tiny store where every employee counts, an employee had called out sick. And no one on their tiny list of employees would step in. The day's shipment had turned out to be way larger than expected, which had forced Katy to scramble for space in the stockroom. Without that additional employee to help out, Katy had found herself lifting the cargo alone, sweating through her business-casual khakis like she was in a sauna.

A sauna owned and operated by the devil himself.

After a few hours of that madness, Katy had given up and left the backroom, only to be hit with a steady stream of irate customers. One had disagreed with Katy about the store's return policy. No, not disagreed. Yelled. One customer had *yelled* at her

9

about the store's return policy. Before Katy could wind down from that experience, another had entered the store, purely to yell about the store's *buyback* policies. And yet another had hounded her as to why one particular novel was $12 when the *used* version right next to it was only $2.

Apparently, where the lady had come from, "new" and "used" were abstract concepts, left only to the highest-ranking philosophers.

Three self-involved customers in the span of two hours. That was three times the store average for a weekday.

And – serving as the icing on the multi-layer cake of suck – another customer had apparently decided to ignore her pixie-stick-addict of a son as he ran through the aisles as if on a bad trip, kicking out a bottom row of books, and then – as if part of his grand finale – pushing out a whole section of books from the top row, as if there had been magical treasure on the other side.

To be perfectly honest, the only thing keeping her from bursting into hysterics over the morning was the fact that she already had six years of this soul-crushing pattern to properly desensitize her.

After a lap around the block, Katy found herself back at the main entrance of South End Collections. With a sigh, Katy grabbed the door's handle and yanked the door open. Hannah looked up from the checkout counter and smiled in lieu of a proper greeting. Katy walked over to the registers and scanned the store.

"Did Rosemary leave with her baby yet?" Katy asked, her voice heavy.

Hannah cocked her head, her brows slightly furrowed.

"*Rosemary's Ba* – ah – never mind. Bad joke." Katy's face scrunched. "Did the brat and his mom leave?"

"The kid who was running around the store?" Hannah laughed. "Yeah. A couple minutes ago."

Katy let out a dramatic sigh before hunching over and leaning her elbows against the edge of the counter, her face dropping into her hands.

"I'm almost mad at myself for not kicking them out." Katy paused to rub her eyes with the tips of her fingers. "I swear that had to have been an act of sabotage. I don't know why, and I don't know from whom, but the reasons were definitely malicious. I'd commend the little incarnate on his strategizing if it had been in someone else's store." Katy took in another breath. "Was the mom at least a paying customer?"

"Yup." Hannah gave her supervisor a distracted answer, her eyes already darting towards incoming customers.

"Please tell me it was something on proper parenting – or local military schools."

"You're out of luck: chick lit."

"*Chick* lit?" Katy raised her eyebrows and coughed. "Should have known." She cleared her throat. "I almost wish I had been around, then, just to pass judgment. Openly pass judgment."

Hannah shrugged her shoulders. A customer walked past Katy and up to the registers. Katy pushed away from the counter to make room and Hannah welcomed the patron with a cheerful, "Hello." Katy gave the man her best customer service smile and turned toward the aisle where the book avalanche had occurred.

Katy walked over to find Ben already organizing the mess.

"Welcome back," said Ben.

"Thanks, I guess," said Katy as she crouched down next to him. She picked up a few scattered books and lined them against the bookshelf's bottom edge. A minute into sorting, Katy dropped to her knees and sat back on her heels. "My God. I'm done with this."

"Really? Looks like you've just started," Ben remarked.

"Oh, ha, ha." Katy rolled her eyes. "I mean *this*. I'm done with *this*. All of this. Customers doing things like this. I'm sick of dealing with it. I don't think it takes that much to be a respectable human being."

Katy pressed her tongue against her teeth. She moved a few more books around before giving up again.

"I mean, seriously. Simple acts of consideration," Katy continued. "And common sense – maybe even logic from time to time. It's not that hard. But they step in here and it's like 'the customer is always right' is their life mantra, or something. I'm going to snap someday, I swear it."

"From the looks of it, I'd say you're snapping right about…now."

"Oh thanks, thanks a lot. And Ben?"

"Yes?"

"I kind of hate you sometimes."

Ben let out an unimpressed snort and grabbed the first set of sorted books. He stood up and lifted the books onto their proper place on the shelf. Katy started lethargically arranging the pile by her feet.

"Don't get me wrong; this place drives me nuts as well," said Ben. "But we all have bad days. And we also have good days – and good customers. And, to be honest, it beats working in a cubicle. At least I'm walking around. Plus, I get a killer discount on my favorite type of entertainment."

Katy paused for a moment.

"I thought you were a movie-buff type of guy."

"C'mon now, I'm not talking about *these*." Ben lifted the next set of books onto the shelf. "I mean watching you go absolutely insane."

"Again with hating you."

Ben shrugged, walked to the end of the aisle, and grabbed an empty pushcart.

"It could be worse," Ben said as he began placing the books meant for the other side onto the cart.

"How's that?"

"You could be working in *clothing* retail."

"Oh, you're quite the optimist."

Katy pressed a palm into her forehead and rubbed her eyes. With a sigh, she started placing the novels in their correct sequence. Her lofty hope of an unremarkable day was long gone now. Her new goal was to clean up the mess without screaming profanities. And even that seemed like a bit of a pipedream.

She could've sworn that it hadn't always been this difficult. It *had* to have been easier when she had first started there. Right?

Everything felt so different now. Working at South End Collections had once been an enjoyable part of her life. When had that stopped? Those first years now felt like they were a figment of her imagination.

Once she had cleaned up her area, Katy walked to the end of the aisle. With her feet still firmly in her aisle, she draped her body around the endcap and stuck her head into the aisle where Ben was unloading his pushcart.

"Need any help?" she asked Ben, holding onto the edge of the bookcase.

"Good as done," he replied, shuffling around books on the upper shelf.

Katy righted herself and began walking towards the stockroom, checking the shelves along the wall for tidiness as she passed, stopping periodically to straighten up a book or two. Suddenly, scrambling around in the backroom didn't seem as unnerving as before. Maybe her original hope of an easy day was plausible after all.

A meek voice called out from behind her: "Excuse me, miss? Miss?"

Maybe not.

Katy turned to see a petite, frail lady, easily in her mid-seventies, a frayed sweater draped over her bony shoulders.

"Yes, ma'am – how can I help you?" Katy smiled weakly.

"Oh, hi there, honey. I was hoping if you knew when the new releases were coming in." The lady clasped her hands together by her waist. "I realized I've read just about everything in your Women's Literature section and I need something fresh."

Katy bit her tongue. *Women's* literature. Ha.

"Well, we do have a vast array of books. I could show you something from…mystery? Maybe historical fiction?"

"Oh, thank you, but I really only like Women's Literature."

Katy couldn't stop herself from raising her eyebrows. Women's Literature. A misleading label. At South End Collections, it was pretty name adapted by the store to encompass romance novels and chick literature, isolating them into one section, keeping the romance novels away from the science fiction and the chick literature away from general fiction.

Great idea. Terrible title.

Katy had suggested a different name, something a little more honest. But, for some reason, her co-workers wouldn't get behind Katy on "Escapism Fluff" – nor were they willing to support "The Opiate of Women Who Need to Reevaluate Their Life Choices".

"Hmm." Katy pressed her lips together. "Well, I can find out for you." Katy tiptoed around the lady and into the owner's office, pulling the binder marked "Expected Deliveries" off one of the shelves. "You're just in luck," she said as she returned with the binder open in her hand. "I'd say we should be getting six Women's Literature titles in the beginning of May."

"And these are all...new releases?"

"Of course."

"Do you know if this is the earliest any store will be getting them?"

Katy's customer-service smile curved into a slight grimace.

"We'll get them the same time the supermarkets do."

"Well, that's a relief to hear. Can you tell me the titles?"

Katy looked down at her binder.

"Let's see...we've got Love at the Sea, Walking in Paris, The Next Door Neighbor, Teaching My Former Teacher, Best Friends for Love, and The Express Espresso. Would you like to know the authors?"

"Oh, that's not important," the lady replied. "But do you know what they'll be about, by any chance?"

Katy looked down at the list. Author names, ISBNs, release dates, expected shipment dates. No plot summaries.

Not that these books ever had plots to begin with. But still...

A sardonic grin crept onto Katy's face.

"Well, I imagine that *Love at the Sea* deals with a beautiful young woman who meets a man while onboard a ship of some nature. There'll be some problem going on that they'll need to solve together. They'll fall in love, possibly be forced away from one another, but eventually they get back together, because true love conquers all."

"Oh, don't tell me the ending," the lady snapped, her eyebrows lowered. She pursed her lips, turning them into a ruby-red dot. "Well, no matter. What about *Walking in Paris*?"

"Hmm, I can see *that* one dealing with a beautiful young woman who meets a man while in Paris. There might be a language barrier or a future distance thing that keeps them from truly connecting. I believe I know how it ends…but I won't spoil it for you."

"Oh, thank you – you're a dear." The lady placed a hand to her chest. "And about the express-o one?"

"This might seem like a long shot, but *that* story probably revolves around a beautiful young woman and a handsome young man meeting at a coffee shop and falling in love." Katy pressed her lips together, stifling a sigh. "Is that all, ma'am?"

The lady looked down for a second.

"Well…I *am* curious about the other ones, but…I'll wait until they come in. I guess it wouldn't hurt to read something from my collection again."

Wouldn't be that much different from the new stuff, either, Katy couldn't help but think.

"Wouldn't hurt one bit," Katy agreed and clapped the binder shut. "Have a good one."

She turned away from the lady and returned to the office. The only clock – save for the one by the registers – hung on the office's back wall. She gazed at the time as she tossed the binder onto the desk and collapsed into the chair. 3:15. Fifteen minutes past three o'clock.

"Three more hours to go. Not even – two forty-five. You can do this. You can *do this*," Katy quietly reassured herself, her head resting against the top of the chair. "Almost done…almost done."

A knock against the doorframe snapped Katy's head back up.

"Katy? Sorry to interrupt." Josh's seemingly pubescent voice squeaked into the room. "Um, I just need to clock in."

Katy sat up, ran a nervous hand through her hair, and glanced up at the clock again.

"You're late," she said in her most nonchalant voice, reaching for the scheduling book and handing it to Josh.

"The T was delayed. Not my fault," Josh mumbled as he wrote in his time and handed the book back.

"And your dialing thumb's been chopped off?" Katy raised an eyebrow. "Seriously though, I don't care if the whole train is on fire. I don't care if *you* are on fire. Call." Katy smirked, checking Josh's entry in the book before initialing it. "And don't give me the 'no service' excuse. My cell works perfectly at Downtown Crossing."

"Okay, then. Next time I'll call. Anything else?"

"Aside from the fact that it's a shipment day and we're already short-staffed? I guess nothing else," said Katy. "Put your stuff away and go see Ben. He'll let you know what you're doing tonight."

"Alright. Sounds good." Josh turned from the office.

"Just be glad you weren't any later – I was starting to contemplate proper flogging techniques," Katy called out. Josh looked over his shoulder and grinned sheepishly as he walked down one of the aisles and away from the office.

Katy pushed herself in the chair with the heels of her feet until she was within arm's reach of the door and nudged the door just enough for it to latch closed. She brought herself back to the desk, returned the scheduling binder to the self, and rubbed her eyes, feeling sillier than any college student coming in late to work.

To be honest, she had completely forgotten that Josh was coming in that day – let alone at 3 – until he made his way into the office.

Katy leaned back in the chair until it wouldn't go any further and hung her head over the backrest. She stared at the world in the disorienting, upside-down way that she used to do as a kid, sitting the wrong way on her parents' couch. The ceiling became the floor and cabinets seemed suspended in the air. The metal safe, for all its heaviness and size, was now hanging upside-down as if it weighed nothing. Her shoulders relaxed and a grin crept up onto her lips. She could spend hours like this, observing a world where she would have to duck under desks and step over doorways.

She had never needed to hide away like this during her first years at South End Collections. By now, secluding herself in the office was becoming a daily ritual. How had she done her job with such a blissful ease in the beginning? Was it because she had just started college and everything had still been new to her? Had she really not been bothered by it all?

She once had such an intense love for this store. She could always find a novel that she hadn't heard of before, or some local book that might never see the shelves of a west coast store. There had been a sense of wonderment for her in that. Something exciting and different. Like a world where light fixtures accent the floor and people dance upside-down on the ceiling. Something new and engaging and stimulating.

Katy gazed from the ceiling back to the clock. Even upside down, the clock's hands let her know her little respite needed to end. There were things that needed to get done. With a sigh, she lifted her head up and re-entered the right-side-up world.

Katy pushed herself off the chair and walked back into the main part of the store. A few customers were quietly flipping through paperbacks. The loudest noises were the *click* of the office door closing and the creaking floorboards from the second floor. There was a lull in the store – possibly the calm before the rush-hour storm. She strolled across the back of the store for a few paces, glancing down each aisle as she passed. Not one book had been pushed out from the shelves in the past hour. Progress was already being made.

Katy wandered down the section designated for science fiction and fantasy and looked up at the top shelving. She reached up to the gap where someone had taken down three or so books – hopefully to buy. Or to steal. Whatever. She was so tired of the store by now that she didn't care *how* the books left. She placed her hand against one end of the gap, straightened the novels to the left, and pushed the bookend closer.

Things were so still now. Katy could just stand there and take in the musk of the bookstore: a faint but ever-present aroma, the combination of brand new books with the more aged ones. Even after everything that had happened that day, there was still a chance that she could find sanctuary in the stock room before her shift was over. The second register needed a new tray of money but, other than that, Katy was in the home stretch. Katy stood there for a moment, watching a few new customers as they started wandering around the first floor, before she began her walk to the checkout area, fingertips trailing the spines of the novels to the left of her.

"Is Hannah in stock now?" Katy asked as she got to the front.

"I'm assuming so. Either way, she went in that general direction." Ben pointed towards the back as a customer came up to the registers.

Katy shook her head.

"Ever the shining emblem of authority. May you never become manager."

"Harsh words," Ben responded, scanning the patron's books. "Hey, if I remember correctly, once upon a time I was a shining emblem of authority to you, too."

"Yeah – for like a minute. Don't let it go to your head." Katy opened the register's drawer with a twist of her key. Katy slipped her fingers underneath the cash tray and pulled it from the drawer. Balancing the tray on her hip, Katy grabbed the checks and $50 bills from beneath the tray and stacked them on top. Katy returned to the office, counted and documented the money, and placed everything in its spot in the safe. Katy slid out a new tray with the allotted cash resting nicely inside and returned to the front.

Katy could see the beginning of the rush hour customers start to trickle in. Katy watched as Ben's newest customer came up to the counter, each arm carrying a stack of books so high that they toppled over when the customer tried to place them on the counter. Ben had to press his hands against the edge of the counter to keep them from sliding over and onto his feet.

Katy plopped the newest tray next to the cash register.

"Looks like you got your hands full. Literally."

Ben rolled his eyes as he re-stacked the books.

"Ha."

Katy unlocked the second register's drawer and slid the tray into place.

"And where is Josh in all this," said Katy.

"I told him that I'd need him at the registers," Ben replied. "I wouldn't be surprised if he fell asleep in the staff room."

Katy scanned the room and gave a half-hearted sigh.

"For someone who was already late to begin with, Josh is taking his sweet time getting ready."

"Eh, the kid's a freshman. It's to be expected."

Katy cocked an eyebrow.

"*I* wasn't like that as a freshman."

"But *you* are anal-retentive."

"Touché," Katy said, nodding her head to one side.

Katy grabbed the calculator from under the counter and began double-checking the money in the tray. She scooped up the change and counted out the pennies, nickels, and dimes. She popped open a few coin rolls and poured them into their respective slots. A line quickly began to form as Katy counted out the one-dollar bills and Ben scanned his customer's mountain of books. A man in his late 60s bypassed the line entirely and went straight over to Katy.

"Hey, lady – can't you take me?" The man glared at Katy.

I can't take your money if I'm counting my own, Katy thought to herself as she lifted the fives out of the tray and passed them from one hand to the other. Five, ten, fifteen, twenty. She lifted her head to the customer. "Sir, I have to open the register first. But I'm almost done and I will be ready then, okay?"

"I don't understand why you don't have both registers open all the time," he responded. "It's not efficient!"

Katy pressed her lips together and dropped the five-dollar bills into the tray. She punched "40" into the calculator and, after making sure she had checked everything, pressed the "equal" button. Everything added up to a perfect $70. She closed the drawer and deliberately looked out past the man and into the line of patrons.

"I'll take whoever's next in line," Katy called out, her eyes squinting with her forced smile.

"What is your issue, lady? I'm right here," the man said.

"Sir, there are people waiting. If you would like to purchase your books, I need you get in line," Katy responded with a level of patience fit for a kindergarten teacher.

"This is ridiculous," the man grunted. "I've been standing here forever. Can't you give an old man a break?"

"Sir, I really need you to get in line," Katy repeated, her fingers tightening around the edge of the counter.

"Unbelievable," the guy muttered, turning and walking to the end of the line. "The gall of young people these days. I swear I've never…"

The lady at the front of the line timidly stepped forward, glancing back at the man before giving a nervous smile to Katy.

"Hi there, ma'am. Did you find everything all right?"

Katy rang up her customers with a watchful eye on the line, counting the number of patrons between the man and the cash registers. If she could properly swing it, she'd have two more customers – one of them being the customer right in front of the surly gentleman, leaving Ben to ring him in.

She made small talk with the first woman in line until Ben had finished ringing up his customer. She then sped through her next customer, desperately trying to time things just right. Katy eyed Ben's side of the counter as she rang in the books of the woman who had been in front of the old man, trying to keep her current patron at her register until the old man walked over to Ben's register. As Ben's customer rummaged through her purse, Katy paused and looked down at one of her own patron's book.

"Oh, *Whispers through Arabian Dawn*." Katy swallowed. "That sounds interesting."

"I know, doesn't it?" The lady smiled. "I just couldn't help myself with this one. Just look at that cover. Have you ever seen a more handsome man?"

Katy gazed at the cover, the ornery old man still in her peripheral vision.

"He is quite handsome," Katy lied. "Reminds me of someone I went to high school with, actually."

"Oh really? It's a small world, isn't it?" The lady replied.

Katy watched as Ben's customer lifted her bag of books and left the store. With a sigh of relief, Katy placed *Whispers through Arabian Dawn* into its own bag and ran the woman's credit card.

"Yes, yes it is."

The old man approached Ben and landed his book on the counter with a heavy *thud*.

"Young man, is there a manager I can speak with?" Katy heard him say.

"The manager is not in today, but maybe I could help you," Ben responded.

Katy could feel her whole face get hot. She bit at the inside of her cheeks, handed the woman her bag, and looked into the line. The only patron left was a girl in a lacey blouse and khakis, her blonde hair gathered into a ponytail.

"Oh, my – Katy?"

Katy's face went slack. The world went silent for a moment. Even the old man's complaints went mute.

"...Rachel?" Katy eventually said. She tucked her hair behind her ears and stared.

"Oh. My. God. Katelyn Sinclaire! I haven't talked to you in like forever! How are you?"

"I, I'm good," Katy stammered. "How about you – how are you?"

"Never better." Rachel placed her books on the counter.

"I'm sorry about that sir," Katy heard Ben say, his deliberately quiet words echoing in her right ear. "We have to be fair to all customers, including those waiting in line."

Rachel stared at Katy, her eyes wide with astonishment.

"Oh my God, I would *never* have expected to run into you here."

"Yeah. Oh my god," Katy said flatly.

"I have never been spoken to so rudely in my life." The man's voice suddenly came into focus. "Who demands that an elderly person stand in a long line like that?"

Katy glanced at Ben before shooting her eyes back up to Rachel.

"So, um, what are you doing here?" Katy asked, her voice tinged with accusation.

"...sure she didn't mean it that way. We try to help customers of all physical abilities. I'm sure this is all just a big misunderstanding..."

Katy cleared her throat.

"It was kind of a spontaneous thing, really," Rachel responded. "I've been gone for so long, and I wanted to get reacquainted with Boston. So I came down to the South End. And – lo and behold – I found this place." Rachel broke off eye contact with Katy to scan the store, pausing briefly at the old man and Ben. "You know I'm just a sucker for independent bookstores."

"...doesn't matter. No one should speak to someone like that. Especially a paying customer."

"No, I didn't know that." Katy began picking up Rachel's items, anxiously shifting them from her right hand to her left. "So you left? Where'd you go?"

"Belfast," Rachel answered, her voice dripping with pride. "Gorgeous city, really is. Full of history, too. Incredible place."

"I really do apologize for..."

"Belfast? Really. What were you doing in Belfast?" Katy spat out. Her brow furrowed and her nose creased. She could taste copper building in the back of her mouth. Please, let there be a domestic version of Belfast – like Venice, California. Or Milan, Ohio.

Please say there's a Belfast, North Carolina.

"Well, me and my friends went to the UK after graduation, actually. We went everywhere – Wales, Scotland, Northern Ireland – and I fell in *love* with Northern Ireland. Just took my heart away. And one of my friends suggested, 'Hey! Why don't you go to grad school here?'"

"…it really speaks of her character that she would ever…"

Katy stared blankly at the books in front of her. If there were a just God in this universe, he wasn't particularly worried about Katy today.

"Oh."

"…I shouldn't have to declare that I'm old just to give some service around here…"

"Did you know that Queen's University's Master's program is only a year long? It was like fate. I just *had* to do it." Rachel twisted the cord of her necklace for emphasis. The Celtic spiral pendant did a few turns before slowing to a stop and started spinning in the opposite direction.

"…I don't get your generation. Only thinking of yourselves. No respect for anyone…"

Katy tried to swallow down the copper taste.

"So how was grad school…in Belfast?"

Belfast. Capital of Northern Ireland. She went to graduate school in Northern Ireland. After traveling around Europe, Rachel went to graduate school. In. Northern. Ireland.

"Please let us know what we can do to make you feel more respected at our store…"

"Amazing! I got my Master's in Women's Studies," Rachel dropped her necklace, the pendant landing against her blouse with a slight bounce. Katy started placing Rachel's books in a plastic bag.

Women's Studies.

"Oh." Katy pressed her tongue against the back of her teeth.

"And how about you? What's going on in your life?"

"You can start by teaching your employees some manners! I was a firefighter for 37 years…"

"Um, you know." Katy could feel the blood rushing to her face. It seemed pretty damn obvious what she was doing in her life, standing behind that counter and punching in the prices of Rachel's books. "You know. Stuff."

"…I risked my life day after day for the citizens of Boston…"

Stuff in the bookstore. What else? She could feel her mouth going dry. While Rachel would take her books, leave the store, and get on with *another* life-altering experience, Katy would be stuck in the store. Today, tomorrow, and for the rest of her natural born life. "Just, heh, you know, working here."

"...My blood, sweat, and tears went into the safety of this city..."

"Oh. Well. That's nice," Rachel responded in monotone.

"...she's just some damn cashier, for Christsake!"

Rachel stopped what she was saying and looked over at the man. The world went mute for the second time, save for a violent buzzing in Katy's ear. Katy was ready to hide in the staff room. Or run out the door. Or scream, "FIRE!" and jump out a window.

Something, anything.

Dear God, let the store implode in on itself so this would stop already.

Katy managed an awkward laugh and shrugged her shoulders.

"But you, I mean...a Master's from Belfast. Impressive. Yeah, so, what's next? Doctorate in Australia?"

Rachel laughed.

Katy wasn't joking.

"Well, um. Well, actually, I've been a public affairs officer for a couple months now, for Mass General. I had interned for them right after Eddington Publishing, actually. When I got back to the States, I called them up about work, and they had an opening – with my name on it." Rachel laughed. "Well, at least that's what my boss had said."

"Oh."

"...If you would like, sir, I can give the manager your name and number, and she can help sort this out with you one-on-one..."

"Yeah, it's a little breakneck, but it makes life interesting. And you meet some of the most intriguing people there...I'd love to tell you all about it. We should catch up sometime!"

"...not worth the effort. I just want you guys to understand how people expect to be treated..."

"Yeah. Of course. This is $38.67, by the way."

Rachel reached into her bag and passed Katy one of her credit cards. Katy swiped it through the clunky black box to the side of the register and punched at its buttons. She eyed the old man as she ran the credit card, who gave her a once over as well before leaving the store.

"Oh my God, I love it!" Rachel pointed to the credit card machine. "You just don't see these anymore. So antique. Like one of those thingies that would roll over the credit card. You know what I mean?"

A new customer came up to Ben, all smiles as she placed her books on the counter.

"Yeah. Of course." Katy handed Rachel back her card, watching from the corner of her eye as the man left the building. "Hey, have a great day."

"Yeah, you too. Listen, feel free to give me a ring. I miss you to pieces." Rachel gave a sincere smile, picked up her books, and walked out the door. Katy stood, watching her leave. The bell at the top corner of the entrance clanged as the door closed, announcing Rachel's departure.

Katy could have sworn that the store had gone quiet again. That, or a sudden vacuum had been created on the first floor. The second option seemed appropriate, as Katy felt like her head was about to explode.

"Who was that?" Ben asked, giving his last customer her bag.

"Huh?"

"The girl you rang up. Looks like you knew her."

"Oh. Yeah." Katy's lips curled upward. "We went to BU together, both class of '03. Known her since my freshman year." Katy looked away from the door and focused on the ground. "We, uh, even interned at a publishing company together." Katy leaned forward, pressing her knuckles against the edge of the counter. "Great girl. Yeah, really great girl. And she apparently has her Master's. That she got in Europe. And now she works at MGH. Isn't that swell."

Katy lightly rapped out a staccato beat against the counter. A new customer walked up to the counter and Katy instinctively took a step back. Ben waved the customer over with a cheerful smile.

"I can take you over here, ma'am," he said.

As if on cue, Katy could hear Josh walking down the stairs. Perfect timing, as per usual.

"Well, then," said Katy, her gaze fixed on the door again, her voice automatic and droning. "I'll be in the backroom."

Katy immediately turned and tried to disappear down the aisles. She swore she could feel everyone's eyes on her as she made her way to the stock room.

Katy placed a palm to the back of her neck and shook her head. She dragged her feet in front of her through the stock room entrance and to the latest shipment, completely ignoring Hannah. She opened the first box she saw and began shoveling out paperbacks with both hands, shelving the books in clumps onto a metal pushcart.

The wearying pattern was soon interrupted by the carton's top flap falling forward as Katy tried pulling out another clump of books. Katy let out a frustrated grunt and shoved the books into the offending flap.

"Stay there," she muttered, blood rushing to her face.

Books. So many books. So many goddamn books that needed to be moved and sorted and recorded into the system. Her grip tightened on the next cluster she took out. She turned from the box and slammed the cluster into the cart.

The noise echoed against the concrete walls, causing Hannah to put down her price gun and stare at Katy. Katy let out a small, wavering grin at Hannah and went back to emptying the box.

All these boxes. All the goddamn boxes. Sci-fi and suspense and horror and self-help. In the end, they're all the same. They're all identical stories that just get printed out in nauseating cycles – yet no one seems to remember the ones from the previous rotation.

She opened up a second box and grabbed an empty cart. Hardcover textbooks. To eventually go to the second floor. With the "Do-It-Yourself"'s and the biographies and anything else that could have ever proven useful.

The second floor, where you had to park the cart at the base of the stairs and bring everything up in assorted handfuls. Because there's no elevator here. Because wouldn't that ruin the rustic look? Wouldn't an upgrade in technology go against the theme of this place, with its defunct cash registers and shitty credit card reader?

Katy placed the books on the second cart seven or eight at a time, her arms aching under the strain. She bit the sides of her tongue as she picked up bigger and bigger handfuls at a faster and faster pace.

Why were there two floors in the first place? This store didn't need to be so damn *tall*. Everything felt narrow and compressed. For God's sake, move somewhere else, where everything can be on one floor. Dumb redbrick building sandwiched between other redbrick buildings. Maybe they could move to a place with some *air*. Or a parking lot. Cars smothered the curb with their bumper-to-bumper parking. There was no way to *get out* unless you climbed over a car.

Katy shifted to the front and yanked the cart back towards the first one with the paperbacks. The yank caused her elbow to slam into one of the edges of the paperback cart, sending a jolt of pain up Katy's arm and a cluster of paperbacks onto the floor.

"Oh fucking *damn* it!" Katy barked out, kicking at the cart and cradling her elbow in her hand. She crouched down and wildly began tossing the books back onto the cart's shelf. Stupid books. Stupid goddamn shitty books that can't ever be where they're supposed to be. With each book she tossed, another slid off and hit the floor again. Katy got up, pushed the cart away from her, and let out an exasperated grunt.

Katy clenched her teeth and balled her hands up into tight fists. She could swear everything was tightening around her, making her want to jump right out of her own skin. Katy eventually unclenched her teeth and looked behind her. Hannah stood with her hands by her side, politely silent. The muffled sound of a cash register drawer opening filled the room.

"…You got this, right?" Katy asked, her voice filled with frenzied awkwardness.

Hannah slowly nodded her head.

Katy nodded to herself.

"Great. Good. Yeah, okay, then." Katy left her pile of books and trudged up the stairs. She marched into the staff room, grabbed her book-bag from her locker, and hurried down the stairs and across the floor.

"Where are you going?" Ben asked.

Katy stopped at the front doors and turned.

"Um, home. I think I'm gonna go home." Katy's eyes scanned the store. "Not feeling so good."

"Well, get better," Josh innocently interjected.

"Yeah. Thanks, Josh. I'll try." Katy readjusted the bag's strap on her shoulder. "Ben, you're okay covering for me, right?"

"Of course," he responded.

"Good, thanks," Katy breathed out.

Ben pursed his lips.

"Are you sure you're okay?" Ben asked, his voice slow and unsure.

"Yeah, fine. Just a little sick to my stomach, is all."

Before anyone could respond, Katy pushed open the doors and spilled onto the sidewalk. She slung her bag over her shoulder and hiked down the street. Around her were the sounds of impatient cars, backfiring mufflers, chattering people.

She felt the blood rush to her face again. The air was humid and muggy. Sweat beads relentlessly clung to her skin. She tried her best to stride down the street like she always did, but in the end, her feet were stomping against pavement, her breath was short and raspy, and her hands were balled up again into frustrated fists.

Chapter 2

The muffled jingle of keys let Katy know that Maria was home.

"Oh, hey." Maria looked into the living room. "You're home early."

Katy dropped her head back against the top edge of the couch.

"Don't ask."

"Not asking, then." Maria placed her purse on the kitchen counter and opened the fridge. "Do we still have those oranges?"

"Clementines," Katy sighed out. "And no. Finished those off yesterday."

"Alright, time for plan B, then."

Katy stared at the sitcom in front of her for the span of two laugh tracks. She turned off the TV, leaned forward, and turned her head toward the kitchen.

"Maria, what would you say has been my biggest accomplishment since graduating?"

"That's a little random," Maria replied, her voice echoing off the inside walls of the fridge.

"Humor me."

"Um...I don't know." Maria emerged from the fridge's innards and shrugged, her eyes still on the food. "Didn't you date the brother of an NFL player?"

"Great." Katy folded back into the couch. "My success is defined through relationships. Also his brother was just on the practice squad."

Maria sighed and put her hands up.

"Well, I don't know. What about Miller?"

The cat, hearing his name, perked its ears up. The rest of his body stayed curled up by the living room window.

"Anyone can adopt a cat."

"But...*this* one has a billion thumbs," Maria remarked, turning and pointing at Miller. "I mean, that's pretty special, right?"

"Hemingway cats are common in this area," Katy muttered.

Maria's eyebrows lowered. She opened her mouth to say something, but stopped. Her gaze narrowed at Katy. Katy instinctively closed her eyes and rolled her head back toward the ceiling. There was no hope in hiding the blotchiness on her face. The skin under her eyes was probably starting to puff up as well. But she could at least hope that Maria hadn't caught the redness in her eyes before she had clamped them shut.

"Hey...is everything alright? You don't look so hot."

"I don't want to talk about it."

"Well, okay, then." Maria let out an exasperated sigh. "We won't talk about it."

Katy listened as Maria moved the various items around in the freezer. After a moment or two of clanks and shuffles, she opened her eyes and rolled her head back towards the kitchen.

"How long have we been out of school?"

Maria closed the freezer door.

"Is this a trick question?"

"Two years," Katy answered, nearly interrupting Maria in the process. "Two years, and I've managed to do absolutely nothing. Other than get a cat." Katy rubbed at her eyes. "Oh, and get promoted to supervisor – at the same job I've had since I was eighteen."

Maria shrugged and opened the refrigerator door again.

"A lot of people do that. It's not that big of a deal."

"It's a big deal to me," Katy countered. "I'm doing basically nothing. Wasting my life, day by day."

"Don't be so dramatic," replied Maria. "You're too young to be having a mid-life crisis."

Katy rubbed at one of her temples.

"That's because I'm having a quarter-life crisis."

"There's no need to be having one of those either," Maria replied. She closed the fridge and looked back at Katy. "You're only 24. No one's asking you to be CEO just yet. Especially not in this economy. Things take time." Maria opened the cabinets by the stove, shuffling around the non-perishables, the metal and glass containers clinking against each other.

Katy fingered the On button of the TV remote before placing it to her side.

"Do you remember Rachel?"

Maria paused.

"Rachel…?"

"Rachel Osterman. Short girl, blonde hair – kind of annoying?"

"Not ringing any bells." Maria pulled out the jar of peanut butter.

"Eh." Katy bit at her bottom lip. "I just had a really un-fun run-in with her today."

Maria held the jar with both hands.

"I'm sorry about that – what happened?"

"Nothing big. Just made a bad day that much worse. She's – ah, forget it." Katy paused and rubbed her eyes. "Not important. Just rattled me up a bit." Katy scratched her neck before placing the remote back on the table and standing up. She walked a few steps over towards Maria and rested her elbows against the counter that separated the living room from the kitchen. "Gonna make anything good?"

Maria scooped up a dollop of peanut butter with a spoon and popped it in her mouth.

"Worth asking," Katy teased. With a quick shove against the edge, Katy stood up from the counter and turned away from the kitchen.

"Where'ya going?" Maria swallowed down her spoonful.

"My room," Katy mumbled.

"Do you feel like going out in a little bit?"

Katy turned back.

"I just had the most terrible day in the history of terrible days. I plan on stewing on my bed for a little bit instead."

"I doubt it was *that* bad," Maria replied. "I'm sure nothing a night out couldn't fix."

"A night in my room with the curtains drawn sounds better."

"C'mon. Me and the girls are gonna see a movie tonight." Maria dug out another scoop of peanut butter.

Katy rubbed her eyes.

"Dare I ask which one?"

"Just Lovers."

Katy dropped her hands by her sides.

"Huh."

"Have you seen it?"

"Um, well, I haven't exactly watched the movie on the screen," Katy responded. "But if you mean 'do I know how it ends', then...yes."

"But, you don't know who the characters are," Maria pointed out. "Or what happens *before* the ending."

Katy cocked an eyebrow.

"Let me take a wild stab: I'll be dealing with either an adorably *snarky* or an adorably *awkward* girl. And she'll make a pact with some guy – who will also be either adorably snarky or adorably awkward – to have sex without the emotional commitments of a relationship. They'll fall for each other eventually, deal with something that drives them apart, and then get back together. How does that sound for knowing what happens?"

Maria coughed out a laugh.

"Well, so, there you go. There won't be any surprises, so who cares? You can just hang out and have fun and forget about your day. Sit and relax, eat some popcorn." Maria shifted her shoulders. "Maybe a hot guy will sit next to you, strike up a conversation..."

"Please," Katy scoffed. "Unlike the characters in this movie, I *don't* plan on solving all my problems with love."

"Oooh!" Maria taunted. "Said with the anger of a character right out of a chick flick. You could play the main character's best friend."

Katy clutched at her chest.

"You cut me deep."

"Please. You're so the stereotypical bitter girl right now." Maria gave her spoon a final lick before tossing it in the sink. "You're one step away from tearing down Valentine's Day decorations."

"Come on – there's a huge difference between being bitter about *love* and being *annoyed* about the *fluff* that people try to pass off as love," Katy replied. "But, now that you mention it, I wouldn't mind ripping down a glittery heart poster or two."

Maria twisted the peanut butter cap through its final rotation. Katy leaned against her bedroom's doorframe and crossed her arms.

"So." Maria tossed the peanut butter jar into the cabinet. "Can I count you in?"

"Not in a million years."

"Well, what if I buy your ticket?"

"I don't take bribes," Katy responded. "Moral code and all."

"I'm not trying to bribe you. I'm trying to be nice," Maria replied. "You obviously need to get out. Come on. You call it fluff, but maybe that's what you need."

"Like a bullet to the head," Katy added.

"No, *not* like a bullet to the head," Maria retorted. "Stop being so difficult. The last thing you should be doing right now is 'stewing'. You need to go out – do stuff! And I'm offering you that completely free." Maria rubbed at her forehead. "I'll buy you a drink afterwards if I have to."

With a groan, Katy uncrossed her arms and hung them in defeat by her hips.

"Make it beforehand and you've got a deal."

"Deal."

Maria shook her head and closed the cabinets.

"Someday you'll appreciate how much I look after you."

"Oh, but I do," Katy responded. "You just can't see it under this layer of suck."

Maria smiled, rolled her eyes, and walked out of the kitchen, undoing the top buttons of her blouse as she made her way around the counter. "Speaking of suck, I need a shower and possibly a delousing before I'm seen in public again."

"Bad day as well?" Katy asked.

"HR had me doing their grunt work." Maria snatched off her heels and held them by their ankle straps. "What can I do? Low man on the totem pole. Nothing I can say."

"How about 'no'?"

"Yeah. That's smart." Maria leaned into her room tossed her shoes onto her bed. "You don't piss off the people in charge of handling your paycheck."

"Touché."

"I'll see you after my shower." Maria continued unbuttoning her shirt as she entered the bathroom.

Katy turned and walked into her room. She barely got two steps in before she plopped onto her bed, her face resting on its side, her feet dangling off the corner edge. Outside, the intermittent passing car filled the room with muted engine noise. In between the random traffic, silence hung in the air, filling every available space as it slowly sank into the room.

Katy allowed herself to sink down as well, to the point that she couldn't imagine ever getting back up. It felt like the right thing to do, lying motionless on her bed. Physical stagnancy to complement life stagnancy. It was almost poetic.

No. Forget that. It *was* poetic, dammit.

Katy let her eyes drift shut, treasuring the moment of peace before Maria would inevitably call for her.

Maria just didn't understand. Her intentions were good, but they were horribly misplaced. Katy was perfectly content being consumed by her misery. Going out wouldn't make her *happy*; it would make her tired. Seeing a romantic comedy wouldn't make her feel better; it would make her annoyed.

Not to mention that Maria was wrong. Wrong, wrong, wrong. Wrong on top of wrong with a dollop of wrong on the side. Okay, sure. She was "only" twenty-four. But so was Rachel. And *Rachel* went to Europe. *Rachel* got to go to Europe and get her Master's. And now *Rachel* is working at one of the best hospitals in the country.

And where was Katy during all of this? Had she even tried finding an actual job after college? Had she tried doing *anything* after college? What had she done in all her twenty-four years?

She was too busy being "just a cashier"; that's what.

And twenty-four turns into twenty-five and twenty-six — which eventually turns into a bitter old lady who expresses her resentment for staying in retail for her entire life by passive-aggressively shooting down customers.

And at "only" twenty-four, Katy was already seeing herself do more and more of that.

Katy scratched at her back before letting her arm collapse loosely by her side. Everything seemed to itch, but she couldn't garner the energy to move her limbs anymore.

Of all the bookstores in the city, why did Rachel have to come to her bookstore? Of all the days for her to come in, why did it have to be that day, and at that exact time? Of all the things Rachel could have done with her life, why did she have to do all of *that*? A Master's degree? Sure. European vacation? Sure. Great job? Fine. But all three? Now, that's just unfair.

But, really, most of all: of all the people who could have possibly come in on that day, at that exact time, having done all those things, why did it have to be Rachel?

It wasn't that Katy out-and-out hated Rachel. Katy just didn't care for her. Rachel was an overachiever: the kind person who could only validate her existence through grades — and the best grades, at that. She was that way in class, and she was that way at Eddington Publishing. It was never enough to be a *good* intern. She had to be the *best*, the director's favorite. But Katy had dealt with it, thinking that people like Rachel typically burned out within the first year of the "real world", and Katy would end up vindicated by living in Europe, or getting her Master's, or finding a wonderful job in an exciting and engaging career.

But what really happened after graduation? Rachel never burned out, and instead continued to accomplish bigger and better things.

And what had Katy accomplished? She spent most of her college life imagining just how far she would go after graduating. Of all the things she had imagined, certainly none of them involved working at the exact same store she had applied to in her freshman year.

If this had been a competition, the announcers would already be calling the game and the people in the stands would already be going home.

She hadn't done a thing since graduating. Not one thing. She hadn't even accomplished the tiniest little goal. Everything was passing her by like the last train out of town.

Twenty-four into twenty-five into twenty-six and beyond.

"That doesn't look comfortable." Maria emerged at the doorway, wrapped in a towel.

"Perfectly comfortable." Katy mumbled into her comforter.

Maria walked over and tapped at Katy's calf with the back of her hand. With a groan, Katy rolled over.

"We're meeting Ashley at 7. Shower's free, now. You have plenty of time to grab one if you'd like."

"I'm good without a shower." Katy sat up only to roll forward and collapse her elbows onto her knees.

"Maybe you could take one anyway."

Katy sat up a little straighter.

"I'm insulted by your insinuation that I smell bad."

"C'mon now. Enough with your defense tactics. Nothing cheers a person up like a hot shower." Maria turned around and headed into the living room. "Well, except maybe a strong drink."

"I said I'm fine," Katy shouted.

"Humor me, then," Maria shouted back.

With a groan, Katy slid off her shoes and traipsed into the bathroom. She closed the door behind her and shed off her work attire, shimmying out of her khaki pants and sliding off her cotton top. Avoiding the medicine cabinet mirror at all costs, Katy leaned over the bathtub and cranked the shower knob past "cold" and three-quarters of the way through "hot". She stepped in only when the water from the showerhead reached a near-boil. She let the water cook her feet for a bit before plunging her head into the steady stream.

Katy hated to admit it, but Maria was right. She still felt like the world was collapsing in on her like a poorly cooked soufflé, but at least her body was less tense. All the steam had caused her face to flush, which would hopefully hide whatever remaining blotchiness that crying had caused. After a few more minutes of standing under the water, Katy turned off the water and stepped out of the shower and into her room, vigorously drying herself before putting on something a little less bland and nondescript as her work clothes.

Maria opened Katy's door, interrupting Katy as she brushed out her hair.

"See? Don't you feel better?"

"Shut up." Katy shook her wet hair one last time before throwing it into a ponytail.

"You'll catch a cold like that," Maria sing-songed.

"I think I'll take the risk," Katy mimicked the song back, throwing on a pair of shoes.

Maria returned to the kitchen and grabbed her purse from the counter. Katy gave Miller a quick scratch behind the ears before turning for the door. Together, they walked out of the apartment and down the stairwell, the carpet underneath them muffling the creaking floorboards. Katy's gaze shifted back and forth from the floor to Maria, periodically taking in a breath as if to say something, only to stop herself halfway through.

Katy opened her mouth again as they reached the first floor.

"Hey – is it alright if I list you as a personal reference?"

Maria turned to face Katy.

"Um, sure – what for?"

"Well, I'm, uh, actually thinking about getting a new job." Katy explained. Maria pushed the main door open and both girls started making their way down the stretch of sidewalk. "I haven't exactly been thrilled working at the bookstore. Maybe this is the wake-up call I need to get out of retail."

"Sounds good to me," said Maria. "Although I can't remember the last time a *real* job asked for 'personal' references."

"Still, in case they do – is it all right?"

"Sure." Maria's high-heeled shoes clacked against the concrete. "I'll just make sure to not tell them about your fits of hysteria. Employers tend to look down on that."

Katy shot Maria a look. Maria shrugged.

"Oh, you're going to tell me you *weren't* crying before I came home?"

Katy shifted her shoulders.

"You forget how long I've known you," Maria added.

"Regardless."

They walked side by side for a block, neither saying a word. The sounds of a trolley rumbling by the B line tracks could be heard from down the street.

"I'll have you know I made sure to leave work before I turned on the waterworks," Katy finally said.

Maria nodded at Katy before crossing the street.

"Keeping the melodrama at home," replied Maria. "I can respect that."

Both girls stepped up onto the train platform, the trolley that they had heard already long gone, slowly traveling down Commonwealth Avenue and into the city.

Chapter 3

Katy took a brief detour through the bookstore when she came in the next morning, meandering through the aisles on the second floor as she made her way to the break room.

GRE-prep books were in the same aisle as the used textbooks. While some were published in 2005, others were dated back upwards of ten years. Katy leafed through a few volumes, unsure exactly what she was looking for. Did schools in Europe recognize GRE test scores? She'd have to find out during her lunch break.

After a minute or two, Katy grabbed one of the older books and tucked it into the crook of her elbow. The more recent copies were upwards of $20, $30, even $40. This one, used and with a publication date of 1998, was only $7. How much could have changed in seven years, anyway? Plus, a cheaper book would alleviate any guilt if she ended up putting grad school on the back burner upon finding an interesting job. Katy walked into the staff room – a tiny one-room, one-bathroom cube located in the far-left corner of the store – and slid the book along with her backpack into her locker.

It was almost 8:30 in the morning and Katy already felt drained. Maria's friends had joined them for drinks beforehand, and Katy's one drink before the movies quickly evolved into three (and, given how infrequently she drank, all three drinks weighed heavy in her stomach). Katy ended up spending most of the movie stuffing popcorn into her mouth, chomping down on the popcorn to mask the lingering aftertaste of her rum and Coke drinks. This resulted in a nauseating combination of rum, Coke, popcorn, and not much else in her stomach. In a moment of proper and poetic timing, Katy had become so queasy that she nearly threw up on the theatre floor right at the moment when the male and female protagonists realized that they were madly in love with each other after all.

Katy could see through the store's second-floor windows that rush hour was in full swing. Boston traffic in the morning was relentless, even on smaller roads like the one that South End Collections was on. Katy trudged down the bookstore's stairwell – an antique, creaky piece of carpentry that descended against the wall and stopped just feet before the cashier area – and began walking toward the back room, where she found Andrea unloading boxes at a steady, methodical pace.

"Good morning," Andrea said.

Katy scanned the area, positively mortified. The stock room was in almost as much disorder as when Katy left it yesterday. What did Hannah do? Price a few more books and then clock out? Really, the question was what *didn't* Hannah do. And that answer was everything.

Well, that's what Katy got for trusting a part-time college student to pick up the slack of a full-time neurotic supervisor.

"Hey there." Katy gave a nervous salutation. "Um, so do you want me to help out with the boxes or should I get the money out for the registers?"

"The registers will take five minutes, tops. *This* –" Andrea held up one of the books for emphasis. "– will take all day. *If* we're lucky."

"Well, then." Katy pressed her lips together. "I guess I'll help with the boxes."

Avoiding Andrea's gaze, Katy walked over to the next carton. She cut the tape, opened the flaps, and grabbed for a pushcart. Katy started loading up the cart, this time with smaller, more careful handfuls.

The stockroom became deafeningly quiet, interrupted only by the noise of books gently landing on the pushcart. Katy kept her eyes on the books, focusing only on the task at hand.

"You left us a pretty mess to clean up," Andrea finally said.

Katy stopped what she was doing and looked up.

"I'm really, really sorry about that. I am," Katy meekly answered. "I just…I felt sick."

"Yeah, yeah…so I read," Andrea replied with a frustrated huff. "I guess I can't fault you too much. Even though we *were* already short-handed yesterday. Just be glad Ben is willing to cover your butt."

Katy's eyebrows darted up.

"Oh?"

"He left a note in my office detailing why you left," said Andrea. "And, by some miracle, he was able to prep the store for the next day, even while shorthanded. That alone is giving us a chance to actually get caught up on this stuff today." Andrea clicked her tongue and shook her head. "Count yourself lucky that we have him around. The kid's got more maturity in him at *twenty*-six then I ever did at *forty*-six."

"I'll definitely have to thank him," Katy replied, her mouth suddenly dry.

"We'll see what we can get done for now." Andrea shifted an empty box over and opened the one underneath it. "Hannah's coming in around 1. Ray's going to make up for calling in sick yesterday by coming in tonight. I called up Evelyn; she might be able to give us a hand as well." Andrea looked into the carton and smiled. "Oh, Professor Greene. You're not coming in for another month. Why are your books arriving now?"

Andrea turned to Katy, holding one of the textbooks in the air.

"Can you believe this guy? Stuck up to think that people will come to a book signing of his newest textbook. Almost every professor I had in college had written probably a whole library's worth of books, and none of them pulled this nonsense. How much do you want to bet he'll force his students to come as part of their assignment?" Andrea tossed the book back into the box. "Eh, what can you do. Revenue's revenue." Andrea bent over and wedged her fingers under the bottom of the box.

"Need any help with that?" Katy asked, placing down the book in her hands.

"That'd be nice," Andrea replied shortly.

Katy scuttled over to the other side of the box and helped lift it up.

"We'll put it in the back, over there," Andrea motioned with her head. Katy turned to see where she was going and began walking in that direction, taking baby steps to keep from tripping.

"Before I forget," Katy said mid-stride, "I have a book I need to you ring in for me."

"Oooh, what are you getting? The latest chick lit?"

Katy turned and faced Andrea long enough to shoot her a look of disgust.

"You know I die a little each time you say that."

"Well," Andrea replied with a smirk. "From *that* indignant tone, I'd say you're purchasing a full-out romance novel."

"Don't forget you're teasing someone who's holding one end of a very heavy box," Katy grunted, shuffling backwards until she was parallel with the back wall. She steadily lowered herself with Andrea, easing the box to the ground before sliding her fingers away.

"But really though. What's on the reading list today?"

"Oh nothing, y'know." Katy could feel her mouth go dry again. "Just a GRE prep book."

"GRE?" Andrea repeated. "Are you thinking of getting your Master's?"

No, Katy couldn't help but think to herself. *I just like studying for unnecessary tests.*

"Um…well yeah. I mean, I figure it's time to take that…um…that next step forward," said Katy, absently nodding along with her reply.

"Oh, that's great! A girl like you really should get an advanced degree. You've always been so smart." Andrea checked the time and walked back to the main stack of boxes. "Are you planning on going back to BU?"

"BU? Oh yeah, of course. I mean, where else would anyone go to study…English?"

Katy pressed her tongue to the roof of her mouth.

"You've got a knack for literature. It makes sense." Andrea opened a box and automatically started placing the books on the overstock shelf. "I can't say it won't be at a loss to me, though. I'd hate to lose you as a full-time supervisor."

Katy let out a muffled "uh huh" while arranging the pushcarts.

"I could still count on you for part-time work, right?"

"Yeah, of course." Katy's voice wavered.

"Ah, I knew I could count on you," Andrea beamed, thumbing the spines of the overstock books on the metal shelves. "It would be just like old times."

Katy repeated, "old times" wordlessly. A new type of nausea took over her. She gripped the handle of the first pushcart, focusing on the cool metal against her skin.

"Alright, it's time for me to set up the registers. If you could record this latest shipment, that would be great." Andrea wiped her forehead before stepping out of the stockroom.

Katy watched through the doorway as Andrea walked over to the registers, popped both of them open, took out the trays, and delivered the trays to her office. Part of her desperately wished she could just bolt out of the store. She wanted to escape onto the sidewalk, feeling the sun on her face and grabbing lungfuls of fresh air, but looking out through the window would have to do for now. She rubbed her eyes, took in a long breath of stagnant bookstore air, and grabbed invoices from the shipment.

Katy hated this part of her job almost as much as she hated dealing with customers. Recording shipment invoices was incredibly tedious, but it required all of her attention. Going on autopilot usually resulted in a major error, which resulted in Katy spending even more time on shipment invoices than she wanted.

Katy sighed and opened the shipment binder. The more that Katy thought about it, however, the more Katy realized that her task was probably like some outdated version of data entry. And, really, who looks down on people who do data entry? At least not like they do with retail junkies. People in data entry work in offices. And they get paid better. And they get health insurance.

And they have access to the internet. Unlike at the store, where, if Katy needed to do something online during the day, she'd have to lug her laptop to work, wait until her lunch break, and steal the wireless internet at the coffee shop down the block.

And that was exactly what Katy was planning to do that day. She just had to pray that Andrea wasn't hard-set on getting all of those books out before Katy could take her break. There were over six carts already queued up, and it took at least a half an hour to put one cart's worth of books away.

Putting books away – a standard part of library work, right? Maybe she could work at a library. Maybe the Boston Public Library. Granted, she'd be putting books away more frequently, but the general atmosphere of a library is so much more relaxed. Librarians might have a stigma all their own, but at least they have the reputation of being book-smart and intelligent. Working at a bookstore tells the outside world that you're either a mindless retail slave or so unjustifiably pretentious that only a bookstore would put up with your spiels about TS Eliot and James Joyce.

"And God help me if anyone here starts raving about James Joyce," Katy muttered to herself, copying over dates, codes, and titles into the binder. Talking to herself was enough to snap her out of her reverie and make her realize that she had just gone on autopilot. She'd have to scan over everything now, just to make sure she hadn't made a mistake.

"Not a fan, I take it." A familiar voice rang into the room, interrupting Katy's work.

Katy raised her head to the tall, slender figure standing in the doorway.

"How long have you been standing there?" Katy asked.

Evelyn stepped into the backroom and closed the door behind her.

"Long enough to find out that you talk to yourself about how much you hate James Joyce," she said.

Katy couldn't help but smirk. Katy had only known Evelyn for the last year or so, but she considered Evelyn one of her closest friends. She worked at the store part-time, spending the rest of her time as an aspiring actor and model, going from audition to audition, casting call to casting call. Andrea had routinely offered Evelyn a full-time position, but Evelyn had always (politely) declined. Katy couldn't help but be slightly envious, if only because Evelyn didn't have to spend as much time at South End Collections as she did.

"You know me. Never have been, never will be." Katy raked a hand through her hair, her eyes scanning the pages in her binder. "Apparently I skipped the class where we all drink the Kool-Aid and become obsessed with books that, in reality, suck."

"Harsh words from an English major." Evelyn smirked, walking over to the carts and scanning the titles. "See, I actually liked *Dubliners*."

"That's because it wasn't forced down your throat like a cyanide pill." Katy did a halfhearted flip-through of the invoices before sighing and restacking them. "You'd hate it too if you spent an entire class finding the symbolism in everything."

"I doubt the entire class was spent on finding symbolism," Evelyn replied.

"You'd think that would be the case, but no..." Katy closed the binder and got up from her seat. "He's buying her a gift! It's symbolic of him trying to get closer to God." Katy turned towards the steel cabinet next to her seat. "She's drinking coffee! It's symbolic of her waking up to reality." Katy opened the filing cabinet and thumbed through the folders. "He took a dump! That's symbolic of...release!"

Katy dropped the invoices into their proper spot and hip-bumped the cabinet closed.

"Well, this is turning out to be a lovely and not-at-all disgusting conversation," Evelyn quipped.

"I only speak the truth."

"The 'truth' sounds more like pent up emotions and resentment," Evelyn replied. "Come help me with the carts instead."

Suppressing a grin, Katy rolled her eyes and joined Evelyn at the carts.

"I see you're in the best of moods."

"I love getting woken up at the crack of dawn by a phone call," Evelyn replied. She held the backroom door open with her elbow as she passed her cart through. "Unless it's to tell me I've landed a gig...or an Oscar nomination...I don't want to hear it."

Katy smiled.

"Well, I'm sure Andrea appreciates it anyway."

"I'd appreciate not working at 10 in the morning unless I've been given a week to prepare," Evelyn protested as she exited with her cart.

"It's already 10?" said Katy. "Sheesh. Time flies when you're forced to do tedious paperwork."

Katy looked down at her cart. A mix of romance and chick lit – a.k.a. "Women's Literature" – on one side, young adult novels on the other. Looked like someone hit pay dirt. With a sigh, she made her way to the Women's Literature aisle and grabbed her first handful.

The one nice thing about putting books away was, unlike recording shipments and inventory, it could mostly be done on autopilot. Smith is in between Sampson and Summers. Last names like Aaronson trump everything in its section, becoming trumped only when somebody figures out a way to begin a name with even more letter As. If there is more than one book written by the author on the shelf, check the title and alphabetize by title. If there is more than one author with the last name, check the first name. Et cetera, et cetera, ad nauseum, ad infinitum.

And – really – the customers were only going to end up moving them out of place anyway, so did it matter if Katy messed up a time or two?

The fluff that filled the "Women's Literature" section was the simplest. Novels fell into two easily sortable categories: part of an incredibly long series of books, or the author's only work. They were either a constant and consistent rehashing of the same characters, locations, and situations...or a would-be writers' only attempt at a novel. Katy wasn't sure what perplexed her more: the writers who only produced one chick lit book, or the writers who continued to shamelessly dish out the same tired drivel.

Katy grabbed her second handful. One of the books was a continuation of a series from one of the more infamous serial authors. She scanned the cover and rolled her eyes.

Coffee and Conversation.

"Oh you *have* to be kidding me." Katy rolled her eyes again for extra emphasis. A customer in Katy's aisle looked over quizzically.

"You alright?" Evelyn called from a few aisles over.

Katy gave a mortified grin to the customer and slinked away to the classics, poetry, and historical fiction aisle, where Evelyn was rhythmically sorting her books.

"Can you believe this nonsense?" Katy turned the book's cover to Evelyn. "How much do you want to bet that the lovebirds in the story meet each other at a coffee shop?"

Evelyn lowered her eyes to the book.

"Or," she stated slowly, "they might just like to...get together at one. And talk. Hence the 'conversation' part."

"Please," Katy scoffed. "You and I both know that any chick lit worth its weight in movie deals always has the gorgeous woman meeting the ridiculously handsome man at a coffee shop." Katy turned the book back to her and tapped at its cover. "Maybe this one will even spice it up a bit and –" Katy feigned a gasp. "— have one of them *working* there."

Katy clasped her hand against her mouth. Evelyn smiled and shook her head.

"I still don't see why you had to cry out like that," Evelyn remarked. "I thought you had stepped in dog poop, or something."

"Well, this is kind of like dog poop, only I didn't step in it." Katy lowered the book to her hips. "Did you know that we're getting another chick lit book in a couple weeks with basically the same title? I guarantee you it's the same storyline. You'd honestly think people would catch on that these books are all the same."

"Well, maybe they have, and they don't care," Evelyn replied. "People still see romantic comedies. Everyone knows the couple will stay together in the end, but they watch it anyway. Entertainment's entertainment, even if it's at the lowest common denominator."

"And it doesn't get any lower than this." Katy quipped.

"At least it's not about sparkly vampires?" Evelyn offered.

"Touché," Katy responded. "I although I still have Young Adult to sort out after this, so I'm sure I'll get my fill of those, too." Katy sighed and looked down at the book. "Well, time to put *Coffee and Conversation* away, next to *Lattes and Love* and *Cappuccinos and…More Conversation*."

"You are ridiculous," Evelyn remarked.

"And you love me for it." Katy flashed Evelyn a winning smile and walked back to her spot in Women's Literature. She slid *Coffee and Conversation* into its rightful place and picked up her next handful of books.

Katy's mind started wandering again before she could finish her set. Now that she thought about it, being a librarian really wouldn't be that much of a step up from book retail. Cleaning up after people, scanning book after book, constantly telling people to "have a nice day" – it was practically the same thing, only the books would be on loan instead of sold off.

But what about being a librarian at a school? Teaching students the Dewy Decimal System (or was it now Library of Congress in schools?) and manning the computer room. That might be fun.

And very few school libraries would have books like *Coffee and Conversation*. Right?

Katy gave an audible sigh. What good would speculating do? Katy didn't know what was available yet, and she wouldn't get a chance to look until her lunch break. But she was anxious – more than a little anxious – to get started with her searching. Part of her worried that any day now, she'd run into someone else – anyone else – from her past, and learn that they were getting their MD, or had just returned from a missionary trip in Tanzania.

Or, maybe she'd run into an old classmate who accidentally got pregnant right out of high school and now worked at McDonald's. Not *everyone* can be absurdly successful. Right? Katy needed that thought to keep things in balance. She tried her best to ignore the nagging feeling that she was more on that end of the spectrum than the other.

After emptying her cart, Katy parked it along the back wall and detoured into the owner's office to check the time. 11:42. Katy slunk back out of the office and dragged her empty cart into the stock room. Katy looked at the rest of the carts, tapping her foot anxiously before finally turning around and walking toward the registers.

"Is it alright if I take my lunch break now?" Katy asked as she rested her elbows on the side edge cashier's counter. A customer came up to Andrea's register and, with a curious glance at Katy, unloaded his armful of books to the counter.

Andrea glanced down at her wristwatch before picking up the customer's books.

"You can't wait fifteen minutes?" Andrea looked over at Katy, her fingers effortlessly finding the buttons on the register.

"Well, starting a cart *now* wouldn't make any sense. You'd then have a cart hanging around unattended for a half hour," Katy reasoned.

"You could always bring the cart back to the stockroom before its finished. Or, if you want, you could face the shelves for a bit." Andrea turned towards the customer. "That will be $39.62, sir." The customer handed her a few twenties and Andrea cradled the cash drawer as it popped out. "Why are you so eager, anyway?"

"I need to use Café Jungle's wi-fi. And it would be nice to beat the lunch rush. At least by a few minutes."

Andrea gave the change to her customer with a sigh.

"Fine, fine. If it's a special occasion, go right ahead." Andrea closed the cash tray and turned her body towards Katy.

"'Special occasion'. You make it sound like I'm going on a field trip."

"I can change my mind if you'd like."

"No, no. I'm good. Grabbing my stuff now." Katy dashed up the stairs and into the staff room. She grabbed her backpack from her locker, slung it over her shoulder, and returned to the front.

"Why do you need to go online so badly, anyway?" Andrea remarked. "You don't strike me as the type to constantly check her email."

"Um, you know – really want to get a jump start on all the grad school stuff." Katy's voice faltered, her backpack already pushing open the door as she slowly backed out. Before Andrea could say anything in response, Katy twirled her body out of the store and onto the sidewalk.

Katy made her way to the coffee shop, walking so fast that she was nearly bouncing down the street. She could smell the heat radiating off of the asphalt. With any luck, they'd have an early summer this year. Springtime in Boston always meant rain, anyway. Katy readjusted her backpack and made her way into the shop.

The aroma of pastries and coffee beans filled the air. The chatter from the patrons around her easily overwhelmed the acoustic rock music that was meekly playing from the overhead speaker system. After a quick glance around, Katy picked a small table by the window.

"Where to begin..." Katy mumbled to herself as she opened her laptop. There were job sites, online classifieds...did she still have access to her university's career center page? Either way, there had to be something. Katy delayed the decision, checking her email three or four times, before searching for job listing websites.

Signing up for the job search sites was the simple part. It involved nothing more than a valid email address and the ability to type. She knew her name, her birthdate, her phone number. Easy stuff. And she already had a résumé. It was over 4 years old, but all it needed was a few alterations and it could be brought up to date. Delete "bookstore associate", replace with "shift supervisor", add a few new duties, and *voilà*. She didn't even have to change the "dates hired" section.

Sure, signing up was easy. It was the searching process that overwhelmed her. She was flying blind, essentially, with random key words and an endless number of vague categories. Why couldn't the websites give Katy a personality test and match her with jobs best suited for her, like some dating sites do? Where was the place where she could just tell them her likes and dislikes and they would come up with her top 10 matches in the Boston area?

If Katy was being honest with herself, it was starting to look like finding a *boyfriend* online would be less stressful than finding an actual *job*.

Category: single female looking for single male. Subcategory: between the ages of 24 and 28. Location: Boston area, Massachusetts.

Matchmaker, matchmaker, make me a match.

"Is it okay if I sit here?" A voice called from beyond the laptop. Katy jerked her eyes away from the screen.

"Um, sure, I guess," she answered reflexively, sitting up straight and readjusting herself in her seat.

"I'm Alex, by the way." The voice spoke again, taking the seat across from her. "I hope you don't mind. Every table's been taken."

"Um, sure thing. No worries," Katy mumbled, looking up just long enough to smile awkwardly and look back down at the table. She glanced at the man in front of her before focusing on the table again, hoping against hope that she wasn't suddenly blushing. His eyes were such an intense shade of blue that it was downright impossible to maintain proper eye contact. She glanced up one more time, pressed her lips tightly together, and locked her eyes back onto her laptop's keyboard.

Why do authors always write about the love interest and their amazing, piercing blue eyes? Really, they're not as cracked up as they're made out to be. They didn't remind Katy of the ocean, nor were they effortlessly hypnotizing her. All they did was make her a little bit uncomfortable and a lot bit self-conscious.

With one last glance at Alex, Katy turned back to her laptop and tried to return to business. She attempted to continue her search, only to quickly give up and just start clicking at random websites. She was constantly aware that Alex was in front of her and that knowledge was distracting her more and more with each passing moment.

He was good-looking, that was obvious enough. He had the height and the hair and the square jaw line, complete with the beginnings of a five o'clock shadow. All the requirements needed for a textbook definition of a handsome man. Check, check, and check.

And she wanted nothing more than to have him out of her head so she could get back to her fruitless job search.

"I don't think I got your name," Alex eventually spoke up, pulling apart his scone more than he was actually eating it.

"I'm sorry. Um, it's – it's Katy," she replied, scratching her shoulder. "Nice to meet you."

"Likewise." Alex bowed his head slightly.

Katy brought her eyes back to her keyboard. She gently moved her finger along the touch pad, watching the pointer do figure eights across the screen. Everyone else's chatter quickly filled up the sudden void created by two strangers sitting silently at a table. Katy pressed her tongue to the roof of her mouth, becoming all too aware that the silence between the two was yet again becoming a contender for space in the room.

"Okay, I have a confession," Alex spoke up again.

Katy snapped to attention.

"When I saw that all the seats were taken, I was just going to go and head back to work."

"Really?"

Katy felt the blood rush to her face. Her fingertips tapped at the edge of her laptop.

"What made you change your mind?" she found herself asking.

"Well, I saw a beautiful young lady by her laptop and I knew that I had to get to know her better." Alex gave Katy a charming smile.

Katy felt a sudden and lethal combination of complete flattery and paralyzing panic, like she had just been chosen by the teacher to present her phenomenal research project to the class. She bit her tongue and pressed her palms into the edge of her computer.

Why don't books ever talk about how *scary* meeting someone new can be? No, they never talk about that. Just entertaining banter and flirtatious glances and maybe some butterflies in the stomach. Perhaps all those impossibly gorgeous women are just so socially proficient that they knew exactly how to handle those types of situations.

"I'd love to meet this beautiful young lady." Katy stared into her screen. "She sounds pretty awesome."

"She does. I think you'd like her."

Katy looked up and blushed.

"You are one smooth talker," she said, immediately wincing as if someone had just stomped on her toes.

Smooth talker? *Smooth talker?* Who even *says* that anymore?

Maybe she should invite him to a speakeasy while she was at it.

Alex shrugged his shoulders and popped a piece of his scone into his mouth.

"You'd be surprised to find out that I'm not always this smooth."

Katy didn't know how to respond. Words – she knew she had some of those somewhere. Thousands upon thousands of words in the English language and she couldn't even scrounge up a few of them to flirt back at an absurdly handsome guy.

Why did it always seem so effortless for everyone else? Flirting was just not her forte. There was nothing that she could draw from to help her. All the memories, all the interactions she's had with people she was comfortable talking to, all the stock responses that she could use to appear socially competent, were betraying her. Katy gave a blushing laugh and went back to looking at her screen. The whirl of an electronic whisk started up behind them. She could smell the giant macadamia cookies and suddenly felt like getting up and buying one, even though she hadn't taken a bite from her sandwich.

"I don't think I've seen you before. Do you live around here?" said Alex after the distant sound of the whisk died down.

"Ah, no. I live in Brighton. But I work here, though," said Katy, before quickly adding: "Well, not *here*, but, I mean, at the bookstore down the street. South End Collections – have you ever been there?"

"I can't say that I have. But then again I don't spend much time here."

"Really?" Katy replied. "So what brings you to the South End?"

Katy pushed a section of hair behind her ear. Her fingers slid down the strands and lightly twisted the pieces at the end.

Houston, we have dialogue.

"I had a meeting with a potential client. And I figured I'd grab something to eat before heading back."

As if to prove his intentions, Alex took one of the larger pieces of his shredded scone and placed it into his mouth.

"Where do you work?" Katy asked.

Conversation? Full steam ahead.

"I'm the director of programming at Trotsky, Inc," Alex responded, eating at his scone at a more comfortable pace. "I'm guessing that you never heard of them. It's a firm near Downtown."

"You caught me, there. I've definitely never heard of them. But it does sound interesting," Katy said, unsure of what program directors even did in the first place. Katy scratched her forehead and looked down at her laptop. Popping up in her peripheral vision, her computer's screen stoically informed her that it was now 12:25. Ten minutes later than it should've been. Would Andrea notice if Katy returned late after leaving so early? If she left now, she'd be back by 12:30, which was when she was originally scheduled to go back to work anyway. Katy's teeth scraped at her lower lip.

"I hate to be the bearer of bad news, but my lunch break's almost up." Katy slowly closed her laptop.

"I'm sorry to hear that," Alex responded, remaining seated. "It was really great talking to you."

"Yeah, likewise." Katy stood up and slid her laptop into her bag.

Alex smiled and ate the last remains of his scone. Katy fumbled around in her bag, occasionally looking up to see if Alex would say anything else. Was the conversation really going to end there? Was he really only interested in spending time with her for 40 whole minutes?

She wasn't offended – not yet, at least – but she couldn't ignore the sinking feeling of disappointment as she stuffed back everything inside the bag, shuffled the edges of her backpack around the laptop, and zipped it closed.

All that talking – all that work *to* talk – all for nothing?

"Hey, uh, before you go, is it possible to get your number?" Alex's voice made its way through Katy's micro-reverie. "I'd love to call you sometime. Maybe we could grab some coffee."

Katy snapped her head up.

"Y'know, seeing that neither of us ordered coffee today," Alex added.

Katy smiled and pushed her chair in, wondering if Alex had been listening in on her internal dialogue and was now acting accordingly.

"Yeah, of course. That'd be great." Katy shifted her backpack onto her shoulders and gave her number to Alex. The sinking feeling that had reached its way to her lower abdomen quickly dissolved into a small wave of embarrassment.

But what is life without a little melodrama?

"I'll call you sometime." Alex slipped his cell phone back into his pocket, picked up the wax sheets that came with his scone and crumpled them into a ball.

"That sounds great," Katy answered, shifting her weight from one foot to the next.

"It was great meeting you." Alex got up and pushed in his seat. "Have fun at the bookstore."

"Heh, I'll try. I'll talk to you later." Katy turned and exited the shop, replaying her interactions with Alex over and over again in her head to the point that she nearly walked into traffic when crossing the street.

She could banter back and forth with her closest friends, she could play the Employee of the Month role when she felt like it (or Passive-Aggressive Employee of the Month when she didn't), but it took every brain cell that wasn't currently focusing on organ function and basic motor skills to talk to someone out of her immediate comfort zone.

And sometimes the parts of her brain in charge of the basic motor skills were needed for basic social pleasantries as well.

What had just happened was above and beyond her comfort zone. She was in a different setting, and with no one familiar that she could fall back on. At least at SEC, she had been there long enough to gain the confidence necessary to interact with customers and co-workers without much effort. At least at parties, she could tag along with Maria and pretend that Maria's friends were her friends too (Maria was the social butterfly of the two anyway, with her infinite list of people to call and her infinite patience for an English major who was once assigned the same freshman dorm room as her). In the bookstore, she could play her role. With Maria around, she had her safety net. Here, she was struggling to stay afloat.

But Alex didn't seem to mind, did he? Who would ask for the number of someone if they thought the person acted like they had been dropped at birth?

Well, someone who had a thing for people who had been dropped at birth, but Alex didn't seem like the type to have such a fetish.

That would be impossible. Guys in pressed khakis can't have weird fetishes.

Katy continued to make her way back to the store. The sun faded behind a passing cloud, dimming the neighborhood around her, before coming back out and brightening the street again. Her shoes stomped against the concrete, anticipating what Andrea would have to say when Katy returned. The store was in plain sight. Katy watched it slowly inch forward towards her as she prepared for the wrath of her boss.

Katy jolted a bit, losing her stride and nearly tripping over her feet as she felt her back pocket come alive. She took a moment to regain balance and composure before pulling out her flip phone, which was vibrating in rhythm to its ring tone.

"Uh…hello?" Katy asked uncertainly. The number on the screen bore no resemblance to any number she was familiar with.

"Hey, it's Alex. From the coffee place?" A voice jovially danced its way into her ear. "I know that was ages ago but…remember me?"

Katy stayed silent for a moment, attempting to squash the bubbling giddiness. Her stomach muscles clenched and her face bunched up.

"Of course!" Katy closed her eyes and responded. "But – just vaguely, you know."

"It's what I get for waiting so long to call a girl back." Alex gave a *tsk-tsk* into the phone. "But I was hoping if you'd let someone you vaguely remember take you out to dinner sometime."

Katy turned back, squinting to see the Café Jungle sign. She was at least a block or so away at this point. The distance made her feel brave.

Brav*er*, at least.

"Well that depends." Katy smirked into the phone. "How many times have you called a girl immediately after meeting, pretending like you haven't called in ages?"

"Um." Alex coughed out his words. "Am I allowed to plead the fifth?"

"I don't know – am I allowed to plead the fifth on dinner?" Katy responded, instantaneously going wide-eyed and smacking herself on the forehead. Somewhere on Tremont Street, a law student was sensing a disturbance in the force. Lawyers in cemeteries all around the greater-Boston area were rolling counter-clockwise in their graves. And Katy was deeply regretting her failed attempt at banter. "How about I pretend the last 30 seconds never happened and I just say yes to dinner?"

"I'd say that'd be great," Alex replied. "Can I make up for lost time by suggesting dinner tomorrow?"

"Tomorrow?" Katy repeated. "I'd love to, but I'm closing the store tomorrow. I don't get out until at least 10:30."

"Well, how about the more traditional Friday or Saturday, then?"

"I have Friday off. That could work for me."

Katy found herself just outside of South End Collections. She stationed herself right by the doorway, facing towards the street, her back to the store.

How late was it now? Ah, hell. It didn't matter.

"So Friday at 7, then?"

"Sounds great," Katy beamed. She turned around and looked through one of the store's windows. Andrea met her gaze and gave her a cold stare from the cash registers. Katy quickly turned back.

"Well, excellent, I'll talk you later," said Alex.

"Alright, I'll talk to you later...as well." Katy felt her face tighten. She snapped closed her phone, slipped her it back into her pocket, and made her way inside, replaying her last statement over and over in her mind.

'I look forward to it.' 'And I'll see you on Friday.' Even an, 'Okay, bye' would've been better.

Good God. Katelyn Viktoria Sinclaire – master linguist. Winston Churchill be damned.

"Do you have any clue what time it is?" Andrea lowered her eyebrows at Katy. Katy stopped in her tracks and gave Andrea her best impression of doe eyes.

"Um...earlier than I hope it is?" Katy squeaked out. She stood stock-still by the cashier's counter, her fingers playing with the straps of her bag.

"It's nearly one," Andrea responded, tapping on the counter.

"Oh." Katy's lips puckered into her teeth. "Um, there's a good reason for that, I promise."

"Oh, I am *all* ears."

"I, um..." Katy lowered her eyebrows.

Was it even worth trying to come up with an excuse? Would anything sound even remotely plausible? Freak cappuccino accident? Mugging? Time warp? Oh, for crying out loud – she saw her on the phone outside of the store.

"Okay, I'll be honest: I met a guy and I lost track of time."

"Oh," Andrea replied, her tone significantly lighter now. "While getting coffee?"

"Well, technically the internet. But, yeah. We ended up sitting across from each other and struck up conversation." Katy's face started warming up. She gave an embarrassed smile, blushing at the fact she was blushing.

Andrea hesitated.

"Well, okay, then," she responded. "If you promise to work a half hour extra tonight, I'll pretend this didn't happen."

Katy should've turned for the staircase then. She should've professed her undying gratitude to her generous and benevolent boss and darted up the staircase before that generous boss changed her generous mind.

"That was extra-kind." Katy's voice permeated the room instead of the sound of her footsteps obligingly turning and walking up the thinly carpeted stairs. "Why the clemency?"

"Believe it or not, I know what it's like. I was young once, too," said Andrea. "Now go back and help Evelyn. We've still got a lot to get done. You're lucky she agreed to stay longer."

Katy finally accepted the act of kindness without any further questioning and brought herself upstairs and into the staff room. She unlocked the padlock to her locker, pushed her bag in, and slipped the lock back through the latch. She walked down the stairs and returned to the back room.

"Welcome back," greeted Evelyn from inside, already pulling out another cart. "I thought you had abandoned ship."

"If only," Katy replied. She looked over her next round of books. Self-Help and Traveler's Guides. Her fingers skirted along the edges of the spines, tapping her fingertips occasionally against the corners of the covers. She grabbed the front of the cart and tugged it behind her, following Evelyn out the door. "Guess who's got a date for Friday?"

Evelyn stopped and turned around.

"No way."

Katy blushed again.

"Yeah way."

Evelyn's jaw dropped.

"When did *that* happen?"

"Just now, during break," Katy answered. "It's why I was so late coming back."

"Get out of here," Evelyn said with a keen smile.

"Seriously."

"Some guy just…asked you out?"

"You make it sound like I had a drive-by proposal." Katy cocked an eyebrow. "We talked. And then he asked for my number."

"Wow, good for you." Evelyn remarked.

"It's only one date," Katy reminded. "We'll see what happens."

"But still, that's pretty awesome," Evelyn went on, turning to face the front again. "I mean, that kind of stuff never happens to me."

"And I don't believe that for a second," Katy said, following Evelyn as they continued to pull their carts down the aisle.

"It's true," Evelyn said over her shoulder. "You'll have to tell me your secret."

"I don't know – personality? Confidence?" Katy bobbed her head from side to side. "Constant public declarations of my incurable nymphomania?"

From behind Katy, a customer gave a curt "excuse me" as he walked past the girls, his eyes on the ground.

"Hi there, sir." Katy's lips curled into her teeth as she attempted to smile. The man mumbled a single syllable in response and quickly turned a corner.

Evelyn pursed her own lips while she watched the customer disappear.

"Well, you must be right," Evelyn remarked, letting her smile break free. "Just a quiet mentioning of it draws them close to you."

"Yup," Katy replied, her tight smile unraveling into a mortified snarl. "Works like a charm."

Katy parked her cart by the stairwell and lugged her first armload of books to the second floor. The overwhelming sense of humiliation abated after a while, and she was allowed to go back to doing her tasks without replaying the scene with the customer over and over in her head.

She was amazed – downright incredulous – that "that kind of stuff" never happened to Evelyn. Evelyn was the model-slash-actress. She was the girl who always looked like her hair had just been professionally done: hair that held a striking shade of red that could never be duplicated by the $10 stuff you buy at the pharmacy (what do the chick lit books call that kind of hair? "Raven red"? "Fiery red"? "'Hey, someone spilled paint on you' red"?) If someone like Evelyn was getting out-courted by someone like Katy, then all chaos had officially broken loose on the world.

Four horsemen be damned. Which might sound a little redundant, but – eh – details.

Katy quickly returned to her routine of pushing shelved books to the side and placing new arrivals in the gaps. The second floor, with its set of windows facing a bustling downtown, was unseasonably quiet. The world around her seemed to have simplified into basic sounds – the creaking of the floorboards, the shuffling of paper against wooden shelves, the muted ding of a cash register drawer opening – allowing Katy to quietly slip into a contemplative reverie, wondering what Alex's last name was, or where he learned how to win girls over by calling them immediately after meeting, only to pretend like it had been weeks since they had met.

Chapter 4

Katy busied herself Wednesday and Thursday with online job sites, creating profiles and searching blindly. She closed the store on Wednesday, opened on Thursday, and spent both lunch breaks at Café Jungle, half sending out her résumés, half hoping to run into Alex again. Much to her disappointment, his chiseled jaw and ironed khakis never walked through the doors while she was there.

When she wasn't working or finding new a place to work, Katy half-heartedly flipped through her GRE book as a type of pre-study studying. The previous owner had scribbled notes in the margins – techniques to memorize word definitions, attempts at solving math problems – and Katy initially regarded them as type of leg-up. This former wannabe-grad-student did all the work already; all Katy had to do was pay attention. But it became pretty apparent that, while Katy might not have a problem with the vocabulary section, she was a long way off with the math section. And no amount of help from the previous owner could help Katy with anything above the most basic algebra questions.

However, getting ready for the date on Friday seemed pretty elementary for her. She didn't need to ransack her closet, wondering if Alex would like her in a dress with ruffles or a dress with fringe. Perhaps it was due to her extreme lack of choices in her wardrobe, but Katy wasn't too worried. She was certain that she would somehow make a complete fool of herself, but at least she wasn't too concerned about her attire. After all, when has a little black dress steered anyone wrong?

It had been a while since she had gone on an actual date, and even longer since she had been on a "first date". In a way, it genuinely shocked her that people still dated. She could've once sworn that it had gone the way of antebellum courting. She probably was in high school the last time a guy asked her out to dinner. After that, her "dates" were meet-ups in dining halls, meet-ups at parties, and the infamous "watch a movie and make out through most of it" get-together.

Ah, the evolution of relationships. What once started as a man humbly going to a girl's home to entertain both the girl and her father had dissolved into just plain "hanging out".

But obviously people still date. She was going on one, after all. Can't really participate in something that doesn't actually exist.

Well, you could if you hallucinate vividly, but that was neither here nor there.

"Look at you," Maria whistled, leaning against the frame of Katy's bedroom door. "Do I detect eyeliner?"

"Shut up." Katy fidgeted with her hair.

"No, really, though – you look great," said Maria. "Where are you guys going?"

"Top of the Hub," Katy replied.

"Wow." Maria raised her eyebrows. "That's impressive." Maria sauntered into the bedroom and sat on the edge of the bed. "Hey, if it doesn't work out, send him my way so he can take me to the Top of the Hub, too."

Katy found herself fidgeting again. The top of the Prudential Tower held one of the more upscale restaurants known as the Top of the Hub. It boasted an exceptional view of the city and a type of higher-class dining experience that Katy just wasn't all that used to. Who honestly took someone to a place that nice for a first date? She was going from dining hall fries to gourmet meals. It felt surreal, to say the least.

She was hoping she could leave that awkward feeling behind when she left the apartment, but her neurotic self-consciousness eagerly followed her down to the B line. She felt like she stuck out amongst the usual crowd waiting for a trolley. It was a Friday evening; she definitely wasn't the only one going out for the night. But this was Brighton; the people getting on board between this part of the city and downtown Boston were college students: mostly BU, but with Northeastern, Boston College, and a smattering of other colleges students staking claim there as well.

There would be kids in casual wear and bar attire. Very few little black dresses.

It was only late April, but Katy was convinced that summer was coming early this year. Her proof was in the sweat that had accumulated around her neck. She swept a nervous palm under her hair and shook her hands out. Around her were people in blue jeans and sweaters. It was too early for any bar-goers and far too early for the club scene, with their shimmering blouses and little skirts.

And there were definitely no little black dresses.

Katy looked off and watched her trolley come around the bend in the road, rattling around the tracks and into full view. Cars drove along at either side, sandwiched between parked vehicles and the grassy medians that separated public transit from private.

Katy gave a sigh of relief as the trolley stopped in front of her. The newer, box-like trolleys made very distinctive starting and stopping sounds, an odd combination of mechanics and harmonized notes. It made the trolley sound like it had been floating above the tracks all along. The hovering noise whirred into its multi-tonal braking sound and a double *bing* preceded the opening doors. Katy gingerly stepped on board and found a seat.

The plan was to meet Alex at the Prudential Center – a shopping plaza built at the base of the tower, filled with expensive clothing stores, a smattering of ground-level restaurants, and a food court to boot – and then walk to the Skywalk area, where they'd board one of the elevators designed to go directly to the top. If everything went according to plan, they'd get in said elevators, be brought up over 50 floors, and enjoy a dinner that was still way too nice for a first date.

Katy hopped off the B line's trolley at Park Street and grabbed an E line one heading out of the city. She felt a little silly going into the heart of downtown Boston only to turn around and go back out only in a slightly different direction. She could've easily gotten off a few stops earlier and simply walked, but she'd be damned if she did any sort of physical activity in dress shoes. Whoever said that flats were the comfortable alternative to heels had to have been a delirious short person. Whether or not her foot tilted up 45 degrees really didn't matter if the edges of the shoe dug into her skin and created blisters at all the pressure points.

The E line stopped right at the Prudential Center. Katy and Alex's meeting destination was graciously across the hall from the subway exit. Katy exited the turnstiles, crossed the hallway, and tried her best to gingerly stand by the clusters of college students and suburban families waiting to eat at the restaurant adjacent to the plaza's entrance.

Right up the stairs was a mega-bookstore. Part of her wanted to pass the time searching through the bookshelves. Another part of her remembered just how high on the blasphemy scale going to a national chain was when you work at an independent store. She decided to sit tight and watch the patrons enter and exit instead.

Even though she was fifteen minutes early, a tiny pit of unjustified dread started forming in her stomach, the feeling working its way out to her fingertips and throat. An equally unjustified idea popped into her mind: what if Alex never showed up at all?

It could happen; she had been stood up before. Granted, back then, it meant she would hang out in the dorm's lobby area for an hour, angrily calling or texting before returning back to her dorm room. But it still happened.

Plus, she barely even knew the guy. How could one face-to-face conversation and a few phone calls create any real rapport? And – honestly – who would take a girl to such an expensive restaurant on a first date?

People were capable of cruel tricks like that. Meet an unsuspecting girl, promise an extravagant date…build up the hype just to see the look on her face when she realizes it was all fake.

Although: how would they be able to see said look if they didn't show up for the date in the first place?

She was already mapping out her exit strategy when Alex approached her, donned in a button-down shirt and khakis, both ironed out to perfection.

"Hey there," he said. "Did you find the place alright?"

"I've lived in Boston for years. If I can't find the Prudential by now, I'd have to have myself committed," Katy replied back.

"I can't argue with that," said Alex with a nonchalant smirk. "Shall we?"

Katy nodded and began walking to the escalators. They made their way through the Prudential Center and to the elevators, which sent them soaring to one of the highest points in the city.

Katy couldn't help but feel intimidated walking into the restaurant. What stood before her after passing through the lobby was an unnervingly beautiful view of the city. Staring right in front of her as she entered the restaurant was the broad side of the Hancock Tower, almost threatening her with its powerful blue-green presence. It was almost as wonderful/intimidating as the perfectly poised waiters with their pressed suits and polite smiles.

Katy and Alex were seated at a table by one of the glass walls. Katy absently played with the elegant napkin that had been elegantly folded over her elegant silverware while she stared in awe over her city. Without even craning her neck, she could see the downtown area, the Charles River, and a small bit of the MIT campus in Cambridge. Everything was in panoramic view for her: the mix of office lights and twilight – and the river effortlessly reflecting all of it. The waitress poured water into their glassware and asked if they would like to order any drinks to start. Katy responded that she was content with water, looking over at the waitress only long enough to say it.

"You know, in all my time living here, I've never once been up to this place," Katy confessed after the waitress left, her gaze still fixed on the window. "I mean, it's kind of like the Duck Tours: something you kind of write off as something for the tourists. But now I wish I had. This view is amazing."

"Did you grow up in Boston?"

"Well, Lowell, technically, but I've been traveling into Boston since forever." Katy finally dragged her eyes away from the view of the city. "I remember when looking for colleges, the only thing I cared about was if it was in Boston. The rest was just details."

"Which school did you eventually choose?" Alex's menu was still closed. Katy mimicked and kept a palm over the edge of hers.

"BU. I really liked it there. It was so close to everything." Katy's fingers drummed on the edge of the menu. "It was just a walk away from the Paradise Rock Club, so that was really useful."

"Oh wow, the Paradise." Alex laughed. "I have to admit I haven't been there in ages."

"Really?" Katy responded. "I have to admit that I don't go there as much as I used to – but, oh man, I loved going there, especially in college." Katy looked down at her hand on the menu and smiled. "I mean, almost all my favorite bands now play there. And most of those bands were huge like a decade or so ago, so I always feel like I am in the presence of real rock royalty," Katy continued, feeling weirdly confident in babbling about herself. "I mean, I guess I have my brother to thank for that; he's way older than me and he got me hooked on all his favorite bands. By the time I was old enough to go to concerts, the ones that didn't break up were playing small venues like the Paradise. I mean, it really worked out for me – I get to see all my bands up close and personal, and for cheap."

"That's definitely the best part of the Paradise," Alex admitted. "But I have to ask: what bands did you see there?"

"Well, I guess any band that had its heyday in the early 90s...you know, Tomcat, The Posts, Telephonic Overload. The usual alternative rock music of yesteryear."

"And your brother got you into them?" Alex asked. "How old is he, if you don't mind me asking."

"Um...almost 32. Why do you ask?"

"Well, because *I* loved the Posts. And Telephonic Overload. I went to see them when they actually sold out major venues," Alex opened his menu, his eyes scanning the options as he spoke. "I think your brother and I would get along great. Although I guess this means I'm way older than you, too."

"Really? How old *are* you?" Katy blurted. She scraped at her lip with her teeth and added: "If you don't mind me asking, of course."

Katy quickly removed her palm from the cover and opened up her menu, burying her head in the main courses section.

"Thirty," Alex admitted into the menu before looking back up. "You don't have to tell me how old you are – just reassure me that you're at least of age."

"Well, how old do you think I am?" Katy temporarily felt free to be coy in light of Alex's small joke.

"Oh that's not fair." Alex cocked an eyebrow. "That's a loaded question if I ever heard one."

Katy felt herself retreating back, to the point that she was actually leaning against her seat. From brave to chicken in two seconds flat.

Take that, every sports car ever.

"I'm 24, just to let you know. So, heh, very much of age." Katy went back to the menu and darted her eyes over appetizers. Fried calamari. Of all the decadent pleasures in the world, nothing tastes as wonderful as fresh calamari in New England. "You don't have to tell me how old you thought I was," she finally added.

"I didn't really think of any particular age, in all honesty," Alex replied. "You look youthful. I mean, you definitely don't look older. That's definitely not what I mean. But…you have an old soul about you. You looked so – I don't know – mature and established."

"I'm going to take a huge leap here and say that you're a terrible judge of character."

"You don't think you're any of that?"

"I think I work at a bookstore," Katy returned flatly.

"You like music from the generation before you, I'm assuming you enjoy reading, and you looking stunning in a simple evening dress," Alex said after a pause. "I'd say that's all the qualifications you need."

"You think I look stunning," was Katy's knee-jerk response. It was initially a question, but the blood rushed to her head at such a fevered pace that it came out more like a semi-hysterical statement.

"Of course I do," Alex replied with little inflexion in his voice, as if someone had asked him if he really thought water was wet.

Katy looked back down at the menu, biting her lip. The waitress, who must have been trained to swoop in at precisely the right time to take people's orders, came in and became the vessel Katy needed to direct her attention somewhere else.

"I'll have the calamari," she told the waitress before the lady could ask.

The rest of the evening went by in a blur. They asked about each other's lives in the classic first date tradition. Where did you go to school, what's your job like, what are your hobbies… Katy talked about her time at BU; Alex talked about the MBA he recently got at Northeastern University. They mildly debated the best and worst albums from their mutually-enjoyed bands. Katy swung her gaze over from time to time back to the city view, using it as her crutch when the conversation would start slowing down, or if she felt too bewildered to figure out a response.

At the end of the night, Alex quietly paid for dinner and both stepped into the next available elevator. They shuffled backwards, their backs almost pressed against the wall as other people made their way in.

While traveling to the ground, Alex slipped his hand into Katy's. Katy kept her eyes on the door, attempting to keep the smirk from becoming too noticeable or the excitement from welling up in her throat. She became keenly aware of his palm, his thumb, his forearm and bicep. She was acutely conscious of the texture of his shirt and the way it brushed against her skin and the exact amount of space between his face and hers. She got so wrapped up in the simple phenomenon of physical contact with someone new that she didn't even notice when the elevator opened to the main area.

From there Alex took her across the street to the Reflection Pool, which lived up to its name, bouncing back the lights from the Christian Science Center like little fallen stars. They walked alongside the pool, the water lapping over the edges and into the basin below, their hands still intertwined, talking quietly and about nothing in particular.

Before they could hit the midway point of the pool, Alex turned to the left and directed them through the section of trees that seemed to sprout straight from the cement in three perfectly parallel rows. It was in between rows two and three that Alex stopped talking and turned to her. It was in between rows two and three that Alex used his free hand to touch Katy's neck and it was in between those rows where he kissed her gently on the lips.

And in between rows two and three, seconds after the shock of the kiss faded, Katy braced herself, blinking a few times, genuinely expecting wake up and find herself back in the stock room at South End Collections.

She was radiantly happy when she stayed exactly where she was. Instead of coming to realize that she had dosed off at work, she found herself moving in, preparing for a second kiss.

Chapter 5

By the next Monday, the surreal memories of her date seemed to fade into blissful and infallible fact. She might still be in the beginning phases of finding a new job (and hopelessly lost in terms of GRE prep), but at least something was going right.

Mass General, Shmass Schmeneral. Did Rachel ever have an amazing evening at an amazing restaurant with an amazing guy and have it end with an amazing first kiss? Yeah, thought so.

"Ooh Benjamin, I have a huge favor to ask of you," Katy downright sang when Ben entered the store. Katy was arranging books in the display bookcase across from the cashier's counter when Ben arrived for his shift.

"And I haven't even put my stuff away," Ben remarked. "Let's hear it."

"Is it possible to use you as a business-slash-personal reference?" Katy moved around the books in the "Editor's Pick" display shelf. The bookshelf hosted a motley assortment of books that Katy, Ben, Evelyn, and Andrea had picked from the shelves and deemed their "picks" (although obviously not enough of a "pick" to buy for themselves). In this situation, "editor" meant nothing more than "experienced bookstore lackey". They were editors in that they contributed to the employee newsletter pinned up on the staff room bulletin board, but, really, that was it.

"I'm lost…explain." Ben took his bag off his shoulder and hung it from his hand.

"Well, you know, references. People who can vouch for the fact that I – well, that I don't suck. I've got Evelyn and Maria, and I was hoping you, too." Katy kept her back to Ben, glancing periodically over her shoulder as she put the final touches on the books.

"I'm still not following."

"For my job hunt. I need references." Katy shrunk back a bit. Admitting it out loud in the store felt like proclaiming atheism in a convent. It just didn't feel right, and she half expected a nun to wrap her on her hands with a ruler.

"Wait, you're job hunting?" Ben's voice tensed up.

"I didn't tell you?" Katy asked sincerely, looked to the ground, and shrugged. "I guess not. It was a recent decision, but yeah. I'm job hunting."

"So, wait, you're planning on leaving soon?" Ben grilled, his mouth hanging slightly open.

Katy put down the books in her hand and turned to face Ben.

"C'mon now, don't give me that kicked puppy look," Katy said with a smirk. "I'm not, like, leaving-the-country leaving. Just trying to find a new job. You know we'll still hang out."

"Says every person who has ever left a job, ever," replied Ben flatly.

Katy nudged Ben with her elbow before turning back to the shelf.

"Come on, you know I'll always find my way to your apartment, even if they have me working, like, 60 hours a week...hell, maybe then I'll have some money and we can actually do something fun."

Ben wrapped the strap of his bookbag once around his palm. Katy picked up the remaining books from her cart and shuffled them from one hand to the next.

"So...wow." Ben swallowed. "Have you told Andrea?"

"Not yet," Katy replied. "I mean, I know I should – but...I don't know. I'm not ready yet. It's like admitting a tattoo to your parents: it's inevitable, but you're not ready for their reaction." Katy shrugged again. "Maybe I should wait until I actually have a new job before I give her the news."

"Understandable," Ben replied, unraveling the bag strap from his hand. A customer approached the cashier's counter, and Katy abandoned her post by the bookshelves to ring him in.

"I, uh, I'm going to put my stuff away now." Ben held up his canvas satchel to Katy before turning and retreating up the stairs. Katy finished up with the customer before finishing up loading her books onto the bookcase. She lined up the books so they appeared somewhat neat, pausing only when a customer approached the registers.

When Ben came back down, Katy took her scheduled break, this time away from the coffee shop and in the staff room, like her usual routine had once been. The only difference between her old routine and her current break was that, today, she valiantly accompanied her sandwich with a call to Alex, who sounded content, if not downright happy, to spend a half hour of his time talking with her. When her break ended, Katy reluctantly ended the conversation and returned to begin her next task for that day: going through the latest batch of donated books.

Although most people sold their old books, South End Collections routinely received donations as well. Sometimes they were from libraries, either ones that were closing down and or ones that were simply cycling out older books. Sometimes they were from people who wanted to do an act of charity (or didn't want to risk the embarrassment of having one of their books denied for buyback by the store). And every once in a while, someone (usually Katy) got to inspect them, organize them, figure out their price, and record them. Price stickers were to be added to the ones that passed inspection. Then, depending on the number of them, the books would be brought out to the floor right afterwards.

Old library books could be as cheap as a dollar. All that hard work and energy, just to sell a one-dollar item. There was something horribly cost-ineffective about it, but the store wasn't called Collections for nothing.

South End Literary Pack Rats.

Katy spent the rest of her time that day in the back room, slowly going through the motions of her tasks. She prepared the afternoon cash register and spent some time idly talking behind the counter with Josh – who had actually showed up on time for his shift – but eventually she retreated back into the stock room. She slowly but surely finished the stacks of donated books – inspected, recorded, and put away. Seven o'clock eventually rolled around, which meant only one more hour until clocking out. There was stuff she could do, including "facing" (a lovely term that basically meant "tidy up the shelves and make sure everything is in its right place"), but she opted to return to the front of the store instead to kill her last hour hanging out with Ben. Josh's shift had just ended and Ben was now manning the registers alone.

This was something she was going to miss: their schedules overlapped three days out of the week, and, during the lulls, Katy essentially got paid to goof around with her best friend.

"Another sorry shift bites the dust," Katy announced to Ben when she entered the register area. "I didn't get to see you much today. How were things at your end?"

"The usual. Nothing new." Ben drooped his eyes a bit with his reply. "Spent the majority of today marking down February's used books."

"Ooh. Markdowns. That's something I won't miss." Katy walked around the counter and sat down on the stool stationed in the back corner. "Or buybacks, or returns, or…well, just about everything."

"I can imagine," Ben half-heartedly replied.

He stood directly behind the registers, staring off and out the window for a bit. People were slowly filling the sidewalks, getting an early start to their Monday night.

"So you really want out, huh?" He stated bluntly.

"Well, I guess. I mean…it's time." Katy shifted in her seat. "You know, time to break out and find something not so…dead-end-y."

"Aw c'mon, it's not *that* bad. You became a supervisor."

"*That's* a feat." Katy rolled her eyes. "I mean, look around you. The store usually has more supervisors working at any given time than regular employees. Promotions are like participation trophies around here."

"Katy," said Ben, his voice lowering in pitch like he was some surrogate father, "seriously, what's wrong? This is just...out of nowhere. Why the sudden change?"

"Nothing. Nothing happened. Maybe I've just reached my expiration date with this place," Katy replied, shifting in her seat. "I don't know. Things like that just happen, I guess. Time for bigger and better things."

"Is it because of that friend? The one who came by last week?"

"'Friend'?" Katy snorted at Ben, her face scrunching up, as a customer approached the counter.

"Okay, whoever." Ben paused to ring in the customer's books, swipe her credit card, and bid her a good evening. "Is that what started this?"

After a moment, Katy shrugged her shoulders.

"I guess. I don't know. I'm just tired." Katy sighed. "Shit, who wouldn't get tired?" Katy turned and gazed out the window. She couldn't see the Prudential building from this angle; just rows and rows of redbrick buildings. "I mean, if anything, it was a wake-up call. Like, 'This is Your Wasted Life'." Katy paused again. "I just don't want a repeat, if that makes any sense. God knows if anyone else from my past comes in flaunting their great, successful lives, I'll shoot myself."

Katy sighed again leaned back against the wall.

A customer came up to Ben, books in hand. He rang up the lady's sale, placed the books in a bag, and watched as she left the store. The silence in the store made Katy's ears ring. The place seemed awfully dead for a Monday.

"You know what blows my mind?" Ben finally spoke up.

"A shotgun?"

"That people look down on working in retail. I don't get it. My degree's not being used, sure, I'll give you that. But it doesn't mean I'm not going anywhere," Ben stated, slowly and deliberately. "Plenty of people don't use their degrees...and I would be miserable with an office job. How does a cubicle validate anything?"

"I know, I know." Katy scratched behind her ear. There was something so bitterly unpleasant about this conversation, like she was trying to break up with a boyfriend and he was busy telling her the merits of relationships. "I just…it's just time for me to find something new."

Ben shrugged, turning back to the register.

"I just hope you're looking for a new job because *you* want to, not because you think working here means you've failed somehow."

Katy looked down at the shelves underneath the registers. Shelves of varying widths and heights. Binders and notepads and pens and rubber bands and trash bags. Spare bookends and dividers. A trash can in one corner. A bin with newly bought-back books in the other. None of them looked appealing.

"I can't spend my whole life in retail," Katy said finally.

"Some people do."

Katy remained silent, nodding to what Ben had said and looking out the window. Dusk was approaching. Street lights, car lights, and office lights seemed to pop into existence. The weather was cooling down. Soon her shift would be over. She would be replaced by one of their part-time employees. Maybe Hannah, but probably Ray, the 20-year-old who had been there for a couple months. How much did she want to bet that after he graduated, he'd find a real job and leave SEC for good?

For someone whose verbal filter malfunctions from time to time, Katy kept an amazing control over her tongue at that moment. She bit her tongue and pursed her lips, her eyes focused on the outside as Ben rang up a few customers. When the customers were gone and the feeling had passed, Katy shifted the conversation onto a new topic. She knew how Ben felt about the store and had censored herself as a result, but what took control of her thoughts and nearly came blurting out into perceivable and audible sounds was one simple reply:

"And those people are just sad."

Chapter 6

No matter what Katy did, the job market maintained an eerie radio silence with her. She had once thought that her supervisor title and her internship at a publishing company would give her a leg-up on the competition. That "leg up" turned out to be more of a "stump hobble", because it took over two months (and nearly a hundred applications) to get even a reply back from any potential employer.

Was the job market that bad? Were the other applicants that much more experienced? Or did two jobs look too scarce on a résumé? She had gone to a good school and had earned good grades. That had to count for *something*.

And maybe it did: after sending her resume to nearly every job in the metro-Boston area, one job finally called her for an interview. The job was an entry-level position at the Department of Telecommunication and Utilities. She would be in charge of keeping track of packages that came in and out of the office, a slight bit of data-entry, filing, faxing, photocopying, and whatever else the director might want her to do (in the job description, the Department of Telecommunication and Utilities called this duty, "assisting the director in her tasks and activities". That quickly translated to "get the director her coffee" in Katy's eyes). They called her phone while she was at work, left a voicemail, and received a call back from Katy as soon as she clocked out of SEC. They scheduled an interview for that Friday.

She shopped around for a proper business jacket and skirt immediately after her phone call with the Department of

Telecommunication and Utilities. She asked Alex for tips on winning people over in interviews – and then immediately started begging for blind encouragement and false promises instead. He gave her whatever advice he had and told her that any company that didn't think Katy was the perfect candidate for the job would be out of their minds.

The department was located in between Downtown Boston and Boston's North End, on the fifth floor of plain concrete building. On the day of the interview, Katy arrived the standard fifteen minutes early, checked in with the receptionist on the first floor, and made her way to her possible new place of employment. She had her references (which was a depressing three names, but she could probably think of more in due time. Would an old baby-sitter or a high school teacher count?), her résumé, and a printout of the job description. All the items were tucked inside a little black folder that she carried alongside her little white clutch purse.

The elevator brought her up four floors and opened up to a short hallway with a pair of glass doors at the end. Katy walked down the hall and through the doors, into a sparsely furnished foyer. The foyer consisted of four chairs and two solid wood doors, both adorned with a small pane of frosted glass with the respective department names stenciled in black. Katy found a chair by the door marked "Department of Telecommunication and Utilities" and waited for the head of human resources – a Mrs. Wanda Prendergast – to come and see her.

The room was abysmally brown: light brown carpeting, beige walls, brown doors, dark brown chairs. It was as if this very foyer was the dying ground for all colors. Only here, they didn't fade together into white, or shrivel into black. They instead became a sucked-out version of themselves. And apparently that version took on the look of rust. Katy couldn't help but feel like she was not so much waiting in the room as she was stuck in it.

Katy fidgeted in her seat, smoothed her hair back behind her shoulders, and checked for what seemed like the eighteenth time at her folder's contents. Katy checked her phone to once again make sure that it had been turned off. Part of her was tempted to turn it back on, just to find out the time.

"Ms. Sinclaire, it's nice to meet you." A curvy lady with a thin, tight mouth and no-nonsense bun walked through the door and stopped right in front of Katy. "If you'll follow me, we can start the interview process."

"That sounds great," Katy replied, shaking the hand of who she assumed to be Mrs. Prendergast with the recommended two-and-a-half firm shakes. The assumed Mrs. Prendergast grabbed the ID dangling from her waist, touched it to the sensor by the door, and kept the door open for Katy. Katy graciously walked through, stopped, and turned to wait for Mrs. Prendergast to enter and lead the way.

"Do you prefer Katelyn, or Kate…" Mrs. Prendergast asked as they entered a small conference room.

"Katy works for me."

"Ah, Katy."

Katy didn't know quite what to make of Mrs. Prendergast's reply. Instead, she sat down, her folder in front of her on the table, her purse on the floor by her chair. The conference room seemed incredibly walled off; the only areas that didn't seem sealed in with concrete were the door and the small window facing out onto the street.

"So, tell me about yourself."

So tell me about yourself. The most common and most exasperating question in the interviewing lexicon. For those who practice their speech beforehand, it is a monotonous repetition that lost all flavor after first few times giving it. For those who had not figured out an answer beforehand, it is a baffling and suddenly insurmountable question, causing the applicant to eventually descend into babbles about random tidbits of their life.

And where was Katy in that speech spectrum? Somewhere in that icky, irky middle. In the place where she did actually think of something to say, but decided that there was no possible way that people actually still asked that horrifying question anymore and proceeded to forget everything.

"Well, I'm, uh, I'm Katy," she began, her hands now off her folder and under the table so Mrs. Prendergast couldn't see them ringing together. "I grew up in the Boston area, and I've always loved the city." She paused for a second, hoping to God Mrs. Prendergast would take mercy and ask another question.

Mrs. Prendergast did not.

"Well, I've been working at a book store – South End Collections – for about six years, and I've been a supervisor for three of them. It's, uh, it's a great job. It really is. Um, lots of responsibility, lots of organization and patience. I also did an internship at Eddington Publishing, and they do a lot of publishing with um…travel guides and, uh things of that nature."

She looked at Prendergast's emotionless glare and gulped.

"It was really great." Katy's voice picked up. "The internship. I mean, if it hadn't been unpaid, I would've been there full-time, during school, everything." Katy could feel the hole that she was digging for herself, but she kept on going in hopes that, if she dug the hole deep enough, she'd make it through to China and somehow everything would be all right.

Katy gave a bit of a laugh and a smile.

No response from Prendergast's end.

"I also have a degree in English. I, uh, graduated *magna cum laude*. And, uh, I love books. Love words, love sentences, love syntax – I mean, I'm terrible at it in practice, but I love it anyway."

A small, hysterical laugh bubbled up from her throat.

"I mean, you have to love it – you spend thousands of dollars on a degree that won't get you a real job. So you gotta love it, or it's not worth the frustrations. Because, I mean, you have to dodge all the 'are you going to teach English?' questions. And it's like, if you ever have a negative opinion about a piece of literature, they instantly brand you a pretentious book snob. Which makes me sad – I love books. I really do. Thrillers and memoirs and historical fiction…I'm actually *not* a fan of most of the classics, so how could I be a book snob?"

Katy realized then that, between her location and China, resides thousands and thousands of miles of liquid hot magma with a solid, impenetrable core. Digging the hole deeper never helped anyone.

"But, um, yeah." Katy coughed. "I'm a very responsible person, very organized. I do my jobs efficiently and with hard work, and I would be perfect for this job."

The lady across the table from her simply smiled in response and went right into the next question.

Mrs. Prendergast must have been able to sense Katy's desperation, the same way hyenas can sense a wounded elephant. She strung Katy along for a little while, asking her a few less difficult questions, allowing Katy to regain just the tiniest bit of confidence and composure, before unleashing the hound of hell question itself:

"So why do you want to work at the Department of Telecommunications and Utilities? Not just why you would be great for us – I'm sure you are – but why would you want to work *here*, specifically."

Katy could feel her face drop. The sinking feeling in her stomach reminded her too much of when a professor would make the entire class explain why they were taking that particular course. And it always seemed to happen with required courses that she had absolutely no interest in. She would always get flustered when it was her turn. She would downright stumble over her words and give an answer that even the least attentive person in the room could spot as bullshit.

And this situation was worse. Much, much worse.

"Why here?" Katy gulped. She had looked at the department's website. She had read the introduction page and everything. But the last thing she did was prepare for such a question. "Well…it's a very important department. Utilities are necessary. I mean everyone has a phone…and everyone has…utilities? I mean, without utilities, no one could take a shower or watch television, and everyone does one or the other – or both. But not at the same time. Usually." Katy coughed. "I just think it's really important to be part of something that has such an impact. Telephones are used by everyone, everyday, and without them, where would we be? How could people call for ambulances without them?"

Katy took in a breath, hoping Prendergast would show a little bit of mercy and end the train wreck. Instead, she just glanced up at her notes long enough to establish eye contact with Katy before going back to writing.

"And the state. It's important to work for the state. I mean, it's the state. We live in it. Being part of something that helps it run is very important."

Was this a game to Prendergast now? Did she want to see just how much of a neurotic pile of ineptitude Katy could dissolve into? What was this lady's angle?

"And that," Katy downright yelled out, her hands digging into the tops of her thighs. "That's why I would love to work at the Department of Telecommunication and Utilities."

Prendergast put down her pen and looked at Katy, giving her a critical one over before clasping her hands lightly on top of the table.

"Well, I think that about wraps up our interview. We have a few more applicants to see, but we should make a decision by the end of the week." Prendergast stood up and began ushering Katy out of the room.

"Do – do you need my list of references? A copy of my résumé?" Katy fumbled for her folder as she stood up.

"That won't be necessary," Mrs. Prendergast replied coldly, walking Katy to the door. "But have a nice afternoon. You'll hear from us soon."

"Yeah, that's great. I look forward to it," Katy responded, nearly bending her folder in half. She gave Mrs. Prendergast another professionally-recommended handshake and left the department. She felt some comfort in the fact that at least she didn't mess her handshakes up, at least not too much. She reminded herself of that when she got into the elevator. She continued to remind herself of that when she said goodbye to the receptionist in the main lobby and left the building. Outside, she focused on the sounds of idling engines, blaring horns, splashing puddles; the smells of asphalt and cigarette smoke; the idea that no one wants to see a girl in tears, so she better keep the swell of emotions to herself.

She wanted to go home. She wanted to crawl on top of her couch and watch television and cry herself exhausted. Only she didn't focus on the crying part. If she thought about it now, she'd start crying over wanting to cry, and everything would unravel on her. So she simply continued on, berating herself for being the type of person who would dissolve into a pile of tears – er, That Thing She Wasn't Going to Think About – after a bad interview.

After a few blocks, Katy crossed the street and made her way into the nearest Green Line stop, through the turnstiles, and onto a B trolley that had mercifully pulled into the station the same time that Katy stepped onto the platform. She got on board, found a single-person seat in one corner of the train car, and collapsed into it, her folder and purse lying limply on her lap. The trolley pulled away from the stop and made its way through the tunnels under Boston.

The knot in Katy's stomach expanded, turning into a pit that weighed down the rest of her body. She felt her chest compress, her lips quiver, and her eyes slightly well up with tears. As the lights and platform of the Park Street station came into view, Katy turned her head into the corner and kept it there until the trolley was long above ground and the monotone voice on the speakers announced her stop.

*

Melodramatic tendencies. Over-sensitivity. Inherent narcissism that turns her into an insufferable, blubbering beast whenever she felt cut down to size. Perpetual Crybaby Syndrome. The emotional stability of a chick lit automaton. Whatever it was that caused her to get so upset, she couldn't fully figure out. But it had been there for years, causing her to do things like cry in class if a teacher yelled at her – or things like numbly let tears stream down her face until her roommate came home, all because some old man yelled at her and a stupid former rival showed her up.

The only difference between this time and her situation a few months earlier with Rachel Osterman was that, this time around, Katy was a little more subdued. She replayed what happened until it stopped mortifying her. She hugged Miller until he scrambled out of her arms. She watched trash TV until her brain hurt. She went through every single thing she had said, reworded them, and eventually came out the victor in her new alternate reality. By the time Maria came home, Katy was whisking a bowl of cake mix.

"I can't tell if this means the interview went really well or really bad," Maria said when she entered the kitchen.

Katy rolled her eyes, grunted, and put down the bowl.

"Uh oh. Outcome number 2?"

"Worse," Katy replied, taking a moment to wipe away the flour from her sweatpants and tank top.

"Outcome number 2-and-a-half?" Maria asked.

"No, worse," said Katy.

"You didn't even go?"

Katy huffed.

"I wish." Katy stared at her tank top. "I made a complete ass out of myself."

"Yikes," Maria grimaced, placing her bag on the counter.

"It was terrible," Katy continued. "Save for maybe puking mid-sentence, the interview could not have gone any worse than it did."

"Oh c'mon – it couldn't have been that bad."

Katy picked up her mixing bowl.

"I started rambling about the importance of electricity."

"Oh," said Maria. "Well – plus side? At least you didn't puke mid-sentence."

Katy threw her elbow into the whisking.

"But it was what – some boring state job?" Maria continued. "I'm sure electricity was the only important thing you could talk about."

Katy paused from her cake batter long enough to shrug.

"It still sucks."

"At least it's over?" Maria half-stated, taking off her high heels in the process. "And it's practice, so you can be amazing at the next interview."

"Doubt it." Katy stopped whisking and placed the bowl close to her face, scanning for lumps. "I'm sure I'll suck just as much at the next interview."

"You'll be fine." Maria walked into her room. From inside the bedroom, Maria shouted out: "I nearly ripped my résumé in half on my first interview, I was so nervous." There was a pause in Maria's speech. After a minute, Maria emerged back out in jeans. "I doubt there is anyone in the world who is right off the bat super-charismatic. That type of stuff takes practice."

"Or a dose of antidepressants," Katy mumbled to herself, emerging from a spot by the bottom cabinet with a glass pan in hand. She placed the baking dish on the stove and turned back to Maria. "I'll be fine. Just, I don't know. I'm really frustrated, I guess."

"Job hunting is frustrating," Maria said, leaning over the counter and grabbing a fingerful of batter from the edge of the bowl. "Are you forgetting how it was for me after graduation? By July, I started questioning if I'd ever land a real job, and forget about how I felt in September or October. But it happened, eventually." She punctuated her statement with sticking her battered finger into her mouth. "I'm gonna grab a spoon if you don't mind." Maria swiveled around the counter into the kitchen area.

"Would it kill you to wait until it's cooked?" Katy remarked.

"It possibly could."

"Then it was nice knowing you. I'll give the police a detailed statement." Katy cocked an eyebrow and snatched the bowl off of the counter. She tilted the bowl over the dish and watched the batter slowly trickle out, collecting in a pile in the middle before spreading out to the edges. "I think I deserve my self-pity cake to be left alone until it's cooked."

"Fine, fine," Maria said, re-licking her finger. "You know I'm rooting for you. You know I am." Maria eyed the bowl one last time. "But I think I'm okay with you making a cake every time you bomb an interview."

"Always the caring friend."

Katy placed the pan in the oven and set the timer. Maria scooted past and opened the fridge.

"Have you tried your old internship? Y'know, to see if they're hiring?"

"Eddington?" Katy turned. "I tried when we graduated. There was nothing there for me then."

"Well, then call them up now. Things can change after a few years." Maria paused to reach into the fridge and take out a carton of milk. "Plus, it's not like they're going to *re*-interview you, or anything. They know you."

"True." At this point, Miller jumped up on the counter, surveying the kitchen before cleaning one of his massive paws. Katy walked over and scratched behind his ear. "It couldn't hurt to try."

*

And try she did. Katy called up Eddington Publishing during her lunch break on Monday. The response was the roughly same one she received two years prior: while they felt she had been a great asset to the company, there was nothing available at that time. But she was more than welcome to check back in at a later date to see if there were any openings.

Katy spent the rest of lunch break reliving the same disappointment she felt when she had first called them about a job. She had interned for them during her junior year and, while it had been unpaid, Katy had genuinely believed it would potentially evolve into a job after graduation. They had loved her as an intern, giving her more and more responsibility until her boss started joking that Katy would soon take over the company if she kept it up.

But the company had a different song to sing after she graduated. They loved her when her work was for free, but they were less eager to take her in when money was involved. They liked her, but not enough to actually pay her.

Once again, the part that was bothering her the most wasn't that the company she had worked 20 hours a week for (and for free, on top of it) didn't want her. Well, it mostly wasn't that. It was the reminder that she was, once again, back in the chaotic job hunt. It was the reminder that, once again, her hard work and time and energy meant nothing in the real world. And it meant that a seemingly straight path out of the woods had come to an abrupt halt, and she was back to aimlessly finding her footing.

Abby Rosmarin

Chapter 7

The rest of her shift that day went by in a haze. Katy went through the motions of her daily tasks. She tried filling her mind with productive thoughts: strategies for interviews, possible changes to her résumé, ways she could get noticed amongst a sea of other applicants. When that didn't work, she resigned herself to just counting down the hours until she could go home again.

The Women's Literature section always became popular as the school year ended and the summer days began, but that day, it seemed even busier than usual. Women and girls alike filled that particular aisle to an uncomfortable capacity.

Katy smirked at the overflowing aisle. In a way, South End Collections thrived during the summer because they made it easy for customers to find the perfect beach read. With all the romance and chick lit sectioned off in one little corner, no one in search of a superficial read had to worry about accidentally buying a book that required critical thought. In a way, Katy enjoyed spending time around the Women's Literature customers that day. Keeping her opinions about those books to herself was a welcome change of pace.

At 6, she clocked out and made her way to Alex's place. Alex lived just outside Boston in Melrose, which required her to take the Orange Line train to the very last stop and walk an additional half mile or so. His apartment was in a small complex just off the main road, in an area so peacefully suburban that it disoriented Katy to think that a subway stop was just around the corner.

Alex's apartment was a simple, one-bedroom, one-bathroom place with contemporary furniture and a modern kitchen. As part of their newly-established routine, Katy would stand at the base of the apartment, ring Alex's apartment to be let in, and make her way to the fifth floor and into his apartment. Usually, the ingredients for whatever meal Alex would be cooking that night would already be laid out on the counter in the kitchen. Katy would usually begin her night by talking with Alex in the kitchen and helping him prepare dinner.

Today, Katy completely bypassed the kitchen and collapsed on his leather couch, her bag dangling by her forearm.

"I take it today didn't go so well," Alex stated, leaning against the wall by the front door.

"That's a nice way of putting it." Katy sat back up and planted her bag on the ground, hunching forward in the process.

"It had to have been bad. I didn't even hear from you during lunch." Alex walked into the living room and sat down on the adjacent armchair.

Katy straightened up a little.

"Oh. I'm sorry about that," Katy replied. "I guess I was preoccupied. Found out that Eddington Publishing has no use for me and it all kind of went to hell from there."

"Wow, I'm sorry," said Alex. "Wait, I think I'm confused. Did you interview for them recently?"

"No, they're a firm I interned for a couple years back," said Katy. "I was hoping that they might want to hire me as an actual employee, but obviously *that* didn't happen."

"I wouldn't take it personally," said Alex. "The economy hasn't been too kind to the publishing world. I'm sure they would hire you if they could."

Katy said nothing and leaned her head against the back of the couch. Alex got up from his armchair and sat down next to her. Katy shifted over and rested her head on Alex's shoulder.

"I just want out of the store so badly. I swear I might just quit and hope for the best," Katy said, her eyes drifting off to the ceiling. "It's just…I'm tired of it. All of it." Katy sighed and shook her head slightly. "Especially the customers. I don't want to deal with anymore dumbass customers. The self-righteous, the inconsiderate, the vapid, the downright stupid...."

"Harsh words," Alex replied. "C'mon now. I'm sure they're not all bad."

Katy snorted.

"Well, they're not all good."

"Well, at least the day is over?"

Katy rolled her eyes.

"Please. It's only going to get worse from here," Katy groaned. "We're at the start of beach read season. Every summer, it's the same thing. We get all these new customers, and they all want some fluffy beach read, which means we get a serious influx of fluffy beach read books to put on our shelves. I swear my soul breaks a little bit each time I look at cover art for a new chick lit novel." Katy rubbed her eyes and groaned again. "Ooooooh, when I don't have to see those books take up so much of the first floor, I'm going to be a seriously happy camper. A camper who is camping as far away from chick literature as possible."

"C'mon, now. Beach reads aren't that bad," said Alex. "At least people are reading."

"Not if what they're reading is *that*. They're better off illiterate."

Alex shook his head.

"I would be shocked if they're as horrible as you say they are."

"The books or the readers?" Katy quipped.

"Oh, ha, ha." Alex mimicked Katy. "You know what I mean. The books."

"Trust me on this one: they really are. It's the same rehashed story in the same rehashed formula. Every. Single. Time."

Alex raised an eyebrow and grinned to himself.

Katy dropped her shoulders and sat up.

"Have you ever even *read* a chick lit book?"

"Well, of course not."

"Then, let me enlighten you."

Katy turned to Alex and tucked her legs under her.

"To start, I'm assuming you have, at some point, watched a romantic comedy, though, right?"

"I guess, sure."

"Well, there you go. It's just like that. Romantic comedies follow one storyline and never deviate. Chick lits are no different." Katy spread her hands wide, as if presenting something. "The formula is completely and totally brainless. I mean, take the main character for one. She always has this super unorthodox name, like Jasameena Butternier. Or, it's an all-American name that is spelled super weirdly. Like Sarah with an 'E' and two 'R's, or something.

"Now, she is either some jet-setting magazine editor, or a painfully average girl that *everyone* thinks is so cute and so smart. But it doesn't even matter who she is, because being with a guy is what the story is about. Always. No self-discovery, no rites of passage, no revelations on life. Just – male companionship. Like a good husband is at the epicenter of a truly happy life." Katy paused long enough to roll her eyes. "Hello, 1950s."

"Well, I can see why that's frustrating," said Alex.

"But you know what the best part is?" Katy continued. "The guy in the book? The love interest? Zero personality. None. Completely boring. No believable faults, no weird mannerisms, nothing. But that's okay, because he's not *supposed* to have personality. He's supposed to be *the perfect guy*! He's supposed to be hot and he's supposed to be devoted. Nothing else. No fanaticism for sports, no penchant for hookers…just – there." Katy jutted her hands out for emphasis.

Alex lowered his eyebrows. Katy continued before Alex could respond: "See, the details change a tiny – oh, I *do mean* tiny – bit from book to book, but essentially the story always is: they meet, they fall in love, something causes them to be apart, and then they get back together." Katy gave another dramatic pause. "They *always* get back together."

Katy smacked her palm against the side of her head.

"Ooh! But there is some variety! How could I forget? Every once in a while, the girl already *has* a boyfriend, but that someone is always a prick who eventually leaves her so that the perfect guy can come in. *Sometimes* this perfect guy is the new guy,

Mr. Zero Personality; but *sometimes* it's the best guy friend who has been secretly in love with her all this time." Katy leaned forward and dropped her voice to a whisper. "And I'll let you in on a little secret: if there's a guy friend in the book, it will always be him. Unless said friend is her gay shopping buddy, the story will always veer onto path number two." Katy leaned back and crossed her arms. "Always the role of guy friends in chick lit. Mark my words: find a straight male friend in a chick lit, not only is he in love with the main character, but he'll turn out to be her soul mate after all."

"Wow." Alex placed a sardonic finger to his lips and acted pensive. "If you put this much passion into the professional world, you'd have your own company by now."

"I mean it, though!" Katy defended. "Every bit of 'women's literature' is just like that. The only difference between chick literature and romance novels is that romance novels are more melodramatic and have more explicit sex scenes."

Alex cocked an eyebrow.

"And how many sex scenes in romantic novels have you been reading?"

"None!" Katy scoffed. "I just…know that."

"Mhmm," Alex continued with a smirk. "Much like how you know the complete ins and outs of a chick literature book?"

Katy crossed her arms.

"Well *that's* neither here nor there."

Alex laughed and shook his head.

"Seriously, you have given me quite the cohesive lesson for today. You could teach a class with what you know."

"Oh, shut up."

"'Topography of the Chick Lit'. I can see it now."

"Correct me if I'm wrong, but didn't I just tell you to shut up?"

"Come on now." Alex got up from his spot and kissed Katy on the forehead. "Enough with the concern over chick lit. No use losing sleep over what people read. Now that you've – hopefully – gotten that out of your system, I'm more interested in the more important things, like dinner. I was thinking that I'd make up a nice pasta dinner. Maybe we can take a walk over to the pond after that. I'm sure that will take your mind off the bookstore, chick lit and all."

Katy leaned backwards until she was lying down on the couch.

"What type?"

"Chicken Alfredo? With a nice side salad to boot?"

"Oh, you are too good." Katy got herself back up and followed Alex to the kitchen. Katy helped make the salad as Alex prepared the rest of the meal. They enjoyed their dinner together without any mention of chick literature and finished the evening with a nighttime stroll.

They walked a mile or two down Main Street, through downtown Melrose, and to the nearby pond, which had become completely and serenely still. The twilight sky bounced the most beautiful shade of navy blue off of the water's surface. They sat down on one of the benches by the waterside. Katy nuzzled her body in the crook of Alex's arm.

"Do you think I'll ever find something?" Katy said after a lull, the sky slowly receding into black night.

"You mean, a job?" Alex asked. He kissed the top of Katy's head, which was leaning on his shoulder.

Katy looked up.

"No, a puppy."

"Well, if you keep trying, I'm sure you could get both," Alex replied. "You'd be a vital asset for any company."

"And I'd be an awesome puppy snuggler."

"I can't disagree with that," said Alex, his head leaning on top of Katy's as the nighttime traffic continued on just a few yards behind them.

Katy scratched the part of her neck exposed to the air. The mosquitoes were probably out in full force at this point.

"I mean, the Red Sox actually won the World Series last year. Anything is possible."

"That is true." Alex replied half-heartedly, which let Katy know that Alex might not be as fervent of a basement fan as Katy was.

Chapter 8

If she wanted to continue her comparison to the Red Sox: right now, she felt like she was perpetually stuck in Game 6 of the 1986 World Series, particularly the part when the ball went right through Bill Buckner's legs.

If she felt up to explaining it, she'd say that the comparison stood because she felt like she kept getting so close to winning, only to trip up at the last minute – because she felt that stupid mistakes were costing her everything, that a few setbacks kept snowballing into a total and irrevocable loss. And, like the Red Sox, it felt like it would take an additional eighteen years before she'd ever actually get what she was after. The only difference was that finding a proper scapegoat for her situation was even more ridiculous than blaming Bill Buckner for the entire World Series loss.

But she didn't feel up to explaining it that much, at least not to anyone else. She had kicked up her searches. She had signed up for multiple job sites and had even begun looking in the traditional classifieds. She had emailed résumé after résumé. She even started contacting every company she applied to for follow-up (something she started doing on the advice of Alex).

She got a few bites. She went on a few interviews. For some of them, the term "crash and burn" seemed too merciful of a description. At least when a plane crashes and burns, no one is expected to live through it and remember what happened.

One interview was for an entry-level marketing job, but the lady in charge treated the interview like Katy was vying for head of sales. The lady grilled Katy about her responsibilities at the book store, asking her questions that Katy had never even thought of before, like: "When you help customers, do you direct their attention to the more expensive items in your store?" or "how often are you able to successfully convince patrons to purchase items that they had not originally planned on purchasing?"

Katy stumbled over her answers, all the while attempting to quell the voice inside her head screaming, "Of course not, you dumb hag! I have a soul! An actual soul!" She then asked Katy what she would do in very specific marketing scenarios – scenarios that only someone with extensive sales and/or bullshitting skills would be able to respond to properly.

Katy left that interview feeling dirty. The only good thing that came from the interview was that, on the frenzied, infinite list of possible career paths, marketing could most likely be crossed off the list. There was something vaguely comforting in the idea that she just might be too nice for marketing.

Even when the interviews were not on a complete death spiral, she could still pinpoint the exact moment in each when the employers would start mentally considering other applicants. In the end, they always asked questions like, 'what is your five-year plan?' or 'why would you like to work here/why would you like to work in this profession?' After her disaster with the Department of Telecommunications and Utilities, she had tried coming up with answers for such questions beforehand, but they always turned into monotonous drivel. Painfully insincere recitations on why being a law firm's receptionist, or a middle school's administrative assistant, or any other nondescript job was just what she was looking for.

Sometimes she just wanted to say, "My publishing internship taught me that I don't completely suck at office work, so I probably won't completely suck here either."

Sometimes her inner voice was the real bandit, sabotaging her without the slightest warning. It couldn't be silenced with the idea that no job could be forever (and anything had to be better than retail). It poked at her, made her doubt the job, made her doubt her abilities, made her panic at the realization that she had no clue what she wanted to do, or if she would ever figure out what she wanted.

The interviews weren't all bad. Some even looked promising. An interviewer at a production company looking for a receptionist seemed very laid back. He asked her a few simple questions, to which she responded with an acceptable level of competence. He gave her a quick tour of the office and spent a good amount of time just chatting with her, even when the interview started to go over schedule. The man conducting the interview seemed to really take to her, and soon called to let her know that she made it through to the next round. The second interview also seemed to go pretty well – if only because there were even fewer questions and more tours of the building.

But it was the promising interviews that provided the most heart-wrenching rejections. Two weeks after her second interview with the production company, she got a standard rejection email. They hadn't even tried to hide the fact that the email was copied from a template. Most of the email body itself was in Arial font. Her name and job title within the email? Times New Roman.

Four hours total of phone calls, interviews, and introductions, and they didn't even have the heart to type out three or four original sentences or at least change around the fonts. But, even then, it paled in comparison to the ones that couldn't even be bothered to contact her and let her know that she didn't get the job.

If she were up to more comparisons, she might compare her situation to the fickleness of the dating world. Because, really, which was worse: going on a disastrous date and knowing there wouldn't be a second, or going on a promising date, only to never hear from the guy again? Or – worse – finding out that he had decided to start dating someone else? Someone hotter and smarter and more socially adaptable?

But she wasn't up to that type of comparing at all. Not after month after month of the same crushing disappointment in the job search world.

"Oh, that'll be the day." Katy sang one Saturday afternoon. Outside, the trees along the edges of the sidewalks were beginning to don orange and red leaves. "Can I say good-bye? Yeah-eah, that'll be that day – this place makes me cry. Yeah-eah, I say I'm gonna leave here. I know it's a lie." Katy turned to Evelyn, her hands to her heart. "Because that'll be the day-ay-ay, when I die."

"That's a bit morbid," Evelyn said in response.

"It's a song of truth," Katy replied. After looking over her shoulder to make sure that Andrea wasn't within listening distance, she added: "I swear the fates are trying to tell me that I'm doomed to be here forever."

"I doubt that," Evelyn said, handing Katy a book on Russian politics to have re-stickered. Both were situated upstairs and had been given the ominous assignment of finding the red-stickered used books and giving them new, lower-priced stickers. "You just started your job hunt right as a ton of people were graduating college. The market was flooded, most likely. I'm sure now that people are going back to school, there'll be more openings."

"Hopefully," Katy murmured. She placed the re-stickered Russian book back and shuffled through the shelves before finding another red sticker. "I just don't like rejection," she added.

"Oh, but everyone else in the world does?" Evelyn replied, tapping Katy's shoulder with the book Evelyn was holding. "For every gig I get, I probably get rejected for twenty. Maybe more. And, to be honest, there's not much difference between auditions and interviews."

"Yeah, but at least at auditions, you're told what to say." Katy pressed the price gun against a hardcover and snapped the trigger back for emphasis.

"Yeah, but – I don't know. It's different," said Evelyn. A few patrons made their way to the second floor and began to wander the aisles. They chatted lightly with each other as they went down one aisle and up another, pausing in their conversation long enough to pass by Katy and Evelyn.

"Have you ever thought of doing it?" Evelyn asked, scratching her temple with her price gun.

Katy cocked an eyebrow.

"Doing what?"

"Auditioning."

"Oh totally," Katy exclaimed with an eye roll. "I think about it everyday. My life *revolves* around it."

"No seriously." Evelyn tapped at Katy's shoulder again, this time with the tip of the price gun. "You're pretty, you're witty, you speak well…why not? There are always casting calls for parts that don't require you to be part of the union. You just email and show up."

"I don't know," Katy replied.

"Actually, it makes sense," Evelyn replied after a pause. "Maybe you've been going about it all wrong. Maybe the office thing isn't for you."

"Maybe the going-on-auditions thing isn't for me, either," Katy countered. "This sounds like something straight out of a bad novel."

"Come on now," said Evelyn. "It could be fun. Imagine it now: you'd become all killer famous and I can be like, 'You know that Katy Sinclaire? She got into acting because of *me*.'"

"Nice to see your actions are completely altruistic."

"Seriously, though! I get emails all the time about open auditions for bit parts. Allow me to forward them to you and I'll shut up about it," said Evelyn. "Come on, at the very least, it'll be something new to do."

"Fine. You beat me into submission," Katy gave in. "It couldn't hurt to try it out."

Evelyn gave a satisfied grin.

"What's the worst that can happen?"

"Famous last words," said Katy

"Or famous first words," Evelyn countered. "I can see it now. That particular chapter of your biography, right before it gets into you being all famous, will end with you saying exactly that, followed by, 'and that was how Katy started auditioning for movie roles.'"

And that *was* how Katy started auditioning – for one single movie role. Within the week, Evelyn had forwarded a casting call looking for actors to play a few small speaking roles in an independent film. Katy, already warming up to the idea of acting, agreed to contact the casting director with her name, age, and a few pictures, as the email had directed. The casting director replied back, settled on a time and date to come in, and instructed Katy to bring in a photo of herself.

"Photo". It's a funny word, as Katy quickly learned the day of the audition. Katy arrived at the auditions half an hour early, just as Evelyn instructed, holding an 8 x 6 snapshot of her sitting on her couch with Miller sitting on her lap. She signed in at the door, scribbling her name on a large clipboard resting on a side table. A man with a large binder nestled in the crook of his arm soon approached her.

"And you are?" he said, angling the binder away from him.

"Um, Katy – Katelyn Sinclaire? I have an audition…" She fingered the snapshot and attempted to meet the eyes of the guy, but he was already scanning his eyes over the papers clipped to the front of his binder.

"Ah, yes, hi Katy." He opened his binder and thumbed over a few pages, pulling out a stapled set of eight. "You'll be auditioning for the role of Lexi. She's supposed to be a bit self-absorbed, very in-your-face and sarcastic." He took his eyes off of the binder and met Katy's long enough to hand over her portion of the script. "Your parts are highlighted. I'll let you know when you're up."

"Um, thank you."

The man smiled briefly in response and then walked away. Katy made her way over to a sleek set of couches and sat down, script and snapshot in her lap. To her left was a petite girl with surrealistically tiny waist and arms. In her lap was a leather portfolio. On top of said portfolio was an 8 x 10 professional headshot on glossy paper. Across from her was another impossibly beautiful woman, her 8 x 10 resting daintily on her purse.

It was at that exact moment when Katy learned what "photo" actually meant. She scanned the room to see that everyone there had some variation of an 8 x 10 headshot, professional and properly lit and edited and printed. Katy felt painfully unprepared and painfully out of her league. It was as if she had gone to a Halloween costume party, wearing cat ears over normal clothing as her "costume", only to realize that everyone else was dressed in elaborate outfits.

Although any person who would be so unadventurous as to wear cat ears and call it a costume deserves that type of humiliation. But somehow that notion didn't comfort Katy much at the moment.

Okay, so her picture wasn't done in a studio somewhere – but why did theirs have to be so much *bigger*? Might as well bring in a poster while you're at it. Katy grinned, imagining someone coming in with a rolled-up movie poster, the head in their headshot technically bigger than the majority of their real-life body. The girl across from Katy glanced up and locked eyes with Katy. Katy pressed her lips together, swallowed, and forced her eyes back down at her script.

She went over her lines again and again, mouthing each word and imagining how Lexi – the self-absorbed and sarcastic minor character in an independent film – would say them. In the end, she found herself vacillating between exaggerating the lines past the point of any believability and saying them as a vaguely modified version of herself.

She doubted that either would win her the role.

"Katy Sinclaire?" The man approached her, his binder now held tightly against his chest with both arms. "You're up."

"Um, thank you. Again."

Katy, nearly folding her "photo" in half, got up and walked through the double doors and into a completely sparse room, save for two sets of tables with four or five people sitting behind them.

"And you're...Katy?" the lady sitting in the middle of the tables asked.

No, I'm Elvis and I've just entered the building, she thought to herself.

Katy nodded daftly.

"Great. I'll take your photo and we can get started."

Katy walked over and handed over her "photo", feeling her limbs lock up with each stilted step. The lady grabbed her snapshot, looked down, looked up, and looked back down again, before moving the photo to the side.

"So, Rick here will be reading off with you." The lady pointed to a chubby man sitting more towards the side of the tables than behind it. "Whenever you're ready."

Katy cleared her throat and gave the go-ahead. She tried her best to recite the lines, but it felt like a roadblock had suddenly been created in her brain, making it impossible to deliver a sneeze, let alone a scripted reply. With the exception of an occasional glance at Rick as he delivered the other character's lines, her eyes were glued to the script.

Should her eyes stay glued to the script? Did they expect her to memorize these lines in a half hour? Can regular actors do that? Is that a requirement to become a SAG member?

Maybe she should've come in even earlier.

Her legs started to tremble. She tensed up her leg muscles, but to no avail. She focused on keeping them still, but found that it only resulted in her losing her place in the script.

For God's sake and all that is holy, stop trembling. Katy wasn't there to tap dance, and she certainly hadn't been asked to imitate how humans react in small tremors. And it was starting to make the rest of her body shake as well. What had she done to deserve such involuntary movement? Maybe her legs believed that Katy was out of her league and was punishing Katy accordingly.

"Hmm, okay," the lady said after Katy finished her part. "Can we do over pages three through eight, and maybe this time be a bit more...realistic? Lexi is a bitch. She always gets her way. Show me that ferociousness."

Katy wanted to say, "But I'm *not* an always-gets-her-way bitch. How can I make it realistic if it's never realistic that I get my own way, even once?" Instead, she took a breath, flipped to page three, and began again. Her legs trembled, sending shockwaves into her arms. Her pages started crinkling. This time around, instead of feeling like her mind had a massive roadblock, Katy felt like she had completely blacked out, taking a backseat while some other – hopefully more confident – part of herself grabbed ahold of the reigns.

From the looks on the people behind the table after she had finished, that part of herself must not have been that confident after all – or she had passed out on top of blacking out and they had just witnessed Katy coming out of a slight coma. The silence filled every space of the austere receptacle they were calling a room.

"Hmm, okay," the lady said again after a moment. "Thank you for your time, Katy. We'll be doing callbacks in about a week, so, if we like you, you'll be hearing from us soon."

"Oh, okay, thanks." Katy forced a smile, but ended up just pushing her bottom lip up and into the edge of her top lip. "Uh, do you want the, uh, script?"

Katy held up the pages as if they wouldn't know what she was talking about.

"That? Just give it to Billy on the way out. Thanks again."

Katy turned and pushed opened one of the double doors, feeling hurried and unsatisfied. The entire process seemed to have ended before it had even begun, but Katy walked back into the waiting area with an incredible uncertainty, as if hours, possibly even whole days, had passed instead. She handed the script to the boy with the binder, who she assumed to be Billy, and promptly left the place.

Her shoes echoed off of the linoleum floors and asylum-white walls as she made her trip down the corridor and over to the elevator. Somewhere in the distance, a slight buzz of the harsh fluorescent lights made its presence known, humming as she pressed the down arrow button. She watched the lights situated at the top of the elevator as they slowly lit up the numbers for floor two, then floor three, then floor four. The elevator slowly crept up until its doors slid open for Katy.

Katy got into the elevator and pressed the button for the first floor, her mouth tightly pursed. What was she supposed to feel right now? Exhilarated? Alive? She was filled with a mix of nerves and disappointment. Her self-esteem had been left behind somewhere in the casting office with her 8 x 6 "photo" of her and her cat. She felt empty and displeased and the second her feet touched the cement of the sidewalk, she grabbed her phone from her purse and called Evelyn.

"I am never going on another audition ever again," Katy stated before Evelyn could even say hello.

"Oh." Evelyn answered. Downtown Boston seemed to whiz by Katy as she stomped down the street.

Katy paused, waiting for Evelyn to respond. When Evelyn, obviously stunned into silence, didn't, Katy picked up where she left off with more gusto than before.

"I can't act. I can't even pretend that I act. I suck. Deaf-mutes with no hands could deliver their lines better." Katy's voice grew tight and terse. "Apparently the only role I'll ever be equipped to play is that of a loser bookstore supervisor. So unless there are any auditions looking for that, I think I'm done forever."

"Don't be so hard on yourself." Evelyn finally spoke up. "I mean, do you get this worked up after every failed interview?"

Katy remained silent.

"Everyone has a rough go the first time around. It's natural," Evelyn continued. "My first audition was terrible. You know why I bugged you about showing up so early? Because my first time, I didn't. At all. I showed up thinking I was the shit with my headshot and my acting résumé, and I ended up having thirty seconds to prepare. And it was terrible. I mean, in high school, you kind of just go up and do whatever. I kind of thought the real world would be like that, too. But I was wrong. I fumbled so bad, it wasn't even funny. I said sentences as questions when they were statements and statements when they were questions. I ran some sentences together and stopped in the middle of other sentences. I wanted to just die afterwards. I thought I had made a complete ass of myself. But it turned out it wasn't as bad as I thought it was."

"Let me guess: you got the job anyway."

"Well, no," Evelyn replied. "But I did get a callback, which at least meant they didn't think I stunk *that* badly. Maybe they'll feel the same for you. I mean, there's still a chance they liked you. Sometimes casting directors are impossible to read."

"This one seemed pretty cut-and-dry."

"Still, it was something new. And now you can say you have auditioned for a movie. How many people can say that?"

Katy huffed on the other line.

"Aw, don't be like that," Evelyn cooed. "Aren't you glad you tried it out though, at least? At least just to say that you did it?"

"I – I guess," Katy said finally. "Just...no more forcing me into doing these types of things anymore."

"Hey now," said Evelyn. "My intentions were good."

"You have so many good intentions, I could pave a road with them," Katy retorted. "Only we know where that road would lead."

"Hey, no worries. I just thought you'd have a good time. And I mean, I'm not saying hold your breath, but there might be a chance that they thought you did pretty well," Evelyn reassured. "They might call you back for a second audition. You never know."

Chapter 9

But after a week, Katy did know. There had been no phone calls, no emails, no contact of any type. Evelyn tried her best to reassure Katy, mentioning that they might have needed longer to figure out who they wanted. But Katy was already certain that the casting director had caught on to her mediocrity.

However, that didn't stop Katy from bringing it to Evelyn's attention that following Saturday, after weeks of hearing absolutely nothing. It was all part of Katy's passive-aggressive way of proving a point.

"You said they might just be taking longer to decide, but it's been way too long," Katy pointed out. "Still nothing."

"I'm sorry about that," Evelyn responded. "I mean, you never really know in this industry."

"I pretty much knew with this one, but thanks for the comforting words."

"Still, I feel bad. You didn't seem that interested in the first place, I made you do it anyway, and it wasn't even enjoyable for you." Evelyn shrugged. "I don't know. I just thought you would've like it."

"Please," Katy replied. "If I got mad at you for every time you cajoled me into trying out something you swore I would like, we wouldn't be friends. Thankfully, I'm not mad, and we still are friends."

Katy stationed herself behind the cashier's counter, with Evelyn organizing the window display and college student Josh upstairs shelving the newly-arrived books. Andrea had called in sick that day, leaving Katy in charge.

"It just sucks that they didn't at least tell me that I didn't get the part," Katy said finally.

"That's actually pretty normal," Evelyn confessed. She paused as Katy rang in a customer's books, swiped their credit card, and sent them on their way. "I mean, most people don't hear back if the casting people end up choosing someone else."

What a semantics wizard. "Choosing someone else." Not "rejecting your sad self in favor of someone more competent."

Evelyn could get a job in public relations with the way she could word things.

A second customer came up to Katy's register with both *Express Espresso* and *Coffee and Conversation* in her hands. Katy gave the customer a tight grin and a "hello" to match, rang in her items, and wished the customer a good afternoon.

"Still sucks though, rejection. Like, thanks for reminding me I'm not good enough for anything," Katy said after the customer left. "Makes me want to curl up in the stock room and never come out. I don't like it."

"Yes, and you're the only one who ever gets disheartened by rejection." Evelyn mockingly lowered her eyebrows.

"Shit. I *knew* I was alone in this world!"

"If Andrea heard you swearing in the store, she'd have a fit."

"A shit-fit?"

"Katy!" Evelyn gave a whispered yelp as a third customer came up to the front of the store. The customer smiled at Evelyn before turning to Katy.

"Nothing I haven't heard before," he reassured Katy as placed his books on the counter.

"Seriously, though..." Evelyn said after the customer left, letting the two words linger in the air.

"And Andrea is *seriously* not here right now," Katy replied. "Which must mean at least one of the four horsemen has started saddling up."

Evelyn smirked.

"It is very unlikely of her. I can't even remember the last time she called out."

"I don't think she ever has, at least not since I started. Bare minimum, she has always been on call. This place is her baby," said Katy. She leaned on the counter and scanned the room. She could see a few customers wandering around, books in hand. "A high-maintenance, incredibly dysfunctional baby. Note to self: never open your own store. You'll work 80 hours a week and start worrying over whether or not your employees are saying potty words. Like 'shit'."

Evelyn rolled her eyes at Katy and left to check on Josh. Katy remained behind the counter, ringing in customers until her shift ended at 6. As per a semi-followed ritual, Katy went straight from work to Ben's apartment. It was a ritual that had been losing ground since Katy's relationship with Alex had started becoming a little more serious, but it was a ritual all the same.

Katy rode the T through Boston and Cambridge and into Somerville, getting off the train at Porter Square. She deliberately avoided the escalators and made her way up the seemingly endless flights of stairs that connected the platform to street level. Such an act felt like something specifically mentioned in the Geneva Convention as cruel and unusual punishment, but it was the closest thing she had to exercise these days. Besides, she liked the fatigued feeling she got when she finally made it to the top. It also made it a lot easier to wait by the crosswalk for the traffics light to change when her legs felt like jelly.

Today, the lights were in her favor almost immediately after she exited the station. Still winded, she crossed the street and made her way down a narrow one-way road. She passed by the small strip mall on her left, complete with a supermarket and an independent bookstore – one that seemed way more organized and up-to-date than South End Collections could ever hope to be. She hung a left around the plaza and snaked her way through the residential streets before arriving at Ben's apartment.

Ben lived on the second floor of a three-story, multi-family home. The front door was always unlocked, so Katy made her way in and up the stairs before tapping a catchy beat on Ben's apartment door.

"Door's unlocked!" Ben's voice called from inside.

Katy opened the door and walked into the living room, where Ben was seated at his computer desk.

"I love how worried you are about break-ins."

"In Slummer-ville? Any burglar with enough brain power to pick a lock is smart enough to go somewhere else for decent merchandise."

"Please, even the bums have MP3 players now," Katy replied and dropped her bag by the sofa. "How has your Saturday been so far?"

"Um..." Ben trailed off and pointed at his computer. "This."

"And who says youth is wasted on the youth." Katy took the moment to stretch her arms up above her head. "As long as it wasn't all video games...or porn. Eh, I don't care if it was porn, but I don't want to hear about it if it was."

"A liberal approach to pornography." Ben raised his eyes to Katy. "You truly must be the perfect girl."

"Because I'm not one of those hyper-sensitive people who denounces porn and bans all walks of life from watching it?" Katy cocked an eyebrow.

Ben blushed.

"Unfortunately some people do pull that," replied Ben.

"Y'know, there's totally a dirty joke that could accompany that 'pull that' statement," Katy added.

Ben let out a full-belly laugh.

"And that's why I would love to have a girlfriend like you," Ben blurted. Ben immediately sat up in his seat and scratched his neck. "Y'know, because my past girlfriends were so uppity about porn. So, um, any new – uh – news about that audition thing?"

"Other than how obvious it is that I didn't get it?" Katy clicked her tongue against her teeth. "Not much. The lack of response is just confirming what I already knew."

"Yikes. I'm sorry about that." Ben stared at his keyboard.

"Eh, don't be. The experience was…different, but I'm glad I did it." Katy draped herself across the nearby armchair and leaned back, crossing her legs over one of the armrests. "Don't get me wrong: Evelyn had pushed me to do it so hard that I thought I was going to trip over my own feet, but she made a good point. Maybe I'm going about this job search thing all wrong. Maybe the office thing really isn't for me."

"Really? I guess so, but, I mean, what else is out there but office jobs and, y'know, SEC?" Ben replied with a bit of force in his voice.

"There's life outside of cubicles and the Collections," Katy answered. "I mean, acting and modeling – that kind of stuff. Which I guess is shit for someone like me, but…still. I mean, I could be a teacher – or a substitute teacher – or I could…I don't know, become a DJ. Maybe I have some untapped talent and all I need is the proper push."

"Proper push?"

"I don't know. Maybe I'm awesome at cooking and just don't know it yet. Maybe I should go into culinary school instead of grad school. Or dance school. Too short for modeling, but dancers are usually short, right?"

"Dancers usually start dancing before they're in kindergarten. Not in their mid-twenties."

"Then I'm a late bloomer. And it's not like I've never danced before."

Ben looked at his computer once last time before gazing back over his chair.

"I've never seen you so obsessed like this. You swear you would be no good at this thing, a failure at that thing, et cetera, et cetera, et cetera. But whatever it is, you want it because it's new. What do you think you are going to gain by leaving SEC?"

Katy rolled her eyes.

"Don't be like that. It's not because it's 'new'. It's a…a first step. I get a new job, and…well, I'll get a better idea as to what I want to do. And I'll probably get paid more, so I can finally do some traveling." Katy readjusted in her seat. "And, I mean, I really haven't gone anywhere, so it would be nice to spend some time in Europe, or even just around America. I mean, hell, what if I'm actually meant to be living in a different part of the world, but I don't know it yet because I've never been there?"

"A city is a city and suburbia is suburbia. Not much changes based on the region of the county," Ben interjected.

"But how do you know unless you've been there?" Katy asked. "Like, DC – I've always wanted to see if I'd like it there. Or San Francisco. Or Chicago. I mean, Chicago would probably be just up my alley. Right by a large body of water, multiple baseball teams…"

"You just don't know what to do with yourself now that the Red Sox are decent," Ben replied.

"I'm not *that* masochistic." Katy lowered her head.

"Jury's still out on that one." Ben swiveled his chair a couple degrees. He bit at the skin around this thumbnail. "But I have to admit I'd hate it if you moved to Chicago…y'know, because then I'd never hear the end of you moping over the Cubs. Boston's got better sports teams, anyway. I don't see the Bears winning the Super Bowl anytime soon."

"Well I'm not going anywhere yet. It's just a thought for now." Katy made herself into a ball in the armchair, hugging her knees into her chest. "So what's the plan for tonight?"

"Anarchy and mayhem, as per usual."

"As long as we don't kill anyone this time. Disposing of bodies is *such* a chore."

"Killjoy."

"That's what I'm good at," Katy responded. "But, in all seriousness, as long as I can get on the T before it shuts down, I'm good."

"You know I can always drive you back if need be."

"True," Katy replied. "But aside from inconveniencing you, I need to get up early tomorrow. Alex turns the big three-one. We've got the entire day planned. So getting to bed wicked late seems like a bad idea."

"Oh," Ben replied, letting the word hang in the air for a moment. "So uh, how, uh, how have things been between you two?"

"Really good, actually. Coming up on about six or so months together." Katy stretched her legs and straightened her back in the chair. "Wow. Definitely doesn't feel like it's been that long."

"You guys must be getting serious then, huh."

"Well, I guess so. I've used the 'B' word around him a few times and he seemed okay with it, so that's definitely a sign of something."

"'B' word?"

"'Boyfriend'."

"Ah. Boyfriend." Ben echoed, tapping his fingers against his chair. After staring off into space for moment, he cleared his throat. "Y'know, if I remember correctly, you haven't seen any of the original Star Wars, am I right?"

Katy shrugged.

"You are right."

"So, since you have to leave so early, I figured we could ixnay the anarchy and we can *finally* get you started on experiencing the holy trilogy."

"Goodie! And then you'll finally stop gaping in shock every time I remind you that I haven't seen the movies!" Katy feigned an excited look.

"We don't *have* to. I just thought it would be a good idea."

"Hey, I'm okay with it. Will pizza be involved?"

"And beer if you see fit."

"I *always* see it as fit."

Ben got up from his chair and walked over to his TV. The TV itself was modest, but the collection of DVDs next to it was anything but. The shelving for it was at least five feet in height with 4 columns of shelves, all filled to maximum capacity with DVDs.

"I still can't believe you haven't seen any of them," Ben said as he scanned through his shelves. "You at least know the basics of Star Wars, right?"

"Sure. Shatner's the captain of the ship, right?"

Ben turned around, dropped his hands to his sides, and stared.

"Kidding – just kidding. Sheesh, you fanatics have no sense of humor sometimes."

"*Fear and Loathing in Las Vegas.* That's when a shopaholic and her best friend go on a road trip to Sin City, right?"

"Apples and oranges. Chick lit's the devil."

"I'm sure there are some Star Wars fans who feel the same way about Star Trek."

Ben stacked a few DVDs on top of his TV and called up the pizzeria to place his order. Katy went into the kitchen and came back with a few cans from the refrigerator before finding a place on one side of Ben's couch. After the deliveryman came with their pizza, Ben joined her on the other side.

"To be honest, I'm amazed you haven't forced me to watch Star Wars sooner," said Katy, opening the pizza box just enough to slip out a slice.

"Seeing as the original Star Wars movies are just three of possibly a hundred classic movies that you've somehow never seen, I'm amazed I even remembered now." Ben mimicked Katy's actions and grabbed himself a piece of pizza.

"Movies and I don't click well. It's an assault on my attention span."

"Waiting for the microwave to finish heating your food is an assault on your attention span."

Katy shrugged again.

"Details."

The sun started setting in the middle of the first movie. The room slowly darkened, to the point where the only sources of light were from the TV and the hall light a few rooms over. The pizza was quickly demolished. After emptying her can of beer, Katy made her way into the kitchen and poured herself a glass of water. Midway through the second movie, Katy folded up her legs and curled herself around the armrest.

"You'll fall asleep if you do that," Ben warned.

"I'm not 10. Big girls can watch movies past their bedtime," Katy replied, resting her elbow on the armrest and holding up her head with her hand. She scratched her neck with her other hand and focused intently on the screen in front of her.

Within half an hour, resting her head on her hand evolved into resting her head on the armrest. Before the movie was over, Katy was drifting in and out of consciousness. Ben looked over to find Katy's eyelids drooping and eventually shutting.

"You're going to miss the end of the movie if you don't sit up," Ben gave another warning.

"Of obviously, but the banana cork has no lids," Katy mumbled into the armrest.

"Katy?"

Katy attempted to say, "what?" but all that came out of her mouth was a mix of mumbles and groans.

"Is someone falling asleep?" Ben patronizingly sing-songed.

"No... yes..."

Ben sighed.

"Might as well. Almost midnight anyway. Come on now, time to get up. God knows what your boyfriend would say if he found out you were sleeping over another guy's house." With that, Ben started collecting the empty beer cans.

"But the monkey never got the call," Katy answered, drifting off into dreamland.

While Katy was falling deeper into sleep, Ben got up and tossed the cans into the recycling bin. After rinsing his hands briefly under the kitchen sink's faucet, he snaked back through the kitchen and the small dining room to find that Katy had stretched her legs out onto Ben's spot on the couch, one arm cradling her head and the other dangling off the sofa. The light coming from the television encased Katy, bathing her in a blue, cherubic light. With a small, fatigued grin, Ben knelt next to her and brushed away the hair that had fallen over Katy's face. He moved his hand from her face to her shoulder, his hand touching her skin slightly, before gently stirring her.

"Did I fall asleep?" Katy popped her head up from the armrest and gave a disoriented scan of her surroundings.

"For a little while," Ben replied softly. "Come on, you're in no shape for the T. Let me drive you home."

"Oh, Mr. White Knight saving me from tripping down the Porter Square steps." Katy sat up and rubbed her eyes. "If I'm going to descend into the bowels of hell, best to do it one step at a time."

"That's the spirit," Ben replied with a small grin.

"Are you sure you're fine to drive? You look as beat as me," Katy said, getting up and walking over to grab her bag.

"I'll be fine. Let's get you home," Ben said and ushered Katy out the door.

Chapter 10

Katy woke with her alarm clock the next morning.

Correction: she woke up five minutes before her alarm clock the next morning. Usually, it was impossible for Katy to obey such an alarm. That morning, however, she was awake before the alarm went off and out of bed by the first of the alarm's beeps. She slipped on her sandals and walked out of the apartment and around the block to the nearest Dunkin Donuts, ordering a coffee large enough to ensure that she wouldn't revert to falling back asleep in her bed. Or in an alleyway.

Yes, she wanted to be up for Alex's birthday, but there was something more. To be honest, she was nervous. The type of nervousness that causes one to flutter their eyes open hours before they need to wake up out of pure anticipation.

This was their first – sort of – holiday together. Their relationship had seen a few vacation holidays – Memorial Day, the Fourth of July, Labor Day – but they were relatively low-key, unromantic, and, furthermore, Katy had found herself working through all of them. But now they were at some sort of sentimental, undeniably-clichéd crossroads. They'd been together for almost half a year – half a year! – now. They had called each other "boyfriend" and "girlfriend". And now they were celebrating a holiday, albeit a fairly self-absorbed and nationally *un*recognized one, together.

It was a step. A next level, if you will.

Katy trudged back up the stairs, biting the straw of her iced coffee and waiting for the caffeine to set in. She fumbled with her keys, reentered the apartment, and set aside the remainder of her coffee in order to take a searing-hot shower. By the time she had dried, dressed, and finished off her coffee, she was ready, if not downright giddy, for the day.

The itinerary for Alex's birthday was fairly simple: first, they'd first enjoy the crisp morning air of downtown Boston until their legs gave out. They'd have a small lunch and a movie to recoup and then enjoy the sights and sounds the city some more until they had dinner with some of his friends from work.

So, on top of everything else, Katy was going to finally meet some of his friends — something that neither of them had done yet, with any of their friends, even after six months of dating. Yet another reason Katy was able to force herself out of bed with her alarm.

To reiterate: today was a big day, symbolically. A level up. A step in some direction.

Hopefully the right type of direction.

Katy set out from her apartment complex, a yellow-brick, five-story establishment wedged between other similar yellow-brick, five-story establishments, and followed the various sidewalks and crosswalks through the neighborhood until she reached Commonwealth Ave. There, she crossed the busy road and waited for her train.

The trolley made its way around the corner, its familiar start-up and slow-down noises transporting her down Commonwealth Avenue and into downtown Boston. Waiting for her just outside of the subway stop was Alex, standing proper against a wall that had been covered from the ground up with advertisements.

"Why hey there, birthday boy!" Katy cooed, extending her arms out for a hug. Alex looked up, grinned, and walked over to accept the hug.

"Good morning," he replied, planting a tender kiss on Katy's lips. "So what do you want to do first?"

Katy slipped her hand into Alex's.

"It's *your* birthday; you decide what we do first. Come on: what do you want to do this morning?"

Alex cocked an eyebrow.

"Okay, you suggest that, and I'm forcing you to go shoe shopping," she said.

"But you hate shoe shopping."

Katy shrugged.

"Casualty of war. I'll deal with it."

Alex gently rubbed the top of Katy's thumb with his.

"How about we strike a truce and grab breakfast?"

Katy pursed her lips.

"Well, the terms of the treaty are a bit shaky...but I'd be willing to call a ceasefire."

Alex sighed out a small chuckle.

"Has anyone ever told you that you're a complete dork?"

Katy widened her eyes and dropped her jaw.

"Who, me? Never. I'm the queen of normal. When they were passing out normals in kindergarten, I took two just to be safe. That's how it works, right?"

Alex laughed and kissed the side of Katy's forehead. Together, they made their way through Beacon Hill to a coffee shop that Alex had introduced Katy to a few months beforehand.

The outside of the café seemed to get swallowed up by the sea of storefront signs surrounding it, but inside hosted dark varnished wooden tables & chairs and a beautiful collection of thickly-framed black & white photographs. The side facing the street was almost all window, giving everyone a peaceful view of the redbrick sidewalks and the thin-trunked trees sprouting up from the sidewalks. The only thing that could rival such a cozy and comfortable setting was the enveloping smells of coffee grounds and baking dough that emanated from the kitchen, past the counter, and into the line of waiting customers. Alex ordered a coffee and a simple pastry. Katy ordered more coffee and a confectionary item covered in chocolate sauce.

"So how does it feel, being so old?" Katy asked after they picked a table and sat down. Katy wrapped her hands around her coffee cup, warming her fingers and palms.

"Now that hurts," Alex replied, his voice a mix of laughter and feigned pain.

"Silly, old people don't have feelings." Katy rolled her eyes and sipped at her coffee. "Didn't you get the memo?"

Alex grinned down at his cup. The tables around them were slowly filling up with other patrons. Outside, the Sunday morning world was finally waking up, with more and more people walking past the coffee shop.

"It's weird," Alex said finally. "Like, I can't explain it fully. Being 30 is...being 30. But being 31...well, now you're in your 30s. Does that make any sense?"

"None whatsoever."

"Figured." Alex gave a small, self-deprecating laugh. "No it's...well, you know how some get upset over turning 30? Like it signals the end of their youth, or something like that. I always saw 30 as just a milestone. Thirty was 30. You were one year over your 20s. That's all. And I didn't really see myself as in my 30s because of said milestone. But now I'm past it. Now I'm 31."

"Are you trying to say that you're now having a third-life crisis?" Katy lowered her gaze and smirked.

"Definitely not, no," Alex countered. "It's just...really weird. I feel like I'm a little different now because I'm 31. Like things I haven't really been thinking about are becoming more and more important." Alex shot his eyes back down at the table and took a meticulous sip of his coffee. He added quickly: "But there you go. You asked. I answered." He gave an apprehensive chuckle. "Or rambled, I guess, is the better word."

"Eh, semantics." Katy shrugged her shoulders and tore into her chocolate-covered breakfast. After finishing their food, both sat back in their seats, taking in the morning and allowing the butter and caffeine that was now swirling maniacally in their stomachs to digest. When they were ready, Katy and Alex got up and ventured out towards the Charles River, hand in hand, spending most of the morning wandering around the city. For lunch, they stopped by a café-bookstore hybrid at the very end of Newbury Street. While Alex had chosen where they had breakfast, Katy was the one who had decided where they would have lunch.

"For someone who is dying to get out of her *own* bookstore, you sure pick an interesting place to eat," Alex admitted after they were seated.

"Ha ha. Come on now. I love bookstores; you know that. I just...don't like working for them anymore."

"True," Alex replied. "Well, you have an interview this week, right? Maybe that'll bring in some good news."

"I hope so. I mean..." Katy trailed off, looking around the café. Everyone around her was talking loudly, bodies hunched over their food. The sights and sounds suddenly felt like a weight on her and a wave of exhaustion soaked into her skin. "...I just need to find something, and soon."

"You will, I know it," Alex reassured.

The waitress soon came by to take their beverage orders. Katy took the opportunity after the waitress left to finally open her menu.

"Maybe it's hopeless, the whole job thing," Katy said, scanning the list of meals. Katy looked up to see Alex lower his eyebrows. "For now, at least. Maybe I should focus on the GREs, or something."

"Are you interested in graduate school?"

"Sure. I mean, why not? Everyone eventually gets their master's."

"Well, not everyone. Depends on what you want to do."

"And grad school is perfect for those who *don't* know," Katy retorted, raising her eyebrows and tilting her face with a smirk. The waitress returned with their drinks and asked about their final choices in food. Alex ordered a sandwich and Katy ordered the first thing her eyes landed on in her menu.

"Well, maybe grad school is a good idea, especially if you're really passionate about a certain subject. I'm assuming you'd get your master's in English?"

"I don't know. Maybe. Maybe I'd go to law school." Katy shrugged. "Hey, maybe I'd be a killer lawyer."

"They have a different set of graduate exams for law school. You know that, right?"

"I know that." Katy shrank back in her seat. "Details." After a moment, Katy sat back up and took a sip from her drink. "Maybe I'd take my GREs and then focus on other things. Like, it couldn't hurt to have GRE scores, right?"

"I'm pretty sure there is a time limit on how long you can go between taking the GREs and applying," Alex warned.

"Oh."

"Maybe studying for the graduate exams would be a useful thing to do in addition to the job search," Alex suggested. "Never hurts to plan more fully for the future."

Katy felt a pit forming in her stomach. She took a slow sip of her soda, her fingers pressing into the sides of the glass.

"I guess it couldn't hurt," Katy said, looking out the window. "Hey, speaking of changing the subject, what time is the movie?"

The waitress came by in due time with their food in hand. After eating, Katy and Alex strolled down the main streets, graciously talking about nothing in particular, before heading over to the cinema and watching the movie that they had agreed upon.

The day before, Alex had facetiously suggested a romantic comedy. Katy, who had been standing at the doorway of Alex's bedroom, reacted by walking into the room and jutting her hand out at Alex.

"Hi, my name's Katy. Obviously we haven't met," she had said.

They had decided on an action movie. Alex had remarked that action flicks were just as predictable as romantic comedies, to which Katy replied, "But at least in action flicks, you get to see things blow up. If the female lead in a rom-com got into a car chase after she realized that she actually loves her best guy friend, I might be more inclined."

After the movie, the two headed downtown to the restaurant. Unlike the Top of the Hub – the fancy establishment Alex first took Katy to, at the top of one of Boston's tallest buildings – this restaurant was situated on the first floor, where the recommended clothing attire was significantly more casual. But it didn't stop Katy from walking in with the same excited apprehension that she had felt on their first date.

Inside the restaurant stood a group of ten or so people, a smattering of both males and females, all dressed in business casual, lightly chatting with each other by the hostess's booth. As Katy and Alex entered, the group stopped their conversations and turned to greet the couple. Alex bid everyone a hello before performing an assembly line of introductions to Katy and his friends and their guests. Katy smiled and nodded and shook their hands and said how nice it was to meet them, wondering to herself just how much she was fumbling up even the most basic of pleasantries. The hostess came to the group after a few more moments and led them to their table.

At the table, Katy sat down and silently watched the conversations unfold. Everyone else at the table traded barbs and made references to things and events that Katy didn't know anything about.

And, really, Katy was all right keeping mum. She sat and watched. She smiled when people laughed and nodded when everyone else was in agreement over something. It was nice observing and keeping to herself and slipping behind her menu from time to time to concentrate on what to order.

Besides, what would she talk about with Alex's friends? She knew nothing about management, or programming, or anything involving an actual career-oriented job. The best she could do was awkwardly answer questions about her life and hope to God that someone starts talking about sports – and she was praying that the first of those two situations never played out that night. She went on enough interviews as of late and didn't feel like participating in the social version of one.

"So Katy," interjected one lady, presumably the wife of one of Alex's friends. "How did you and Alex meet?"

Shit.

"Oh, we um, we actually met at a coffee shop," Katy replied, twisting around the hair elastic on her wrist.

"Aw, that's so great. It seems like nobody meets on chance anymore."

Katy tucked a nonexistent lock of hair behind her ear.

"Yeah, it's nice."

So, how about them Red Sox?

"So, how long have you guys been dating?" The woman continued.

"A little over six months."

"Oooh, nice," the woman responded.

Katy smiled awkwardly.

Patriots. New England Patriots. Hey, it *is* football season as well, everyone; let's direct the conversation over that way.

"So, are wedding bells around the corner?" Another woman jabbed.

Oh, for the love of God.

"Actually, we drunkenly eloped in Vegas," Katy deadpanned. "I thought Alex told you guys."

Alex grinned sheepishly.

The second woman's jaw dropped.

"Oh my God, really?"

All the muscles in Katy's face lost their hold.

"No. I was joking."

The second lady's stared blankly before furrowing her brows and shaking her head.

On second thought: Katy didn't even want to talk about sports now. Nope, she was perfectly fine not talking at all. Just go back to talking amongst yourselves, friends of Alex. It's okay to leave Katy out of the conversations. Pay no attention to the girl behind the curtain and all that jazz.

"Already making jokes about marriage," one of the guys said before raising his beer to his lips. "You know what they say about girls who do *that.*"

The table laughed. Alex gave another bashful grin and Katy tried her best to make her eye-roll look facetious. After a moment, one of the other guys at the table brought up the recent Patriots/Dolphins game and Katy slipped behind her menu once again.

Something in her had switched and her wallflower tendencies were taking a serious stronghold. She now just wanted to stay in her spot, enjoy her meal, and leave the restaurant without having to suffer any more interactions.

Maybe it was a bit of an overreaction, but it had already been well established that Katy was queen of overreacting. Regardless, "When are you getting married?" was such a stock response – a clichéd and banal question doled out without much consideration. Specifically, it was one of the most obnoxious stock responses one could give. If one was in a relationship, the question centered on marriage. If one was already married, the question centered on children. What could they ask after that? Grandchildren? Retirement?

"Say, when are you planning to go into a nursing home?"

So, it might have been an overreaction, but it didn't stop Katy from absolutely cringing at such hackneyed questions. Maybe it was because she had always received such stock responses after admitting she majored in English ("So what are you going to do with your degree?" "Are you going to teach English?"). But Katy swore it was because they were trivial and meaningless and the words amounted to nothing more than, "Hey, I participated in this conversation!" She dealt with it at the parties, the family get-togethers, and, on occasion, at interviews where the employer had attempted to be light-hearted and social – but, at the end of the day, she'd rather be silly and sarcastic and sincere with the few people she was close to than petty and insincere with many people that she wasn't.

Deep down inside, Katy knew that the woman across the table didn't mean anything from it. However, that didn't take away from the fact that the comment made Katy switch from shy to full out uninvolved.

And when was that food coming? She could always stuff her face with food and no one would bother her, then.

At least she should have been happy that they hadn't asked her what she did for a living yet.

"So Katy, I forgot to ask: what do you do for a living?"

God? Just as an FYI: You're not as funny as You think You are.

*

127

"I hope you had a good time," Alex said after they had left the restaurant, his hand slipping into Katy's.

"It was nice, yeah. I had a good time." Katy nodded.

"Good, I'm glad," Alex replied. Both of them strolled through the Common, the nighttime darkness settling in everywhere in the park except for small pools of light created by the street lamps. Everything was quieter. People's voices barely traveled to where Alex and Katy were. No shouting, nor crashes, no cacophonies of any sort. Even the traffic seemed muted and distant.

"You didn't speak too much during dinner, so I just wanted to make sure you didn't have a bad time," Alex suddenly explained.

"I was fine," Katy responded. She lowered her eyebrows, took in a quick breath, and added: "And I mean that in the actual definition. Not in the 'fine means I'm miserable' way. I had a pretty decent time. I mean, there just wasn't much for me to talk about, but I'm perfectly happy with staying silent. Beats getting asked what I do with my English degree, or when I'm getting married."

"Well, they're not the *worst* questions in the world." Alex scanned the area of the park in front of them.

"But they're the most meaningless," Katy responded. "They're unoriginal, they have no thought behind them…it just makes me feel like I'm getting interviewed."

"You have a point," Alex conceded. "But isn't that how all types of relationships work, social or otherwise? You say the trite, meaningless things and so you can move on to more serious things?"

Katy shrugged.

"Did *we* say trite, meaningless things when we first started going out?"

"Probably."

"Really? I could've sworn we didn't." Katy paused. "At the very least, you didn't ask me those types of dumbass questions, right?"

Alex paused.

"Probably not."

"Good. Then I rest my case."

Together, they walked up a small hill at the heart of the Common and around the statue that rested at the top before heading back down towards the playground and the Frog Pond. The fall air was slowly becoming more sharp and crisp. The benches that lined the pathways were littered with leaves.

"The questions aren't...*that* 'dumbassed'," Alex mumbled into the quiet air.

"Okay, okay, they're not," Katy laughed out, looping her other arm around Alex and snuggling in. "They're all perfectly deep and meaningful and not at all inane. Now can we please start talking about something else?

"Like what?"

"Like how badly the Dolphins got trounced by the Patriots?"

"I thought they talked about that during dinner."

"But I was busy being quiet then," Katy said with a smile. She hugged into Alex's shoulder again and they crossed the street together.

Chapter 11

That following Tuesday, Katy had her next interview – and possibly her *last* interview for quite some time, considering how her job search had been going. Every interview had been either a complete disaster from the get-go or deceivingly promising. After dealing with disappointment after disappointment after disappointment, Katy just couldn't see herself continuing on after this one.

Katy was also fed up with scheduling all of her interviews on her days off. This time, she scheduled the interview during her regularly-scheduled work hours and requested to take the morning off instead. It was simply getting to be too much to lose one of her few free days to stressing over an interview that never really delivered, anyway. Although it turned into a bit of a hassle – Andrea had decided to schedule her vacation for that week as well – by the time the interview date rolled around, Katy was in the clear.

Not that it mattered: Katy was willing to play hooky, just to see what would happen. Part of her was just so fed up and tired and stressed with the whole process that she was curious as to what would happen if she just didn't show up to work at all.

And besides, Andrea wouldn't be there to yell at her, so who cared?

Katy got off the train and onto street level, trying her best to take in the blue skies and fresh morning air. She made her way through Cambridge and to her final destination at Maurice Fielding Publishing, a major publishing firm with a branch located just outside of Harvard Square. The air was unseasonably warm, making Katy feel like she was in the heart of spring instead of the middle of fall. She took the weather as a good omen. Maybe it meant that this interview might finally – finally – be the one that landed her a job.

And, hey, it could happen, especially if the nice weather could calm her down enough so she could go into her interview *sans* nerves. At the very least, if the interview bombed, she could always take a nice, long walk before heading back to work.

The four-story, white-brick building was on a tiny street with redbrick sidewalks. Tall, glinting windows decorated every side on every floor. Katy smiled as she entered. All those windows must give everyone such a lovely view of the neighborhood. Katy could get used to a view like that.

The first thing Katy noticed when she entered the firm was how modern and stylish and colorful everything looked. The lobby-area furniture was sleek: angular leather chairs surrounded a glass tabletop, which was held up by an elaborate set of blue, spiraled posts. Deep red shelves lined the walls, all filled with the various awards that they had won and books that they had published. The lobby was separated from the rest of the floor by a frosted glass wall and a sliding glass door. She loved how everything felt completely vibrant and alive and transparent and freeing.

Katy stood by the elevators and peered surreptitiously through the glass. The walls in the heart of the firm were covered with beautiful abstract paintings. From her view by the elevator, she could see almost all of the firm, which took up the entire fourth floor. The tall windows that Katy had admired from the outside were lined with colorful wooden frames on the inside. The offices and meeting rooms were only on two sides of the building, which gave two open views of Cambridge for the rest of the workplace to enjoy. The offices and meeting rooms were sectioned off with glass walls decorated with small, frosted circles. The entire floor had a feeling of openness to it. The only parts that did not have color were the cubicles, which were a pure white instead of the standard-issue beige.

Katy took a breath, walked in, and checked in. The receptionist greeted her with a smile and led her to one of the meeting rooms. Once inside the meeting room, Katy sat down in one of the swivel chairs. She gingerly placed her purse on the floor and her folder on the table. After a few moments, a lady wearing a white bottom-up blouse and jeans walked into the room.

"Hey there, Katelyn – or do you like Kate?"

"Katy, actually," Katy replied, before quickly adding: "But I mean, you can call me whatever you want."

"Why would I want to call you something you hate?" she asked matter-of-factly. "I'm Tabby, by the way."

Tabby leaned over the table and shook Katy's hand. Katy tried her best to stand up and lean over, but ended up in an awkward semi-squatting position instead.

"Let me tell you, I hate it when people call me Tabitha." Tabby pulled out her chair as Katy sat back down. "So you can trust me on this one: I like to make sure that I'm not calling someone by their full name when they have a nickname that they like way better."

"Well, that's really good to know," Katy replied with a smile, her posture rigid and straight, her back a solid two inches from the backrest.

Tabby sat down, placed a manila folder in front of her, and leaned into her backrest.

"I know interviews are supposed to be all formal and what have you, but I just want to let you know now that this isn't the case here. So you can relax. We are usually flooded with résumés even when we *don't* have openings, so if we pick you to interview, it usually means we already know you can do the job. I just want to get to know you and see if you'd be a good match for our team."

"Kind of like a date," said Katy, relaxing her posture for a moment before immediately sitting back up.

"Only – unfortunately – no free food and booze," Tabby retorted, opening her folder. "So, I see you have previous experience in the publishing world, which is definitely good."

"Um, yeah: I worked at Eddington Publishing." Katy placed her hands on her folder. "It was a really great internship. I got a lot of wonderful hands-on experience preparing manuscripts for clients and, um –"

"Don't worry. I can read your job description on your résumé perfectly fine on my own." Tabby sat up and leaned over the table a bit. "Hun, you're still in twenty-questions-interview mode. You know you can relax a bit, right? Answering a bunch of meaningless questions never accomplishes much anyway. At best, it shows that you're either really good at bullshitting or really good at memorizing. Now, honestly, just tell me about yourself. And not in the formal, business way. Tell me about your college. Tell me about your bookstore job, or how much retail sucks."

"Retail isn't really that bad. It's great to work with customers." Katy gave a weak smile.

Tabby leaned farther over.

"Like I said: relax. Don't worry about being proper." Tabby pushed herself back and stretched out. "Come on now – retail sucks!"

Katy eyebrows briefly flicked up.

"Retail does suck. A lot." Katy sat back slightly. "The customers drive me crazy sometimes. And the pay is terrible. And I mean, don't get me wrong, I love books and I love my co-workers, but…I don't know. Half of the time I'm selling books that are just…" Katy licked her lips and shook her head. "See, books to me are about gaining new perspectives on the world and on people… About getting a better understanding of things. You are not going to learn anything new about the human condition if you're constantly reading romance novels or chick lit. Like, everything is all fluff and fun – the only thing anyone could ever really gain from that stuff is a complete misunderstanding of how relationships actually work." Katy paused before sitting straight up. "I mean, not that there's anything *wrong* with chick literature. I mean, if that's what you like."

"You wouldn't catch me dead with it," Tabby replied. "And trust me: I know how you feel. I used to be a bookstore slave, too. I know how bookstores work. They want the college educated employees, especially the English majors, because they'll be more informed about all the great and interesting books available. But they pay you poverty wages because, in the end, you're just there to stock the shelves. No one really wants to hear your opinions on literature. Let's face it: there's a reason why most bookstores have, like, two rows devoted to dime store paperback novels." Tabby swiveled Katy's résumé around on the tabletop, letting it slow to a stop before giving it a sharp tap. "But y'know – the biggest thing that always bothered me was how chick lit was never cordoned off as well."

"Me too," Katy replied with instantly regrettable gusto. "I mean, it can be so frustrating going into most bookstores unless I already know exactly which book I want to get. And, even then, it's depressing to see a really awesome book right next to books that have titles like *The Shopaholic Diva.*"

"Ah, shopaholics. I hate it when people are addicted to shopahol," Tabby deadpanned.

"Definitely sounds like something you'd have to go to rehab for," Katy replied, using most of her energy to suppress a rogue grin.

"You know, maybe that's what those books are actually about: addiction to prescription drugs." Tabby tapped at the table again. "Maybe we've been missing the whole point all along. Shoe shopping and obsessing over boyfriends – those are just symptoms of withdrawals from their shopahol."

Katy nodded with a laugh before looking back down at her folder. She had nothing more to contribute and an awkward silence was about to creep in.

"So tell me," Tabby interrupted the impending silence. "What bands do you like?"

The rest of the interview seemed to fly by. Katy talked about the music she liked, the movies she loved, and the places she wanted to travel to someday. When she mentioned San Francisco as one of said places, Tabby perked up.

"Oh, I love San Francisco. It is just such a beautiful town, and I honestly never get sick of seeing the Golden Gate Bridge." Tabby drummed at her manila folder. "I don't know if you knew this, but we actually have a branch there. We have branches in almost every little corner of America. If we hire you, you could always spend some time at one of our other offices. Y'know, we do that from time to time, especially when certain projects need that extra help. We're all one big happy family, as they say. You know, minus the alcoholism and awkward reunions."

Katy found herself fully leaning back in her chair, nearly in a reverie with all the possibilities. The idea of spending time in California sounded almost too good to be true. She hadn't even been hired yet, and she was already fantasizing about traveling opportunities.

After the interview was over, Tabby took Katy around for a small tour of the place. Tabby showed her the various printing rooms and introduced her to the different teams at the office. Photographs and drawings were tacked up on rolling bulletin boards. Papers and folders were shuffled into little bins and upright organizers. Everyone seemed so determined and fast-paced and laid-back and social, all at the same time. The more Katy walked around, the more sure she was that she wanted this job.

The realization struck Katy with such an intensity that she stopped listening to what Tabby was saying. It wasn't that she wanted *a* job. She wanted *this* job, at *this* corporation. She wanted to dress in jeans and a nice blouse and send projects to clients and third-party editors. She wanted to talk to the people in charge of printing. She wanted to be the assistant to the supervisor like she read about in the job description. She wanted to travel to San Francisco – and whatever other towns hosted Maurice Fielding Publishing – and help out fellow coworkers.

To go back to that first date comparison from so long ago: Katy was already falling head over heels and contemplating a future together before the first date was even over.

After the tour, Tabby led Katy back to the lobby area.

"So we do have a few more applicants to interview, but our goal is to get back to everyone within a week or two at most," Tabby explained. "But you really are a phenomenal person, and it was great meeting you."

"And likewise. It was great meeting you too," Katy replied, her folder resting casually by her hips.

Tabby bid Katy goodbye and waited until Katy was in the elevator before going back inside the main office. Katy leaned against the back wall of the elevator, tenderly watching the numbers above the door light up and dim.

She was good at organizing, and she was good at dealing with people. And she had always loved working with Ben and Evelyn and Andrea on the South End Collection's newsletter, even if it was nothing more than a glorified piece of bulletin board entertainment for the coworkers to absently look at in the break room. It just felt right to her. Everything felt right. And she felt energized. She could work from opening to close every single night at South End Collections if it meant that, at the end of two weeks, she'd have a new job at Maurice Fielding.

Katy took her time returning to the train station, walking slowly, gleefully taking in everything about the day. The smell of the leaves reminded her of the mornings she would spend with her high school friends, grabbing coffee and driving for what felt like forever to the nearest beach, just so that they could watch the Atlantic waves hit the sand.

She felt just as carefree and adventurous as she did when she was 17. There was the tiniest chill accumulating under the trees and canopies that would evaporate every time Katy walked out from under the shade and into the warm sunlight. The streets had only a few passing cars. The sidewalks were full of people idly enjoying the late morning.

Katy eventually got on the train and made her way to South End Collections. For the first time in what felt like a long while, Katy enjoyed her walk to the store, with the buildings all lined up, squished together side-by-side, as if they were expecting to get a group picture to be taken. She even enjoyed the crosswalk light at Tremont Street that seemed to take an eternity to change. There was almost a skip in her step as she walked into the bookstore. She opened the door with gusto, the little bell at the top nearly singing Katy's arrival.

"Hey there," Ben said from one of the aisles, an armload of books in hand. "How'd the interview go?"

"Really good. Like, really, really good."

Katy slung the purse off her shoulder and shimmied off her jacket.

"The place is so cool and the lady I talked to was so nice," she continued. "I don't want to jinx it or anything, but I think I really have a shot at it."

"Hey, that's great," Ben softly replied.

"Oh, and thanks again for covering. Andrea was ready to have a heart attack over it." Katy tossed her jacket and purse strap over her forearm.

"Well, what's an interim manager supposed to do in a time of need but sacrifice some of his own time to save the day?" Ben gave a broad smile that proudly showed off his top and bottom teeth.

"I still can't believe she put you in charge while she's gone."

"I still can't believe you blatantly lied to her about why you needed a half day."

"It wasn't a *blatant* lie; I told her I was going on an interview. I just...changed the location, is all."

"Huge difference between 'admissions advisor' and 'possible new boss', especially from the point of view of your *current* boss."

"With all the sick days and sudden vacations she's been taking, I shouldn't even *have* to give a reason," Katy countered. "Slightly hypocritical, if you ask me. Plus, would she have even noticed? She always seems like she has half of her mind somewhere else now, anyway."

"You have a point." Ben turned around and began walking back down the aisle to his pushcart. Katy followed.

"But you're definitely one of her favorite employees. You know that, right?" Ben continued.

Katy faltered.

"Yeah, but...what happens if I tell her I'm looking for a new job and I don't get one? Nothing builds work relationships better than essentially saying, 'hey I'm looking to replace you' and then sticking around when you can't find anything better."

"Well, from the sound of it, you might not have to worry about that. Sounds like you'll be getting a new job after all," Ben replied with a weak smile and a new armload of books.

Katy followed a silent Ben back to his spot in the aisle, her tongue pressed against the roof of her mouth, periodically taking in a large breath as if to say something.

"Why do you think Andrea is on vacation now?" Katy finally settled on what to say. "I mean, out of no where, and in the middle of fall, no less."

"Nervous breakdown? Fall rush too busy this year? I don't know." Ben kept his eyes on the shelf. "Shouldn't you be getting ready to actually work? I mean, I'll take an extra hour of work to just talk with you, but – yeah." Ben coughed. "Shouldn't you be getting ready for work?"

"Fine." Katy shifted and readjusted the jacket on her arm. "I'll put my stuff away and start being all productive."

Katy turned, trudged up the stairs, and entered the break room. She opened her locker, placed her things inside, and slowly closed it, latching the door shut by leaning her back against the metal.

The sounds from the refrigerator filled the area with its muted buzz. She scanned the sparse room, bringing her eyes from the refrigerator to the small plastic table and finally to the bulletin board above the table. Her gaze rested on the few pages pinned onto the board by thumbtacks, also known as the South End Collection's newsletter. The current issue had Ben's reviews on a few books, Andrea's blurb on store-related news, and Katy's commentary on public transit etiquette. Save for Andrea's blurb, there was never any proper rhyme or reason to the newsletter. To be frank, it seemed more pathetic and self-congratulatory than anything else. But where would Katy be if she didn't have that extra little activity? And Katy had always been good at collecting tidbits for the newsletter and figuring out what would fit best onto the page. That had to be a sign of something.

Right?

Katy walked down the stairs, relieved Ben of his duties, and went about her shift with a peculiar alacrity. She wasn't just calm.

She wasn't just optimistic. She couldn't put her finger on it, but she felt something different, something that drove her to unload the carts of books with zero complaints, to use extra patience with customers, and to be extra mindful with her tasks.

Katy concluded after the second cart was finished that what she was feeling was the satisfying sensation of knowing that things were slowly but surely starting to fall into place. Details about her future were becoming a little less vague, a little less confusing, and a little less bewildering. She had a great boyfriend, good friends, an idea as to what she might want to pursue as her career, and a opportunity to finally do something more with her life than just sort and stack books.

If she gave any thought as to how almost all stories – including the most standard chick lit novel – worked, she would have kept a watchful eye out then, understanding that this was the exact moment when everything starts to go horribly wrong. But what she cared about right then and there was savoring the moment, thinking positive thoughts about her latest job prospect, and periodically reminding herself, for once, she wasn't constantly counting down the minutes until she could clock out.

Chapter 12

When she did clock out, Katy continued the celebratory walk that she had started after the interview and ventured north. She wandered around downtown Boston, whimsically going wherever the winds took her. When her legs finally tired out, she settled on the nearest T stop and eventually caught a B trolley home.

Katy opened the door of her apartment to find Maria in the kitchen, stirring away at a large pot on the stove.

"Do my eyes deceive me? Is Maria Johnson actually cooking?" Katy closed the door and dropped her bag by the wall directly across from the kitchen.

"Two ingredients barely counts as cooking," Maria replied, lifting up the can of Alfredo sauce for emphasis.

"Still. A step up. I'm so proud of you." Katy walked behind Maria and to the refrigerator.

"I know. I'm growing into such a fine young woman." Maria continued stirring.

"Eh, I wouldn't go that far."

Katy opened the fridge and pushed around the different containers before finding her orange juice. Holding the carton in one hand while fishing through the fridge with the other, Katy asked, "So how was your day, besides your need to better your culinary skills?"

"It was good. You know, the usual," Maria said, keeping her eyes on her stirred pasta. "I mean, I got asked out, but other than that, the usual."

"Oh, a date?" Katy turned from the fridge and cocked an eyebrow. "Wait – is that why you're cooking? Are you expecting *company* tonight?"

"No, I'm not expecting *company* tonight." Maria stopped stirring and lowered her spoon. "I just…wanted some fettuccini."

"Well then – details!" Katy closed the refrigerator door and leaned against it. "About the boy; not your fettuccini. Tell me who he is. Tell me what he looks like. Tell me where he's taking you."

Katy watched as Maria went back to stirring.

"Or…is he a she?" Katy held the orange juice against her chest. "Is that why you're being so secretive? You switched teams? You go, girl!"

"*He* is a new temp and he's…he's nice. I don't know where he's taking me yet, but we're going out on Friday." Maria twirled the stirring spoon and pulled out a rogue piece of fettuccini. She blew on the spoon, cautiously tasting the pasta before reaching into the cabinets for the colander.

"Uh oh. He's 'nice'? Yikes." Katy put down the orange juice container and crossed her arms. "You can be honest with me. Is he a creep? Is he hideous? Do you need me to fake a doctor's note so you can get out of it?"

"No," Maria replied, placing the colander into the sink. "He's cute. He's really cute. I just don't know how I feel about him yet, is all. I mean, we get along pretty well, but, I don't know."

"Well, at least you're giving him a chance, and that's the important part." Katy opened the cabinet next to the fridge and pulled out a cup.

"I hope so." Maria let out a small sigh into her fettuccini.

Katy paused with the glass in her hand, surveying Maria's face.

"Uh oh. Do *not* tell me you're thinking too much about it." Katy unscrewed the top of the orange juice container, her eyes locked on Maria. Maria shrugged her shoulders, raised her eyebrows, and gave her fettuccini another sigh.

"Ah man, pretend I didn't even ask you about it," Katy quickly added. "Thinking too much will get you in trouble. You should know that."

"I can't help *but* think too much," Maria replied. "I don't exactly go on *date*-dates." Maria lifted the pot and poured everything into the colander. "I mean, it's all going through my head — what if there's no chemistry, but what if I like him and I just have my guard up, what if he changes his mind about me, what if I'm thinking too much and should just shut up for a moment...it's all there."

"I'm sure your mind is telling you this as well, but: you'll be fine. Just, be calm. Everyone freaks out a bit when they first start dating someone."

"I'm definitely not 'everyone'," Maria replied.

"Well, close enough to everyone. I mean, movies and books and — shit, maybe *everything* entertainment-related — makes us think that love happens in one certain way and in one certain way only. No other way counts. So of course it's gonna cause some anxiety when time itself doesn't stop the moment you two first meet."

"I guess so." Maria shimmied the sieve one last time before dumping the pasta back into the pot.

"Seriously!" Katy continued. "I mean, love cannot not be all fireworks and trumpets blazing and heaving bosoms and whatever other garbage that goes on in that pandering smut."

Maria gave another shrug and dumped the Alfredo sauce in the pot with one big shake of the jar.

"I mean it," Katy continued. "Think about it: when everything goes exactly like some banal storyline, how much of it is falling in love and how much of it is fulfilling an *obsession* with love?" Katy sighed. "I don't know; maybe *I'm* the one who is thinking about this too much. But, who knows. Maybe actual love is different. Maybe it's a bit more...boring." Katy raised her glass to her face, blithely gazing into her beverage. "Hell, maybe it's something that comes about slowly, like a gradual understanding of something."

Maria turned from the stove.

"You *have* been thinking about it too much."

"So?" Katy took a quick sip from her glass. "It's good advice, isn't it?"

Maria cocked an eyebrow.

"Katy, is there something you'd like to share about your current experiences with love?"

Katy nearly spat out her orange juice.

"No. I'm good. C'mon, now. This is about what's going on with *you*."

"Are you sure?" Maria pressed. "Because I'm talking about first date jitters, and you're expounding on the realities of love."

"Shut up." Katy crossed her arms. "Besides, maybe I'm just rambling so you'll feel better about your own situation. Ever thought of that?"

Maria laughed.

"I don't know if you've ever considered law school, but take my advice: never become a lawyer. You're shit at creating a defense."

*

Thursday afternoon, Maria called Katy right as Katy was getting ready to leave for work.

"Can I ask you a huge favor?"

"Do I have to dispose of a body?"

"No," Maria retorted. "Well, not yet at least. I wanted to know if you were free tonight."

"Sure, why do you ask?"

"I just wanted to know if you wanted to hang out."

"Of course," said Katy. "When would that ever be a favor?"

"When it involves going to a club."

Katy sucked in her breath, her entire face scrunching up.

"As in a nightclub? Really?"

"This is why it's a favor," Maria replied. "I need you to come with me."

"That desperate to share lemon drops?"

"No." Maria sighed. "Just — okay. So, Jacob asked me to go out to a club with him."

"Jacob being…the nice guy?"

"Yes. That Jacob." Maria sighed again. "I guess his friend is DJing tonight or something and he was going to show his support."

"So…I'm not sure where I come in."

"You come in because I panicked and turned to everyone else in the room and invited them as well."

"Well, then." Katy plopped back on her bed and rubbed her eyes. "How did that go?"

"This girl from marketing piped in and said she'd go and everyone else stayed silent," Maria answered.

"So…"

"So that's even worse," Maria whisper-yelled into the phone. "Now it's going to be him and me and Amanda when he obviously just wanted me to go."

"And, if I went, I'd be there to boost up your numbers to make things less awkward."

"Yes!" Maria whisper-exclaimed. "I knew you'd get it."

"Just putting this out there: for someone who isn't sure how she feels about a guy, you're certainly worried about a simple night out at a club."

"Irrelevant," Maria hissed before taking in a breath. "Please, I really need you there. I'll be in your debt forever."

"Forever? Don't give a girl like me that window of opportunity."

"Well, I would be," Maria replied. "Oh – you could bring Alex."

"And make it a double date? With…Amanda in tow?"

"Well, Jacob doesn't have to know you guys are going out. Not yet, at least," Maria offered. "And I could always dance with Alex, you could always dance with Jacob. Make it look like a low key deal, y'know?"

"I feel like I'm being invited to a swinger's soiree." Katy let out a defeated sigh. "I'll ask. He'll probably say no, but I'll ask."

"If he says no, are you still coming?"

Katy looked around the room, gathering her thoughts before answering.

"I'll still go. If you need me, I'll be there."

Maria downright beamed through the telephone.

"I knew I could count on you."

"Yeah, yeah, yeah, I'm the hero of the day." Katy got up and grabbed her bag. "And now I'm off to save the day at the bookstore, one crap bestseller at a time."

Katy exited her room, grabbed her bag, gave her usual goodbye pats to Miller, and trudged down the stairs. As soon as she made her way to the sidewalk, Katy released the death grip that she didn't even realize she had on her phone in the first place and called Alex.

"Hey sweetheart, how are you?" Alex answered the phone with.

Katy shifted her bag onto her shoulders.

"I'm good. I was curious if you were free tonight."

"Uh, I might be staying late to work on a presentation, actually," Alex said after a moment. "But, I mean, there's always a chance I won't be. Why?"

"Um, well I was curious if you could do me a favor," Katy replied quickly, rubbing at her eyes. "And come with me to a nightclub tonight."

Alex hesitated for longer this time.

"A nightclub?"

"I mean, Maria – y'know, my roommate? – wants me to come with her tonight. It's a long story, but, well, I wanted to know if you would come with me."

Alex gave out a small, nervous laugh.

"I have to be honest. I never liked the nightclub scene. Plus, I stopped going out on weeknights long ago." Alex paused again. "And I thought you hated nightclubs, too."

"I do, I do." Katy anxiously scratched the side of her neck. "Maria just wanted us to come as kind of like a moral support."

"Normally, I would be in favor of moral support," Alex responded. "But nightclubs are loud, overpriced, sweaty...and I hate being around drunk people. Especially drunk college students, which I'm sure the place will be full of. I'm sorry, but it's just not for me."

"It's all right," Katy sighed out. "Don't worry about it. Just figured I'd ask."

"Hey, no harm in asking," Alex replied. The sound of a keyboard clanking in the background soon dominated the conversation. It was all Katy could hear until Alex spoke up again: "You know, I have to say I'm surprised you'd be okay with it. You always struck me as someone who was way too mature for those kind of things."

"Yeah. Yeah, I do. You're right. I am," Katy stammered. "You know, I won't go either. Maria can always owe me some other time."

"That's good to know. I have to admit I wouldn't be all that comfortable with you in a room filled with a bunch of drunk guys wanting to dance with you." The keys kept clanging in the background. "But hey, I really need to get back to work. I'll see you tomorrow?"

"Of course." Katy kept silent while she looked for traffic and crossed the street. "I'm actually heading off to work, myself. I'll see you on Friday."

"Okay, then, have a good day at work."

"You too."

Both remained silent. Katy stepped onto the trolley platform, her toes digging into the soles of her shoes.

"Okay, I'll see you then."

"Sounds good. Bye."

Katy bit her lip and waited for her train.

Katy allowed herself to fall into the usual routine at work that day, to the point that she almost felt like she was outside of herself, allowing her basic motor functions to go on auto pilot and her stock responses to take the place of actual conversations. Every once in a while, she wondered about when she would hear back from Maurice Fielding Publishing. But, for the most part, she kept her mind blank. She worried that, if she thought about it too much, she'd end up jinxing herself. And that was the last thing she wanted to do.

Maria called and left a voice message, reminding Katy of their plans for that night. Katy called back while on her break, assuring Maria that she'd meet up with them as soon as she got out.

Part of her remembered telling Alex she wouldn't go. Another part of her impulsively decided that there was no harm in going without his knowledge, so long as it was just for a little while. A third part of her also remembered that she would be going to a nightclub dressed in work clothes. Not exactly an outfit meant for the nightlife.

As soon as the store closed, Katy stashed her messenger bag in her locker – taking out only her wallet, phone, and keys, and stuffing them into her coat pockets – and left for the nightclub, hoping against hope that no one would pay attention to her long-sleeved cotton shirt and khakis.

Katy met Maria outside of the club. She, Jacob, and Amanda were already in line, the muted club music pulsating through the walls. Katy gave her hellos and surreptitiously cut in line to join them.

Maria introduced Katy to her two coworkers. Maria slurred a few words together in the middle of the introductions. She stopped, giggled, and apologized, admitting that they all had gone out for drinks immediately after work and she was already a bit tipsy.

Katy tried her best to involve herself in conversation, specifically the conversations between Jacob and Maria, only to find herself as the third wheel alongside Amanda. The amusement over two people acting as the third wheel kept Katy's nerves at bay as they paid the exorbitant cover charge and made their way inside.

The bass of the music permeated through everything. Katy could feel her jacket vibrate in rhythm to the song playing as she handed it off at coat check. People seemed to be spilling out of every door, congregating where they could with brightly colored drinks in their hands. With the music already thumping at her insides, Katy followed the rest of the group into the main room.

Katy hooked onto Maria's arm as they snaked through the crowds of people. Everywhere, in every possible inch of space, there were sweaty people swaying and jumping and grinding up

against whoever was closest. Maria and the rest made their way to
where the bartenders were and ordered their drinks.

"Ordering" quickly turned into, "screaming simple blocks
of words over a crowd of people to the bartender." Maria handed
the bartender a few twenties, shouting somewhat coherently that
she was paying for the first round. Before Katy could thank her,
Maria grabbed her and Jacob's drink. Katy managed to get a hand
around hers and Amanda's. By the time Katy turned around,
Maria and Jacob were already making their way to the DJ booth,
flirtatiously linked arm in arm.

"So much for it being a group thing, huh?" Katy shouted
to Amanda as she handed Amanda her drink.

"What?"

"Never mind."

"What?"

Katy rolled her eyes and brought the beer bottle to her lips
instead. Amanda gulped down her drink, swung her arm back to
place the bottle on the bar counter, and shouted something that
resembled a, "see you on the dance floor!" (that, or "Neo's gonna
be sore!" One of the two.) Katy smiled and watched Amanda
fade into the crowd while the club music thumped against her
temples and pulsated through her ribcage. After her own bottle
was empty, Katy contemplated venturing out onto the dance floor
as well. By the DJ booth, Jacob was already introducing Maria to
the man behind the turntables.

After a moment, Katy turned back to the bartender. She
decided on another drink instead.

Katy continued to stand in the back and observe while
periodically ordering a drink. Katy ignored everything – the
awkwardness of the situation, the fact that Maria begged for Katy's
help only to completely abandon her, the understanding that she
was in a sweaty, loud nightclub for absolutely no reason – by
constantly gulping down her drinks. It certainly seemed more
productive than looking around the room, comparing herself to the
girls in the little dresses and remembering just how out of place she
was.

Her fifth drink helped numb the pounding vibrations that Jacob's DJ friend seemed to be sending directly to her via his stereo system, but her mind couldn't help but race. What was Alex doing now? Would this have been more fun if Alex had come? If he had come, would she have been able to abandon everyone the way that Maria had abandoned her? Would she have been home by now – or, at the very least, somewhere quieter?

Katy turned away from the dance floor again, closed her eyes in order to concentrate, and shouted what she wanted to the bartender. She grabbed her drink and turned back to wax romantical.

She missed Alex. She hated that she was here, alone, with no one around to even attempt to have a conversation with, her best friend obviously not in need of her help. She was miserable and hot and woozy and she just wanted to be with Alex, now more than ever.

Eventually, Maria and Jacob made their way back to the bar to order their next drink, Maria giggling profusely, Jacob's hand on Maria's back. Neither of them acknowledged the wallflower off to the side. With gritted teeth, Katy walked over and leaned into Maria's ear.

"I'm going home!" Katy declared, using Maria's shoulder to keep herself from falling over.

"Are you sure?" Maria shouted back.

Katy nodded emphatically in reply.

"Okay! I hope you had fun though!" In proper nightclub etiquette, Maria spoke in slow, enunciated syllables.

"Yeah! Sure! See you tomorrow!" Katy shouted back. Without acknowledging Jacob or even caring where Amanda went, Katy turned, her mind completely focused on making it through the crowds and grabbing her coat at coat check.

Everything around her seemed to mesh together. The walls and the floor and the ceiling and the strobe lights and the booming music and the people dancing and grinding together. She slowly made her way to the other side of the room, got her coat, and spilled out into the cold night. Her drunken lungs gulped at the outside air, as if fresh air could sober her up, or at least prevent her from getting sick.

With her coat now around her shoulders, Katy immediately reached into one of its pockets, drew out her phone, and flipped it open. Her eyes squinted at the screen as she slowly pressed the number two on her speed dial. She listened intently to the ringing sound, her phone now pressed tightly against her cheek.

"Hello?" A groggy but familiar voice answered.

"Alex! Alexander! Hel-lo!" Katy chirped.

"Katy? What's going on? Are you all right?" Alex replied, his voice still sluggish and mumbling.

"I…just wanted to call you up because I missed you," Katy sang into the phone. "Oh my God, Alexander, I missed you so much. So much! The entire time I was in there I was like, 'I miss Alex. I wonder what he's doing.' And then I realized that you might be missing me, too. Or – or you might think I was dead! Dead!"

"Why would I think you were dead?" Alex asked, slowly and deliberately.

"Because I didn't call!" Katy exclaimed, her free hand jutting up into the air. "At a dark and mysterious clu-u-u-ub and I don't even call! So now I called, and now you know I'm not dead. I mean, what if I didn't call and you started thinking I was lying in a ditch. That would suck! And then you'd be worried and I wouldn't want you to be worried."

"It's nice that you put my feelings first," Alex replied in monotone. "You do know it's 2 in the morning, right?"

"Yes!" Katy shook her head at the phone. "…No! But that's not the point. The point is that I missed you and I just needed to call you and tell you that I love you. I think I really love you, like, so so much and I think I've been too chickenshit to say anything because once you tell a guy you love them – well that's when they become fuckheads. And I didn't want you to become a fuckhead."

"Katy, how much did you have to drink?"

"Like, *a* drink," Katy replied, eyes widening. "One – one! – drink! I'm not drunk! Nope, nope, nope!"

Katy, amused with how her lips felt when she said "nope", began to mouth the word, accentuating the "p" sound.

"Katelyn – are you drunk?"

"Of course!"

Alex's sigh filled Katy's eardrums.

"Are you home yet?"

"No. No! Just got out! Total shitfest in that nightclub, oh my God. Someone should let Jacob's friend know that he DJs at a shitty nightclub. Hey, it's after midnight! T is good and cl-o-o-o-o-o-sed! I need to get a cab! Okay, I love you, bye-bye!"

Katy snapped her cell phone shut, threw it in her pocket, and began jogging down the street with one arm waving. A cab eventually pulled over and Katy hopped into the backseat.

Chapter 13

At ten o'clock the next morning, Katy started cursing herself for not pulling down the shades in her bedroom.

Her eyes strained open, only to immediately shut against the invasion of sunshine that had infiltrated her room and declared all-out war on her eyes.

What a day to not be overcast and raining.

Katy turned to face her pillow, only to be greeted with a sloshing wave of nausea. Despite being attacked on two separate fronts, Katy mustered enough energy to slither out of her bed. Groping around with her eyes half closed, she hobbled over to her window shade and tugged it closed. She briefly thought about returning to bed, but the idea of lying back down sent a brand new wave of nausea through her. Instead, she trudged into the kitchen for whatever type of bread that she could find.

Bread. All she wanted was bread. Wheat bread, rye bread, banana bread – to fill her stomach with wonderful bready goodness and to take away all the sick feelings. She grabbed at the bags on top of the fridge, pulling down the hotdog buns and the loaf of sliced white bread, and meandered towards the living room area.

Miller trotted out of Katy's room and into living room, jumping on the couch and finding a place to rest. Katy watched with a foggy fascination, as if recalibrating her brain to recognize and understand moving objects. She trudged to the window shades in the living room, dragged them down as well, and gently sat down on the couch next to Miller. Miller lifted his head and purred softly at Katy's arrival. She gave him a few scratches behind the ear before opening the sliced bread bag, removing a slice, and taking a few cautious bites.

After a few minutes, Katy felt up to turning on the television. With the volume on low, Katy watched whatever the TV set provided her – infomercials, daytime talk shows, failed reality series, the whole kit and caboodle. Katy sat with her eyes half open, feeling a type of misery that can only be processed by sitting in a near catatonic state, barely registering any sight, smell, or touch.

Sometime in the afternoon, Katy got up from the couch, lethargically looking around for her phone. It wasn't plugged in with its charger and Katy couldn't remember where she put her bag. It took her a while to remember that her bag was back at the bookstore and that she had shoved the essentials into her coat pockets. She grabbed her coat – which was lying in a crumpled pile by her closet – pulled out her flip phone, and sent Alex a message, telling him that she couldn't wait to see him. She then found her place back at the couch and continued her comatose television watching.

With her phone in her hand, Katy contemplated sending Maria a message. She paused for a moment, figuring out whether her message should be sarcastic, passive-aggressive, or humorously forgiving. She wondered if Maria was going through her workday with the same hangover that Katy was experiencing. After a moment of deliberation, Katy slid her phone onto the coffee table and mindlessly ate another slice of bread.

She couldn't help but feel a little bit silly for drinking so much. She had been too angry that night to remember her limits, and too embarrassed by the whole thing to acknowledge the telltale woozy feeling – the one that would essentially warn her, "the next drink you order better be a water or you're gonna be in a trouble." She drank herself into oblivion and it was pure luck that she even made it home all right. She had allowed emotions dictate the amount of alcohol she consumed. Was that one of the first signs of alcoholism? Or maybe just the first sign of being really dumb.

Being in the apartment felt odd. Fridays always had a surreal quality to Katy, especially when she tried watching TV. The soap operas, the daytime talk shows, the commercials hounding her to go back to school and finally get that associate's degree – they made her feel like she should be at work instead.

But the television was not the reason Katy felt so strange today. She couldn't put her finger on it, but somehow everything just felt off.

After the ninth law firm commercial inquiring about any accidents that Katy might have been in (through not fault of her own!), Katy turned off the television, crawled back into bed, and took a semi-nauseous nap. After a few hours, Katy woke up, slid out of her clothes, and made her way to the shower. The hot water helped clear her mind and sooth her stomach. She reveled in her first feel-good moment of the day, holding her head under the showerhead and letting the water pelt her forehead.

Eventually, she got out and padded around the apartment in her towel, happy that her nausea was finally fading. The sun was starting to set and the apartment was slowly filling with darkness, save for where the bathroom light flooded through. Katy switched on the light in her bedroom, changed into her clothes, and left for Alex's place.

On the way down the stairs of her apartment complex, Katy fished out her phone, flipped it open, and called Alex. After a few rings, a curt "yeah?" let her know that he had picked up.

"Hey sweetie," Katy cooed into the phone, waiting for Alex to respond. When he didn't, she coughed and continued: "I just wanted to let you know that I'm leaving my place now and I'll see you soon."

"Okay. I will see you then, Katy."

A silence flooded the airwaves.

"Um, okay, sweetie, I'll, uh, see you then!"

Katy hung up her phone, her lips pressed together in a tight line. To say Alex was distant on the phone would've been an understatement, and Katy couldn't help but feel despondent about it. Was it a bad day at work? Did he not get a proper night's sleep? Did he –

Shit.

Details from the night before hit her quicker and more suddenly than any cheap shot of vodka could ever hope to. A new type of nausea hit Katy's stomach as she approached the green line stop and waited for her trolley.

Who *wouldn't* be pissed about getting woken up in the middle of the night by some incoherent numbskull straight out of a nightclub – even more so when that numbskull is your girlfriend? Or, more importantly, when the incoherent numbskull girlfriend had previously said that she wasn't even going to a club in the first place. She had lied and went anyway and proceeded to wake him up with a drunk-dial just to let him know that she was a liar, liar, pants on fire.

Shit, shit, shit, shit, shit.

It felt like everything ground to a halt in her body. Her lungs stopped, the muscles in her face went slack. It was downright clichéd, but Katy could've sworn her heart stopped as well. At the very least, how else could she explain feeling like blood had stopped flowing through her body?

She swayed back and forth on the trolley platform, simultaneously anxious to see Alex and dreading the very moment when she would arrive. All actions and interactions – from paying her fare, finding a seat, and switching subway lines at the appropriate stop – had slipped into the unconscious. Katy drifted along, her skin covered in a cold sweat, everything in a complete haze. At Alex's stop, her body instinctively walked off the train, down a set of stairs, and across the pedestrian bridge.

Her mind was in a hysterical conflict, urging her to get to Alex's apartment as quickly as possible – as well as get the hell away from there as quickly as possible, find a new boyfriend, and never have to face Alex's inevitable disappointment. Alex was a naturally more reserved man, but his ultra-reserved tone on the phone let her know that she was in for it big time.

When she arrived at his building, her hand instinctively rose up and pressed the intercom buzzer for Alex's apartment. Without a reply, Alex buzzed her in. Her unconscious mind continued to do all the work for her and commanded her feet to climb the stairs.

"Hi, sweetie," said Katy as Alex answered the door, her mind still a couple layers separated from reality.

"Hi." Alex replied in monotone, pushing the door open for Katy to catch as he made his way into the living room.

"So, um…" Katy pressed a dry tongue against the roof of her mouth. "How was work?"

"Not that great. Didn't get much done. Tired…for some reason." Alex turned to Katy and crossed his arms.

Everything inside Katy felt like it had suddenly dropped away, descending down through every apartment floor and burrowing into the ground.

"Oh."

"Yeah." Alex's mouth tightened. "Plus, all day I had this nagging feeling that my girlfriend had outright lied to me."

Katy quickly realized that her previous feeling was misguided. Everything inside her had *not* dropped away. Some things had stayed behind. She knew that because it had just drained out at that very moment.

"O-oh."

"Should we talk about this now or should we wait until after dinner?"

If Katy had not been so overwhelmed with guilt and dread, she would've laughed. Who could have an appetite in this atmosphere?

"We should talk now."

"Fine then." Alex walked over to one of his kitchen stools, hiked up the sides of his pants, and sat down with his hands intertwined. "Who should start?"

Katy kept her eyes on the floor. The silence bore into her from every other direction.

"I am so sorry," Katy eventually blurted out. "I mean it. I really didn't plan on going. Honest. I just…"

"Honest? You're honestly going to lie to me again and tell me you didn't plan on going?" Alex interrupted. "You're going to excuse a lie with another lie? Is that how much you value our relationship?"

Katy could feel her face flush.

"I don't know why I said I wouldn't go. I...I don't know."

"You knew I wouldn't approve," Alex replied matter-of-factly.

Katy stopped her panic for a split second, just to repeat his last word in her mind. *Approve?*

Katy took in a shaky breath.

"I guess I just...I wanted make everyone happy. And I messed up."

"And by making everyone happy you decided to lie to your boyfriend and go get drunk at some club and go dancing with strangers?"

"I never danced! I didn't!" Katy interjected, as if that was the only line of defense she had. "I just stood there and watched everyone else have a good time."

"And that's what you consider a good time, huh," said Alex, a tone of finality in his voice.

"No!" Katy yelped out, as if someone had just punched her. "Come on, you know me. That's – that's not what I do. I don't even *like* clubs." Katy felt her entire body flood with heat. Something inside of her was switching from flight to fight.

"But you'll pretend to, to make Maria happy."

"Well, yeah! That's what friends do," Katy responded, her tone slipping from apologetic to defensive. "Like you never did anything that went against your character to help out a friend."

"I wouldn't lie to my girlfriend and then do something she wouldn't like."

"I'm sorry! Oh my God, I'm sorry." Katy let out a shaky laugh and put a palm to her forehead. "How many times can I say I'm sorry about lying? I wasn't thinking."

"That's not good enough for me," Alex replied. "What happens when you do something else because you were 'not thinking'?"

"What?" Katy tried to keep her voice down, but it was fruitless. "What are you even *talking* about?"

"I just expect more from you." Alex's tone remained subdued.

"More?" Katy cried out. "When I have ever done something like this before? Never! In all the time we've been dating, never. I made a mistake and I said I'm sorry! I said I'm sorry a million times! What else do you want me to do?"

"We shouldn't be having these discussions in the first place," he stated coldly. "You should be wanting to do these things without me pushing you to do it."

Katy threw her hands in the air. She knew she messed up, but this was taking it to another level.

"I don't even know what you're talking about!" she cried out.

"If you really hated drinking and going out and staying late, you would've told Maria you weren't able to go. I highly doubt her life was on the line, so I think some part of you likes that lifestyle."

Katy grabbed at her scalp.

"You are making some seriously random conclusions. Where is this even *coming* from?"

"You know I don't do things like go out and drink, and you know I wouldn't approve of you drinking like that."

A wave of anger surged up Katy's spine. There was that word again! *Approve.*

"I don't deliberately go out and get wasted," Katy maintained. "That was a fluke."

Katy looked at Alex, whose expression had become completely unresponsive.

"What?" Katy exclaimed, her whole face getting hot. "Oh my God, what? I'm sorry. I'm sorry that I lied and went to a club, and I'm sorry that I woke you up in the middle of the night. It was a shitty thing to do and I'm sorry. I'm sorry, I'm sorry, I'm sorry. But don't you dare accuse me of being some alcoholic in disguise. That's not fair!"

The words seemed to hang in the air. Katy let out a long sigh. All of the drive that kept her in fight mode dissipated with her breath.

"I'm just...disappointed," Alex said after a moment.

Katy threw up one of her hands again.

"Of what?"

"You."

Katy rubbed at her eyes, shaking her head as she took in another breath.

"You just said that you were trying to make everybody happy," Alex went on. "So either you've been pretending to be someone you're not with Maria, or you've been pretending to be someone you're not with me."

Katy threw her head back, exasperated.

"What?" she downright whispered.

"I'd like to think I'm a good judge of character," said Alex, "and I thought I knew who you were. But now...how do I know if you haven't been pretending to be what you thought I wanted all this time?"

"You are getting all of this...from one lousy mistake?" Katy responded. She pressed one of her hands against a wall, feeling like she would faint otherwise. "Where...where is this all even coming from?"

"It's...something I've been thinking about for a while," Alex said after a pause. "I mean you scoffed at the idea of marriage..."

"What?" Katy shot back, her eyes widening. "What are you talking about?"

"Marriage. You hated that my friends had asked you if we would get married."

"They were being facetious, and I thought it was annoying." After a moment, Katy added: "And I never said marriage was stupid. The mindless banter — *that's* what I found stupid."

Alex pursed his lips and shook his head.

Katy looked Alex up and down before asking slowly: "Is this what this is all about? Is this why you're so upset? You're trying to figure out if I'm – what – wife material?"

"It's not as simple as that."

Now it was Katy's turn to shake her head.

"Did turning 31 really mess you up that badly? That you're finding a stupid mistake as a sign that...that..." Katy let the sentence linger in the air. She wasn't exactly sure how to finish it, or if she was ready for what would have been said.

Silence hung in the air, suffocating Katy as it filled the room. Both looked to the ground, painfully aware that the conversation was quickly leading them down a path that neither of them wanted to venture toward.

After a moment, Alex got up and kissed Katy's forehead.

"Can we just...forget about this?" he asked quietly.

Katy cast her eyes down, unsure how to respond.

"I'm sorry," Alex continued. "I know I'm making mountains out of molehills. I'm sorry I brought this whole thing up. It was an overreaction."

After a moment, Katy returned his gaze.

"I'm sorry, too. I really am. This whole thing is so stupid..."

Alex pulled her in closer and wrapped his arms around her. Katy hugged back, her head pressed into his chest, wondering if they had stopped soon enough to place the lid back on Pandora's box.

Abby Rosmarin

Chapter 14

Using work in the early morning as her excuse, Katy took the one of the last trains back into the city that night. She curled up in one of the corner seats in the train car and gazed heavily out the window. The midnight world swirled around her in a parade of scattered lights and reflections before the train went underground, where concrete walls and nondescript darkness replaced her view.

Katy got off one line and slipped onto another, her bag feeling like it had gained twenty pounds instantaneously. Aside from a mumbling drunk, the train car was deathly silent. The fluorescent lights bounced off of the scuffed metal of the seats, the linoleum floors, the advertisements that had been scribbled over in marker.

She sat by the door of the trolley, again looking toward the outside, but focusing on nothing. The trolley made its way aboveground, starting and stopping its way through Boston University. A few girls with drunken giggles got on, only to get off four blocks down the road. The conductor mumbled something under his breath as he let the girls off and ran through a red light for the trolley. The automated voice announcing Katy's stop snapped her out of her reverie just enough for her to murmur a "thanks" to the conductor, step unto the street, and make her way up the hill until a familiar apartment complex came into view.

Katy stepped in the apartment to find a Maria sitting cross-legged on the couch, twirling her spoon in a bowl of ice cream as she watched television.

"I didn't expect you back tonight," were the first words to come out of Maria's mouth.

Katy bit at the inside of her cheek.

"Change of plans, I guess."

Maria kept silent as she looked at Katy, her spoon tapping lightly against the ice cream bowl.

Katy forced a smile onto her face.

"And you!" Katy exclaimed with regrettable gusto. "I wouldn't have expected you to be home so early, either."

"Well that's how dates work, right?" Maria blushed. "First dates, at least? Nice dinner, fun activity, home by 11?"

Katy licked her lips.

"I'm glad you're having a good time with this guy."

Katy walked into the kitchen and placed her bag on the counter. The TV filled in the silence of the room with a commercial for a strip-tease exercise program, with free "exercise pole" included.

"Katy, what happened," Maria eventually said.

"What do you mean?" Katy used her most innocent inflection while the back of her neck heated up.

"I wish you wouldn't do that," Maria said slowly.

"Do what?"

"Be so guarded when something is obviously bothering you. You know I'm always here for you."

"I'm fine."

Maria got up from the couch.

"You know you can't use 'I'm fine' to another woman. It doesn't work on us. Come on, now." Maria walked up to the counter and rested her elbows on it. "I promise, this time, I'll wait a whole week before I alert the presses."

Katy shrugged and opened the fridge.

"I just have to go in early tomorrow, is all," Katy said flatly.

"You always stay over Alex's, no matter how early you have to get up in the morning," Maria countered. "If you don't want to talk about the fight –"

"Who said there was a fight?" Katy retorted, her voice a solid decibel louder, before retreating her gaze to the ground.

"Is there any other reason why you're here?"

Katy sighed and rolled her eyes.

"I don't want to talk about it."

"There are two things I know about Katelyn Sinclaire. Well, three if you count the fact that no one ever spells your name right." Maria looked up facetiously, saw Katy's expressionless face, and instantly dropped the smirk. "One, that you cannot handle it when people see the side of you that isn't sarcastic and whatever. Two, that, for all your guardedness, you actually feel better when you talk about whatever's bothering you."

Katy sighed.

"I hate that you're right."

Maria gave a peppy smile.

"That's what I'm here for." Maria let the smile fade away before adding: "But really, what happened?"

Katy closed the fridge and pressed her back against it.

"Just like you thought," Katy replied. "A fight."

"Sweetie, I'm so sorry," Maria replied. "About what?"

"It's…stupid." Katy rubbed her eyes. "I accidentally drunk-dialed him last night, after the club. And he was pissed about it."

"Pissed about a drunk dial?" Maria raised an eyebrow. "Well, that's kind of ridiculous."

Katy rolled her eyes before staring at the wall next to the fridge.

"I might have previously told him that I wasn't going to go to the club."

"Oh," Maria replied.

"It's just so stupid." Katy pinched at the corners of her eyes. "He told me he didn't like nightclubs and when he asked me if I was going…I don't know, I froze."

"You didn't want him thinking less of you," Maria stated.

Katy pressed her lips together and gave out a muffled "hmph."

"So you lied, and then woke him up in the middle of the night and got caught in your lie," said Maria. "Everyone makes mistakes. Were you even doing anything at the club?"

Katy shook her head.

"Aside from drinking by myself? Nope."

Maria sighed.

"He does have a right to be annoyed with the situation, and maybe even argue a little over it...but really? He got so pissed off that he kicked you out?"

"No, he didn't kick me out," Katy replied slowly. "I left on my own."

"Was the fight that bad?" Maria asked.

"I mean, it was the worst fight we've ever had," said Katy. "Well, to be honest, it was the *first* fight we've ever had. I just felt so uncomfortable there, like I was suffocating."

Miller trotted into the kitchen and rubbed up against Katy's feet. She bent down, picked him up, and buried the side of her face into his back.

"I...I think he's trying to figure out if I'm marriage material," Katy said finally. "And I think last night made him worry that he could not ever marry me."

"Wait, what?" Maria answered incredulously. "He got all this...all from a drunk dial?"

"He kept going on about how I'm pretending to be someone I'm not." Katy rested her chin on Miller's shoulder. "Apparently I made some off-hand remark about a marriage joke and he took it as a sign that I never wanted to get married."

"Oh, wow," Maria responded. "Katy, that really is dickish of him to be making these assumptions all off of one mistake." Maria drummed at the countertop. "But, to be honest, I can't say I'm not surprised."

Katy lifted her chin off of Miller.

"What do you mean?"

"He's, what, 30 now?"

"31."

"I wouldn't be surprised if he's starting to think about the rest of his life." Maria dragged a finger across the counter, her eyes moving from the countertop to Katy's solemn expression. "People usually get married and start having families at this point. Everyone around him is probably settling down. I mean, that gives him no right to freak out, but...I don't know. He might be worried that you're too young for him." Maria sighed and pushed herself away from the counter. "It's the whole idea of 'shit or get off the pot'. Maybe he's trying to…I don't know, figure out the state of the bathroom, if that makes any sense."

Katy gave a weak laugh and hugged Miller tighter.

"Leave the metaphors to the English majors."

"I'm just saying…" Maria trailed off and looked back down at the counter. "Well…do you?"

Katy dropped Miller to the ground.

"Do I what?"

"Want to get married?"

"Someday, yeah."

"To Alex?"

Katy shrugged.

"Well, maybe. I don't know," Katy answered. "Somewhere down the line, maybe. But not right now. Not anytime soon. We've only been together for 6 months."

Maria remained silent.

"Are you telling me I need to break up with him?"

Katy didn't mean for her voice to break in the middle of her sentence.

"No, of course not," Maria replied. "That's not what I mean at all. I just mean – well, I'm taking a huge guess here in saying that you and Alex never talked about marriage before."

"Again, we've only been together for, like, six months. Of course not."

"Where a relationship is supposed to be at that point when you are 24 is totally different from where a relationship is supposed when you are 31. At least if you're thinking about marriage," said Maria. "And I'm assuming that you still want to be with him."

Katy nodded, crossing her arms tightly over her chest.

"I think it would be a good idea to just…bring the topic up. Let him know that you want to be with him, but that you're also not ready for marriage. Not anytime soon," Maria advised. "If he can live with that, then that's fine. If not, then it's for the best if you guys end it then, before things get really involved."

"I guess," Katy said, avoiding eye contact with Maria. After a few moments, she added: "You know, I should get to bed. It's getting way late and I have to work early tomorrow."

Maria stared at Katy before responding with: "Yeah, you should get some rest."

"Good. I'll see you tomorrow, then. Technically today. Ha ha."

Maria straightened her back.

"Please think over what I said," Maria stated slowly. "I know it sucks, but it's better to face this head-on."

Katy avoided Maria's gaze, gave a rushed, "Okay, good night," and retreated into her room, where she escaped out of her clothes and into the security of her bed.

*

Katy woke up well before her alarm went off – although, to be fair, calling it "waking up" would be a misnomer. More accurately, Katy had given up all hope of getting any real sleep and had stumbled out of bed well before her alarm went off. The entire night was spent in thirty-minute nap intervals, followed by an hour or more of lying in bed and staring at the ceiling. With muffled grunt, Katy grabbed the khakis that were crumpled up by her bed and slumped to the kitchen for a glass of orange juice before making her way out the door and to work.

Katy was greeted by a smirking Hannah, who was sitting on the metal bench just outside South End Collections.

"Did you hear?" Hannah asked, standing up the second Katy was within the general vicinity of the store.

"I didn't." Katy got out her keys and fumbled around the key ring for the one to unlock the store's front entrance. "Hear what?"

"About Andrea," Hannah glowed. "I found out yesterday."

Katy inserted the key, turned it half a revolution, and opened the door.

"What happened yesterday?"

"Well, nothing actually happened yesterday," Hannah said as she followed Katy inside. "But I now know why Andrea has been MIA."

Katy shrugged off her bag and trotted upstairs.

"Well, okay: why then?"

"Andrea got *married*."

Katy stopped and turned.

"Married?"

"Yeah, *married*. And that last minute vaca a little while ago? Her impromptu honeymoon. She apparently had this, like, insane whirlwind romance and they decided to elope."

Katy gave a pained smirk. What unbelievable and unrealistic timing.

"Wow. I'm just...wow. Good for her." Katy continued up the stairs and unlocked the employee's lounge.

"Has Andrea ever been married before?" Hannah finally asked as she placed her purse in her locker.

"Not that I know of," Katy answered. "I mean, not since I've known her. And she has never mentioned a divorce or anything. For all I know, this store has been her whole life." Katy paused and closed her locker door. "So this is probably her first."

"Wow." Hannah raised her eyebrows and followed Katy back downstairs. "Could you imagine not getting married until you're in your 50s?"

Katy shrugged her shoulders.

"That is a pretty long while to wait."

Katy held open the office door and let Hannah inside.

"I know she'll probably tell you all about it, but I couldn't wait," said Hannah. "She was telling me and Ben that she wants to do something soon, like a mini-reception or what have you."

"Oh."

"Still don't get why she was so secretive about it, though."

"I wish I could tell you," Katy replied, kneeling down, her eyes already on the money safe.

The only time people kept relationships so secretive is when they thought others would disapprove. Katy opened the safe, pulled out the cash register trays, and placed them on top of the table. They were already prepared, the bills and coins already in their proper spots and with the proper amount. Katy couldn't remember the last time Andrea closed the store and decided to prepare the trays for the next day as well. If this were any indication, Andrea was pretty happy about her recent events. Katy stacked the two drawers on top of each other and made her way to the front of the store.

"I wonder what he looks like," Hannah said when they reached the front.

"She didn't mention that?" Katy asked, handing Hannah one of the trays and unlocking Hannah's register.

"She was too busy gushing about her vacation." Hannah replied, slipping her drawer in.

"Well, we'll find out eventually, won't we?" Katy's upper lip curled inward as she smiled, exposing more gum than teeth. She silently counted out the money in both trays, verifying that it was the right amount.

"Alright, I'm going to scan the first floor," Katy said after she finished counting. "You check the second floor. Be back when it's time to open."

"Sounds good," Hannah replied and made her way upstairs.

Katy quickly retreated into the aisles, her fingers tracing the outlines of the books as she walked by them. She weaved in and out, absently checking to see if anything was out of place. The "Women's Literature" section came into view and Katy found herself scanning the titles, wondering if any of them had stories about boyfriends looking for a wife around the exact same time their boss gets married out of no where.

Of course not. The females in chick literature are never questioning what levels of commitment they're ready for. They're never stressed out over the confusion and uncertainty of everything. They go shoe shopping, they gossip with their best friend, and they fall deeply and dramatically in love with someone who is obviously compatible with them on every level. And, if not, then at least you know from the very beginning that the straight male friend is actually the girl's soulmate and that, by the three-quarter mark, she'll realize it as well. Either way, everyone will all live happily ever after. There's no sense of dread – certainly no conversation that could potentially unveil a fatal flaw in the relationship – and no complex, painful confusion.

No. Just shopping and gossip and martinis. A vapid and ignorant existence.

Lucky girls.

Katy almost slapped herself for the last thought. God, woman, get yourself together. Have you no self-respect? That type drivel was meant for the pathetic and the lovesick. Predictable stories with predictable outcomes so that those who live in a more uncertain world can have a sense of security, however fleeting it may be.

Katy peered into the office before closing the door. It was 9 a.m. Time to open up. She grabbed the binder she needed, wandered to the front, found Hannah by her register, and unlocked the door.

"I'll be dealing with the new buybacks if you need me," Katy informed and made her way into the stock room.

Once inside, Katy pulled up a chair and the box of used books. She opened the binder and began writing down what they had bought back, how much the store paid in the buyback, and what their new prices would be. Katy was on autopilot, shifting books from one hand to the other and making a pile on the ground. Katy only knew she was done when she reached into the box, only to find it empty. She meandered to one of the metallic shelves to grab the price gun and began sticking price tags to the used books' covers. She paused her task twice, once to fill in for Hannah while she had her break and once to unlock the second register when Josh came in. She eventually finished the pricing and loaded an empty cart with the books. She was halfway through filling the cart when Evelyn popped her head in.

"Hey you," she cooed.

"Oh, hey." Katy blinked and rubbed at her eyes. "What time is it?"

"Two. Time for me to temporarily be in charge while you take your break."

Evelyn walked over and picked up one of the used books.

"So, Hannah told me the big news," Evelyn continued. "Sounds carefully planned and thought out. Not at all sporadic."

Katy let out a nervous laugh.

"Tell me about it."

"I didn't even know she was dating."

"I don't think anyone did." Katy put down the price gun and stood up, sighing audibly. "I don't know. I just hope she's happy."

"Well, Hannah's definitely happy for her, at the very least."

"Or she's happy that she was one of the first to find out."

Evelyn laughed and shook her head.

"You have a point there. But, seriously, though. This whole situation is right out of left field. It always seemed like Andrea had the store and that was...kind of it," said Evelyn. "But she really did need something else going on, outside of the store. Something in her personal life. I just hope it doesn't blow up in her face."

"I doubt any of us are hoping that it does," Katy retorted.

"Again, point," Evelyn replied. "But, regardless: go on your break. And take a nap while you're at it. You look exhausted."

Katy leaned backwards, stretching her arms up and behind her.

"Just practicing my best zombie impersonation," she said and exited out of the stock room and up the stairs. She entered the break room and grabbed her bag from her locker, only to quickly realize that she hadn't packed herself any type of lunch. With a groan, she fumbled for her wallet and pulled out a few dollars. With slight hesitation, Katy reached back into her bag for her phone, wondering if Alex had called, or, at the very least, sent her a text message. She flipped open her phone to find a voicemail alert, front and center on her screen. Feeling her face go cold, Katy mechanically checked her voicemail.

"You have – one – new voicemail," the automated lady informed.

"Hi there," said a familiar-enough voice. "This is Tabby from Maurice Fielding. I just wanted to get back to you and let you know that we unfortunately chose someone else for the job position. But I wanted to let you know that I think you really would be a great addition to the company and I'm going to keep your résumé on file in case any other jobs open up."

Katy closed her phone, placed the money back in her wallet, and sat back down.

"I'll keep your résumé on file in case any other jobs open up." But Katy knew no jobs would come up. No jobs ever came up. They always give that line, time after time, but they never really mean it. Yeah, maybe she'll work there when another job opens up. And maybe she'll stumble upon a lifetime supply of teddy bears and rainbows on her way home from the unemployment office.

Katy hunched over in her chair. She collapsed her head into her hands, her face scrunched up, trying like hell to keep from crying. Because if she started to cry about this, she would start crying about Alex, about her job, about how hopeless and confused and stressed out and anxious and uncertain she had become and then she wouldn't be able to stop. She slid her forehead from her hands to the tabletop, her palms pressed against the back of her head.

Katy eventually opened her eyes and looked up, squinting and blinking until she remembered where she was. South End Collections. Break room. It was Saturday. And – according to the clock – already 2:28. Did she fall asleep? Must've. Heh. There went that day's break. Maybe she could force down a few chips from the vending machine in her remaining minutes. Maybe a soda or two would help energize her. Katy took a deep breath, stood up, and began walking. After a lap around the room, Katy leaned against one of the walls, gathering herself.

Within seconds, a surge of anger swept through her body. She clenched her teeth and stomped her foot on the ground.

It wasn't fair. Wasn't goddamn fair. Why did all this shit have to happen all at once, and to her? Not Rachel, the hyper-competitive classmate. Not any of the slew of the jerks, the jackasses, the all-around douches that Katy had to deal with on a daily basis. No. Her. Just her.

Katy breathed in again, this time deeper. She bit her tongue and closed her eyes and focused on keeping calm. Just like with crying, if she started with the anger and the self-pity, she wouldn't be able to stop.

But still, it wasn't fair.

Katy exited the break room and made her way back downstairs, only to be intercepted by Evelyn.

"Hey you," said Evelyn, stopping midway up the stairs. "Oh my goodness…you look like hell."

"I'm fine."

Evelyn paused.

"Are you sure?" Evelyn pressed. "You joke about being a zombie, but you actually look like one right now."

"I'm positive I'm fine, just as I'm positive I'm not a zombie," Katy replied, raking her hair back with her nails. "Just dozed off while on break, and now I'm groggy as hell."

"Yikes. I hate when that happens," said Evelyn. "But I was coming up for a reason. Hannah's clocking out. Do you want a crack at the registers or would you like me to take over?"

"You go right ahead," Katy replied. "I'm in no mood to deal with whiny customers. I might actually go full-zombie and bite them."

"And no one would want that," Evelyn laughed.

"Because that's how the zombie apocalypse starts." Katy gathered her hair by the base of her neck. "Y'know, I think I'm going to face the shelves a bit before diving into buybacks again."

"Do what makes you happy," Evelyn replied. "I doubt Andrea would mind if we get a bit behind on the checklist today."

"Apparently Andrea wouldn't mind a lot things," Katy mumbled, before adding: "You go relieve Hannah. I'm gonna get lost in the self-help section."

"Sounds good," replied Evelyn. Before turning to go down the stairs, Evelyn advised: "You really should get some coffee, or something. I promise I'll look the other way if you want to slip out."

"And I promise I'm fine," Katy responded, closing her eyes. "Go let Hannah leave before she starts demanding time and a half."

Evelyn turned and went back downstairs. Katy turned in the opposite direction and went back upstairs, walking past the history section until she hit the "do-it-yourself and self-help" section – a.k.a. the least populated area in the store, a.k.a. the farthest point away from the stairs and closest point to the windows. Katy fumbled at a few books before retreating back and sitting on the ledge of the windowsill.

Cars were parked on either side of the road, each spot adorned with parking meters standing by the passenger side. Even with the colder air coming in, people were still eating in the outside areas of the nearby restaurants. Katy looked past the redbrick buildings, over the roofs and at the Prudential and Hancock Towers, both standing over Katy's area of Boston like two authoritarian parents. All around her was tar and brick and pavement. She could hear a few people on her floor, shuffling through books and flipping through pages. It was only a matter of time before someone would pass by her and see her sallow face. She knew she needed to get back to work. If only she could get over the feeling that everything was slowly crumbling around her.

Chapter 15

Katy spent the weekend without any contact from Alex – which worked for her, because she had no desire to contact him, either. She didn't call him after work on Saturday, opting to go straight home and into her room instead. She got up on Sunday and immediately curled up on the couch, absentmindedly watching TV.

Sometime around 11 that Sunday morning, Maria came out of her room and immediately jumped into the shower.

"How long have you been up?" Maria asked when she came out of the bathroom.

"I don't know – 8-ish?"

"Any plans for today?" Maria asked.

Katy gestured to the TV.

"So, nothing with Alex?" Maria asked slowly.

Katy laughed.

"Yeah, because *that* sounds like fun."

"Katy," said Maria. "Have you at least called him recently?"

"Eh…can I plea the fifth?"

Maria readjusted the towel under her arm.

"You know that I just want what's best for you, right?"

"You make it sound like I have an addiction or something."

"Come on now…you know I'm the last one to try and dictate your life," said Maria. "But if I know you like I think I know you, then…" Maria paused and sighed. "Listen, just make sure you talk with Alex, okay? Obviously a bomb's been dropped. Acting like it never happened will only make it worse."

"Yes, Mom, I'll talk to my boyfriend. And I'll wash behind my ears and study my multiplication tables and eat all my dinner before having dessert." Katy feigned an eye-roll and changed the channel.

Maria sighed again.

"I've lived with you for the last six years. Your defense tactics don't work on me."

"I know." Katy rolled her eyes again, this time in defeat. "And I will call him. Eventually. Can't I just stew for a bit?"

"Be careful that 'a bit' doesn't turn into 'until something blows up'," Maria warned before entering her bedroom and closing the door behind her.

Katy stretched out across the couch and reached her arm out, her hand grasping around the side table until she felt her phone. With a halfhearted sigh, she sent Alex a message asking if they wanted to hang out the next day.

*

Katy was back on the orange line again, back on the same sidewalks and back by Alex's place, ringing for his apartment like so many times before. Instead of hitting the buzzer, Alex took the elevator down to meet her at the door.

"Hey there," said Alex with a kiss for Katy. "How was your day?"

"Exhausting," Katy found herself saying. "Mondays are kind of rough."

"Mondays are rough for everyone, I think," Alex replied and led her to the elevator.

Katy's face tightened before she asked: "So...how was your day?"

"The same. Sometimes it feels like Mondays are spent just replying to all the emails that accumulated over the weekend." Alex pushed the button for his floor and stood back, his hands clasped behind him. Katy mirrored Alex and clasped her hands behind her.

"I can imagine," Katy finally replied. The elevator doors opened and Katy followed Alex into his apartment.

Katy's hand traced against the wall by his door, imagining a reality where she never looked at this wall, this area by the door, this apartment, ever again. How could she bring up something so loaded? And Alex hadn't acted the least bit cold or distant so far, though, right? Why bring it up when everything was basically back to normal?

"So, what's on tap for tonight?" Katy asked, shrugging off her jacket.

"I figured we could go to this little Mexican restaurant down the street. I heard they make the best enchiladas."

"Really," Katy said, tossing her coat on one of the kitchen stools. "And it's just down the street? I can't believe we haven't gone yet."

"Had no interest in it before, I guess," Alex replied. "Always good to venture into the unknown every once in a while. Try new things, see what you like."

"Ah."

An uneasy silence barged into the room, knocking into every corner of the kitchen and living room area and socking Katy square in the stomach. Katy could feel the words that she needed to say bubbling in her stomach. They became so prevalent and forceful that she swore that if her mind went blank even for a second, they'd come bursting out.

"So..." Katy said instead, moving closer to Alex. "Feel like killing a few minutes?"

Alex grin went askew.

"'Kill a few minutes'?"

Katy stepped back with a forced smirk.

"Well, yeah. We could, y'know..." Katy stammered. "Work up an appetite?"

Alex's sideways grin transformed into an awkward smile.

"I don't think I've ever seen you so...this, before."

"Well, I mean, we don't have to," Katy replied, her face suddenly getting hot. "I was just – I was just thinking of things we could do. Beforehand." Katy swallowed. The newly-formed lump in her throat remained. "And hey, speaking of changing the subject – anything new happening with you?"

"Um, nothing major," Alex answered, slowly and deliberately.

"Well, then, let's find something else to talk about," Katy replied, the cadence of her voice matching her heartbeat in speed.

"Um, ok," Alex said slowly. After a moment, he raised his eyebrows gently and added: "Well, then: let me ask about your job search. How is that coming along?"

"Heh." Katy felt her face go red. "It's kind of non-existent."

Alex tilted his head to the side.

"What do you mean?"

Katy coughed.

"Um, can we go back to innuendos and euphemisms again?"

"Katy, tell me what's going on."

"Nothing, nothing," Katy replied. "Just, I don't think the job search is right for me, right now."

Alex raised an eyebrow.

"A new job isn't right for you?"

"Well, I mean the job market," Katy replied, her words unraveling faster than she could think. "It's really tough out there. And I don't think it's for me, y'know, just yet. Maybe I should do grad school instead."

"And is that what you really want?"

Katy shrugged and hugged herself across the waist.

"I don't know what I want."

"If you don't know what you want, maybe you shouldn't be making such absolute decisions."

Katy took in a breath and turned into the kitchen, the words bubbling in her stomach again. Only this time, they weren't tinged with frenzied guilt. She could feel the venom surging up, wanting to take what she had to say and use it as a weapon, if only because she had no other line of defense.

Alex took a step closer to Katy.

"C'mon now," he said. "I'm just trying to give you good advice."

Katy closed her eyes and shrugged her shoulders.

"Well, maybe I don't need advice."

"You obviously have no idea what you want." Alex crossed his arms. "So maybe you do."

Blood rushed to Katy's face, making it hard for her to focus on anything.

"You know, I do not need you constantly hounding me about my future," she found herself saying.

"I'm not trying to hound you about your future," said Alex. "I just don't want you to be stuck in a job you hate for your entire life. You are better than that."

With Alex in front of her, kitchen counters to the sides of her and a wall right behind her, Katy thought she was going to collapse from the crushing claustrophobia.

"And what if I'm not?"

Alex dropped his arms to his sides.

"How could you even say that?" Alex replied. "You *are* better than that. You are smart and resourceful and capable of so many different things. And you're wasting your time working a dead-end job in retail." Alex took another step closer.

Katy reflexively took a step back. Oh God, she felt so trapped. She wanted to tell Alex that she didn't want him treating her like a child. But if she said that, she knew she'd slip up and blurt out everything else: that she wasn't ready to get married, that it wasn't fair for him to be looking down on her – because he couldn't have been any better than she was at 24. And if the tables were turned, he wouldn't think it was fair if she had expected him to act *her* age all the time.

"I don't want to fight," Katy eventually mumbled, her eyes on the ground. "Can we just go out to dinner?"

Alex opened his mouth before closing it tight. He sighed, looked around, and said, "Of course. I shouldn't have even brought it up like that."

"It's okay. I think we've all been a bit stressed out," said Katy. Both stood in the kitchen, surveying the countertops before Katy added: "So does this mean we can have make-up sex now?"

Alex hunched slightly as he laughed, as if someone had punched the laughter right out of him.

"I do not know what's gotten into you today."

"Guys aren't supposed to complain about stuff like this. If a girl talks about sex, a guy isn't supposed to question why." She tried to execute it as a joke, but her defensive mood added barbs to the end of every word.

"I guess not," Alex said with a slight eyebrow twitch.

Katy rubbed her eyes.

"I'm sorry."

"You have nothing to be sorry about."

Katy stepped forward and wrapped her hands behind Alex's neck and silently stared at him, one corner of her mouth upturned.

"I love you," she said meekly, her words sounding more like a question than a statement.

"So I found out at two in the morning last week," Alex razzed.

Don't bring that up, don't bring that up – oh God, why did he bring that up?

Katy attempted to swallow the lump in her throat. No such luck.

"I mean it, though," Katy pressed, her eyes now on the ground. "I love you."

"I love you, too," Alex replied, touching the back of her neck. "Is this why you've been so…this, tonight? Didn't know how I'd react to you telling me this when sober?"

Katy gave her best upper-gum-showing smile, her upper lip snarling under her nose.

"Yup. You caught me."

*

For the first time in what felt like ages, Katy hung out with Ben. Their weekly hangout sessions had gone from downright-ritualistic to downright-infrequent, but Katy had made sure to make plans with Ben that week. When her shift ended on Wednesday, Katy hopped on the T to Ben's apartment. After unsuccessfully attempting to open the front door, Katy rang the buzzer.

"Stepping up the security around here, huh?" Katy said to Ben when he opened the front door.

"New neighbors upstairs. Vigilant about locking the doors behind them," Ben replied.

"Well, it's getting a bit too cold to be waiting outside like this," Katy continued. "It's getting too cold, period. You'll have to start picking me up at Porter soon."

"Like I'd allow my spot to get taken," Ben replied, tilting his head over to the curb where his car was parked. "Get a scarf."

"Oh I'm definitely feeling the love here," Katy said as she walked into the foyer and up the stairs. She turned back towards Ben as she reached the top. "But you're paying my hospital bills if I get pneumonia."

"Yeah, because you're so fragile that a ten minute walk would land you in the ER." Ben swirled his keys around his index finger before catching them in his palm. "Like I said: get a scarf."

"Ouch," Katy replied, moving to the side so Ben could open his door.

"Sometimes tough love is the best love."

"You'd make a great drill instructor," replied Katy. "So, what's on tap for tonight?"

"Y'know, the usual. Assorted drafts, soda, water...oh you meant what the plans were."

"If you actually had those things on tap, I'd be coming over all the time." Katy tossed her bag into a corner and followed Ben into the kitchen.

"Speaking of which – soda?" Ben asked, opening his fridge.

"Sure," said Katy, leaning against one of the counters.

"Any preference?"

Katy shrugged.

"Whatever you've got."

"Alright, then. Previously opened Coke it is."

"Oh, you're hysterical. Has anyone ever told you that?"

"I tell myself that every chance I get," Ben replied and handed Katy an unopened can.

Katy followed Ben into the living room and plopped down on his couch.

"God, I didn't think I could get through work today," she let out as her back hit the sofa.

Ben stood in the archway.

"That bad?"

"Nothing unusual," said Katy. "I just don't have the energy."

"Now that you mention it: you looked like you were really dragging on Monday," Ben responded, tapping his own can of soda. "Is everything all right?"

Katy leaned her head back.

"Oh, peachy keen."

"Uh oh." Ben raised his eyebrows. "Is there a body somewhere that I need to hide?"

"I'm just..." Katy stopped and closed her eyes. "Meh."

"I'm sorry you're so...'meh'," said Ben. "Anything I can do to help?"

"No, it's all right, I'm..." Katy trailed off. After a moment, Katy sat up, clasping her soda with both hands. "Do you think Andrea made the right choice?"

"About getting married?" Ben asked. "I guess so. I mean, she's been beaming about it ever since she got back. I thought she was going to burst into dance yesterday, so I'm assuming she's happy."

"Just makes me wonder when the other shoe is going to drop."

"Why would the other shoe drop?" Ben asked.

"Because that's what happens in relationships," Katy retorted. "Especially ones that seem all perfect like that at first."

Ben paused.

"Is everything all right with you and – um – with Alex?"

Katy's face dropped and shoulders slumped.

"What makes you say that?"

"Really?" Ben asked. "Do you want the long version or the short version?"

Katy sighed.

"Let's go with the short."

"That was rhetorical, you know."

"And I'm taking it literal," Katy replied, staring at her soda. "…you know."

"Well, then, y'know, because I know you." Ben tapped at the side of his can again. "Because I know you're not one to actually talk about the issues in your personal life, even if there's something going on, and I know under normal circumstances, you wouldn't be this hung up on something like Andrea's marriage."

Katy crossed her arms.

"What makes you say I'm hung up on it?"

"You've been bringing it up every time Andrea is out of hearing range."

"Oh."

"So I repeat: is everything okay?"

Katy leaned back on the couch.

"Meh."

"Again, I'm sorry things are 'meh'," said Ben. "You know…I'm always here if you ever need me. I might even be able to give you some helpful male insight."

"Your vagina begs to differ."

"Oh now that's just mean," Ben replied. "My vagina would totally agree that I'm great at giving the male perspective."

Katy's grin lifted her cheeks towards her eyes. She sat back and sighed.

"I think I can handle a *meh* situation on my own, but if it gets past *meh*, you'll be the first one I call."

"Hey, that's what I'm here for." Ben flashed a toothy smile.

Katy stretched out.

"I'm glad that you're the level-headed one. God knows where I'd be without you."

"Hiding dead bodies all by yourself, is where," Ben replied, still standing across the living room and under the arch.

Chapter 16

It's funny what happens to a relationship when something big is not discussed. The elephant in the room can do some pretty gnarly stuff if it's never addressed. The relationship changes; the way both people act in the relationship changes. There's the eggshell-walking, the tip-toeing around any hot button topics. There's the sudden argument that always ends far too abruptly, lest it potentially venture into undesirable territory. Things are ignored, if not flat-out denied. But there's always a tension in the air – a tension that can't ever really be talked about without discussing the underlying problem causing everything in the first place. So nothing is discussed and everything feels like it's on high alert.

Katy hadn't had that before. Her previous boyfriends had no qualms about discussing problems – usually as they were breaking up with her. Like most young adults, they believed relationships were either awesome or over – no time for the grown-up concepts of introspection and compromise. She had never had to question the long-term future of a relationship before she met Alex. Her meager dating past made her unequipped to know what to do next.

But Katy also noticed that, as the days went on, a sense of normalcy eventually found its way back, along with the attitude that the problem might not need to be talked about in the first place. The problem at hand had been unofficially shoved under the rug and Katy was more than happy to believe that the bump protruding from under the carpet was just an error in the flooring. And Katy was more than willing to believe that Alex had just had a brief moment of panic after the nightclub fiasco, that he wasn't itching to get married anytime soon, and that everything was just fine in their relationship.

Katy was working the day of Andrea's quasi-reception get-together. The night before, she had stayed over at Alex's. There had been no fights, no tension…Alex didn't even bring up Katy's job search or her plans for the future. She woke up in his bed, relieved and refreshed, ready to commute to work and open up the store on a Sunday, even though that particular task usually topped her list of workplace annoyances.

The trees were letting go of the last of their foliage, littering the redbrick sidewalks with fragments of red, gold, and brown. The air still had the crisp newness of early morning; the empty roads a reminder that the rest of Boston hadn't woken up yet.

Today wouldn't be that bad. She was up early when she'd rather sleep in, she was opening the store on a Sunday, and, thanks to a lost charger, her phone had been dead since Friday, but Katy was optimistic. She'd be able to close up shop early that day. There was a chance that Ben would come by to give everyone a ride, and she knew that Ben would inevitably pitch in to help close the store, even with him working off the clock.

At this point, Katy knew four things about Andrea's new husband: his name was Tom, they met at Andrea's sister's birthday party, he was five years Andrea's junior, and he was an acting and vocal coach. Andrea had gushed about other things, but Katy labeled those as purely subjective – that he was so sweet and kind and intelligent and talented and blah, blah, blah. She would decide on her own if Tom matched any of these criteria. And once she learned more about Mr. Tom WhatsHisFace (including things like, say, his last name), she'd surely be less apprehensive.

But, no matter how she tried, she still couldn't get over the change in Andrea's personality. Andrea Peterson (or Andrea WhatsHisFace – did she take his last name when they got married?) was synonymous with intelligent, rational behavior. Her straight-thinking was what helped her start South End Collections, shape the business when she had no prior experience, keep the bookstore going through rougher times, and survive as a businesswoman for the past twenty-five years.

Does a logical, calculated woman secretly marry a man that she had only known for a few months, and then hightail it across the country on an impromptu vacation?

Katy's reverie was interrupted by the sounds of shouting that were wafting down the street, coming from the general direction of the store. Most of it was garbled to Katy, but the word "asshole" was loud, pronounced, and easily recognizable. Katy walked to the intersection. From her spot at the corner of the sidewalk, Katy could see Hannah across the street, slumped over on the bench by the store, her phone clenched in her hands.

"No. That's bullshit. How can you not see that that's bullshit? Oh my God – I don't even want to talk to you right now." Hannah looked up and saw Katy in the crosswalk, approaching the store. Katy did her best to keep her eyes fixed on the front door and front door only. Hannah continued in a whisper: "Listen, I have to go. No, I have to work. I'm not lying. Some of us actually have jobs." Hannah looked up one more time before covering her head. "Stop it. Just, shut up. I have to go now. Bye." Hannah snapped her flip phone shut before standing up with a jolt.

"Hey," Katy almost whispered, her eyes focused completely on her bag as she searched for her keys.

"Hey."

Katy pulled out her keys, unlocked the door, and held it open for Hannah. Hannah stomped through the doorway and into the store, where she made a beeline for the break room.

Katy quietly followed along before eventually clearing her throat.

"I hope I wasn't um, late, getting here."

"No. I'm just...I got here early," Hannah replied curtly, taking out her anatomy book before shoving her purse in her locker and slamming the door.

"Anything you want to talk about?" Katy asked.

Hannah huffed out a sigh.

"No...it's just stupid, anyway."

"It's quite alright," replied Katy. Katy gave Hannah a small nudge. "But don't you forget – I'm not just a supervisor. I'm also a friend."

Hannah giggled out a snicker and hugged her anatomy book.

"You are so weird."

"It's what I do best," Katy remarked and made her way down to the office. After setting up the registers, Katy wandered the back room a bit, contemplating what she could get done that morning before quickly deciding that she would do none of it. When it was time to unlock, Katy stayed up front, fumbling around with the "Editors' Pick" books and arranging them around in various and sundry fashions. Hannah kept her head in her anatomy book, snapping up only to quickly ring in a customer's books and send them on her way.

Before lunchtime had even hit, Katy strolled behind the counter and unlocked the second register.

"What are you doing?" Hannah asked. Katy kept her eyes on the second register, imagining that Hannah didn't mean for her words to come out as harshly as they did.

"I'm in no mood to process buybacks, so I figured I'd come do some cashier work," Katy replied. "Anatomy doesn't look like it's an easy class. I assume finals week is probably around the corner. Besides, I doubt Andrea will care if nothing gets done today, anyway."

"Oh." Hannah's face softened. "Well, thanks. That's really nice of you."

"Hey, I'm not just a supervisor. I'm also a philanthropist."

Hannah glanced over incredulously, her lips poised to say something, but instead gave a smile and went back to her textbook.

Katy rang in customers, with Hannah pitching in whenever a line started to form. After a few hours, Hannah closed her book, sighed, and pulled the metal stool closer to the counter. Without any customers by the cash register area, the atmosphere grew tense and anxious.

"You wouldn't have, by any chance, seen a phone charger around these parts, have you?" Katy broke the silence with.

"Um, no. Why do you ask?"

"I think I lost mine. And no one seems to have the same phone as me," Katy replied. "I'm not ready to admit defeat and buy a new one just yet. I'm hoping it just dropped out of my bag at some point."

"Ah."

Katy drummed the counter, rang in a customer, and watched him leave the building.

"So. What was going on this morning?" Katy finally asked.

"Nothing, nothing." Hannah rolled her eyes. "Just a stupid fight."

"Well, regardless, I'm sorry," said Katy. She pursed her lips. "Do you mind me asking what it was about? I mean, it's totally cool if you don't want to talk about it."

"No, no, it's okay," Hannah replied. "It was just…stupid things."

"I would figure," Katy replied. "I don't think there's anything more tragic than a stupid fight about *serious* things."

"My boyfriend is…" Hannah trailed off before checking around her and looking back at Katy. "He's just being an idiot with money."

"Yikes."

Hannah sighed again.

"He's been bitching nonstop about having no money, asking if I can spot him for groceries and whatnot. And this morning? I found this crazy-expensive imported beer in his fridge."

"Ouch."

"I know, right? The worst part is that he sees nothing wrong with investing all his money on booze, but he can barely make rent? I told him that I was through helping him with money, and he flipped out on me. He said I was being selfish." Hannah rolled her eyes again. "Yeah, *I'm* the selfish one."

"I'm sorry about that, Hannah. That really is unfair," Katy said, pausing to ring in another customer.

"It's bullshit, but whatever. He's been an extra douche lately ever since he found out that I got accepted to NYU for grad."

"Oh, hey: congrats on that!" Katy exclaimed.

"Thanks," Hannah replied with a halfhearted shrug. "I wish *he* had been that excited when I told him the news."

"Why would he be upset about it?"

"Because he hates New York and wants to go back to his hometown after we graduate," Hannah said and fell silent, staring down at her lap.

"Oh. Yikes." Katy paused and rang in a few more customers before directing another to where sci-fi and fantasy could be found. "How long have you two been together?"

"Since freshman year," Hannah replied coolly. "But apparently I became a senior and he's still suck in his freshman mindset." Hannah sighed. "Whatever. If he keeps this up, then I'm obviously going to have to end it. Simple as that."

Katy silently nodded, biting her lip. She desperately searched for a reply, and was more than thankful when a customer approached Katy with a question, breaking her from the conversation.

"Hey, you're totally free to take your break at any time if you want," Katy added, after talking with the customer.

*

Katy returned to her apartment around 11 p.m. The rest of her shift was easy enough. She acquiesced to her assigned duties and began processing buybacks when Evelyn clocked in, and she rushed through all of her closing duties when Ben stopped by to pick everyone up.

The dinner itself seemed to go pretty well. Mr. Tom WhatsHisFace with the questionable criteria turned out to be Mr. Tom Decker, who appeared to be an overall nice guy. As she learned that night, Mr. Decker had previously lived in LA, but moved to Boston for a change of pace. He apparently had been struggling in LA, but was creating a nice niche for himself in Boston, specifically with the college scene. Andrea's sister was one of Tom's first clients in Boston and had invited Tom to her birthday as a way to help him meet new people. Andrea's sister introduced her to Tom that night and the rest, as they say, is history.

And Andrea seemed happy. And that's what was important, right? The glow in Andrea's face was genuine and Katy couldn't detect any ulterior motives in Tom. At least, not yet. She was able to accept the situation at hand – or at least she was able to *start* accepting the situation at hand – with the stipulation that, if Tom did anything to hurt Andrea, Katy would be the first to track him down. Then she really would need Ben to help her hide a body.

But it was a great night, filled with laughter and music and an overwhelming feeling of love. There was no denying the light in each other's eyes as they looked at each other. There was no denying that this was the path that Andrea was on right now.

Katy traipsed into her room, shimmied off her shirt, and threw it into the hamper. She scanned her room, noticing that she had been ignoring the "throwing in hamper" step with the majority of her clothes as of late. She mechanically grabbed the clothes on the ground, scooping them into her arms and tossing them in the hamper.

Clothes were scattered all over the place. It seemed like there was more clothing on the ground than there was in her closet. Some were piled on her desk; other hung from her chair. A few pieces were draped across her bed as if they created a second blanket. She grabbed everything that wasn't folded or hung up and tossed them into the hamper.

Katy lifted a pair of crumpled jeans in one corner, revealing a cell phone charger underneath.

Katy breathed a sigh of relief.

"Finally!" She went into her bag to grab her phone and plug it in.

She turned the phone on to find that she had five voicemails. Two were from Alex, before she had been able to email him about her dead phone, asking her what the plans were for Friday. In between the two was a message from Maria, asking to grab bacon if Katy was going to the supermarket. The fourth one was from Andrea, confirming the dinner.

"Hey there, Katy," the fifth message began after Andrea's message had ended. "It's Tabby again, from Maurice Fielding. I wanted to let you know that a job opened up in our San Francisco office."

A job? A *job*? Katy looked around for a pen and paper, only to find that her phone charger tethered her to the wall, with her messenger bag across the room. She turned toward the whiteboard on the wall behind her and grabbed a dry-erase marker from its tray.

"JOB!!!! SAN FRAN!" Katy wrote on the board.

"...assistant. It is quite similar to the position you interviewed for here, only you'd be focusing more on purchasing artwork and gathering permissions from the artists and writers. Please call me back whenever you get this and we can set up a phone interview with Erica King, from human resources at the San Francisco branch. I really think you'd be a great addition to the team, so I hope you'd consider it. I already put in a good word for you, so you're already head and shoulders above the rest. Give me a call back at 617..."

Katy scribbled on the board. "SAME TYPE JOB – ARTWORK AND PERMISSIONS – CALL TABBY!!" and hit repeat on the voicemail two more times just to be sure that she had the right number down.

Katy put down her phone and bounced onto the bed. San Francisco? Was this really happening? Was this real life?

San Francisco. San Francisco, as in the Golden Gate Bridge, the trolleys, the hilly & windy roads, the Pacific Ocean. The Pier 39. The Alcatraz. The one of the top places she had always wanted to travel to. She'd be a quick plane ride away from Hollywood, where she could see the Walk of Fame and movie studios and maybe even a movie star or two.

Working at a publishing firm in California. There was something glamorous about it all.

Katy smiled contently. She couldn't wait to call up Tabby. Oh, she wanted to call now, right now. Would she wake up

Tabby? Was the number her office number or personal cell phone number? Would it even be possible for Katy to get some sleep before she called? She could barely breathe, let alone fight the compulsion to call now, beg for the job, pack her bags, and buy a plane ticket.

She closed her eyes and took in the sounds of the city outside. Even in the dead of night, cars still passed outside her apartment, with the occasional honk or holler from the driver. Would all this sound different in California?

Katy breathed out before locking up her lungs and sitting up straight.

Wait – could she really do this?

Sure, it sounded all fun and exciting at first, but could she really just pack up and leave and move across the country?

What about Alex? And her friends? Her roommate and her apartment and Miller – would Miller be okay living somewhere new? Miller had lived in this apartment his entire life – could he handle San Francisco? What would happen if he ever got outside? Brighton was a familiar neighborhood, but a place like San Francisco would be something completely different. She wouldn't know where to start looking. And would Miller be okay without Maria around? Would *Katy* be okay without Maria around? Katy had never lived without a roommate, specifically without *Maria* as her roommate. Would Katy be okay living alone, or, worse, living alongside a complete stranger?

All the packing and traveling and shipping – and all the little things that can (and do) go wrong when you move across the country. What if a box of her stuff got lost?

Plus, she'd have to get a new license – and a car, probably. She hadn't owned a car since high school.

And Alex. A long distance relationship was definitely out of the question, especially with how things had been between the two. They had been on such shaky ground for the longest time and only now had things started to look up. They would almost certainly break up if she suddenly lived on the opposite side of the country. Good relationships become strained when one moves even just a couple hours away. Imagine how hers would turn out if she moved so far away that the only way he could see her was through a day-long plane ride.

Was it worth the risk, the sacrifice? Did she really want to *live* in San Francisco?

Maybe the city was more of a "nice place to visit" type of situation. Could she make such a commitment, only to realize that she didn't want to live there after all? Then she'd be stuck in an alien city knowing essentially nobody and feeling miserable.

Stuck in an alien city and very much single for essentially no reason.

It would be totally okay if she didn't jump on this opportunity, right? There were other publishing companies in Boston. There will be other job opportunities. Why go all the way to California and uproot – and potentially ruin – everything just for one little job?

Maybe she had to think about it; maybe she had to give herself time to figure out just how she would let Tabby down. She slipped off the rest of her clothes and grabbed her towel, which lay crumpled on the floor. She walked into the shower and let the hot water hit her face as she figured out just what she would say on Monday.

"Tabby, I want to thank you for the opportunity to work at your San Francisco office. After some consideration, however, I unfortunately have to decline your offer. I have decided instead to pursue other endeavors."

Chapter 17

Katy approached her Monday shift with unexpected gusto. She didn't seem to mind that it was a shipment day. She didn't even mind that Ray had called in sick (again) and Josh was late (again). She already knew Ray was avoiding working on a shipment day and Josh was...well, being Josh. And she was okay with it. She accepted that that was their personalities and, if push came to shove, she could always shorten their hours and hire someone new. And maybe Andrea would let her try her hand at the hiring process. The world suddenly felt full of little but different possibilities.

She helped out customers and answered questions with a friendlier tone in her voice. She didn't even grit her teeth or murmur passive-aggressive remarks when a few self-entitled patrons became irate because their needs weren't being immediately and exactly met.

It wasn't until at her lunch break that she realized why she was feeling so energized.

She first pegged it on her voice message to Tabby. It felt so empowering, crossing off the idea of working in other cities, knowing at the very least there was one avenue she wasn't going down.

But it wasn't just the feeling of empowerment. The phone call had really shifted things for her. Everything now felt so homey. She was finally appreciating what she had been taking for granted all this time. Everything had now taken on a new gloss of familiarity and she felt so safe and secure in it.

She wanted to say it felt predictable, but "predictable" can have such a horrible connotation. And there was nothing negative about how she felt. There was no worry, no stress — no anxiety over the uncertain.

Yeah, that was it. She didn't feel plagued by the unknown anymore. She wasn't grasping for straws that were not even there in the first place.

Everything had been so fruitless and had felt so unsure when she was job searching. She felt like the world around her had been tossed into the air and held in suspension, waiting for some indeterminate event to make everything magically fall into place. But nothing happened, and things never fell into place. And now she knew at least one thing: she wanted to stay both in Boston and with Alex. Katy was sure that everything else would fall into place at some point, on its own terms.

San Francisco, Chicago, Austin…these cities could wait. Or, better, she and Alex could visit them. On vacation.

Yeah, maybe that's what they needed: a vacation together. Nothing patches things up like spending some time away from the usual sights and sounds. Right?

"Um, ma'am?" A curt voice spoke up from behind Katy.

Katy turned.

"Yes? Can I help you?"

A stout woman with graying hair crossed her arms.

"Are you trying to rip me off?" she snapped.

Katy looked around her, stunned.

"Me?"

"I'm talking to you, aren't I?"

"Um, I guess so." Katy swallowed. "What did I do to rip you off?"

"I found two copies of the same book on your shelf. One at full price — another at only $5. Why are you making people pay for full price when there's a cheaper one right next to it?"

Katy gave her best customer service smile.

"The $5 one is most likely a used book. They're a cheaper alternative." Katy added after a breath: "I prefer buying used books myself, actually."

"Why would I want it *used?* What's wrong with the $5 book?"

Katy's smile dropped.

"Nothing. Nothing at all. We don't sell used books that have any major defects. It's just that it was…pre-owned. Like with cars."

The customer huffed.

"Well I'm not going to pay $14 when there's a cheaper copy next to it."

"Ma'am, you are more than welcome to buy the used book. I'm sure it would suit you just fine."

"Well you're a bit quick to judge," the lady snapped. "Maybe I prefer my books undamaged."

"Like I mentioned before, we don't sell books with any major defects."

"Yeah, but what about *minor* defects?"

"Ma'am, I can check the used copy just in case we missed anything."

"But I don't want the used one."

Katy paused.

"I'm sorry, but I'm not sure what you're asking for, then."

"I want the $14 book at $5. It's ridiculous for you to expect me to pay that much."

"Ma'am, I'm sorry, but we can't change the prices on the new books."

"So you're telling me I could buy the $14 book, sell it back to you guys, and then buy it at $5?"

"Technically, you could." Katy swallowed. "But you'd lose money and it would be a lot easier just to buy the used book. I'm sure there's nothing wrong with it."

The customer dropped her arms and placed her hands on her waist.

"I want to talk to your manager."

"I'm sorry?"

"I said I want to talk to your manager. Obviously I'm not getting proper service here."

Katy's eyebrows lowered in confusion.

"I'm sorry if I did anything to offend you, ma'am, but she'll tell you the same things I did."

"And stop calling me ma'am. You make me feel like a grandma," the customer replied, self-consciously touching the side of her head.

"Of course," said Katy. "I'm sorry I couldn't help you."

"Like hell. Where is your manager?"

"She doesn't come in today, but she'll be in tomorrow."

"Fine, I want her name and yours as well." The customer fished through her purse and pulled out a small notepad.

"Um, uh," Katy stammered. "Andrea. Andrea Decker. That's the manager. And I'm Katy."

The customer huffed.

"You better believe I'll be in tomorrow. The nerve of you people to run a scam like this."

Katy watched as the customer turned around, marched down the aisle, and out the door, the bell on the doorframe clanging violently as she left. Katy unconsciously followed the lady's trail, stopping herself only when she reached the beginning of the aisle.

"What was that about?" Ben asked from behind the registers.

"Apparently I pissed her off by not letting her get a book for cheaper." Katy approached the side of the cashiers' station, her elbows on the counter and her head hanging to one side.

"Why was she demanding a cheaper book?"

"Apparently she doesn't understand the difference between 'new' and 'used'." Katy rubbed her eyes. "You know, I need to focus on the positive: before this incident, I hadn't had to explain the difference between 'new' and 'used' in at least a month. I think that's a record. I should at least be thankful for that."

Ben nodded in response, his eyes on bagging a patron's books. Another customer looked sympathetically at Katy before going over to Josh, who was manning the first cash register.

"I'm sorry," Ben finally replied.

Katy straightened her back and stretched.

"It's okay," she replied. "Maybe this is a sign that I should be in the stock room instead. God knows we're still a bit backed up."

Ben smiled at an approaching customer before turning back to Katy.

"Well, I am *more* than willing to let you finish up on all the paperwork, if you'd like."

"Has anyone ever told you how altruistic you are?" Katy replied flatly.

"No, but I assume it's because my good deeds render them speechless."

"And you're level-headed to boot." Katy replied, watching as a few new customers entered the building.

She tapped on the counter before turning towards the back room.

"All right, off I go."

*

Maria was already in casual wear, sitting on her bed with her laptop on her crossed legs when Katy came in to the apartment. Maria strained her neck to catch Katy's gaze before pushing aside her computer and jumping off her bed.

"Hey you! Congratulations!" Maria exclaimed.

Katy stopped in the middle of the living room.

"What do you mean?"

"I saw on your whiteboard," Maria replied. "San Francisco? That's so intense."

"Oh, that." Katy winced. "I mean, it's not like it's a given that I'd get the job."

"Are you kidding me?" said Maria. "If this is the same company you were talking about before, of course you'll get it. They seemed to absolutely love you. Besides, it's not like they'd contact just anyone for a cross-country job." Maria paused. When Katy said nothing, Maria asked: "So, when's the interview?"

Katy stared at the carpet.

"Um, there is no interview," she mumbled out.

Maria gave a quizzical look.

"So, is that like, a good thing or a bad thing?"

"I don't know."

"Wait," Maria replied slowly. "You *are* going to take the job, right?"

"Um…"

"Katy."

Katy scanned the ceiling before lowering her eyes back to the floor.

"Oh my God." Maria's voice dropped an octave. "Why?"

Katy nervously laughed.

"Why what?"

Maria's face tightened.

"Why aren't you at least checking this job out?"

"I just – didn't feel like it."

"Didn't *feel* like it? You have got to be kidding me!" Maria pressed her fingers into her temples. "You've been desperate for a new place to work, you've been itching to visit California…Well, here's your chance to *work* in California, and suddenly you don't feel like it?"

Katy pressed her tongue to the roof of her mouth.

"It's…it's more complicated than that."

"How in the hell can it be more complicated? This is a chance of a lifetime."

Katy stammered over a few incoherent syllables before falling silent.

"Have you talked with Alex?" Maria asked, her voice suddenly softer.

"About the job?" Katy asked innocently.

"You know what I mean."

Katy could feel Maria's eyes on her as she shoved her hands into her pockets.

"Sometimes I wish I didn't know you so well," Maria muttered.

Katy took her hands out of her pockets and meekly threw them up.

"It's complicated."

It was then that Katy realized how dark the apartment was, save for a few lamps here and there to interrupt the darkness with pools of harsh light. The sun had long gone down, and even the streetlamps couldn't stop the outside night from looking like a black wall. The windows were closed and the air suddenly felt stale.

"You're going to miss out on so much in life if you always avoid risk," Maria said finally.

Katy focused on the windows.

"Maybe some risks should be avoided."

"I just don't want you compromising yourself because you're afraid to lose Alex. If you're meant to be with him, you're meant to be with him. Hell, look at your boss," said Maria. "Apparently love comes at whatever age it's meant to come."

"And you don't think Andrea just got married because she's 50 and lonely?" Katy looked back at Maria.

Maria sighed.

"If you want to look at it that way, I can't stop you. You've obviously taken her marriage pretty negatively since you've found out."

Katy huffed.

"You do know that marrying too young is not a better alternative than marrying too old," Maria said slowly. "Right?"

Katy remained silent.

Maria took a step back. "It's not my business. I know it's not. But...I can't help but worry. I really hope you reconsider the job."

Katy shifted her weight from one foot to the other.

"It's too late, anyway. I already called up and said no."

"Then call them again. Take it back. Or, maybe, take this as a learning experience," Maria replied. "There. That's my advice. Take this as a learning experience. Talk with Alex and don't be so damn afraid to step out of your comfort zone."

Katy kept shifting her weight and biting at the inside of her cheek. After a moment, Katy said: "Has anyone ever told you that you talk like a chick lit cliché?"

Maria groaned.

"Oh, none of *that* right now."

"Okay, okay. I've learned my lesson," Katy said, rolling her eyes. "Now, can I take a shower and get the smell of retail off of me?"

Maria sighed and shook her head.

"Of course." Maria turned and walked into the kitchen. "I'm making chicken cacciatore tonight, if you're interested," Maria added, her voice taking on an almost unnatural bounce.

Katy smiled.

"Well look at you," she remarked. "You're becoming quite the domestic."

"It's straight out of a box. I'm just adding the chicken." Maria blushed. "Go take your shower."

Katy walked into the bathroom, threw off her clothes, and stepped into the shower before the water had even heated up. She winced initially, baby-stepping away from the downpour of cold water before shoving her face in it, holding her breath until the temperature changed and steam started to fill the room.

Leave it to Maria to pop even the simplest bubble. But Katy wasn't compromising, was she? No, she was having an epiphany. Yeah, an epiphany. That's like the exact opposite of a compromise. Well, it might not be the *exact* opposite of a compromise, but they're definitely not synonyms!

If anything, Katy was figuring out that maybe she had been barking up the wrong tree all along. All this worrying about what to do with her life and she thought it all could get solved primarily through a new job? And what good would *that* do? Maria worked as an assistant to an event coordinator. And Maria complained about her job almost as much as Katy did.

Maybe it was best to take a breather from the career world. Besides, what Katy went through might not even have been be a quarter-life crisis anyway. The first half of Generation Y is projected to live well into their 100s. So, maybe that was just a fifth-life crisis. She had time to figure things out. And she had been so set on forcing things to fall into place that she had forgotten that things can and will happen naturally.

And what was wrong with making a relationship more of a priority than a job? People did that every day. And what was the saying, again? No one dies wishing they spent more time at the office?

And she wasn't *solving* her problems by focusing on Alex. Who said she was doing that? That's right: no one did. And no one should. Because she was solving her problems on her own terms and she knew perfectly well that a relationship is never a substitution for an actual solution.

Right?

The clanking in the kitchen let Katy know that, if she kept this mental vomit going for any much longer, she'd miss out on delicious chicken straight off of the oven. With a sigh, she turned off the water and stepped out.

Chapter 18

The days and weeks carried on. It was easy for Katy to get lost in the tide, to let time get away from her, to find herself one day at a Saturday shift when she could've sworn she had just done a Saturday shift the day before. Even seeing Alex turned into a mechanical routine that felt no different than the one before it or the one after it.

Katy would allow the days to bleed into one another. As she saw it, she had made the decision to stop focusing so much on a new job, and this was her taking a step back and letting time sort everything out. She was tired of wondering when things would fall into place – or wondering if she would have to *force* them in place – and was ready for something else to take control.

It was a Tuesday when Rachel made her return.

Rachel Osterman, the former classmate of Katy's. To be honest, Katy was surprised that she hadn't been making weekly appearances to rub her great job and great education and great life in Katy's face. But then again, Mass General was across town. Or maybe Rachel was simply too busy with her great everything to show up some former college classmate time and time again.

"Oh my God, Katy, I was hoping to run into you." Rachel's voice pierced into the back of Katy's skull.

Katy turned away from her pushcart with a plastered smiled on her face.

"Rachel. How good to see you."

"And likewise! How are you!"

"Y'know. Alright," Katy replied. "How about you?"

"Never been better," said Rachel, before adding: "I see you're still working at the store."

Katy pushed her bottom lip up, closing the plastered smile into an awkward grin.

"Yeah. Same old, same old, I guess. And how about you? Still at…" Katy paused and feigned a dismissive look. "Where were you working at, again?"

Rachel laughed.

"Mass General. And, yeah, it's going great. Definitely couldn't see myself anywhere else."

"Ah." Katy let the silence fall between them before turning to the pushcart and grabbing a handful of books.

"So, what have you been doing?" Rachel asked after a moment.

"Um." Katy cocked a grin and nervously chuckled. "Putting new books away."

"Oh," Rachel replied. "I meant, in general. Like, what else is going on in your life?"

"Oh," Katy reacted. "Um, not much. Just, y'know, working, hanging out." Katy trailed away before blurting out: "I have a boyfriend."

Rachel beamed.

"Well, congratulations. How long have you guys been together?"

Katy cleared her throat.

"About 9 or so months. We met back in April."

"Oh, young love. How exciting," Rachel continued her gigantic smile. "So what does he do?"

"He's a director of programming at a software company," Katy answered. "Atrowksi, Inc. I don't know if you've ever heard of them."

"Well, I definitely haven't, but I'm sure they're important."

Katy let out a forceful cough, as if she had been punched in the stomach by Rachel's words.

"W-well yeah," Katy stammered, focusing on the books she had in her arms. "He really likes it there. He's kind of one of the guys in charge, so there's a lot riding on him."

"Wow, good for him."

Katy was certain that Rachel's smile was slowly morphing into a smug grin. She was sure of it. Damn sure.

"It's the single life for me, I'm afraid," Rachel continued. "Someday I'll have time to find a boyfriend. But right now, I feel like my life is taking me down so many different and great paths, I barely have time to breathe, let alone go out on a date." Rachel shifted the purse on her shoulder. "I'm going to go browse the books for a bit. But it was great seeing you again."

"Yeah," Katy replied flatly. "You too."

"I'll probably see you before I leave, but if I don't, take care," said Rachel. "And I'm glad you've found yourself in the right environment to find a steady boyfriend. It sounds like he's great."

Katy could feel her jaw unhinge and drop from its original position.

"Okay," was all she could get out.

Rachel scrunched her face with an unsure smile before replying with: "Well, okay, later!" and leaving the aisle.

Flushed, Katy finished the cart she was working on as quickly as she could and retreated into the stock room. She made herself look busy by rearranging the remaining push carts and reorganizing the books stacked on them. She flipped through the files in the iron cabinet, stopping every once in a while to pick one up and scan through it, her eyes never really settling on the ink on the paper.

After a few more minutes, Katy peered out onto the main floor, timidly scanning the area. When it seemed like Rachel was no longer in the building – or at least no longer on the first floor – Katy pulled out another cart and pulled it to the appropriate aisle. But after a few trips to the shelves, Katy abandoned the cart and headed straight into Andrea's office, collapsing into the desk chair and hanging her head back.

Did Rachel mean to be so brutal? Or was Katy's life so pathetic that just referencing it point blank felt like an insult? Was this all in Katy's imagination? Was Rachel actually trying to gloat about what she had, or was she just trying to talk with an old classmate?

Had there even been a competition to begin with?

Katy sat limply in her seat, taking in tiny, defeated breaths and looking off into nowhere. All at once she remembered why she had wanted to get out of South End Collections in the first place.

It was embarrassing.

Embarrassing to still be working at her very first job – a job she got as a teenager. Embarrassing to be so stagnant in her life, working just for a paycheck, living just to clock out, and doing nothing that ever challenged her. It was embarrassing that she had been spending her prime years coddling impatient customers and vacuuming worn out carpets. Her biggest responsibility was counting out forty dollars in coins & in small bills for cash registers and yelling at college-aged employees when they didn't show up on time – overlooking the fact that they didn't show up on time because the job was just something to pay the bills with until they graduated and moved on to something better.

What the hell was she doing?

But it wasn't the embarrassment that drained Katy of her energy and emotion. It was the fact that she felt stuck. There was no place else to go, no other thing to do. She already went down the road of, "maybe I'll go to grad school, or maybe I'll go job searching, or maybe I'll move to a new city." Been there, done that, wound up in the same place that she began at. Stuck, stuck, stuck.

And even if she knew what she wanted to do, there was nothing out there for her. No jobs, no prospects, nothing. She was just a silly girl with her English degree who only felt on top of her game when she was trading barbs with her coworkers and badmouthing crappy novels. A silly girl who thought she could step out her front door and just magically figure out her path in life, simply because she finally realized she actually had to do something about it. A silly, stupid, little girl who was hopelessly lost and too convinced of herself to even notice.

Katy sat in that chair for as long as she could, until Andrea opened the door.

"Oh, there you are," said Andrea. "I was wondering where you had gone to."

Katy sat up.

"Just taking a breather," she said.

"Take a breather after we get all those books put away," Andrea jibbed. "Unless you're suffering from a major illness, and, in that case, you should probably be in a hospital then. Not in my office spreading germs."

Katy felt a bit of color come back to her face. With a slight renewal of motivation, Katy stood up.

"But what if I *want* to spread germs?" Katy countered. "Leave my mark on this place by giving everyone the flu."

"If you can finish up all the push carts before the end of your shift, you can give everyone the Ebola virus for all I care," Andrea responded.

"Don't make jokes like that. You know I'll hold you to it." Katy gave her most confident grin before exiting the office and making her way back into the main floor, where her abandoned cart awaited her.

After her shift ended, Katy left the building as quickly as she could and downright spilled out onto the sidewalk. The sun had already set and the moon was completely hidden behind a thick layer of clouds. The wind whipped and twirled in between the buildings, reminding everyone just how cold it was. Walking briskly, Katy fished for her phone and called Alex.

"Hello?" said a homey voice.

"Hey, there," Katy cooed. "How are you?"

"Um, I'm doing pretty well. Stuck at the office, but all in all okay." Noise on the other end of the phone went dead for a second. "How about you?"

"Eh, I," Katy began before cutting herself off. "I'm doing pretty well. Not too bad. I was hoping we could hang out tonight."

"Oooh, tonight. Tonight...doesn't work," Alex answered slowly.

"Oh, I'm sorry sweetie," Katy responded. "Is everything alright?"

"Yeah, yeah. Just, a lot of work right now."

Katy swallowed.

"Well, maybe tomorrow, then?"

"We'll see. Right now, I'm swamped," Alex replied. "Um, is it okay if I get back to work? Honestly, I really am busy."

"Of course." Her first answer came out as a whimper. Katy coughed and repeated herself: "Of course. I'll talk to you soon."

Katy bit her lip as the conversation lulled. That should have been the time when she could tell him, "I love you." But, in reality, she hadn't said it since that first time she said it stone sober. Things had been so tense and fragile during that time and – afterwards – it never really felt right to repeat the sentiment. There was never really an opportunity to say it and it felt forced to add it on to her good-byes.

"Okay then, I'll talk to you later," said Alex.

"Okay. Bye."

Katy tossed her phone back into her bag and shoved her hands into her coat pockets. Usually she would grab an orange line train and transfer over to catch a green line trolley home. Tonight, she felt like walking to the green line instead. Hell, maybe she'd just walk home. Did she even know a route home? She'd figure it out. She knew her way to BU and that was in the same direction as her apartment. And who cares if she got lost? If she were really that worried about her destination, she would've made the smarter choice of public transportation in the first place.

But when had she ever been intelligent about paths and destinations? Oh, Mr. Subtext, you've won yet another round.

Every road and backstreet felt like a wind tunnel. Every gust of wind cut against her skin, ambushing its way through the weaving in her clothing. The once-majestic brick townhouses and sidewalks now felt empty and uninviting. Even as she made her way into Copley Square, where the antique streetlamps were replaced with neon lights and the grandeur of the public library, Katy felt disconnected, focusing only on her breath and the cold and the next footstep she'd have to make.

Katy wanted to bemoan not seeing Alex – and that night, of all nights. But what use would seeing him have done? She had given up professing any possible job woe to him for the past couple months. She had given up professing – well – just about everything to him for the past couple months. She had been treading so lightly with him, lest she misstep and find that the ground beneath her wasn't as stable as she thought it was. She knew there was no way she could bring up wanting to leave SEC again. It was an area of contention, a topic that could quickly lead them in a direction that she wanted to steer clear from.

Her mind was blank as she made her way up Commonwealth Ave, walking parallel with the green line trolleys that could've brought her home much, much sooner. By the time she arrived in her neighborhood, she only had one thought in her mind. A thought that played on repeat because she was too emotionally drained to think of anything else:

"Everything is one big, goddamn mess right now."

*

It wasn't until Friday that Katy was able to see Alex again. They traded text messages and had a few phone conversations, but, aside from that, Katy felt like they were on opposite ends of distant worlds. In fact, had it not been such a routine for them, Katy wondered if they would even have seen each other on Friday in the first place.

Katy felt betrayed. How could she not feel a bit betrayed? Alex picked that week of all weeks to go lone wolf on her. It didn't matter if he was overwhelmed with work, or that Katy never fully communicated how badly she needed to see him. The timing was terrible. Absolutely terrible.

But Friday was Friday and they always saw each other on Friday. So she had that, right?

Katy's phone went off just as she was gathering her things to see Alex.

"Hey there," breathed out Alex's voice. "Have you already left yet?"

"No, not yet," Katy replied. "Almost, though."

"Listen, is it alright if we meet at your place instead?"

Katy paused.

"Sure. Is anything going on?"

"Um, nothing, nothing," Alex stammered. "Just wanted a change of scenery, I guess."

"Well, sure, come on over. I'll see you soon?"

"Yeah, I'll see you then."

"Okay." Katy searched her mind for something – some combination of words unknown to even Katy, but could only find: "Bye."

"Bye."

Everything felt off. Everything felt off and nothing felt right. But then again, what was more peculiar? The fact that Alex wanted to meet at Katy's or the fact that Alex almost never came to Katy's in the first place? It was something she had to drive out of her mind, because if she started thinking about that, then she'd start thinking about how she was always the one traveling out to meet Alex – and that fit right into Alex's previous accusation of passivity and…again, something that needed to be driven out of her mind.

So, baseball. How about baseball? Would Katy like to think about baseball? Or football? Or get a song or two stuck in her head?

Lord Almighty, what in the hell was she doing to herself?

Alex pressed her apartment's intercom within the hour. Instead of buzzing him in, Katy trampled down the two flights of stairs to meet him at the door.

"You didn't have to come all the way down here," Alex greeted Katy with.

"Buzzer's broken," Katy lied and reflexively leaned in for a kiss.

Alex leaned in as well, giving back the kiss before saying, "Is it okay if we go up to your apartment now?"

"Yeah, yeah, of course," Katy replied and started climbing the stairs, the words that she hadn't yet said tripping over themselves in her mind. Alex followed her inside the apartment and closed the door behind him.

"So, what's on tap for tonight?" Katy gave her best cheerful impression.

Alex's pressed his lips together.

"I think we need to talk."

The carpet, the floorboards, the entire building itself gave out from under her. It was a miracle that her body was still standing in the same spot. It was a miracle that Maria's door was still hinged to the same spot as well – a piece of information she only gathered because, somewhere in the distance, she heard Maria's door click shut.

Katy's mouth went dry.

"What do we need to talk about?" she asked meekly.

"What we should have addressed a while ago."

The blood didn't just drain from Katy's body. It was downright sucked out from her system, leaving her with barely enough energy to reply with an, "Oh."

"We have to face the truth. At the end of the day, things were brought to light. Things that neither of us…" Alex trailed off. "Things that we have avoided since. But that doesn't mean they've gone away. They kind of just…festered. And we never addressed them again, because I think we were both afraid."

Katy wobbled back and forth on her feet. Red blood cells, white blood cells, center of gravity – all had rapidly gone AWOL.

"Afraid?"

"Yeah, afraid," Alex answered, looking at the ground. "Afraid that it spelled the end of our relationship."

Katy bit the inside of her cheek. She held her breath and frantically started blinking, hoping to stave off what she knew was coming. She had just been drained of practically everything; why couldn't she be drained of her tears as well? This time, Katy didn't even have the energy to reply with, "Oh." She simply hummed out a syllable between her lips.

Alex cringed and rubbed the back of his neck.

"We've both been kidding ourselves." Alex paused, his eyes on the floor. "And it kills me. It absolutely kills me to admit this. But the fact is that we are on two separate paths and it's just not working anymore."

"Not working anymore?" Katy unconsciously repeated. "Th-then we'll fix it."

"Katy, we've been going through the motions for too long," Alex sighed. "There's something fundamentally flawed about us. Our dynamic. I don't think it will ever work. I'm sorry."

And, like that, all of her blood came rushing back, slamming into Katy's head with such force that she thought she would faint. They collided into her skull, crashing against her skin, pushing hot tears with such force that they jumped from her eyes, missing her reddening cheeks entirely.

"But we can!" Katy blurted out.

"Katy…"

"No!" Katy snapped. "No, no, no! This has been an issue for, what, a few months? That's nothing! It's a speed bump, but we can work through it!" Katy's voice rose with every sentence.

"It's not as simple as that…" Alex began.

"But it *is*!" Katy pleaded. "It *is* as simple as that!" Katy pressed the palms of her hands against her eyes. "This isn't fair! Alex, this isn't fair! I want nothing more than for us to be together. After all I've done, after sacrificing——." Katy stopped herself, her lips curving inwards. After sacrificing what, Katy? After sacrificing a job in San Francisco? Because, aside from Maria, nobody knows about it. Are you really going to bring it up now? Are you going to be the manipulative bitch? Would he even believe it?

Katy tried to begin again, but her throat was closing up. A solid wall of tears blinded her eyes. She could feel she was losing ground.

"Please don't think that I am happy about this," Alex stated solemnly.

"If you're not, then do something about it!" Katy coughed out.

"Maybe it's hard for you to see now, but when you're my age, you begin to understand that not all relationships can work, even with the best of intentions."

"Is that it?" Katy yelled. "Is all this because you don't think I'm grown up enough? Then I'll act grown up enough!"

Alex pinched the bridge of his nose.

"I don't want you to act," he replied. "I want you to be who you are."

"And who the fuck is that?" Katy was almost screaming at this point. She swung her arms out until they ran parallel with the floor. "I don't know what you fucking *want!*"

Alex paused, looking Katy directly in the eye.

"Exactly."

Katy's hands fell to her sides.

"What?"

"You're young. You're still so unsure of everything," Alex spoke, his voice soft and gentle. "And I'm not saying that's a bad thing. It isn't. I was the same way when I was your age. It took me years to come into my own and figure out who I was." Alex took in a long breath. "But I can't do that. I can't wait four, five years. And it would be unfair of me to make you figure things out sooner. Because you can't. No one can. And if you try to, you'll just end up resenting me." Alex shook his head. "And if I try to wait around, I'll just end up resenting you."

Katy stood across from Alex, saying nothing, taking in short, weak breaths. Her face was soaked with tears by now, but it didn't matter to her. She felt no need to wipe them away.

"So that's it?" Katy eventually squeaked out.

"I'm sorry."

Alex and Katy stood there, both looking at the ground. The rest of the apartment was deathly still, its silence echoing off the walls and furniture. Katy couldn't tell if the world was spinning, sinking, or staying exactly where it was, in a newly-formed hell that she suddenly found herself in.

"I should go," Alex said finally. Katy said nothing and kept her eyes on the ground.

Her gaze remained there as she heard Alex's footsteps slowly reach the door, where the sounds of the door opening, closing, and latching followed.

As soon as the sounds of the hallway floorboards creaking faded away, Katy turned and dragged herself into her room and fell onto her bed. Her body curled up into the fetal position. A pulsating ringing in her ears now replaced all of the previous sounds, drowning out every possible thought. It nearly drowned out the sound of Maria's door as it opened and Maria's footsteps as she walked to Katy's room, stopping at the doorframe. Katy made no effort to acknowledge her roommate. She simply closed her eyes and focused on the ringing in her ears as the comforter below her slowly became soaked with tears.

Chapter 19

She called in sick on that next morning. She spent the day inside her room, on her bed, numb and catatonic. Miller curled up in one corner, sleeping soundly while Katy stared off into space.

It felt like her axel, her foundation, whatever it was that was keeping her steady, had been snapped in half. She sat against the wall by her bed, oblivious to the time and space around her. She didn't want to read, or turn on the radio, or go into the living room and mindlessly watch TV. She didn't even dare to move, for fear she would crumble into jagged and uneven pieces with her first step on the ground.

Everything, save for the back of her mind, was blank. There were no thoughts, no sensations, not even a rogue tear or two. The back of her mind, however, made up for the lack of activity everywhere else. Her semi-conscious thoughts were speeding by so fast that the ideas quickly lost their individual character and became one blurry entity, like a time-lapsed photograph of speeding cars on a racetrack.

Not like it mattered if the thoughts were recognizable and distinguishable. They were all the usual, clichéd ramblings that every girl has when the rug is pulled out from under her. "This can't be happening, this has to be a dream, he will realize his mistake," *et cetera, et cetera, et cetera, ad nauseum, ad nauseum, ad nauseum.*

The afternoon sun infected the opposing wall of her bedroom, the light stretching across the wall and onto the ceiling. Outside, someone was having a heated conversation, shouting out terse sentences that were heavily peppered with "fucking" and "shit" and "oh my God". It felt like the woman was yelling directly at the sky, throwing her words in the air so that they curved into Katy's window and landed on her floor with a thud.

Welcome to the Brighton neighborhood on a Saturday. What was the girl getting so worked up about? Did she stay out too late and was now fighting with her roommate, her friend, her mother, over her actions? Or did she have an argument last night with her boyfriend and was continuing the conversation the next morning via the telephone? Maybe that boyfriend decided to abandon ship and she was aggressively going after him, giving her a piece of his mind, letting him know that he couldn't just walk away without a fight. A real fight. Not a few yelped words and then acquiescent silence.

Around one in the afternoon, Maria knocked gingerly on the door.

"Hey," she downright whispered. "Is it okay if I come in?"

"Help yourself," Katy murmured.

Maria opened the door slowly, one hand on the doorknob and the other pressed flatly against the door.

"Hey there," she nearly cooed.

"Hey there, roomie," Katy said, pulling her knees to her chest with a pained grin. "How was your Friday?"

Maria scratched behind her ear.

"I canceled plans."

"Well, that's a shame." Katy rolled her eyes towards Maria. "You should be out, having fun, with your great boyfriend."

Maria hugged herself at her waist. She opened her mouth slightly, revealing that she was pressing her tongue against the roof of her mouth.

"I am so, so sorry," said Maria after a moment.

"What do you have to be sorry for?" Katy stated. "You didn't do anything."

"It doesn't matter," Maria replied. "Katy, I'm sorry that…I'm sorry about yesterday. That was not fair to you. At all."

Katy breathed in slowly, collecting her thoughts. As she brought her thoughts to the surface, a fresh batch of tears joined them. She pressed her lips together, trying feebly to keep her lower lip from quivering. She looked up to attempt a snide remark, but Maria was already on the bed, pulling Katy in for a hug. After a moment of bewilderment, Katy wrapped her arms Maria and pressed her cheek into Maria's shoulder.

"It's *not* fair," Katy blurted out, her tears clouding her vision again. Every formerly-unconscious thought was now in the forefront, reminding Katy over and over again that she had lost something – something important – and it wasn't coming back and she was the fool who let it get away.

Maria rubbed Katy's back, saying nothing until the tears subsided and Katy was able to lean back against the wall again, immediately drained of any and all energy. Maria sat by Katy while Katy mustered up enough strength to wipe her cheeks with the palm of her hand.

"Hey, let me take you to get ice cream or something. My treat," said Maria after a moment.

"I don't feel like going out," Katy stated flatly.

"Then let me run to the store and grab a few pints," said Maria. "Any flavor you want."

Katy paused, swallowing meekly around the lump in her throat.

"Cookie dough?" she asked finally.

"Your wish is my command." Maria slowly pushed herself off the bed. "Will you be alright while I'm gone?"

"I'll only throw *one* loud party. I promise." Katy placed her right hand over her heart.

"Good to know you still have your snarky humor," Maria said, showing off a relieved grin. "I'll be back in a few minutes."

"No rush," Katy replied.

Katy placed her head against the wall immediately after Maria left the room. Her eyelids drooped, much to the delight of her aching eyes. After crying like she had just done, Katy would usually feel silly, with a hint of guilt and shame. Today, she just felt tired. Tired and empty and even more lethargic than before. She wanted to feel some profound sadness. She wanted to be swallowed in anguish, the kind that inspires volumes of poetry about lost romance. She wanted throw herself on the floor and overwhelm her senses with heartache as if she were in a Jane Austin novel.

But she had none of that. Just emptiness and despair.

That was it. Nothing else.

Katy must've dozed off, because the sound of Maria unlocking the door jostled her enough to open her eyes again. Katy rubbed at the bags under her eyes before sitting up and crossing her legs as Maria arrived with the ice cream.

"One cookie dough for you, one double-chocolate for me," Maria announced, sitting on the edge of the bed and handing Katy her pint.

Katy opened the lid, stared at the ice cream, and looked over at Maria.

"I might be stewing in my own despair, but I still need a spoon."

"Oh my God, I'm an idiot. Be right back," Maria said and dashed into the kitchen, returning with two metal spoons in hand.

"Why, thank you," Katy said, skimming the surface of her pint with the edge of her spoon. She lifted the spoonful into her mouth, holding the ice cream against her tongue, but the taste fell flat, acting more as a poor imitation of her favorite comfort food than anything else. She swallowed the ice cream, thankful that at least it was cool against her throat.

"You're better off," Maria said after a few spoonfuls. "You really are."

"Why would you say that?" Katy went monotone, her eyes focused on her slowly melting pint.

"You just are," Maria replied slowly. "I mean, he refused to see the bigger picture. So intent on settling down that he runs the second you don't act as grown up as he is. He's in his thirties; of course he's going to be more grown up than you. It's just absurd."

The muscles in Katy's face went limp as she stirred at her ice cream. A wave of restlessness washed over her, temporarily replacing her emptiness with a sudden and undeniable anger. She wanted to tell Maria off. She wanted to tell Maria that Maria knew nothing. That Maria had no business to talk about love, with her precious new relationship with precious Jacob. She wanted to scream out that it was more complicated than that – that Alex was kind and intelligent and believed in her abilities. She wanted to lament over how she had to be drunk out of her mind before her stupid, guarded little self would even allow herself to admit her feelings. That it was her stupid, guarded self who was too afraid to confront the issues that needed to be fixed and it was those stupid problems that brought about the end of the relationship in the first place. She wanted to tell Maria that it was Alex who would be better off. Not her. She was lost – lost, lost, desperately lost – without Alex.

Her anger subsided and a brief moment of pure, beautiful anguish passed by her before leaving her empty yet again.

"Maybe," Katy muttered into the cardboard container and took another tasteless bite.

Chapter 20

Time was a funny concept for her in the days after her break-up. The individual days were slow and tedious, but as a whole they seemed to blur together, to the point that she could barely tell what day it was.

The first few days were identifiable enough. Sunday, she called Evelyn, crying on her end of the line as she detailed how Alex had dumped her. Monday was her first day back. She told Ben with reluctant tears rolling down her cheeks about the breakup. She was given a hug and the ability to do whatever she felt up to, with Ben promising that he wouldn't tell a soul if Katy wanted to play hooky that day. By Tuesday, Andrea already had found out and greeted Katy with a warm, motherly hug, telling Katy that Andrea had been there, done that, time and time again, as a young adult herself. Katy hung out with Ben that Wednesday night, drank a few more beers than she should have, and cried on his shoulder, confessing that she didn't know what to do next.

It was easy the first few days, with everyone gently making sure that Katy was all right. But, by Friday, everyone had gone quiet. Maybe they were hoping that Katy would just go back to normal. Maybe they didn't want to bring it up and potentially make Katy cry again.

But that wasn't what she wanted. She wanted a group of people around her, constantly bringing up the subject and giving her hugs and offering their condolences. She didn't want to be the only one feeling sorry for herself. She didn't want to admit that, in the end, no one else was really affected by it. That there were limits to people's consoling; that people were only willing to stop and hold her hand for so long. She didn't want to admit that other people had their owns lives, most with their own new and happy relationships. Was her heartbreak not enough to get them out of their own cloud nine? Or were they worried that break-ups were contagious – that spending too much time talking or thinking about it would cause them to suffer the same fate?

Either way, life was more than willing to move on, and, at that point, Katy was more than willing to let it all speed by her.

Katy felt like she was experiencing life behind a screen. Everything felt like it was on autopilot and she was nothing more than a weary passenger looking out the window. Cash registers were prepared. Timesheets were initialed. Boxes were unloaded and paperwork was filed. Books were put away, straightened up, reorganized, re-priced, bought in, and sold away. She clocked in and out, went home, came back, clocked in and out, and so on, and so forth.

Katy found herself torn on days when business was slow and she was behind the cash registers. She hated being up front, in the public eye, with nothing to do but look out the window. But a part of her happily got lost in reverie, straining to see the café down the street – a place that she would punish herself with by walking past it day after day – or gazing at the sidewalk in front of her, imagining Alex coming by the store, flowers in hand, confessing the mistake he made and making everything right again.

She couldn't stop herself from wanting to look out the window, to remember and imagine and mourn. But it didn't mean that she liked it.

And what *was* there to like in such self-punishment? God, what was wrong with her? Why was she doing this to herself? If there was anything she knew by now, it was that guys only return with flowers in their hands, begging to be taken back, in bad chick lit books. And she had proclaimed time and time again that those fluff stories were for those who didn't want to recognize and live in reality – for those who weren't ready to admit that love operated on a more realistic, more boring, and more tragic plane of existence.

Was this some sort of payback? For all the years of poking fun at the "Women's Literature" section and judging those who religiously and voraciously ate up each and every book that came onto those shelves? Did the patrons who relentlessly bugged her to check on release dates – the ones who demanded for her to go in the back room to look for more chick lit novels – did they all meet and decide that the best revenge would be to make Katy just as pathetic as the most pathetic of chick lit protagonists? To make her pine while gazing out windows, to make her feel like her entire world had collapsed solely because of heartbreak?

But then again, wasn't that exactly what had happened?

Around the one-month anniversary of the break-up, Katy received a bit of email from one of the job search sites that she had once frequented, reminding her that she had not logged in for three months. The email informed her that she needed to log in soon or her account would soon be deleted. Katy logged in and browsed half-heartedly before logging back out, getting up, and leaving her laptop entirely.

It was downright laughable to think that she could job search now. She needed to first wake up from whatever bad romantic coma she had slipped into before she could even think about looking at jobs – jobs that she probably wouldn't even care about in the first place.

And, really, who cares? A job you hate is a job you hate. No one ever seems happy with their jobs, be it in a cubicle or behind a cash register. Everyone lives for the days off and dreads the days when they have to return. Everyone cherishes vacations, as if they work all year simply so they can get to get a week away from having to be there day after day after day. What was the point?

What was the point of any of it? At least at South End Collections, she had her friends. At least there, she could sound wittier than she actually was through her snarky comments about books and customers. She could complain and commiserate and conspire with Ben or Evelyn, or talk with one of the college kids like Hannah or Josh. She was surrounded by books – books she could buy at a serious discount – and she was in Boston. Good, old, comfortable Boston. And good, old, comfortable South End Collections.

So, honestly: who cares?

Plus, Katy liked observing the changes going on at the bookstore. And what was wrong with a bit of observing? Active participation was overrated. If Katy had left when she had first wanted to, she would've never witnessed the shifting dynamic, as Andrea slowly scaled back her own hours and promoted Evelyn to full-time supervisor. There was a rumor that Andrea might even promote someone to an assistant manager – an unheard of title at the store until then. There was change happening, and Katy would've missed all of it.

And Andrea seemed happy – thrilled, even – with her new married life. It was like finding a husband had awoken all the other good parts about life. So, good on her.

Yup, good on her.

Good on everyone else.

Let everyone else make something of themselves and their lives. The pathetic Katelyn Sinclaire will gladly take a step back and observe, like a cat lady from her porch.

*

The last Monday in February was a shipment day for Katy. The air was cold, the winds were rough, the skies were gray, and the filthy snow was accumulating everywhere it could. Katy and Hannah were stuck rushing boxes into the backroom as quickly as possible. The only plus side was that Ben and Evelyn were working that day as well.

She at least had that.

Katy meandered through her day, checking packing slips and organizing invoices, opening boxes and looking over books. By the start of the afternoon, a few carts were prepared to go out onto the floor. And Katy, opting once again to put away books instead of working the cash registers, absentmindedly pulled her cart out of the storage room. She turned the corner at the door and continued to walk backwards. Within two steps, she bumped into a customer, her back colliding into the side of the person behind her. Katy let go of the cart and dug her heels into the ground. The cart, following the rules of momentum, proceeded to collide into Katy's stomach.

"Sorry, sorry. I didn't see you there." Katy fought through the windedness and turned to the customer.

"Oh no, no problem!" A middle-aged lady said with a beaming smile. "I was hoping to talk to someone who works here."

"Oh, okay, then." Katy rubbed her stomach. "Um, how can I help you?"

The lady clasped her hands by her collarbone.

"Well, I see that you got in a bunch of new books. Do you know when you'll get a shipment of used books?"

"Actually, we usually don't get any used book shipments," Katy replied.

The lady scrunched her face in confusion.

"So...how do you get them, then?"

"Oh, it's simply through our buyback system." Katy paused. When the lady continued to stare back blankly, Katy continued: "It's basically when we buy books back from customers. Sometimes we'll get large donations, or old library books, but there's no set schedule to them."

"Oh," the woman said tersely. "So...you can't tell me what type of used books you'll be getting next week?"

Katy pushed her tongue against the back of her teeth.

"No. But, you are more than welcome to come back next week and see what we have. We get new ones in almost daily."

"Wait, now you're saying the books are new?"

"No, no," Katy rescinded, placing a cold hand on her hot neck. "I just meant that they're new to *us*. And we're usually very good about getting the used books out onto the floor as quickly as possible."

"Huh. 'Usually' good? So you're saying sometimes you guys...forget?"

"No, no – I mean, we're always very good about getting the used books out onto the floor for the customers."

"Well, where do you guys keep the used books that *aren't* on the main floor yet? In that room?" the woman said, pointing just past Katy.

"Our stock room?" Katy's voice almost faltered with fatigue. "Yeah, they do."

"Well, can I see what you have right now, then?" the woman inquired.

"Actually, the stock room is for employees only. I'm sorry about that." Katy could feel herself deflating with each patient response.

The lady opened her palms towards Katy and gave her a patronizing smile.

"Well, I might become a paying customer. That has to count for something."

"The books in the back haven't been processed yet. But they will be out soon."

The lady stared at Katy with a furrowed brow.

"Well, let me look at them. If there's one I like, you can process it then, and then I'll buy it."

"I'm sorry ma'am, but it just doesn't work that way. But you can always come back and see what new books we have out."

The lady – the sweet, once-upon-a-five-minutes-ago broad-smiling lady – crossed her arms as if Katy had just told her to shovel snow with her tongue.

"And how do you suppose I'll know which ones are new?"

"Well, I –" Katy stopped what she was saying and sighed. "I'm sure someone will be able to help you then."

The lady huffed.

"And they say Mom n' Pop shops are supposed to be kinder to customers. I think I'll take my business somewhere else."

The woman abruptly turned from Katy, stormed down the aisle, and exited the store.

"And we will surely miss your business," Katy muttered to herself, crossing her own arms as a type of belated victory. She parked her cart against the wall and made her way to the front of the store.

"Did you just see the crazed woman who walked out that door?" Katy said after a quick scan to make sure that the entrance area was empty.

"You'll have to be more specific," Ben said from behind the counter.

"Middle-aged, looks sweet, but actually has the demeanor of a feral cat?"

"Again, you'll have to be more specific. Remember where you are right now."

Katy placed her elbows on the counter and her head in her hands.

"Well, you look completely exhausted," Evelyn said from her spot at the beginning of the rightmost aisle. She was sitting cross-legged by her cart, slowly placing books on the bottom shelf.

"That's an understatement," Katy groaned into her hands before looking up at Ben. "So how is it over here on the Western front?"

"Fittingly, all quiet," Ben replied. "The place went dead after the lunchtime rush, so I assigned Hannah to facing shelves instead."

"Y'know, I used to think having to organize book after book after book was a tedious and cruel assignment." Katy rubbed at her eyes. "But it honestly beats having to talk to customers."

"C'mon now. They're not all that bad," Ben replied.

"This woman did a full 180 on me the second I couldn't give her the moon, the stars, and the kitchen sink to boot."

"Better than a full 360." Ben opened the cash register drawer and sorted through credit card receipts. "And what would anyone do with a sink and some celestial bodies?"

"Whatever it is, I guarantee you that it would be more fun than talking to that lady," Katy said and walked behind the counter.

"Shouldn't you be working?" Ben asked, eyeing her as she hopped up on one of the stools.

"Self-imposed break. I think I deserve it," Katy responded.

"Well, as long as you're here, I was curious if you had anything in mind for tomorrow," said Ben.

"What's happening tomorrow?" Evelyn poked her head out to ask.

"Just our usual hanging out," Ben replied.

"You guys really need to invite me sometime." Evelyn got up from her spot and shook out her legs. "Provided that I can actually *find* some free time to hang out."

"You're more than welcome to join us tomorrow," said Ben. "We usually plan something awesome, and then order pizza and watch movies instead." Ben reopened the cash drawer and slipped the receipts back under the tray. "Mark my words, though. Someday we'll actually do all those awesome things."

"And what's not awesome about pizza?" Katy quipped.

"Everything's awesome about pizza. But, ideally, I'd rather be doing something awesome *while* eating said pizza," Ben responded.

"We could always kick hobos."

Evelyn gave Katy and Ben an incredulous look.

"What?" she laughed out.

"Please, that's so 1920s," Ben responded.

"Okay, then," Katy tried again. "Let's kick drunkards. It's not like it would be hard to find them."

Evelyn laughed again.

"You guys are so normal."

"What are you talking about? I'm the King of Normal. I even made sure they put that on my driver's license," said Ben.

"Normal is overrated anyway," Katy responded. "I mean, what sounds like a more fun night: kicking drunkards or…making cookies?"

"Oh, we could make cookies!" Ben raised his eyebrows and smirked.

Katy's eyes widened.

"Ooh, yes! But the age-old question remains: chocolate chip or oatmeal raisin?"

"Chocolate chip, obviously," Ben replied. "Don't even mention something as blasphemous as oatmeal raisin around me."

"Just making sure you still have good taste."

"Okay, as fun as this dorkfest is, I think I left a pile of books on the second floor," Evelyn said, heading for the stairs. "Katy, if you're that strapped for work, you could always help me out."

"Or you could face," Ben added.

"Do you ever think of how weird that term sounds out of context?" Katy asked.

"I gotta admit: it does sound dirty," Ben replied. "Sounds like you're trying to make out with a hardcover."

"Only you two would come to that conclusion," Evelyn remarked.

"I try to avoid both about equally. Y'know, organizing or making out with books. They both sound equally unenjoyable," said Katy. She gave a broad smile to Evelyn before adding: "I can always help you upstairs if you'd like. I'll let Hannah deal with whether or not they're in the right place."

"Have fun," said Ben. With that, Katy started to follow Evelyn to the second floor. Evelyn walked up the stairs and to a piled stack of books, all the while smiling and shaking her head.

"What?" Katy said, finally, staring at Evelyn.

"You two..." Evelyn began and trailed off.

"'You two' what? You two nerds, you two losers, U2 the band..."

"You two are ridiculous. That's all." Evelyn rolled her eyes and smiled.

"Yeah, but in the awesome way," Katy scoffed and picked up the first few books from the stack. Biographies, biographies, and more biographies. She couldn't remember the last time she sold a biography book, but somehow they were disappearing off the shelves and being replaced by new ones. Katy shifted the books onto one arm and began making room for them on the shelf with her free hand. The second floor was nearly empty, which made the squeaking noises of metal bookends on metal shelves echo against every corner.

"Okay, I have to say it," Evelyn said after a few minutes.

"Say what?" Katy asked.

"I cannot believe you and Ben have not gotten together yet."

Katy raised an eyebrow before focusing back on her books. "Yeah, okay."

"I'm dead serious, here," Evelyn pressed. "You guys have been friends for, what, almost six years now? It blows my mind."

"Well, it shouldn't, because we're friends." Katy slid another book onto the shelf. "Y'know, the definition of 'friends'? Usually involves not 'getting together'."

"Oh, fun, the 'just friends' card." Evelyn rolled her eyes. "Please, you guys vibe so well it's almost sickening. You guys get along great, you love hanging out together, you are always there for the other person…"

"Well that's some sound philosophy on figuring out who is date-worthy," Katy replied, placing another book on the shelf. "With *that* mentality, I definitely should be dating Ben. I should also be dating Andrea, my roommate, you…"

"Knock it off. I'm serious," Evelyn asserted. "You guys are so good together. Better then some boyfriends and girlfriends. I really cannot believe that you guys haven't hooked up yet."

"So, you're trying to tell me that I need to date my best guy friend because he's most likely my perfect match." Katy turned to Evelyn, drumming her fingers on the book in her arms. "I might be a nut, but I'm not nutty enough to actually believe advice straight out of a chick lit cliché."

"Well, maybe they have that happen in books because there's some truth to it," said Evelyn. "You're supposed to become friends with someone first before dating them, anyway."

"But you also don't date everyone that you become friends with."

Evelyn rolled her eyes.

"Do I need to start quoting 80s movies over here? You guys are perfect for each other. Besides, it's obvious that Ben's hopelessly in love with you."

Katy scoffed again.

"'Hopelessly in love'? Now we really are in the land of crap chick lit."

"I'm serious." Evelyn lowered her eyebrows. "The guy totally has feelings for you. And I'm pretty sure you have feelings for him as well. Maybe you just need to wake up and see it."

"And maybe *you're* seeing things that just aren't there." Katy placed another book on the shelves.

"I'd be willing to bet good money that, subconsciously, you do feel the same way and have just been hiding it all these years."

Katy took in a breath, searching for something to say. She found that her repertoire of snarky comebacks was suddenly empty. When she saw that the pile of books was almost gone, she decided on: "I think you can get the rest of these. I'm going to start with my cart again. What I can get done today won't have to get done tomorrow."

"Deflecting is not going to work."

"Really?" Katy turned and started walking in the opposite direction. "Because it looks like it's working for me right now."

Katy made a sharp turn at one of the aisles, taking the long way back to the stairs, her fingers grazing against the books' spines as she slowly walked by. She felt off, like she had just been told she was actually adopted. She found a temporary solace in the rattling sound she was creating as her hand traipsed from book to book, her fingertips going over each curve and crevasse, her skin conscious of the different textures of each book as she passed. Katy reached the end of the aisle and continued on until she reached the windows, pressing her forehead against the cold glass until it felt like her skull was about to go numb. When she realized she wouldn't be able to shake off the weird feeling, she turned around yet again and approached the stairs.

But something stopped Katy, causing her to pause at the top step and listen to the faint muffle of Ben's voice. She sat down, elbows on her knees, peering down to watch as Ben talked to an older lady by the Editor's Choice self, pointing out the different books that he had chosen. The old lady seemed to latch on to every word, nodding and smiling as Ben picked up and put down his selections.

The words were inaudible, but she could imagine Ben whole-heartedly recommending the books to the lady. Maybe he would confess that he was more of a movie person – and hey, if a movie buff was recommending a book, then it must really be good. His whole face lit up as he talked, his brown eyes almost getting lost behind his full cheeks when he smiled his big, sincere smile. Katy couldn't help but smile back, as if Ben were talking to her instead, speaking gently but passionately about the things he loved, about the books that he couldn't help but read, since underneath his dopey grin, he was an intellectual, probably smarter than Katy had given him credit for until that very moment.

And all at once, Katy could feel herself waking up. The dulled hues of her surroundings burst into life and she was aware of every edge, color, and detail around Ben. Katy broke her gaze long enough to notice that the whole store seemed to come alive with light. Even the snow outside was brighter, a little whiter as it huddled together by the edge of the sidewalk and on top of the parking meters. With one last look at Ben, Katy stood up. Her entire chest expanded and contracted for one long, involuntary sigh.

Sigh?

Did she just sigh?

Like, romantic-novels-heaving-bosoms type of sigh?

"Well, shit," Katy muttered to herself, rolling her eyes and biting her lip to hide her smile as she walked down the stairs and to her cart.

Chapter 21

Katy woke up before her alarm, caught a green line trolley at a time when she would usually be puttering around her apartment, and anxiously wandered the Back Bay neighborhood. After a few laps around the block, she gave up and decided to come into work a half hour early.

Her mind was racing, going way faster than her fine motor skills, making unlocking the front door difficult and making locking the door behind her downright impossible. Her mind was also running faster than her *gross* motor skills, transforming a walk up the stairs to the break room into an Olympic sport. She tripped upwards and over, from her own feet to the stairs and onto the worn out carpet. She could barely lift the latch to her break room locker and she found herself slamming its door shut.

She was in desperate need of something to do. She could try vacuuming the floors, even though it had been done last night – most likely by Ben, who always left the store in pristine shape for the next day's openers. When Ben closed the shop, Katy never had to worry about registers that hadn't been closed out, or books that hadn't been put away. He was easily the most conscientious person she had ever known.

Why did it take her so long to see Ben like this?

It made sense, now that she thought about it. Being with him was always effortless. There was never any pretending around Ben. When Katy was upset, Ben knew it. When Katy felt snarky, Ben openly got the brunt of it, and countered it with his own brand of gentle wit. And he had never ordered her around, acting like he already knew what was right and wrong. He knew – just somehow, someway, psychic-network-levels *knew* – that she responded best with support and subtle advice. Something that Alex never understood.

Hell, Alex would outright hound her if she didn't follow his exact recommendations.

And then there was the *coldness* – the removed, stoic attitude that Alex assumed every time they had an issue. And it seemed like the more and more Katy got upset about something, the more and more Alex withdrew. And what type of relationship could thrive on *that*? So the hell with Alex and his wife-finding ways. Send it to hell. All the way to hell, with a pit stop in New Jersey just for good measure.

But what was she going to do that night? How was she going to navigate through the situation, knowing what she knew now, feeling how she felt now? What was she going to do? Make a crappy joke or two? Pretend that nothing had changed? Admit her feelings in a mushy pile of tears? Cancel hanging out completely? Ravish him senseless on the kitchen floor? What was she going to do, and could she make it through work without bursting?

Katy snapped back into the present with the sound of the deadbolt on the front door unlocking. Hannah was scheduled to open with Katy, and Hannah didn't have a key. Just Andrea and the supervisors. Katy barreled down the stairs, wondering exactly who was coming through the front door.

"It's just me, Katy," Andrea's voice echoed from the first floor.

Katy was bewildered at the sight of Andrea. With the marriage and honeymoon and her steadily decreasing time at the store, Andrea had turned into a shadow figure instead of the store's manager.

"What are you doing here?" Katy blurted out.

"Hannah called out. Poor thing's a wreck," Andrea answered as she took off her coat and started down an aisle towards her office.

"Oh no – what happened?" Katy followed obediently behind.

"She didn't go into the details." Andrea opened the door and draped her coat over a filing cabinet. "But she sounded pretty upset about something."

"Oh, wow," Katy responded, looking to the floor.

"But, hey, it feels like I never get to see you anymore, anyway, so I'm okay with subbing in for her," said Andrea. Andrea turned and added: "Have you set up the registers yet?"

"No, not yet."

"So what *has* been done this morning?" Andrea asked, grabbing the binder filled with timesheets.

"Um, nothing, nothing yet," Katy stammered.

"Just got in too, then, huh?" Andrea smirked.

Katy's face scrunched.

"Yeah. Something like that."

*

Hannah ended up showing sometime in the afternoon.

She entered the bookstore, her face slightly blotchy, and walked right over to Andrea. Andrea was taking inventory on the first floor, checking and re-checking her lists and scribbling down notes, when Hannah approached.

"Hey, um – hey, Andrea," Hannah said hoarsely. Katy watched on from the cash registers, almost handing a man back his credit card without swiping it first in the process.

"Hannah, I'm so glad to see you," Andrea replied. "How are you feeling?"

"I don't eve – heh, I'm okay. Better." Hannah smiled. "I'm sorry about calling out last minute."

"Don't worry about it. Things happen." Andrea gave Hannah her renowned managerial smile. "You know you don't have to be here right now, anyway. Everything's all set."

"I know, but, I hate that I had missed my hours. Is there any way I can do something this afternoon?"

Andrea paused.

"Don't you have class this afternoon?"

"I don't feel like classes right now," Hannah said flatly.

"Hannah, I can't in good conscience…" Andrea began.

Hannah crossed her arms.

"I mean it. I don't feel like going to class. I don't feel like anything. If I don't work, I'll just go back and be miserable in my apartment. And I just want to make up the hours I missed. I hate that I'm losing money because of…all this."

Andrea looked around and took in a deep breath.

"Well, Ray's coming in soon. You can help Katy with inventory after she opens his register. Does that sound good?"

"I'll take it," Hannah replied, her words flowing out of her mouth with a defeated sigh.

Hannah went up to the break room and stayed there. A half hour or so later, Ray came in for his shift. Katy opened his register, snagged Hannah from the break room, and went back downstairs to continue what Andrea had started.

"Have you done inventory before?" Katy asked.

"Not on my own, but I've seen it." Hannah's words tumbled into the air, as if they had been accidentally swept out by her breathing.

"It's exactly how it looks, only more boring," Katy replied, flipping through the lists. She genuinely wanted to go slowly through inventory with Hannah, but part of her just wanted to blast through the inventory as quickly as possible. She could barely keep her mind on her work, and inventory was easily the worst thing to do when her mind was elsewhere. It was a tedious enough task even when her mind was exactly where it needed to be.

"I can go for boring," Hannah mumbled, her eye cast lethargically on the shelves of books.

Katy bit at the insides of her cheek, flipping through the pages but paying attention to none of them. Finally, she said: "You know, I'm always here if you want to talk."

"I appreciate it, but, really, I'm okay."

"Alright, then. Offer's always on the table if you change your mind," Katy replied. "Now Andrea left off right about here. You can pull out the books one-by-one and I'll check them against the list."

Hannah pulled out the first book and blurted out: "He stole money from me."

Katy lowered her brows.

"Who was?"

"My boyfr—." Hannah began. "My ex."

"Yikes." Katy found that that was the only response she could think of.

Hannah pushed the book back in and pulled out another.

"And you know, I thought I would be okay with him," she continued. "Like, my boyfriend is a leech, but there are worse things a guy can be." Hannah bit her lip and shook her head. "Yeah, totally worse things. Like a thief."

"Sheesh. I'm so sorry."

"Just so unfair. Here I was, working my ass off, being responsible, and I had to mother him because he couldn't handle finances."

Katy nodded, unsure of what she could say.

"Like, it's one thing to always hit me up for money. It's another to steal when I say no," said Hannah. "Like, I caught him red-handed taking out all the cash in my wallet. Not even some: all. I call him out on it and he throws a hissy fit, saying that it's my fault he had to do that in the first place."

"Wow, I'm…I'm sorry about all that." Katy hugged the clipboard holding the list.

"I think we fought until one in the morning last night. But it needed to be done. I needed him out of my life." Hannah raised her hands as if mocking surrender before grabbing another book. "And whatever. Who cares? Y'know what? I'm ready to go to grad school as a single woman. I spent most of my undergrad life in this shitty relationship. It's time that I figure out who I am without having such a leech in tow."

"It's a good attitude to have," Katy said uneasily.

Inventory was far from finished when Katy's shift was over, but Katy had no interest in working late. She left at exactly six and sped-walked to the trains before making her way to Porter Square, where Ben's apartment awaited. Katy darted up the escalators leading out of the train station until she reached street level, where she risked getting ran over as she determinedly crossed the various roads to get to Ben's part of the neighborhood. She nearly bumped her head against Ben's front door as she tried opening it, before remembering that the front door was now locked. She rang for Ben's apartment, still out of breath.

"Jesus, did you run here?" Ben raised an eyebrow when he opened the front door.

"Just trying to keep warm!" Katy responded downright manically before clearing her throat and continuing in a more subdued tone: "I never thought I'd be so ready for spring."

"Spring? 'Spring'? What is this odd word that you speak off?" Ben moved to the side and let Katy in. "New England only has two seasons: summer and winter. We don't get *spring* here; we get a few days when New England is so confused that it forgets to give us either of the two seasons. And it usually rains during that time."

"Okay, then, I never thought I'd welcome summer." Katy rolled her eyes and walked up the stairs, her feet unintentionally stomping against the wood.

"You say that now, but you'll be ready for the arctic chill come July." Ben snuck by Katy at the top of the stairs to open the door. Katy took a step back, quietly breathing in the scent of the laundry detergent from his shirt and the shampoo from his hair. He stepped to the side to let Katy go in first. For a split second, she wasn't sure if she could move her legs at all. Katy inevitably took a few steps in, stopped by his weathered dining room table, and took off her coat and hat, her eyes squarely on the chair in front of her.

"I don't know about you, but I'm in need of a drink," Ben said warmly.

"I could definitely use a drink." Katy nearly spat out the words.

"A drink it is. Shall we?"

"We shall," Katy said and followed Ben into the kitchen. The world was bouncing around her with every step she took, to the point that she thought she would bump into a wall before she'd ever get to the doorway.

Ben opened the fridge.

"I've got the usual. Feel like a beer?"

"I feel like Katy," Katy replied, her banter with Ben on autopilot. "But I'll take a beer."

"I see work hasn't depleted you of your wit just yet." Ben reached into the refrigerator and pulled out a bottle.

Katy grabbed the bottle, careful not to touch Ben's hand. She didn't know what would happen if they touched, even for a second. She pressed her palm onto the top of the bottle, unscrewed the cap, and took a bitter gulp.

"So, how *was* work today?" Ben pulled out a second beer and opened it.

"Oh, the usual," Katy replied. "Andrea made a guest appearance, actually." Katy was about to explain Hannah's situation, but thought better of it. What luck would come from that, talking about a nasty breakup at a time like this?

"Really?" Ben smiled. "I think we're seeing Haley's Comet with more frequency these days."

"Tell me about it," she said. "At this rate, she'll be finding herself an assistant manager before the weather warms up."

"Not if those guest appearances keep happening," Ben replied. "But seriously, though: wouldn't that be cool? One of us as assistant manager? There's always been some disconnect between her and the rest of us. Like, she's owner and manager, and we very much work under her. I feel like one of us becoming assistant manager would only make things easier. Fill in the gap a bit."

"Who says she'll pick one of us?" Katy asked, squinting into her bottle.

"You think she'd hire a complete nobody over her loyal employees?" Ben cocked an eyebrow. "Please. I've been there for almost 7 years, you for almost as much. We've earned it."

"I guess so," Katy stated, before she found herself saying: "I think you'd make a terrific assistant manager." She regretted the words and the flowery way they formed in her mouth as quickly as they came out.

"Oh, why thank you. I'm flattered, truly." Ben dramatically hugged the beer to his chest.

Katy's gaze lingered on Ben for a second longer than was comfortable before stuttering out: "So, how was your day off?"

"The usual. Slept in, lounged. Oh! There's this awesome store a couple miles from here that sells used movies and stuff." Ben put down his beer on the counter. "And, like, imported films that you really can't get anywhere else. I went by there today. They were hosting this really cool..."

Ben continued on, but Katy was no longer hearing the words. His lips moved, but the movement itself took up more of Katy's consciousness than the sounds they were making. She felt like whatever barrier that had been keeping Ben and Katy on opposite sides of the kitchen was crumbling, and she had a few vital seconds to take advantage of it.

Do it, do it, do it. Don't be such a wimp. Live a little. The instigating voice filled her head and she suddenly went dizzy, feeling like she was about to get crushed from the pressure of her potential actions. Everything was weighing on her. She felt like she was no longer in Ben's kitchen anymore, but on the edge of the cliff, and being egged on to jump over into an immediate free-fall.

Katy lifted a shaky hand and took a rapid series of gulps from the beer. Instead of putting her arm back by her side, she shifted her weight and placed the bottle behind her. And almost instantly, that barrier had shattered, leaving Katy exposed to take a few perilous steps forward. Her mind, once racing and second-guessing to the point of passing out, cleared. Everything cleared. Time itself seemed to slow down. With her brain devoid of any thought or emotion, her body automatically did what her brain had been too scared to do and she walked across the kitchen.

Ben stopped whatever he was saying and silently looked at Katy. Katy, on a path she knew she could only go forward on, slipped a hand around Ben's neck and leaned in, connecting her smooth lips with his. She held onto the kiss for a moment, feeling Ben's lips move to kiss back. She sensation of his lips moving under hers filled her with electricity. Just the idea – the idea! – of his muscles working in sync with hers, even just the tiniest muscles in his lips was enough to make her want to pass out.

The smallest lull after the kiss was enough to make Katy move her head away, second-guesses poking at the back of her mind. She looked at Ben – specifically, she looked at Ben looking back at her – and broke out in a small, embarrassed laugh.

"What?" She breathed out.

"Nothing." Ben's face was blank, almost star-struck. "Nothing at all."

This time it was Ben's turn to move in for a kiss. Katy closed her eyes, feeling like she really was freefalling, and wrapped her arms around Ben.

Katy started pulling Ben out of the kitchen, through the dining area, and around the corner, as if the bedroom had become a black hole and Katy was defenseless against the pull. Katy and Ben fumbled at each other's clothes, trying unsuccessfully to undress and kiss and walk at the same time. Their lips parted just long enough to let out a few self-conscious laughs before hands awkwardly groped for belt buckles, bra straps, and zippers.

Katy sat on the bed and pulled herself backwards towards the center. Ben leaned over and crawled on top. There was a moment – a small pause – where the tiniest conversation would've been appropriate. Maybe a declaration of feelings. Or statement of incredulity. But that stuff's for the bad romance novels, right? The books fail to mention how awkward sex really is, so the writers ignore the shaky hands and funny noises and add in passionate conversation instead.

But who needed conversation now? Katy's mind was filled with the idea of Ben, her skin acutely aware of every touch. She was rendered speechless by love and lust and exhilaration, and God knows what type of sentences could come out of a mind in that state. Instead of words, Katy pulled Ben closer, her body intent on getting what it wanted, and pressed herself upward, reveling in the skin upon skin, the sensations she had never given a second thought to before.

*

A small shiver stirred Katy. The room was ten degrees below comfort and Katy's semi-conscious body was groping around for blankets. After a few unsuccessful tries, her hands grasped the edge of a comforter and pulled it tightly around her body. Her back, once exposed to the frigid air, was now singing the praises of insulation. Katy's body curled into the fetal position, enjoying the warmth that was slowly building under the blankets. After a moment, Katy stretched out her legs in an attempt to fall back into a blissful sleep, but was interrupted by her feet bumping against skin. A moan emanated from behind her.

"Sorry, sweetie," Katy mumbled and rolled onto her back. After a few moments, Katy gave up on the idea of falling back asleep and started fluttering her eyes open.

Katy blinked a few times before staring up at the ceiling. Her brows lowered in confusion. Whose ceiling was this? Whose *room* was this? This wasn't her bed. This wasn't Alex's bed. Where was she?

Seriously, where in the hell was she?

Katy rubbed at her eyes in a feeble attempt to stave off the sudden and confusing panic. She sat up and rubbed her eyes again, hoping that fully waking up would solve everything. With another shaky breath, Katy surveyed the room and looked down at the figure in the bed next to her. She squinted and focused with bewilderment. Her brain was misfiring and she couldn't put a name to a face. In her half-awake state, she probably wouldn't even have been able to put a name to her own face.

After a moment, her brain answered simply: "Ben."

Oh, Ben, Katy thought to herself. *Ben's room. Alright.*

With that, she laid back down and closed her eyes.

After a half second, Katy's eyes flung open.

Ben?!

Katy slapped a hand against her forehead so hard that it caused Ben to moan again in his sleep. For a brief moment, the world became a vacuum. Life itself seemed to pause. Then, all at once, the reality of the situation exploded all around her and everything came rushing back, filling Katy with a sinking nausea. She covered her mouth with her hands.

Oh God, what had she done?

Was she drunk? No, she wasn't, not by anyone's standards. Unless stupidity and impulsivity counted as a type of alcohol.

What in the hell had she been thinking?

Was Katy that malleable? That impulsive? Or had she been that dumb to think that rebounding wouldn't happen to her?

Katy slithered out of the bed, cringing both at the cold floor and at her unclothed state. She snatched up her clothes and threw them on in a frenzied fashion, as if she had been caught naked in public.

What a stupid, stupid girl. The thought played again and again, cruelly looping through her mind as she trudged down the stairs and onto the sidewalk. The air around her felt thick. It was beyond thick: the air around her felt like it was made out of gelatin. Her movements were slow and labored. Her breathing was shallow. Her muscles hung limply, as if the skin itself was the only thing keeping everything from completely falling apart.

The scenery around her changed slowly and tediously. Eventually Porter Square came into view, mocking her from a block away. She crossed the street, entered the train station, and stepped onto first set the escalators. She paid her fare and slumped by the banister of the second escalator as it slowly descended. She stood by the edge of the T platform, waiting for one of the first trains of the morning to show up. A train ultimately arrived and Katy mechanically went inside. The car was empty – deserted, even. Katy walked to the nearest corner seat and sat with her back against the adjacent wall, her legs drawn to her chest, and her forehead against the windowpane.

The train pulled out of the station. Katy's body rocked back and forth with the train's movements, her eyes focusing past her reflection and onto the dark walls of the tunnel. She wanted to cry, but couldn't muster up the strength to do it. She was tired of – and angry at – and disgusted with – herself. And she couldn't even gather up a few tears to humiliate herself in public with? The hell was wrong with her.

And at this moment of sheer stupidity, who was she thinking about? Who was she missing? Who was she dying to call up, to beg for a second chance, to admit again just how much she loved him?

Stupid, stupid, stupid girl.

She remembered the thrill she got when Alex had slipped his hand into Katy's after their first dinner together. How foreign their bodies felt to each other at the time! How scary and new and exciting everything was. And then things fell into the familiar before falling straight into hell. Because it was gone. All gone. Leave your keys in the mailbox and tell us where we can send your security deposit. Gone, gone, forever gone.

And her impulsive self probably ruined the best friendship she would ever have. She couldn't even picture the previous night without feeling sick.

Stupid, ignoramus, dumbass little bitch. Everything was ruined.

A wave of sorrow hit Katy and, for a brief second while the train emerged from underground and rattled over the Charles River, Katy clenched her face in anticipation of tears. But nothing came. The train crossed the bridge and went into the tunnel and that was it.

Katy transferred over to the green line and assumed the same fetal position, this time in a new corner. The same asinine, gut-punching thoughts played through her mind as the trolley went from stop to stop, station to station, eventually going from underground to aboveground, eventually making its way to Katy's neighborhood. Katy got off the trolley – the bitter morning air making her want to throw up – trudged up the street, entered her apartment, and shrugged off her bag, her coat, her snow-soaked shoes. Katy kneeled down and fished her phone out.

A few rings lead to Andrea's voicemail greeting. Of course it would. It was barely 6:30 in the morning. Why would she be awake at such a time? This was exactly what Katy was hoping for.

"Hey Andrea, it's Katy. I hate to be doing this last minute, but I don't think I can make it today. I feel..." Katy paused, choking back a few tardy tears. "I feel wretched. It – it might be the flu. I'll let you know tonight how I'm feeling. Okay? I'm sorry, Andrea. I'll talk to you later. Bye."

Katy walked over to the television, thought better of it, and turned to go into her room instead. Her bedroom welcomed her like a cavern, its lights off and shades already drawn. Katy undid the top button on her jeans before recoiling as if she had touched decaying matter. Katy rubbed her eyes, slid down her jeans in the most pragmatic way possible, and crawled into her bed. Maria's muted alarm went off in the distance by the time Katy started dozing back to sleep.

Abby Rosmarin

Chapter 22

The apartment was filled with harsh afternoon light and nothing much else by the time Katy woke up. Her gaze glided around the room, going from wall to wall, from one side of the ceiling to the other. Everything felt so heavy.

No, nix that. Nothing felt heavy. Everything felt *pushed* — pushed downward, like something was on top of Katy, keeping her from even lifting an arm. Her chest felt crushed, her lungs felt constricted. Only the driving need to mindlessly watch television helped her out of bed and into the living room, where she instantly plopped down on the couch, grabbed a throw pillow, and slid back down into a lying position. She reached out one hand to the coffee table, grabbed the remote, and turned on the TV.

The TV channels and shows seemed to melt together. She watched a biography series on Andrew Jackson, dozed off a little bit in the middle of an infomercial, and finally decided to sit up sometime in the middle of a reality show program. Somewhere through her media journey, Miller joined her on the couch, curling up in a loose ball a few feet away from her. After flipping through a few more channels, Katy got up, fixed herself a breakfast/lunch of graham crackers and jam, and went straight back to the couch.

The worst was that Katy couldn't even pinpoint how she felt. If she were upset with the situation, then at least she could cry about it. She was good at that. If she were angry with herself, then at least she could kick at the bottom of a wall until her toes hurt. She was *very* good at that. But the way she felt now? It was more nondescript than anything else. She just felt drained. Drained and sluggish.

In the back of her mind she knew that, if she thought about things, truly thought about it all, she would break down and possibly never recover. She would hate herself for being impulsive and grow despondent over her lost relationship & potentially ruined friendship and become immobilized with emotion. But she didn't have the energy for it. She couldn't even form a single, static thought. Forget fully fathoming what she had done.

Once in a while, the events from the night before would pop back into her mind and a militant wave of mortification would wash over her, overwhelming her with embarrassment and guilt. But it would recede as quickly as it crashed in and Katy would become listless again.

The afternoon melted away while Katy sat around in the living room. The sun soon set, leaving the TV and the muted glow of street lamps as the only source of light in the apartment. Every once in a while, Katy would turn down the volume on the TV. The apartment felt cave-like, dark and silent, and Katy would envelop herself in it. She felt like those times would have been good moments to cry, but the tears never came. Only a slight silliness over wanting such despair.

A set of jingling keys disrupted one of these moments. Katy turned as the main door opened and hallway light spilled into the apartment. Maria turned on the main lights and immediately jumped back.

"Jesus, I didn't even know you were here," Maria gasped out, one hand clutching at her chest. "You scared the shit out of me."

"Sorry about that." Katy clicked her cheek against the side of her teeth.

"You're never home this early on Wednesdays." Maria placed her bag and keys on the counter dividing the kitchen and living room. "Punch out early?"

"Never went," Katy replied, turning off the muted television.

"Ooh," said Maria as she opened the refrigerator. Maria pulled out the orange juice and cupped the carton with both hands. "Well, that makes sense. You didn't get home until the crack of dawn. Wild night or something?"

Katy closed her eyes.

"No, not exactly."

"Oh," Maria replied. "Just a late night, then?"

Katy winced.

"Kind of."

"'Kind of?" Maria replied. "Uh oh. What happened?"

Katy took in a breath, cut it short, and rolled her eyes.

Maria tapped her fingers a few times against the orange juice carton.

"Really, you can tell me anything. You know that, right?"

"I know, I know. I just..." Katy trailed off and sighed out a groan, falling silent and opting to look out the window instead.

"Whatever it is, let it out. You'll feel better."

"It's...embarrassing."

"Then I'll destroy any evidence of it ever happening." Maria paused and scanned Katy's face. "C'mon. After all these years, you know I'd be the last to judge —"

"Ben and I slept together," Katy blurted out.

"Oh." Maria placed the carton on the counter and crossed her arms. "Um..." Her top arm popped up and scratched the base of her neck. "Well, how'd that go?"

Katy leaned her head back.

"It felt like sleeping with a stepbrother."

"Oh."

Katy rubbed her eyes with one hand before pinching the bridge of her nose. She slid the hand over her head and let it land against the wall behind her.

"How'd that happen?" Maria said after a moment.

"Long story. Long, long, long story," Katy replied. "I was an idiot, is all."

"Well...things like that happen." Maria walked over and leaned against the wall across from the couch. "You recently had a major break-up...and Ben totally has a crush on you..."

Katy winced again.

"Was it *that* obvious?"

Maria raised her palms up and shrugged.

"Well, I mean the signs were always there," said Maria. "But that's not the point. The point is that it was kind of an inevitable rebound."

Katy dropped her hands by her sides.

"But that's the thing. I wasn't planning on it to be rebound. If I thought it was going to be rebound, I never would've done it." Katy sighed. "It's just, for a split second, I really was convinced he was…"

"The one?" Maria finished.

"Well, not that." Katy repositioned herself. "Or, I don't know."

"Take it from somebody with experience in this," said Maria. "Not all rebounds are intentionally casual hook-ups. The heart is complicated like that."

"I guess," Katy replied and cast her eyes to the carpet.

They stayed like that in silence, Katy's eyes fixed on the ground in front of her. After a few more moments, Maria walked back to the kitchen and poured herself a glass of juice. Katy could hear her fiddle with the cabinets, shuffling around the different boxes and cans. Katy leaned over for the remote, thought better of it, and pushed herself back.

"Hey, Maria?"

Maria stopped in the middle of pulling down a box of instant mashed potatoes from the cabinet.

"Yeah?"

"Can I ask you something?"

Maria closed the cabinet door.

"Of course."

Katy raised her eyes to the ceiling.

"Assuming this had never happened, do you think Ben and I would've made a good couple?"

Maria set the instant mashed potatoes down.

"No."

Katy gave a defeated laugh.

"That was a quick answer."

"Because I didn't need to deliberate," Maria answered. "Don't get me wrong – you guys get along great. Always have. On paper it probably makes perfect sense. But it's such a sibling-like bond, especially on your side. It's a really good friendship, but something would get lost in translation if it went romantic."

Katy sighed and leaned forward, her elbows on her knees.

"It's not fair."

"I know, hun."

"I mean, I thought that this was how things went," Katy continued. "You're always supposed to be friends with someone first. So who would be a better fit than someone you've been friends with for years? Someone you know and are comfortable with. Like, at the end of the day, the best guy for you is the guy friend who was right under your nose the whole time."

"Maybe. That's just not the case for you," Maria stated bluntly, shrugging her shoulders at the end of her statement. "But it's okay to be disappointed about it."

Katy got up, walked over to the kitchen, and plopped her elbows on the counter's raised edges, her chin immediately landing in her hands.

"This just sucks."

"I'm sorry," Maria replied softly. "It won't be like this forever, though."

"I feel like I messed up a really good friendship for forever, though." Katy tilted her head to one side.

"Maybe," said Maria. "Maybe not. I mean, if you just confront him, apologize, and explain what was going on in your head...I think things are salvageable. They might be weird for a bit, but you've guys have been so close. One crappy night can't mess things up forever."

"Maybe," Katy replied.

"When do you work together again?"

Katy snorted.

"Tomorrow."

"No time like the present." Maria bit at a corner of her lip. "Well, no time like tomorrow, to be precise."

"I'm looking forward to *that* conversation," Katy mumbled.

"But it's a conversation that does need to happen," Maria replied.

Katy nodded, absently scanning the counter as she did.

Maria unhooked a large metal spoon from the kitchen wall and added, "I'm making a gigantic pot of mashed potatoes if you're interested."

"A pot of spuds?" Katy smirked. "What happened to the culinary Maria?"

"You're telling me that delicious mashed potatoes are not culinary?"

"That's exactly what I'm telling you."

"Well, I think they're delicious. Head chefs be damned."

Katy smiled.

"Can we have Oreos for dessert?"

"Like I'd have it any other way."

Katy spent the rest of the night hanging out with Maria, eating processed food and channel surfing on the TV. She went to bed feeling like she could take on the next day.

Well, that was a blatant lie. But she did feel like she could at least survive the talk that she'd have to have with Ben the next day. It would suck – well, duh, it would suck – but what else could she do? And she was ready to see him again – to apologize for everything, pretend like she never saw him naked, and hopefully move on with life. She was ready for that. Right? The fact that she fell asleep by midnight without any difficulties had to have been a good sign, right?

Even though Katy was working a later shift that Thursday, she woke up long before even Maria's alarm went off. She jumped in the shower, bringing the water heat up to an uncomfortable level. She threw on her typical retail clothes and decided to go out and get herself some coffee before work.

Katy wandered around her neighborhood, ordered her coffee, and decided to venture down the hill to Commonwealth Ave. As soon she came near the street and saw the trolley that she routinely caught for work, her blood turned to sludge. Without any hesitation, Katy grabbed her phone out of her bag and called up Andrea.

"Hey Katy," a familiar voice chirped.

"Um, hey, Andrea. It's, uh, Katy."

Andrea paused.

"Hey. Katy. How are you?"

Katy forced up a cough. Did she cough in her voicemail message yesterday?

"Still sick."

"Ooh. I'm sorry to hear that. How're you feeling?"

"Um...sick."

"Well, I didn't know if there was a fever, or if you felt nauseas. It is flu season. Have you gotten your shot yet?"

"Maybe it's the flu. I don't know." A gust of wind reminded Katy where she was and she quickly retreated into the foyer of a nearby apartment. "I'm sorry I have to call out again."

Katy could hear Andrea's sigh on the other end of the line as clearly as if she were standing next to Andrea.

"I can call Evelyn, see if she'll cover you."

"She's always been so helpful," Katy added with positive zest. After a lack of reply on Andrea's end, Katy added: "I really do appreciate this. I'm sorry I have to call out a second day in a row."

"These things happen. No worries," Andrea replied. "Get better, okay?"

"I'll try my best."

Katy hung up her phone, pushed it into her coat pocket, turned away from Commonwealth Ave, and walked back up to her street. She still felt like wandering, but now she had a strong urge to stay within the residential parts and as far away from the busy roads as possible.

The world around her was still very much the victim of winter. The dirtied snow piled up on the edges of the sidewalks like makeshift guardrails. The snow had partially melted, only to freeze over, leaving the snowdrifts and sidewalks with a hardened, slippery glaze. The cars that parked along the sides of the road were caked in salt. People were already out that morning, walking down to the main road to take public transit to work, or standing by their cars, exasperatingly scraping at their windshields.

The wind was sharp, pushing the coldness with all its might against anything in its way. Katy countered the cold with long, slow sips of her coffee. She could feel the ice and snow under her sneakers and walked flatfoot to avoiding falling. She circled around her block before wandering down a few random streets.

If only she could quit her job and get paid to walk around like this. If only she could quit her job and get paid to do whatever she wanted. Now would be a good time to find out that she had actually been born a trust fund baby. Without hesitation, she would quit her job and essentially get paid to exist. Or, if that weren't a viable option, now would be a good time to win the lottery.

The buzzing in her coat snapped her out of her reverie. Katy fished out her phone, cringed at the display screen, and flipped it open.

"Hey Evelyn," Katy answered.

"Katy, can I ask you something?"

Katy's face scrunched.

"Um sure."

"Is everything all right?"

"Of course it is," Katy responded, adding: "Aside from being sick, of course."

"I mean, are you actually all right?"

"I said I'm fine."

Evelyn paused.

"I don't mean to sound blunt, but..." Evelyn trailed off and paused again.

"Yes?" Katy asked after the pause overstayed its welcome.

"Are you actually sick?"

"Um, of course I am." Katy answered before getting interrupted by a blaring horn in the distance.

"Uh, huh," Evelyn answered. "So that's why you're outside when it's below freezing?"

"I'm inside," Katy defended. "I just have my window down."

"Uh, huh." Evelyn repeated. "What's going on?"

"Why would you think that something's going on?" Katy shot back with regrettable quickness.

Evelyn paused again.

"You never call in sick. You'd rather give the whole staff measles than take a personal day. And here you are, taking two in a row when you're obviously not dying. What's going on?"

A sudden current of anger surged through Katy's body.

I took your advice and it backfired, she thought bitterly, with such force that it almost made its way to her mouth.

"I'm fine."

"Then you wouldn't mind me coming over with some chicken noodle soup then, right?" Evelyn replied. "Maybe a thermometer?"

Katy nearly slipped on the sidewalk.

"Who said I had a fever?"

"Katy, I'm coming over," Evelyn stated flatly. "Either I'm going to be tending to a sick friend or I'm going to be talking to a friend who's got something going on. Either way, I'm coming over."

"Please, this isn't a good time," Katy replied. "I'll see you soon though, okay?"

"And this isn't a good time for me to fill in for someone who's faking sick, but I'm doing it anyway," Evelyn snapped, before adding softly: "I know something's the matter. And I know you won't tell me over the phone."

"Really, I'm fine."

"Then you won't mind me coming over."

Katy huffed.

"Maybe I'll be too sick to buzz you in."

"Katelyn Sinclaire, unless you want me to call up Andrea and tell her that I'm positive that you're playing hooky, you'll let me come over."

Katy sighed.

"Fine, fine. I give."

"I'm going to head out soon, so finish up on whatever you're doing outside and get back inside."

"I am inside."

"Katelyn…"

Katy faltered.

"It was a health walk."

Evelyn sighed.

"I'll see you soon."

Katy made her way back to the apartment. Maria had long left for work when Katy returned. The only entities in the apartment now were a girl still in her winter wear, an apathetic cat, and the dread of an impending visit.

And what could – or would – Evelyn say? Evelyn was a smart girl. She could probably put two and two together. Hell, she was the one who put two and two together in the first place, anyway. So why even have the conversation? Unless it was to tell Katy what to do next.

Obviously, she was good at doing that.

In the back of her mind, Katy knew she was being irrational. She knew it was unfair to pin everything on one measly suggestion from a well-meaning friend. But the back of her mind could shove it for all she cared.

Katy's irrational thinking seemed to hit critical mass just as her intercom buzzed, with Evelyn waiting patiently to be let in. Katy silently pushed the button to unlock the main door, pushing down with extra force, to the point that the tip of her index finger hurt. After a moment, Katy heard knocking on her front door. She opened it, scanned her eyes over a bundled-up Evelyn, and turned back to the living room.

"Welcome," Katy gave as her monotone greeting.

"Thanks, I guess." Evelyn closed the door behind her and began unwrapping her scarf.

Katy looked over Evelyn again.

"You didn't bring any soup."

"Why waste the money?" Evelyn shrugged off her coat. "I figured you weren't sick, anyway."

Katy slumped against the doorframe of her bedroom.

"So what would you like to do instead? Bake cookies? Parcheesi?"

"This really isn't the time. This is serious." Evelyn stayed in the foyer by her fallen coat and scarf. "I'm worried."

"What would have you worried?"

Evelyn rubbed the back of her neck.

"You refuse to show up at work. Two days in a row. Ben was morose as hell yesterday. After Monday's conversation, it doesn't take a genius to know what's up."

"So if you already know what's up, why bother being here?" Katy replied, crossing her arms. Katy knew the subject would get brought up, but she hadn't anticipated the acrid feeling bubbling up in her mouth.

"I'm worried," said Evelyn. "You guys are like the best of friends and I don't want that getting ruined."

"Yeah, you were so worried about that when you rammed the idea of romance down my throat." Katy tried swallowing the bitter taste in her mouth, but found that she had no spit.

Evelyn gently threw up her hands.

"Everything was there," she reasoned. "At least I thought it was. I thought all you needed was a step in the right direction."

"A shove is more like it," Katy spat back.

"I was just presenting the facts," Evelyn remarked defensively. "I didn't demand that you sleep with him the next time you saw him."

"But you should've known better!" Katy yelled out. The words echoed off the walls, startling Katy enough to quiet her voice. "I just got out of a serious relationship. And I'm still so messed up because of it." Katy stopped and pressed her lips together. Verbalizing what she had been trying to deny all along was too much, and she wasn't ready to cry in front of Evelyn. Not now, not when Katy wanted to be mad at her. "Anyone who is half as smart as you think you are would've waited before unloading that bit of false information."

"I'm sorry about that. I genuinely thought you were already over Alex. I did," said Evelyn. "But how can it be false information? I was just telling you what I saw. And for crying out loud – can you blame me? You and Ben basically had verbal sex with each other on a daily basis."

"Do you *have* to use that term?" Katy cringed. "It's calling joking around! Banter, for fuck's sake!"

"Anyone within a ten foot radius could have seen that you two had crazy chemistry," Evelyn replied. "And since Ben obviously had feelings for you, I only thought it was fair to put the idea in your head."

"Do you see the problem there?" Katy snapped. "You're always pushing me to do stuff that you are so sure is best for me. It doesn't matter if it'll actually be beneficial, just if you think it will be. And now...now I lost my best friend and...it's basically all your fault."

"Oh, cut it with the dramatics. That's why I'm here in the first place," said Evelyn. "If you keep avoiding the shifts you have with Ben, you'll just be making a bad situation worse. I need you to talk with him, sort it out. Apologize. Do something."

Katy lowered her eyebrows.

"I get it," she said. "You came here to, once again, tell me what to do."

Evelyn pressed her lips together and sighed.

"You're upset. I understand. And maybe I'm the last person you want advice from right now. But that doesn't make what I have to say any less important. Try to talk with him. If not today, then at least the next time you two work together. And I'm not saying this because you think I'm some control freak right now." Evelyn paused. "I just want everything to be all right."

"Fat chance of that happening," Katy muttered.

Evelyn sighed again and picked up her coat.

"I'm going to head out now. Maybe you'll understand what I'm trying to say when you've calm down." Evelyn shimmied on her coat and rewrapped her scarf around her neck. "Ben's already there now. Maybe you could drop by."

Katy clenched her teeth.

"Can you quit it with your suggestions?"

"My bad." Evelyn picked up her purse and looked Katy over once more. "I'll talk to you later, okay?"

Katy answered with a twitch of her eyebrow. Evelyn opened her mouth as if to say something more, before closing it and letting herself out.

Katy watched the door shut before turning around and flopping on the couch. Katy grabbed the remote and turned on the TV with extra force. She was suddenly aware of how the cloth of the couch felt against her skin and the way her body sunk into it.

After a few commercials, Miller made his way out of Maria's bedroom. He trotted over to the couch and nudged his head under Katy's remote hand. She scratched behind Miller's ear before stroking his side and dropping her hand back down. She stayed in that position, mulling things over in the back of her mind, while the rest of her focused on the television.

Her right hand clicked mechanically at the remote, flipping randomly through channels. An infomercial selling high-performance blenders. A mid-day medical talk show where the host pointed out all the different ways food at the grocery store can kill you. A history special about the civil war. Commercials about going back to school and getting your associate's online, regardless of your situation ("No high school diploma? We might be able to help!"). Commercials for law firms, vocational schools, electric wheelchairs, patent lawyers – commercials meant for very specific demographics, the usual suspects who stayed home on a weekday. After a while, Katy nodded off. She woke up after what she thought was merely seconds, only to realize that two hours had passed. She woke up groggy and disoriented, yet determined to put her winter clothes back on and get outside.

Katy sat up, trudged over to the closet by the front door, and started placing things on her without really registering what she was doing. She was relying almost entirely on muscle memory, because her conscious mind was definitely not controlling anything. After her coat was on and her scarf was tightly wound, she grabbed her bag and went outside again.

The world had long-since woken up at this point, but the air was still crisp. The air still whipped and slammed itself against anything in its way, sending icy shards into any unprotected piece of skin. Katy made her way down the hill to Commonwealth Ave.

Katy stopped at the corner, numbly studying the trolley tracks that divided the street. Without making anything that her brain could register as a proper decision, Katy turned and began to walk parallel with the tracks from the sidewalk in the direction of downtown Boston.

All around her was snow and dirty cars and Boston University students making their way down the sidewalks or across the street. The sun was cordoned off by a layer of gray sky. They weren't even clouds, discernable in texture and color. The sky was just a solid, dirty shade of gray. Katy almost thought the sky was trying to mimic the snow on the ground, but even the snow demonstrated the full scope of shades, from pure white to soot black. The sunless skies did highlight the pallid world that the snow had created, however. Even the colors of the cars and restaurant signs were muted.

Katy kept walking, her feet occasionally sliding on a patch of ice that hadn't been properly salted. Commonwealth Ave eventually connected with Kenmore Square. Katy walked through the area, crossing streets when need be, and continued down the street as she tromped under a few highway overpasses and across Massachusetts Avenue.

The sky's slowly darkening gray and the way traffic was picking up let Katy know that rush hour was beginning. It was nearing the end of the day. Ben's shift would almost be done. Some portion of her unconsciousness commanded her legs to walk a little faster. God only knows how long she'd been out already.

Katy mindlessly turned right and followed the road across several of Boston's tourist attractions: Newbury St, Copley Square, the Boston Public Library, Neiman Marcus. The paved sidewalks turned to icy redbrick and the journey became slightly more perilous. The increasingly slippery sidewalks forced Katy out of whatever muted reverie she had been in for the past few hours and into where she needed to put her feet.

The streetlamps in this part of town looked as rustic and old-fashioned as the redbrick homes that stood behind them. The sky gave up the gray for a diluted black, the lights from the lamps bouncing off the snowdrifts and onto the streets. Katy waited at the corner to cross Tremont Street, hung a left after a few blocks, and found herself in front of South End Collections.

She knew where she was going all along. At least part of her knew. But now that she was there, every fiber of her being understood why, and panic quickly swept in. Katy ducked down and sat on the bench by the door. She'd rather talk after he had finished his shift and was away from everyone else. Away from customers, away from whatever underlings they had scheduled to help out that day – and especially away from Evelyn. She wasn't ready to see Evelyn again yet.

It seemed like an eternity, waiting on the cold bench and staring off into nothing. Her head jerked up in anticipation every single time she heard the front door's bell chime. And, every time, when she saw that it was a customer coming or going, she dropped her head back to its original position.

Part of her felt like a fool for being outside like this. What if Evelyn went on break and saw Katy there? Then she'd have no choice but to confront and be confronted. And Katy wasn't even sure if she had made it in time. For all she knew, it could be past six and Ben was already on his way home. Or maybe today was the day he went out the back door and walked down the alleyway instead. But Katy wasn't about to check the time or the back alley. Her legs and arms felt paralyzed – frozen – to the bench.

After what felt like the one millionth jingling of the front door's bell, Katy's head snapped up to see a 5'10" man dressed in a thin woolen hat and a coat that couldn't possibly shield him from the wind.

"Ben?" Katy squeaked out.

Ben raised his eyebrows and darted his head to the side before looking down and at Katy.

"What are you doing out here?" he asked, his raised eyebrows now furrowed.

"I wanted to talk to you."

Ben adjusted his stance on the sidewalk.

"Oh."

Katy stood up and opened her mouth, but found nothing coming out. She gave a grimaced sigh and rolled her eyes, praying she'd find what she needed to say. Why didn't she spend that ridiculously long walk thinking about what she'd actually tell him? What's a better way of saying, "Hey, sorry for sleeping with you when I knew you had a crush on me, only to realize that I only see you as a friend"?

What's a better way of wording that?

Ben crossed his arms.

"Listen, it's okay," he said. "I get it. A girl doesn't leave first thing in the morning and then avoid you because she was happy with her decision."

Tears began to form around Katy's eyes.

"It's more than that. It's…it's complicated. I just…" Katy expected the rest of the sentence to come out, but the words just hung there until they faded into the distance.

"I'm just not happy about this," said Ben. "At all. You didn't seem like the type to do something like that."

"I'm not…I'm really not…" Katy found herself murmuring.

Ben stood there for a moment, looking over Katy. After a few seconds, Ben started to laugh in a way that Katy had never heard before.

"It sucks, you know? I care about you, a lot." Ben raised a hand and cradled his neck with it. "Jesus, I think I fell for you the second you first came into the store."

"Ben…"

"And I get it. I'm the friend," he interrupted. "I'm *always* the friend. I'm resigned to it. And it wouldn't be the first time I loved –" Ben paused, his face contorting as if he had bitten into something rotten. "– cared, for someone who didn't feel the same. It sucks, but that's just how things are sometimes." Ben laughed again. "Just – geez, Katy – you got my hopes up."

"I didn't mean to…" Katy squeaked out.

Ben stood to the side as the door opened. A customer silently made his way past the two and across the street.

Ben placed a fist to his mouth, gazing after the customer, before turning back, his face reddened.

"Did you even know I had feelings for you?" His hand darted away from his mouth and accusingly at Katy. "No, don't answer that. 'Cause I know either way, I'll get pissed. Either you were oblivious even after all we've been through, or you understood fully and decided that I was an easy target. So don't answer that."

"Ben..."

"Honestly? Just stop. I thought I'd be upset seeing you again. But now I see that I'm just angry. Angry and disappointed. So to keep me from getting even more upset, I'm going to go now."

"But..."

"No. Goodnight."

Ben turned and walked away from Katy, turning down the first street that intersected with the store's. Katy turned and looked through one of the shop's front windows and saw Evelyn and Josh staring out at her from the registers.

Suddenly, being near the store suffocated her, like everything surrounding it was sucking the air out of her. She turned and ran in the opposite direction, hoping to get as far as she could before well-meaning Evelyn and well-meaning Josh came out and wanted to know if everything was okay.

Because everything was not. Any idiot who was semi-literate in body language could tell you that everything was definitely not okay.

Katy kept running down the street, her shoes smacking against the redbrick until one of them hit a patch of ice. Katy's feet flung out from under her, causing Katy to career and crash into a snow bank.

"Goddammit!" Katy cried out. Ignoring anyone who could possibly be within ear- or eyeshot, Katy cried out another string of swears. She pulled her legs into her chest, dropped her head in between them, squeezed her eyes closed, and sobbed.

Abby Rosmarin

Chapter 23

And that was just how it was. Katy returned to work the next day, reminding herself over and over and over again that at least she wouldn't be working with Ben until the following Tuesday. Evelyn, in all her infinite wisdom, dropped the issue of Ben. And that must've been hard – c'mon, think of all the things Evelyn could've said to Katy? "Don't worry, he'll calm down." "Things will look up. You just need to be patient." "Give him space. Oh, and by the way, you're a vapid bitch for sleeping with your best friend."

And that was just how it would be. Ben ignored her presence and Katy dreaded the days they worked together. Day after day, she retreated into the stock room, desperately trying to spend the endless hours sorting and resorting, checking paperwork, and sitting in Andrea's office, leaning back in the chair, gazing morosely at the office with her head upside down.

Katy avoided any and all work that needed to be done near the cash registers. Andrea would probably reprimand her if Andrea ever cared to come in and observe employee performances. But so what? What was the worse that could happen? Katy would get fired? At this point, Katy was almost hoping for it. She started dreading work in a way that she never had before. It went far beyond the usual hesitation. She'd step into the store and feel like the walls were about to close in on her.

The worst was when Ben stopped giving her the silent treatment and started giving her terse statements and commands. He'd ask to her to continue inventory and she'd want to start crying. The silent treatment at least hinted that he was upset. To be perfectly trite: it showed that he cared. But the apathy? That's what really got to her. That told her that he had shut her out completely. She wanted to do something, say something – *anything* – to change everything around and make things like how they were before. But time and time again, she was at a loss for words. That is, the times when she wasn't holding herself back from scrambling out of the door, never to return.

She wished she could tell him what had been forming in a small part of her mind – a portion that couldn't quite translate the thought into concrete words and was therefore kept locked inside. What she wanted to tell him was that she had figured it out. After weeks and weeks of agony and second-guessing and trying her best to forget that infamous night, she had figured it out.

It wasn't rebound that caused her to go at Ben like she was a Russian spy bent on seducing the president. Her break-up with Alex might've played into it a little bit. It might've caused her to jump to conclusions and hope for a quick fix. But the underlying reason wasn't that.

It was bad storylines. Bad, predictable storylines.

She had given it some thought about it before, but now she was ready to admit it to herself. How many movies – how many books and television shows – had the best guy friend turn out to be the one after all? The protagonist, after countless and fruitless romantic endeavors, realizes that her best friend – the one she had shared everything with since the beginning and felt completely comfortable around – was actually the one for her, and she had fallen in love without realizing it. And the reader knows from the get-go that the guy friend has always had a not-so-subtle crush on the protagonist. They get together and life is perfect. Everything is solved. All loose ends are tied up.

But then again, in chick literature, if the storyline doesn't include this soul mate of a best friend, then the original love interest that had broken her heart always comes back in the end. And she wasn't foolish enough to think that Alex would ever be returning with those flowers in his hand, begging for her forgiveness.

And where was the storyline where the protagonist wakes up after having sex with her best guy friend and realizes that, in retrospect, it had felt like having sex with a relative? Where was the part where the protagonist finally understands that sometimes people are friends and only friends for a reason?

All those tired and overused tropes had long ago implanted that idea into her brain. An idea just subtle enough that she didn't even think about acting on it until she was completely lost in life and staring at her best friend from the safety of a bookstore stairwell. All her talk about chick literature being unrealistic went out the door because, in the end, chick literature had won and she had been convinced that going after Ben was the exact route to go down.

It was sometime in March when Katy came home to find an email from one of the job search sites that she had once used. The content of the email informed her that, once again, she hadn't logged into the site in a while and that a login was required in order to keep her account. Katy looked over the email one more time before deleting it and checking on something else.

Job sites had long ago proven their uselessness to Katy. So many false leads and dead ends – it wasn't worth it. Katy still believed that she would have more luck looking for a significant other on a dating website than she ever would looking for a meaningful job on a job site.

Matchmaker, matchmaker: make me a match.

Katy couldn't remember exactly when her fingers started typing out the address of a well-known dating website. It felt like something inside her had suddenly snapped into focus and was now propelling her forward. She went from idly clicking at links to creating a profile. Was it the realization that the online dating world faired better than the online job market? To some part of her, that actually made sense.

Because, seriously – what was the worst thing to happen? For all she knew, the ever-mysterious and elusive "one" could be right around the corner in the form of a single man online. Katy typed away, answering all the questions that she knew she could answer easily – a lot more easily than "what are your job skills?" or "what is your dream career?" Name, age, a little bit about herself...upload a picture and *violá*, she was done. And the true beauty was that she didn't have to search if she didn't want to. Unlike the job sites – where she was always hunting after *them* – she could just sit back and see who would email her.

And, within a day, she did get such an email. He introduced himself as Randy. His "About Me" on his profile portrayed him as a sweet guy with an administrative assistant job and a cat in the Boston area. His picture revealed a sheepish grin and a possible fear of getting his picture taken. After a few emails back and forth, Randy admitted that he wasn't a fan of communicating via the internet and asked for her number. After a moment of hesitation, Katy gave it to him.

Within minutes of sending the message containing her contact information, Katy's phone lit up with a brand new number on its screen.

"Hello?" Katy answered gingerly.

"Ah...h-hello. Um, Katy?" A slow yet nervous voice responded.

"Yes, this is her..." Katy trailed off.

"Oh, good, good then. Um, this is Randy. Do you remember me?"

The question struck Katy oddly.

No, no I don't remember you. I have the memory of a goldfish. And what's this contraption that I'm holding by my ear?

"Of course. How are you?" Katy responded instead.

"Oh, good, good..." Randy answered. After a pause, he quickly added: "Oh, oh – and you? How are you?"

"Doing alright. Can't complain." Katy started pacing around her bedroom. There was something about the cadence in his voice that was making her anxious.

"Good..." Randy answered.

Silence quickly took over the conversation. Katy's pacing soon expanded out into the living room.

"So, is there anything you would like to talk about?" Randy asked.

"Well, now that you mentioned it," Katy quipped, "I could always fancy a casual chat about nuclear disarmament."

Randy paused.

"Oh. Okay."

Katy cleared her throat.

"I was just joking."

When Randy didn't respond, Katy continued: "Just I'm usually not asked so frankly what I'd like to talk about. So, I answered with a joke."

"Ah. Well, it – it was funny."

Katy started pacing into the kitchen.

"So, I see you're an administrative assistant," Katy said and immediately grimaced. Was this a conversation or a phone interview?

"Oh, yes. Yeah, I like it."

Now it was Katy's turn to respond with: "Oh. Okay."

Katy walked over to the windows in the living room.

"So – do you like any bands? What music do you like?" Katy could hear Maria's keys jingling behind the front door.

"Um. Oh you know. I like everything."

"Everyone says they like everything," Katy responded, "but no one really does. There's always some genre that they hate."

"That's true."

Katy pressed her palm against her forehead.

"So, are there any genres that you don't like?"

"Oh, well, I don't know. I can't think of any right now."

"Oh."

Another pause filled the conversation. Katy turned around to see Maria placing her bag on top of the kitchen counter and focusing her gaze over toward Katy. Katy turned back to the window.

"We should go on a date," he said.

"What?" Katy yelped.

"To get to know each other. I believe a date is an appropriate thing to do now."

Katy stammered over her words. She placed a hand on the cold windowpane.

"Um, you know, I'll get back to you on that. Details and whatnot," she coughed out. "Well, you know, I really gotta go. But it was, um, great, talking with you."

"Oh. Okay, then. I guess I will talk to you later."

"Yeah, I guess so. Bye." Katy snapped shut her phone and looked over exasperatingly at Maria.

"So…what exactly did I just walk in on?" Maria asked.

"Only the most awkward phone conversation in the history of the entire world," Katy responded.

"Yikes." Maria shimmied off her coat and turned to open the coat closet. "Who was on the other line?"

"Um." Katy cocked her head to one side in an effort to find the words that she wanted to say. "Some guy."

"Really?" Maria gave an unsure smirk. "Some guy?"

"Yeah, some guy."

"Do I know him?" Maria asked.

"No, I don't believe so."

"Well, how'd you meet him?"

Katy felt a blush wash over her face.

"Off a dating site."

"A dating site?" Maria repeated. "What were you doing on a dating site?"

"Um…" Katy could swear there was a reason when she had signed up, but she was hard-pressed to find one now. "Just because, I guess."

"I gotta admit, hun, I don't think that's such a great idea," Maria said slowly.

"Because I end up having ridiculous conversations like that?" Katy offered.

"Because I don't think it's such a great idea," Maria repeated. Maria closed her eyes and scratched her forehead before continuing: "You had a really bad break-up a few months ago. You and Ben haven't been on speaking terms for a while, now. I mean, the last thing you should be doing is looking for someone to date."

"What's wrong with looking for someone to date?" Katy responded defensively.

Maria shook her head.

"Because you don't operate like that," she said. "I mean, Jesus, you were miserable at the bookstore, and looking for a new job – like, an actual career. And it seemed like the second things got serious with Alex, you dropped that completely. I mean, hell – remembering that publishing job? You had a job offer in San Francisco and you decided to just give it up. And I am willing to bet money that part of the reason why you gave it up was because you were so focused on your relationship problems."

Katy bit the inside of her cheek.

"It was a job interview. It wasn't a full-out offer."

"You're missing the point." Maria paused, before laughing quietly. "It's kind of ironic. You always get on books and movies that have everything revolve around the main character's love life. But here you are, living out the most flawed chick lit I've ever come across." Maria laughed again. "I mean, finding a boyfriend and letting everything else just fall by the wayside, thinking you've fallen for your best guy friend...minus the part where it's all gone to hell, it has all been one big chick lit cliché." Maria paused and smirked. "And here I am, the roommate-slash-best female friend who always lets you know when you've screwed up. Now *I'm* a chick lit cliché as well."

Katy shrugged her shoulders and looked at the ground.

"I finally got under your skin with all that chick lit stuff, huh," Katy said finally.

"Doesn't mean I'm going to start hating it."

"But I did get under your skin," Katy repeated.

"You're missing the point again."

The apartment quickly filled up with silence after that. Katy looked back down at her feet, unsure what to do with them next.

"Do you really think my life has turned into one gigantic chick lit cliché?" Katy asked quietly.

Maria breathed out a sigh.

"Not fully. Just, that you seem to be going down the same path that most of those characters go down," said Maria. "The only difference is that real life doesn't work the way made-up stories do."

Katy looked to her right and out through the living room windows. After a moment she turned back.

"What do you think I should do?" Katy asked.

"If this were a story, this is the part where I'd say something like, 'Only you can decide what's next.' But since this isn't a book or a movie, I'm going to tell you exactly what to do, which is get your shit back together."

Katy broke into a smile.

"What would I do without you?" she asked.

"You'd be antagonist-less, I'll tell you that," Maria responded. "And I know this is bad timing, but: Jacob's coming over tonight. Is that all right?"

"If I say no, will you cancel?"

"Of course not."

"Well, then," Katy laughed. "You drive a hard bargain, but: yeah, it's okay for him to come over."

"Thank you." Maria smiled.

"Would you like me to disappear?" Katy smirked.

"Of course not. You're always welcome," Maria replied. "But if you stay in the living room, I'm putting on a romantic comedy."

"Now why would you want to punish your boyfriend like that, after all we've talked about?" Katy shook her head.

"Because you didn't actually get under my skin about all that chick lit stuff."

"I have failed as a friend," Katy stated. She smiled, shook her head, and added: "Actually, it's all right. I've got some things to do anyway."

"Well, have fun, then," Maria replied.

Katy retreated to her room to grab her bag. She came back out, put on her coat, and made her way outside. Ben didn't get out of work on Sundays until 6, so, as long as she opted for public transit this time instead of semi-consciously walking, she would definitely get to the store in time. She might've previously veered off track and landed straight into chick lit land, but how many chick lits had the main character recognize how unpredictable life is and then apologize to those she had hurt when she tried forcing things to fit into place?

Chapter 24

The sun had set by the time Katy got off the train. Ben wouldn't be getting off his shift for another hour or so. Katy contemplated avoiding the store until Ben got off work, but she quickly nixed the idea. She wasn't ready to risk losing her motivation, nor was she ready for a repeat of their last major interaction. She continued on with a militant pace, her mind now blank. She crossed the street to South End Collections and gingerly opened the door, her eyes already on the front desk to see if Ben was manning the registers.

"Hey, Josh," Katy said to the person who was actually manning the registers.

"Hey Katy – how've you been?" Josh greeted.

Katy searched around the room.

"Been pretty good. How about you?"

"Eh, other than midterms, all right," Josh replied. "Are you working tonight?"

"Nah, not tonight. Just decided to drop by. Do you know where Ben is, by any chance?"

"I believe on the second floor with Evelyn. They're reorganizing the books, or something like that."

"Sounds like fun," Katy said, her head now in the direction of the stairs. "I'll talk to you later, okay?"

"Of course. Later."

Katy rushed up the stairs and across the floor, her eyes darting down each aisle before finding Evelyn and Ben by a pile off books.

"Hey," Katy heard herself say.

Ben and Evelyn turned around. Surprised expressions smacked both of their faces, leaving both of them with raised eyebrows and slacked jaws.

"Hey," Evelyn responded. Evelyn's words snapped Ben out of his stunned reverie and instantly returned his attention to the stack of books on the ground.

"Hey," Ben said in monotone, his face already toward the books.

Katy swallowed.

"Um, Ben? Can I talk with you, for a minute?"

"Okay, shoot." Ben's gazed remained downwards as he picked up his clipboard.

Katy pursed her lips.

"Alone? Maybe in the break room?"

"Why? We can talk here." Ben picked up a pen, scribbled something on the clipboard, and set both back down, never once looking up.

Katy rolled her eyes to the ceiling, desperately searching for the right words but finding her lips trembling instead.

Evelyn brushed her hands against her jeans.

"You know, I'm going to check on Josh. Heavens knows he shouldn't be left to his own devices for too long."

Ben shot a look aimed directly at Evelyn. Evelyn ignored it and focused on Katy.

"I'll see you guys in a few," she said with a tone of finality that Katy had never heard before, and exited the second floor.

Katy turned, pressed her back against one of the bookshelves, and slid down to the floor so she could be at eye level with Ben.

"Ben..." Katy began.

"Mhmm," Ben brashly hummed out, his eyes still locked on the ground. He shuffled a few books around before picking up the clipboard again. He scribbled something else on the paper before placing it back down and picking up a few more books. He turned to the shelves, pushed a few books around, and returned to the pile on the ground. He then picked a few up from the pile, intently studying the titles.

"Please stop," Katy said.

Ben placed down the books and looked over.

Katy stared back, her lips suddenly paralyzed. Everything seemed to freeze. The whole store seemed to go silent.

Katy closed her eyes.

"I'm sorry."

Ben shrugged and picked up a few more books, narrowing his eyes at their titles.

"Sorry for what?"

"Ben..." Katy said more firmly. "I'm sorry."

Ben put down the books again and crossed his arms, his back now slumped against the opposing bookshelf, his eyes back on Katy.

"It was an impulsive move and I wasn't considering how you'd feel and it was wrong and I'm sorry," Katy said, trying her best not to retreat from his stare.

Ben pursed his lips and crossed his arms tighter.

"But I want to let you know that..." Katy looked away, pressing a palm to her forehead before sliding it over her hair. "That I didn't see it as rebound – that I genuinely thought something was there and that I had to act on it, and now."

Ben shifted his shoulders.

"Oh."

"I just...the breakup with Alex really did mess me up," Katy looked back up. "I wasn't ready to admit it to myself, but it really did. I felt like I had given everything to him and once he was gone, I wasn't sure where to go next. And instead of facing it, I pushed it under the rug."

She watched as Ben's face tightened. Katy broke his gaze, stared at the carpet, and coughed.

"Look, I don't know if Evelyn mentioned this, but she was the actually one who brought up the idea in the first place." Katy stopped and winced. "I'm not trying to say that I'm blaming her. I'm just trying to set up the background. I guess."

Katy paused. When Ben said nothing, she continued: "But when she told me that we were obviously meant for each other, I latched onto it. I was still hurting and that just made sense. I mean, why not? It seems like common hat that the best friend eventually becomes something more. And part of me really wanted it to be so. It made things so much easier. I mean…I can't tell you how much it sucked waking up the next morning and realizing that I was wrong." Katy scraped her lower lip with her teeth and shook her head. "I didn't want it to be. I didn't want to recognize that I had blindly ran on what I was just hoping to be true. I didn't want to recognize that, suddenly, it wasn't."

Katy stared at Ben, searching for a response. He shifted his shoulders, readjusted his legs, and continued his silence.

"But that's just it: I *had* been impulsive. I didn't take a second to think. That, in the end, while some friendships are meant to turn romantic, some aren't. Sometimes people are just meant to be friends." Katy sighed. "I was too busy avoiding what I should have been dealing with to even consider the latter."

"But how can you say that?" Ben blurted out. He took in a breath and hooked one hand over his shoulder. "I mean, how can you just assume we're the latter? What if Evelyn hadn't said anything – or what if you hadn't been so quick to react? What if this is all just shitty timing? What then?"

Katy scraped at her bottom lip again. This wasn't anything that she hadn't already thought about before. She had found an answer for herself, but was it good enough for Ben? She had yet to find a better one, so it would have to do.

"Does it matter at this point?" Katy asked slowly. "If we play the 'what if' game, we'll go insane. Our friendship will suffer. Things will become too complicated and nothing good could come from it." Katy rubbed her eyes. "What happened, happened, and that's it. Maybe the best thing is to just move forward from this, try to go back to normal –"

"I love you," Ben stated flatly. "And, if you didn't already figure that out by now, now you know that I love you. Maybe our friendship worked when you didn't know – or at least when you pretended you didn't know. But that is in the open now and there's no real way of going back. Our friendship is already ruined."

"I don't think so," Katy responded.

"Why?"

"You say that either I didn't know or I pretended that I didn't." Katy paused, her eyes scanning around the room. "I have to be honest. I didn't know. At least, not consciously. But I think, somewhere in the back of my mind, I always kind of knew you had feelings for me. And it never stopped me from being your friend. But it also didn't make me want to take things to the next level." Katy shrugged. "I don't know. Maybe you're right. But I'd rather we at least try to fix our friendship than give up and decide that things will always be weird." Katy closed her eyes again. "I don't want to lose my best friend. And, even if it's a long shot to end all long shots, I still want to try and be friends again."

Ben tightened his mouth into a skewed dot.

"What if I can't?"

Katy's face dropped.

"What do you mean?"

"Maybe you can go on about starting over again, but I don't know if I can," Ben said squarely. "There are lines that get crossed." Ben closed his eyes and leaned his head back until it rested against the shelves. "Things were a lot easier when I believed I didn't have a chance with you. But you got my hopes up. You broke my heart. Intentional or not, that is what happened. And I don't know if I'm ready to be friends again."

Katy sat there, staring at the ground, pressing her lips together. She felt like the world outside their swatch of carpet had disappeared from existence altogether. Her body felt weighted down, anchored to where she was sitting, the vast nothingness outside of their bubble pressing down on her. Katy became very aware of her breathing, which seemed to slow down with every intake. She burdened her mind for what to say next, desperately trying to find the words that could put the conversation back on track towards reconciliation.

"This sucks," she said finally.

"I know."

Katy kept observing her heavy, sluggish breathing. Ribcage out, ribcage in. Lungs taking in shallow, winded bits of air.

"Can we at least be civil?" Katy said after a moment, her words quickening with each syllable. "For God's sake, we see each other all the time. The solution can't be to pretend the other doesn't exist." Katy stopped herself as her words edged toward pure hysteria and continued on more slowly. "Can we at least do that? And see where it goes from there?"

Ben rubbed at his eyes and sighed.

"I guess there really isn't any alternative, is there?"

"Not unless you feel like quitting."

"Hey, I like my job, thank you very much," Ben replied. Ben smirked and opened his mouth to say something, only to let it hang in suspension. After a moment, he said: "So that's that then, huh?"

"I guess," Katy said, still feeling weighted down to the floor. "I don't want it to be, though."

Both sat there for a while in silence, their eyes half closed.

"I really need to finish this project before I punch out," Ben said finally, pushing himself back up.

Katy grabbed a shelf for support and did the same.

"Have fun with that." She brushed away the imaginary dust on her jeans. "I'll see you tomorrow, then."

"As per usual," Ben replied.

Katy grabbed her bag and started walking back down the aisle. As she reached the end, something stopped her and compelled her to turn around. She could feel the words bubbling inside of her, rushing up to break the surface. There was no way she could keep those words down, regardless of how they might sound.

"Ben?"

Ben turned his head towards Katy.

"Hmm?"

"I really hope we can be friends again."

Ben turned back to his clipboard and nodded his head.

"We'll see."

*

By the time Katy got home, Maria and Jacob were already snuggling together on the couch. The lights were off, but the living room shimmered with a blue aura given off by the television. Katy quietly shut the front door behind her and tiptoed into her room, giving out a quick walk-by greeting as she retreated into her room and closed her bedroom door behind her as well.

Once inside, Katy grabbed her laptop and sat her on bed, her back pressed against the wall. She decided that, in the spirit of trying to piece things back together, she would try one more time to look at graduate schools.

She started out her search with the same fervor that had sparked her trek to the bookstore to talk with Ben. But after a few clicks around a few websites, Katy shut her laptop.

She was being quite meticulous, searching for schools based on location and campus amenities, but the second she wondered whether or not she should search for schools based on what she would get her Master's in, she stopped and asked herself the proverbial, "What am I doing?" The answer made her close her laptop and put it back on her desk.

And what *was* she doing? Here she was, looking at all these different schools, located all around America and beyond. And for what? She couldn't even decide on a field of study. She did not want to be yet another college graduate slinking into grad school because she didn't know what else to do.

The more she thought about it, the more she realized that she didn't want to go to graduate school. It was an option that she had played with because it seemed like a surefire way to prove that she could achieve something. But, at best, it would have only helped her in postponing the real world – where, regardless, she would have had to make actual life decisions.

This wasn't the route she wanted to go down. If she didn't feel satisfied working at the bookstore, then it was time to start up the job search again. If she didn't like the direction her life was going, then she had to figure out a way to change that path. For her, going back to school would only delay the inevitable and she would only be going back for that exact reason. If she found a job that required extra schooling, so be it. But she'd cross that bridge when she reached it. Right now the focus needed to be on what she actually wanted to do next, and what she needed to do to get herself to where she wanted to be. And one of those steps involved calling back Tabby. The San Francisco job was more than likely filled by now, but at least she could plead her case. If any other type of job popped up, she'd at least be able to go for it, even if she stumbled and failed miserably along the way.

Chapter 25

It didn't surprise Katy when she found out that there were no job positions open at Maurice Fielding Publishing. But Tabby was empathetic and promised that she'd keep Katy in mind for any upcoming jobs at any of their branches. Katy expressed her gratitude, but understood fully that lightening doesn't strike twice. What she had given up might never come back around again.

Not letting the phone call deter her, Katy finished that day by logging back into the job sites that she had once frequented. Her focus was on publishing jobs, both in and out Boston, but she decided to keep her eye out for other things as well. She felt like she would enjoy publishing, but who knew what else might strike her fancy? What if she'd enjoy grant writing or perhaps even technical writing? There was so much out there and, for once, she wasn't afraid to step her foot into unknown territory. Life figures itself out. The important thing for her to do was to just keep going forward and recognize opportunities when they presented themselves.

It was sometime after that revelation that Katy recognized how much emphasis she had been putting on finding a new job. It was obvious that she was trying to do more than just get out of retail. She was trying to find out who she was and what she wanted do with her life. But there was (hopefully) more to life than just a career. There were so many things that she wanted to do – things that she had been putting off doing. It was then that she decided that she would put a bit of her paycheck away every week so that, within a year's time, she would finally have enough money to take a trip to Europe. She wanted to start with the UK, and, if she could continue saving, maybe spend a little time every year, or every other year, in a different part of Europe.

It could be done. She knew it could be done. She just needed to keep focused. She was the only one who could make it happen; no one else was going to save the money for her.

Work at South End Collections carried on. The hang out nights between Katy and Ben were still on an indefinite hiatus. Their usual banter was still on leave as well. But Ben did his best to remain friendly. And Katy did her best to be patient. She recognized that her wanting Ben to just magically become best friends with her again was a selfish wish – that Ben would return when he was ready, if ever.

Around the end of April, Andrea dropped a bombshell. She announced that she was officially promoting Ben to assistant manager.

The fact that Ben was the one promoted to assistant manager wasn't the bombshell. Ben had been there the longest and was definitely the most dedicated. What Andrea revealed next was: once Ben learned the ropes, Andrea would be stepping down. She'd still own the store and still be in charge of some of the major overhead like the accounting responsibilities, but she would step down as the main person in charge and Ben would then be promoted to manager.

"My heart's no longer in it," she explained. "As you can see, I've become less and less of a presence here at the Collections. But Ben has been nothing short of stellar and I know he'll make an amazing manager."

"But what will you do with all your free time?" quipped Evelyn.

"Paint," Andrea answered matter-of-factly.

"Really." The word slipped out of Katy's mouth.

"Yeah, really," Andrea responded. "I've always loved to paint, and I think it would be nice to devote more time to it, especially if I'm not working 50-plus hours a week."

"Wow. I just. Wow." Katy had been trying to be more deliberate with what she said, but her statements were downright unconscious rambles at that point.

"I'll still be around," Andrea reassured. "It's just time for me to move on toward that next chapter in my life."

In a sense, Katy wasn't that shocked. Something had clicked in Andrea after her wedding. Maybe getting married was what she needed to wake up and realize that she didn't want to be spending every waking moment at the store anymore. She had something else in her life and that something else helped her realize that she wanted something new, something different.

And why not? Katy was sure that, once upon a time, owning a bookstore was Andrea's ultimate dream. And how many people get to pursue their dreams and make them a reality? But somewhere along the line, the dream had turned into a routine. And maybe that routine had started to overshadow all her other dreams. Maybe finding that person to share her life with was a dream of Andrea's as well, a dream she thought would never happen. And maybe fulfilling that goal made Andrea want to move on and do something new. Pursue a different dream.

And again, Katy thought to herself, why not? Dreams don't always die. Sometimes they're satiated and just fade away. Maybe that's what happened with Andrea and South End Collections. And maybe it was time to go after a different dream, even if that one eventually turned into routine, too. Going after a series of dreams – and being unafraid to ditch the ones that stopped being dreams long ago – was an almost admirable way to live a life. It beats many of the alternatives.

Even though Katy was okay with the changes, it still took a few weeks before she would talk with Ben about it. Maybe it was because it would involve talking in a way that required more depth than the conversations they had been having as of late. Maybe it was because that, while Katy was ready to move on and out, Ben wasn't planning on going anywhere, and he was okay with that. Maybe it was bewildering to realize that she and her best friend were on completely different paths in life.

But then again, when the time finally came, Katy didn't even approach the conversation with the expectation that she'd be talking about Ben's new promotion. It simply just slipped out after a particularly long conversation with a patron, who was dissatisfied not only with the store's return policy, but the store's hours, buyback policy, and lack of an elevator.

"...And Barnes and Noble's has escalators. It doesn't inconvenience me to go there instead!" the lady threatened.

"I'm sorry to disappoint you, ma'am, but there's just no place to put an elevator," Katy said in her most fake-flight attendant voice. "I guess we could always knock out a wall and build it outside. But that will take a while."

"Well, then I guess I'll just go to Barnes and Noble's instead," the woman replied curtly.

"Well, I hope you have a wonderful time there." Katy smiled.

As the lady turned and walked out the door, Katy slumped against the Editor's Pick shelf.

"And you want to be the *manager* to this insanity?" Katy sighed out.

Ben, who had been arranging the books in the window display, shrugged.

"Yeah, I do, actually," Ben answered. "I'm pretty psyched about it. I mean, for one, I'll be making way more money – and essentially for the things I do already."

"Only when customers demand to see a manager, they'll be coming to you."

Ben shrugged again.

"Oh well. Hazard of the trade." Ben placed one last book by the window before fully turning around. "I really am excited for this. I mean, there are a lot of things I'd love to do with this store. Maybe bring in more authors, and not just local professors. I'd love to rearrange some shelves, maybe make some room for a children's area – or maybe just more room up front. I've got some great ideas, and as long as Andrea gives me the okay, I'd love to flesh them out."

"I can't believe it," Katy mumbled.

"Can't believe what?"

I can't believe you genuinely like working here, Katy almost said.

"Nothing, nothing," Katy replied, scanning the front windows before pushing herself away from the shelves. "Your ideas sound really cool."

I can't believe that this is as good as it gets for you.

She paused again, this time looking at the cashier's area and the adjacent stairs. Hannah had recently quit in preparation for her upcoming graduation and her move to New York. A new kid – some freshman from Emerson whose name escaped her at the moment – had just been hired in her place. He had only been at the store for a week, but already had the routine down pat.

"If I want to empty out another cart before I clock out, I better start now," Katy finally stated.

"Everyone loves a shipment day," Ben stated, almost mumbling the words to himself.

Katy responded by nodding to no one and making her way back to the storage room.

*

The end of her shift came just as it felt like her knees were ready to give out on her. She hobbled down the road to catch an orange line train, transferred over to the green line, and took a trolley outbound until her neighborhood came into view. She got off and waited until the trolley continued down its tracks before crossing the street. The sun had already set, but the air was dense with lingering humidity. It was going to be a warm May. Katy could only hope that they'd get at least a few weeks of spring before summer barged in.

Katy focused on her apartment building as it came into view, particularly on the darkened figure on the stoop. Katy and Maria had lucked out and never once dealt with a robbery or mugging, but that never stopped Katy from getting apprehensive whenever it was late at night and an aforementioned dark figure was in sight.

Katy got closer, her heart racing, her mind praying fervently that it was just a neighbor smoking. She didn't get her wish as she closed in and saw a familiar figure who, when seeing Katy approach the front steps, stood up with flowers in hand.

"Hey," Alex said quietly.

"Hi." Katy's face went numb.

"Um, I – uh," Alex stammered. "I would've called, but I deleted your number when we uh – when we broke up." Alex raked his fingers through his hair. "So I guess you can say I regret that now."

"Oh."

Katy's ears started to burn as the world around her became less and less focused, to the point where everything outside of a five-foot radius was blurred. Katy started to doubt if a world outside of those front steps even existed at all.

"Well, uh, these are for you." Alex lifted his arm, revealing the bouquet.

Katy delicately wrapped her fingers at the top and waited until the bouquet was cradled against her chest before moving one hand down towards the stems.

"Um...thank you."

Alex looked away while taking in a breath.

"I'll just start by saying that, after being as brash as I was, I really wanted to make sure about this before coming." Alex looked away again. "Listen, I've been...I've been thinking. I feel like I went into our relationship with certain expectations and certain prejudices and I abandoned you the second things didn't seem to be going my way. And that's just not fair – to you or to me. Relationships don't work the way you expect them to and I..." Alex rubbed a hand across his mouth and slightly pulled at his lips as he moved his hand down. "It was a mistake to just leave you like that." Alex pushed his hand past his mouth and through his hair again. "It was a mistake to leave you, period."

Katy's hands started trembling, to the point that she was sure she'd drop the flowers.

"Oh."

"We had something, I know it," Alex continued. "We vibed off each other in a way that...that I hadn't had before." The rhythm of his words quickened. "I don't care if I'm 40 when I marry. I don't care if I'm 80 when I marry. I don't care. I love you, Katy. It kills me that I just let you go like that. It was stupid and selfish and hasty of me." Alex paused to take in a slow breath. "I hope you can give me another chance."

Katy looked down at the flowers. Her grip tightened on them in order to make them stop dancing around under her shaking hands. She could hear the plastic crinkle as her hands changed from trembling palms to solid fists.

"I can't," Katy stated.

Although Katy was looking down, she could tell that it was Alex's turn to stare in disbelief.

"What?"

"I can't." Katy took one last glimpse at the flowers before looking up at Alex. "Listen – I do love you. Even after all this time apart, I'm still in love with you. But I just can't."

Alex's brows lowered, his lips curling inward.

"Why?"

"Because," Katy answered, pausing long enough to snort out a passive laugh. "Because, I don't know, a million reasons. Because it hurt too much when you dumped me. Because you broke my heart. Because there really was something flawed about our relationship in the first place. Because..." Katy closed her eyes and took in a breath. "Because it's just not a good idea for me to be in a relationship right now. Especially in a relationship with you."

Katy let one hand go from the flowers so she could place a palm against her forehead.

"I mean, I recognize that I have no clue what I'm doing," she continued. "I'm trying to figure out so many things and, when I was with you, I was just all about you." Katy laughed again and shook her head. "I mean, shit, there was a job waiting for me in San Francisco and I turned it down because I didn't want to risk our relationship."

"I didn't know that," Alex said flatly.

"I know you didn't. Because I never told you," Katy replied. "God, if that isn't a sign that I'm a little messed up right now, I don't know what is. There's so much that I need to do that

I…if I just get back with you, I'll stay exactly where I am. I won't try and figure anything out and I'll just be content that I'm in love."

"But…isn't that enough?" Alex asked slowly.

Katy pressed her tongue against the back of her teeth, scanning her eyes over this apparent stranger who had just suggested something that she'd never thought the actual Alex would ever suggest.

"No. It's not."

Alex pressed his lips together. The world around Katy seemed to come back into focus, shifting slowly back into reality, amplifying exponentially, to the point that the pitch-black neighborhood was now crisp with life around her. She could hear the cars driving a few streets over. She could see the apartment lights shine through the windows and out into the night's air.

"Do you think that there's a chance we'll ever get back together – sometime?" Alex asked, his voice almost alien to Katy now.

"I don't know," Katy answered. "All I know is that I need to figure out who the hell I am before I can be in a relationship." Katy pushed her arms out, presenting the bouquet to Alex. "You might want your flowers back."

"Keep them," Alex replied, starting down the steps. Once he got to the sidewalk, he stopped and turned back. "If you ever change your mind, I'll just be a phone call away."

"I deleted your number two months ago," Katy stated numbly, her eyes on the stairs in front of her.

"Oh," Alex replied, thrusting his hands into his pockets. "I'll see you around, then."

Alex turned around and made his way down the hill. Katy watched for a moment, his body slowly fading into the darkness, before turning back toward her apartment building. With every ounce of self-control, she steadied her hand to unlock the main door, enter the building, and slowly walk up the stairs.

Katy opened the front door to an empty apartment. Only Miller and the light above the oven occupied the place. Maria must've already headed out. It was just as well. Katy closed the door, latching it shut with her back before sliding down to the ground.

Katy rested her head against the door. Somewhere in between unlocking the door and stepping inside, Katy had started crying. But at some point – perhaps maybe even at the exact same time – Katy had started smiling. Katy placed the flowers on the ground and closed her eyes, smiling and crying and thinking about absolutely nothing.

Abby Rosmarin

Chapter 26

After a tepid June, a hot July month stormed in and caught everyone off guard. It crept up at first, slowly replacing cooler days with warmer temperatures, before charging right through and taking over, declaring itself known.

Maybe it was because she would always be an English major at heart, but Katy couldn't help but draw parallels between the weather and the current events of her life. Things crept in slowly at first, tiny changes here and there, before everything charged in at once and Katy found herself packing up her side of the apartment.

Katy had filled her time during the spring with as many adventures as she could find. She deliberately signed herself up for things that she would never normally do – salsa dancing, indoor rock climbing, sushi making – and allowed Maria to drag her to whatever Maria was doing that particular evening. She complemented her fervent job search with a fervent life search. As hokey as it sounded, Katy needed that balance, a proper reminder that there was more to life than how she got her paycheck.

By the end of June, a Chicago firm responded back to Katy. Their receptionist was going back to school in the fall and they would need a replacement by the end of August. Katy immediately contacted them back and set up a phone interview. A few short days later, Katy got the call letting her know that she had landed the position. The job was more clerical than anything – not directly related to publishing, exactly – but Katy did not hesitate to take the job. While the idea of moving to Chicago scared her enough to want to call back and immediately decline out of pure fear, her response to the company was a thrilled and assertive, "Yes!"

She spent the next week on a new type of search: a search for a place to live. She was eventually able to find a sublet in a decent part of town. It would only be for a few months, but it was at least a place where Katy could call home until she found something more permanent.

If Maria was upset that she was losing her longtime roommate, she definitely didn't show it. But, deep down inside, Katy knew that she was essentially abandoning Maria, leaving her with barely enough time to find a new roommate, and definitely no time to properly find a smaller apartment to live in.

But then again, Maria had never been at a loss for friends. She was the social butterfly of the two: a girl who could easily find a friend who needed a new place to live – or a girl who could easily make friends with a brand new roommate. And there was always Jacob, if their relationship was ready to go to that level. And who knew: it very well could be. For all of Katy's romantic trials and tribulations, Maria's relationship had been relatively drama-free.

Katy decided to continue working at South End Collections until the end of July. She would then have a couple weeks to just enjoy Boston, finalize the packing and shipping of her possessions, and take a moment to breathe before hopping on a plane and starting on a brand new chapter in her life.

Katy gave her notice a full month in advance. And she gave it twice: once to Ben, and another time to Andrea, since it only seemed right that Katy would tell her former boss face to face that she was quitting South End Collections.

Andrea was disappointed. It was clear as day that she was disappointed. She had had a different idea as to what Katy would do with her life. But, really, what was she expecting? Did she think Katy was going to go to grad school, get her Master's in English, continue working at South End Collections – and then what? What would she do after that? What would either of them do after that?

Ben made sure that both he and Evelyn were scheduled to work on Katy's last day. It came at the cost of the new employee's hours, but Katy didn't feel all that guilty about it. She barely knew the new guy and she was filled with enough sentimentality that she didn't want to spend her last day with someone who was just starting out their time at the bookstore.

Her last day, for the most part, went along like any other day. Or, at least it mimicked many aspects of any other day. Katy opened up the store with nervous anticipation, bouncing from point to point like the entire store was filled to the brim with electricity, like something was about to pop. But she went along her tasks, only now with the understanding that this was most likely the last time she'd ever be doing them. The last time she'd unlock the front door. The last time she'd check the stock room before opening.

But, in general, the day had all of the usual events as any day before it. Irate customers. Malfunctioning registers. Loud customers. Aching feet from standing all day. Impatient customers. And customers who would've sworn that Katy had a direct line to every major author and publishing house in the country.

"I cannot *believe* you carry Beverly Brown-Samson," one customer approached Katy as she was resorting some misplaced books.

"Well, we do," Katy replied slowly, her lips puckered in confusion.

"I mean, she's total crap," the customer – a girl in a dark green beanie hat, no older than 20 years old – went on. "It's the same rehashed chick lit over and over again. The same useless female protagonist and the same perfect love interest. I don't know how she keeps making the bestseller's lists."

"Well, from a business standpoint, if she's a bestseller, it would make sense for us to have her books, then." Katy cocked an eyebrow and smirked. "But I totally get what you mean."

"I just worry for the people who read this drivel," the girl in the beanie went on. "I mean, how vapid can you be? What could you possibly learn about the human condition with a girl who just pines over her high school sweetheart until she's back with him again?"

Katy gave a knowing shrug of her shoulders.

"Well, that's one of the reasons why it has its own section, as opposed to being shuffled in with the rest of general literature."

The girl squinted her eyes and rubbed her forehead.

"If I owned a bookstore, I wouldn't even *have* that section," the girl remarked. "I'd take that financial hit. Just on principle alone, I wouldn't carry them. I'm amazed you guys do."

Katy let out a small laugh and shook her head before saying, "Well, we always have the 'Editor's Pick' shelf by the cash registers. There's usually some good finds in there. I'm sure there's something on the human condition there."

"You know, I'll check that out," she replied. "That kind of makes up for this 'Women's' Section." The girl snorted. "Like any real 'woman' would subject themselves to such trivial crap. Am I right?"

Katy pursed her lips to contain a rogue smile.

"I hear you," said Katy. "But, if you don't mind, I just need to get behind you to put a few of these books away."

"Oh, no problem. No problem at all." The girl with the beanie gingerly stepped to the side and made her way to the front of the store. Katy sighed to herself and slowly parted the books on the shelf to make room for the books in her arms.

"You're going to miss that, you know."

Katy turned the other way to see Evelyn leaning against one of the bookshelves.

"How long have you been standing there?"

"Just got here, but I could hear your customer from the aisle over," Evelyn replied. "Is it just me, or did her rant sound a bit familiar to you?"

Katy turned back to the shelves.

"Oh, shut up."

Evelyn shrugged against the bookshelf and pushed herself to an upright position.

"I can't believe you're moving across the country, just to be a receptionist."

"I can't believe they even considered me for it," Katy admitted. "But I'm glad they did."

"Really, though?" Evelyn replied. "Will it worth being a solid time zone away from all your friends?"

"I know it seems ridiculous, but I'm glad I did it." Katy placed the final book in her hand on the shelf before fully turning towards Evelyn. "As I see it, if something else opens up at the company, a current employee is going to have a better chance at getting it than a complete nobody. This is my way in."

Evelyn paused.

"You could have always just searched for longer here. I mean, there's like a million publishing firms in Boston."

Katy closed her eyes, shook her head, and smiled. She wasn't sure exactly what to say now.

"Or New York," Evelyn continued. "If there's a million in Boston, there's probably a billion in New York. And then you're only a bus ride away."

"You know, I think someone might be worried that she'll miss me," Katy said finally.

"Well, duh, I'm going to miss you," Evelyn countered. "This place won't be the same without you."

Katy bit her lower lip.

"I know, I know…but living in a new city – even for a short while – has always been one of the few things that I knew I wanted," Katy explained. "And as much as I love Boston, I feel like if I stay here, I might get back into old habits and never really venture out of my comfort zone. A new city is an adventure, and I'm beginning to like the idea of me as someone who is adventurous."

Evelyn huffed.

"Then go skydiving."

"If the plane engines fail, I might end up doing that, too."

A smile broke through on Evelyn's face, to the point that Evelyn had no choice but to start laughing. And Katy laughed along with her – not because she thought what she said was all that funny – but because Evelyn's laugh was so contagious that laughing along with her seemed like the natural thing to do. But the corners of Katy's mouth started turning downwards and the laughter took on a sad undertone. Katy's heart was pounding by the end of it. This was probably one of the last times she was going to laugh alongside Evelyn like that for quite some time.

This really was the end.

After that realization, Katy's last few hours dragged. The store was filled again with that same condensed electricity and she went at a snail's pace, feeling almost heartbroken that everything she did really was for the last time. It was the last time she'd help out on registers. It was the last time she'd count out the money before opening a new register. It was the last time a customer nagged her about the price of used books versus new.

Well, Katy at least hoped that that one was the last time. She had a hard time imagining she'd miss the customers giving her the third degree.

But even then – even when she focused on how much she wouldn't miss the customers – Katy was at a loss. It wasn't *all* bad, working here. If it had actually been hell, she would've quit before she hit her sophomore year. There was a lot she was going to miss.

But maybe how she felt could be blamed – at least in part – on the fear of flying out to a new state. Maybe it was so heartbreaking because it was easier than dealing with actual reality. Maybe she was romanticizing the store because it was finally over and something completely unknown lay ahead.

But who cared, at that point. She knew she would genuinely miss Andrea and Evelyn…and especially Ben, even though their friendship had never really found its way back to normal. She was going to miss cracking jokes with her friends – and even the college student employees, even though they never seemed to get her sense of humor. She was going to miss walking through the Back Bay and crossing Tremont Street and being surrounded by what she loved most about her city.

To put it simply: she was going to miss her city. No amount of finality could inaccurately romanticize that.

The last half hour was the worst. All work seemed to stop. She was too busy counting down the minutes, knowing all too well that soon everyone would have to say their good-byes. Katy partially wished that Ben would temporarily shut down the store while she finished her shift and bid her farewells, but she knew that type of thing didn't happen in real life.

About ten minutes before her shift ended, Katy wandered into the break room, scooping up whatever items she had left sitting around. The newest newsletter was up, pinned to the bulletin board next to the restaurant menus and a copy of the employee schedule. Along Ben's movie reviews and Evelyn's mini-editorial on the movie industry in Massachusetts, there was a little blurb wishing Katy the best of luck on her new life. There was also a belated wish of good fortune for Hannah, even though she would probably never see it.

But hey, that's what you get when your newsletter only comes out every three or so months. Ben wanted to make it more frequent, and make it public to the customers. Now that he was manager, Katy knew he'd probably put that into effect as soon as possible.

Katy sat there in the break room, taking everything in. She knew this wasn't the last time she'd be here. She'd visit. She'd definitely visit. But it would never be like this, never again. And maybe that was for the best.

No, it was for the best. This chapter had been begging to be closed for a long time, and Katy was finally ready to do so, even though the act alone was scaring her silly.

Not much had changed in the break room since Katy had started working there. Same refrigerator, same lockers, same table and chairs. But Katy couldn't help but feel a bit heartbroken over leaving it all behind, leaving it – leaving the entire store – to potentially change and evolve without her.

Katy took one last look before sighing just loud enough that the sound filled in the emptiness in the room. She made her way out and into the aisles to finish one last bit of organizing before properly punching out.

When the time came, Katy decided to start with Evelyn with her good-byes. She found Evelyn in the stock room, flipping over a few of the shipment receipts.

"Time already?" Evelyn pouted sincerely, putting down her pen.

"I'm afraid so," Katy replied.

Evelyn got up and wrapped Katy in a tight hug.

"I mean it when I say I'm going to miss you," Evelyn said into Katy's shoulder. "We need to grab a drink before you actually fly out."

"Deal. And I'm going to miss you too," Katy said, hugging back tighter. "But you're more than welcome to come out to Chicago. Once I find an actual apartment, you are always welcome there, for as long as you'd like." Katy broke from the hug. "Hell, you could probably even move down to Chicago, if you want. I'll probably need a roommate. And I'm sure Chicago has the same number of acting jobs – maybe even more so."

Evelyn shrugged.

"Eh, I think I'm done with that. Going from casting call to casting call is getting to be too much now. As far as I'm concerned, I think I'm semi-retired."

"Wow," Katy remarked. "I never thought I'd see the day."

"I never thought I would too, but I think it's time for something new," said Evelyn.

"Like what?"

Evelyn shrugged again.

"Eh, I'll figure that out eventually."

Katy hugged Evelyn one more time before heading up to the front. Ben was on registers that day. She prayed that there was no rush of customers. She wasn't ready to say good-bye in between ringing in and buying back books, especially since she knew she wouldn't really get a chance outside of work to say her good-byes to him.

"All right," Katy said flatly as she walked behind the counter. Thankfully there wasn't a customer in sight. "I'm off."

Ben nodded.

"I can't believe it's actually happening," he said.

Both stood there for a while, seemingly stuck in their spots. Katy felt like there were a million things she wanted to say, and every single one of those one million things were bottlenecking in her brain.

"Yeah," was the only thing that made it out.

"This place won't be the same without you," Ben said quietly.

"Yeah, who will be around to make fun of bad books?" Katy forced a smile, but could feel the corners of her mouth turning downwards again.

"If you ever change your mind, there'll always be a spot here for you here," Ben replied after another silence.

"Good to know I'll always have employment in Boston," Katy replied, and the conversation dropped, followed immediately by an uneasy silence.

Katy wanted to step forward and hug Beg. She wanted to rest her head against his shoulder and take in the familiar smell of his shirts. She wanted to go back in time and erase everything that happened in February and make it so their friendship had never changed.

But could it have stayed on that path forever? Would Ben eventually have outgrown his feelings and moved on? Even if her mistake had been wiped from the records, things would've probably come to a head anyway. And Katy had to remind herself that playing the "what if" game was only going to drive her mad. Whatever had happened, happened, and there was no way to sugar coat it or cover it up.

"Well, here's to hoping I don't fail too badly at my new job," Katy replied, picking up the conversation again.

"I know you'll be great." Ben smiled, and Katy couldn't help but smile back.

"Thanks. I definitely need that."

"Hey, it's what I'm here for. Moral support and all that stuff."

Katy looked around the store before returning back to Ben.

"I'll call you soon, okay? Let you know how I'm doing in Chicago?"

Ben's lower lip pushed upward into his smile, turning his smile into a tired grin.

"I'd like that," he said.

"And you'll have to tell me what's going on at the store," Katy continued. "Save all the good crazy customer stories for me in case I ever think about getting into retail again."

"You know I will," said Ben with a warm look in his eyes.

Before the conversation could drop again, before Katy could return the gaze, before Katy could bring herself to finally give Ben one last hug – even though they hadn't so much as shook hands in months – Katy picked up her book bag.

"All right. I'll talk to you soon, okay?"

"Promise?"

Katy raked her teeth across her lower lip.

"I promise."

Katy turned, stepped down onto the main floor, around the counters, and out of the store one last time. The front door's bell gave a muted chime as Katy stepped out onto the sidewalk and made her way down the street.

The roads were still bustling, even though rush hour traffic was starting to taper off. Around her were girls carrying shopping bags by their hips, ladies and gentlemen dressed in their suits with starched-white shirts and blouses, people driving down the streets and honking at every infraction on the road. Above in an apartment somewhere, someone had opened a window and cranked up the volume on their radio, flooding the street with samba music. People of all shapes and sizes were pouring into and out of stores and restaurants, making their way up and down the front steps of their apartment buildings, rushing down the sidewalk at the usual Bostonian breakneck pace. For once, Katy found herself walking slower than the rest, taking in each and every sound of the city, even – especially – the sound her shoes made as they hit the redbrick sidewalk and pushed off to take another step forward.

Acknowledgements

First and foremost, a gigantic thank you to my editor-in-chief, my conspirator, my IT guy, and (last but not least) my husband, Isaac. This book would not be what it is today without you. I would not be the writer I am today without you. I would not be *who* I am today without you. A thank you is not nearly sufficient for all that you do, but that's what you're going to get in this book. So, suck on that.

Another thank you to Jess Kristnofe, my writing partner in crime, my platonic partner in crime. Thank you for everything, including inadvertently living out Katy's life before you had even read the manuscript (although your job in Chicago is way cooler than Katy's).

Thank you to Barbara Shapiro, who was the first to take this far-fetched college student's idea and help shape it to be what it is today. Thank you for going above and beyond for me. Thank you for pointing out the potential. And thank you, thank you, *thank you* for pressuring me to finish this.

Thank you to Michelle Bilodeau, Jeremy Boviard, Rachael Alden (I swear naming the nemesis character "Rachel" was pure coincidence), Chris Markle, Daniel Baker, Christian Rena Morris, Kendyl Maher-Trumble, and everyone else from the most important writer's workshop I would ever be a part of. And to those I forgot: that's what you get for not friending me on social networking sites!

To Maria Rosmarin, a "Maria" that Maria could only dream of being. Thanks for being one of the first readers, and thanks for being an awesome-sister-in-law.

A huge thanks to Bri Stanley Rosmarin, Josiah Rosmarin, Pam Godbois, Sharon McLaughlin Marrama, Robin Croskery Howard, Deb Shaw, Jen Cody Pennington, Abbey Shearer, Catrina Lavoie, Daryle Hillsgrove, Ashley Barajas, Chelsey Gensel, Andrea Taco, Erica Mukhaylov, Julie Tamanaco, Ian Doyle, and Donna Tarasovich for being my early readers. Your reviews, critiques, outside eyes, and just overall support are worth more to me than I can begin to describe. So I won't. I've done enough writing for this book.

And, last but not least, a thank you to Sandra Bullock. Once upon a time, I learned about an (at that time) upcoming movie. An eyeroll and a, "Gee, I wonder how *that* movie ends!" later, I had the beginning ideas for this book. Without you and without that movie, this book wouldn't exist.

(By the way, I eventually saw *that* movie. And I loved it.)

About the Author

Abby Rosmarin is a lot of things, including someone who writes about herself in the third person. A model, a registered yoga teacher, a Bostonian at heart no matter where she lives, Abby is also the author of *I'm Just Here for the Free Scrutiny: One Model's Tale of Insanity and Inanity in the Wonderful World of Fashion,* available where all e-books are sold. Abby currently lives in the mountains of New Hampshire with her husband, her cats, and a multitude of potential story ideas in her head. Abby can be found on Twitter @thatabbyrose and on her blog at thatabbyrose.wordpress.com.